C000081214

SO
ALL IS
PEACE

SO
ALL IS
PEACE

A NOVEL

VANDANA SINGH-LAL

PENGUIN
VIKING
An imprint of Penguin Random House

VIKING

USA | Canada | UK | Ireland | Australia
New Zealand | India | South Africa | China

Viking is part of the Penguin Random House group of companies
whose addresses can be found at global.penguinrandomhouse.com

Published by Penguin Random House India Pvt. Ltd
7th Floor, Infinity Tower C, DLF Cyber City,
Gurgaon 122 002, Haryana, India

First published in Viking by Penguin Random House India 2019

10 9 8 7 6 5 4 3 2 1

ISBN 9780670093717

For sale in the Indian Subcontinent only

Typeset in Adobe Caslon Pro by Manipal Technologies Limited, Manipal
Printed at Thomson Press India Ltd, New Delhi

www.penguin.co.in

To Mummy, Daddy, Pranay, Avie and Aria.
For Everything.

'I was much distressed by next door people who had twin babies and played the violin; but one of the twins died, and the other has eaten the fiddle—so all is peace.'

Edward Lear

Contents

August 2003

Eleven years ago

Prologue in Paris

'I can see your future,' Papa smiled at the painting in the Louvre. 'Yes, in ten years, you two will probably look like this. Bilkul aisi hi,' he nodded, still looking at the painting.

I raised myself slightly on my toes to read the title and the artist's name over Papa's shoulder. We were fifteen then—my twin sister Layla and I—and already almost a head taller than Papa. 'The Two Sisters, Théodore Chassériau, 1843', the embossed letters on the gold plate read. The painting was beautiful, as were the women in the painting in that smooth, plastic perfect way of romantic art. But even at that age, when I took every compliment that came my way at face value, never examining it too closely for motives or intentions, and never doubting its sincerity, I was not delusional enough to believe that the sisters in the painting looked anything like us. For one, they were white, not the shade of dark walnut-brown that we were. For another, although the two women were dressed in matching gathered gold gowns, their hair tied in similar neat chignons, their necks adorned with identical necklaces and their shoulders covered with matching embroidered red shawls, they were not completely alike. Not like Layla and I were. One of the sisters even looked older than the other. But I knew what Papa meant. The taller Chassériau woman's eyes had the same slightly disdainful, slightly exasperated, the all-knowing expression that Layla, older to me by a mere five minutes and wiser by a full five hundred years, with her voracious reading and her ferocious memory, often wore. And the slightly shorter (younger?) woman in the painting clutched to her sister like I knew I did mentally to Layla. Only mentally, I thought. Secretly. Surely, I had never been this physically obvious. And yet I must have been obvious enough for Papa to notice.

I turned around, as usual, to gauge my sister's reaction to Papa's remark before formulating my own reply. But I couldn't spot Layla. Even that early in the morning, the Louvre had got surprisingly crowded in the few minutes I had spent looking at the painting. I noticed for the first time that the red of the painted walls of the rooms there bled through the alleys, hallways, and staircases like an insidious communal rumour, forming the backdrop of the paintings and sculptures forever frozen in time, and I realized with sudden dread that we could easily lose one another in the stream of frenzied people flowing through the museum's cavernous, human culture encompassing depths. And the human I was concerned with had worn the same shade of red as the walls!

Until that moment of panic, I had still been basking in the glow of filial felicity that had emanated from Papa ever since the woman in the blue, red and white Air France counter at the Delhi airport had upgraded us to business class on our flight to Paris yesterday. 'The economy class is full,' she had said. Very cool, very business class-like, after giving Layla and me a perfunctory glance from behind her winged eyelashes as if she dispensed such largesse to every twin as a matter of course. The wide arc of Papa's smile had immediately split his round face into two almost equal halves, and he had pirouetted and succeeded in fitting in a makeshift French bow even in that place clotted with impatient passengers and unwieldly luggage. 'Merciiii,' he had said, his voice shinning almost embarrassingly bright as he had offered one half of his repertoire of French in gratitude. The other half of Papa's French lexicon was 'Bonjour' but he knew not to use that at the end of a conversation, even though it was morning; and since we had been about to embark on fulfilling his life-long dream of visiting Paris (that moveable feast of a city, that centre of everything that is magnificent in the world, everything worth living for—art, culture, fashion, food, fame, fun!) in such an unexpected style, it had been a very good one indeed.

So, technically, today was our first day in Paris, and yet here we were, already ticking off the *second* item on Papa's things-to-do-in-Paris list this early in the morning, because we had done the first—visiting the Eiffel Tower— almost from the plane itself. It had still been a bright 6 pm when we had landed at the bustling and not quite the stylish Charles de Gaulle airport of my imagination; people had looked more anxious and worse dressed and the airport, despite being in a 'foreign' country, had worn the same, disappointingly utilitarian florescent-concrete look as the Delhi airport we had left behind eight hours ago. In order to make the most of every precious moment of our expensive four-day Paris trip, Papa had decided that we would visit the Eiffel Tower immediately. 'We have gained an extra five and a half hours of life!' He had proclaimed as he wound his watch back. 'So, if the time of our death is fixed, but we travel from place to place, never actually being in that particular time at any place, can we evade death forever? Or is the time of death fixed with reference to a particular *time zone* even though we may not be in that zone then?' Layla had mouthed out of Papa's hearing. She had been disgruntled by his rushing about, but even she did not have the heart to dent his aura of goodwill. And this was still a time in our lives when we could speak of life and death lightly. Almost frivolously.

Ignoring the niggling suspicion that our bodies were not quite fooled by the light and were ready to fold in for the midnight that it was in Delhi, we had trooped out of our hotel almost as soon as we had hauled our two suitcases up three floors of the narrow, winding, wrought iron stairs into our tiny double room with a fantastic view (and an extra bed for Papa); Papa allowing us only a few impatient minutes to change into the dresses and the high-heeled sandals—our first ever—that Layla had convinced Mamma to buy for our sojourn into La Ville Lumière, as she had grandiosely put it.

We had caught a glimpse of the Eiffel Tower against the Parisian sky from our hotel window in our few minutes there and we had been so sure that we would be able to find our way to it that we had not even bothered to take along the bright magenta map of Paris—advertising the pleasures of Moulin Rouge on its cover; a place that was *not* on Papa's to-do list—that we had picked up at the airport. We would be done with the sight-seeing in about an hour, Papa had said, and would have our dinner after that; certain that our business class food would easily be able to see us through that time. But we hadn't, and it hadn't. In one hour, we had not even reached the 'site'. We had sashayed and walked and had eventually dragged ourselves from one street to the next, from one curved corner to another in that everlasting Parisian daylight with the Tower always tantalizingly within our sight on the horizon, but never actually there. 'Maybe the Eiffel Tower is just a hologram,' Layla had said. 'You know, a giant hoax of that very imaginative Monsieur Gustave Eiffel. And, of course, like in *Emperor's New Clothes*, nobody will admit that they have not actually been to it. Especially not the tourists, because who would admit to *not* seeing the Eiffel Tower, *the* Eiffel Tower, in their super-expensive Paris trip?' And, there had been many rejoinders in my head— there were no holograms in the nineteenth century, I could have said. Or there are no holograms that can project such a complex image in daylight even now—but the balls of my feet were so sore by then in my unfamiliar high heels that I had not been able to say anything. Not one word.

Papa had ignored Layla's patter and my increasingly desperate silence, and had trudged on and on until after over two hours of walking, we had arrived at the rolling greens of Parc du Champ de Mars and there it was: the Eiffel Tower in all its breath-taking glory; its fairy-tale lights beginning to cascade and sparkle as if only for us. But as I had stood there looking at that unapologetic, unselfconsciously dominating presence, the pain in my feet and the tumult of my circadian rhythm had penetrated in and, like an errant air bubble injected by an inefficient nurse that causes an embolism mid-beat, it had made me have the epiphany that that is how my life was going to be; its beauty forever marred by ache, its moments of ecstasy shadowed by agony. I was wrong, of course. My moments of happiness reached a point and snapped off. Just like that. Never presaged and never returned.

Later, as I had walked under the gaze of shiny, gilded sculptures, past slivers of stylish Parisians on our way back from the Eiffel Tower with my sandals in my hand because Papa could not afford to take a cab, I *could not* walk with those heels on and none of us dared to try to decipher the intricacies of the Parisian public transport, I had been awash with an aching sense of 'what if'. What if the life I had been granted been the same as the life I had dreamt of? What if instead of being the imposter who desecrated rue Cler and Pont Alexandre III with her bare feet, I was one of the bona-fide Parisians who, at that very moment, was living inside the intricate balustrade encircled flats that lined the streets with their white lace-curtained, appropriately French windows thrown open to the elements, whose streaming yellow lights against the lapis blue of the late evening sky, evoked images of fashionable families in linen summer dresses full of laughter and elegance and Vivaldi strings, and who was sitting down for her meal of white wine, red meat, blue cheese and companionable light-hearted, off the cuff kisses? We, on the other hand, barely spoke to each other in our exhaustion, skipped dinner and almost as soon as we reached the room, I drifted into a dreamless, dry-eyed, headachy sleep interspersed with uncomfortably bright lights.

But this morning, although the diffused sunlight had streamed in almost too early because we had forgotten to draw the blinds at night, I had woken up refreshed and joyous in the room that smelled of lavender and roasted coffee beans. The complimentary hotel breakfast, though cold, comprised sausages, croissant, coffee and the best cheeses I had ever tasted, adding to my sense of everything being perfect in the world. Until now.

I looked around, unwilling to tell Papa about my anxiety about Layla that was so new, it felt unreal and separated like in a story. This was the first time in my life that I was worried for her. Her biting intellect, her incessant reasoning, her increasing inclination to cut through bullshit, had never allowed me any space to want to protect her or to worry about her under any circumstances. Dealing with my own inadequacies and vulnerabilities kept me occupied enough. But here we were on our first trip abroad and I understood, for all of Layla's supreme self-assurance, she couldn't possibly possess enough arsenal to take on the malevolent forces that must exist in this entirely alien world. The realization that she would not be able to take on the very familiar world that, unknown to us then, contained even more unpropitious elements, came later. Much later. And in a way that flattened everything in its wake, allowing us no chance to ruminate or reconcile. Or to even properly comprehend.

What if we were unable to find Layla? We had taken no pictures yesterday, the little seven-euro disposable camera Papa had bought at the airport being useless for low light photography. So, except for her passport picture taken three years ago that showed a twelve-year-old girl with braces, we didn't have a single photograph of Layla to show in case we lost her, I thought. Quite irrationally, as it were, because just then a man with neatly folded grey hair and slightly frayed, albeit trendy, retro linen summer jacket stopped short in front of me, looked confused, and turned his head slightly in the direction he had come from, and I realized that they did not need Layla's photograph. All they needed was *moi*. Her clone. Her doppelgänger.

I followed the man's gaze and there she was—my glorious sister—in front of another painting of two women who again looked like each other. I found out later that *Gabrielle d'Estrées et une de ses sœurs* or 'Gabrielle d'Estrées and one of her sisters' too was, as the name suggested, a painting of two sisters. The sisters in this painting were naked and one was pinching the other's nipple (and when we reached the painting, Papa passed it quietly, making no comments on their likeness to us or our ever growing up to look like them). Even from that distance, even to my untrained eyes, the lines of the painting looked deftly rendered and very compelling but what was much more compelling was the sight of my twin sister, who stood separated from the crowd looking at the painting, her head tilted at an angle, her long spine curved slightly back and

with the light above the painting highlighting the stray
strands of brown in her long, springy, mostly black hair;
she looked like an exquisite painting herself. She seemed to
sense my presence and gave me a half smile without turning
fully to look at me and I was filled with an overwhelming
sense of pride. Proud of her, of course, but mostly proud of
me because it was then that I understood for the first time
that perhaps less regal, perhaps less assured but I was that
luminous person too. And nothing could take that away
from me, not even the presence of another me—separated
by less than half a degree.

What I did not understand then was that the glow of
Paris was not only because of my sister's (and my) shiny
presence or even because of Papa's unbridled joy. Although
I was inured to the heat of Paris, having just come out
of grittier, dustier, drier and much more scorching Delhi
summer, even I was not immune to the white-hot relentless
sunshine of that Parisian summer of 2003 when the heat
wave sweeping through France was probably killing some
people inside their homes, on the very streets, at the very
time, we were walking past them. But we did not realize it
then, because there was no television in our tiny room. The
French newspapers splayed untidily in the dark-maroon-
velvet-cushioned lobby of our hotel were just another part
of the quirky French decor to our mostly un-Frenched
selves and although we came across signs that read: POUR
RECHERCHÉ UNE VICTIM PARISIENNE DE
LA CANICULE, LA VILLE DE PARIS A MIS EN
PLACE UN NUMERO VERT: 0800 800 750; Layla's
painstaking and uncertain translation: For-the-victims-

of-the-Parisian-heat-wave,-the-city-of-Paris-has-set-up-a-green . . . green . . . umm . . . new? number 0800 800 750—robbed the words of any real meaning.

But Mamma, who had stayed behind in Delhi with Little Neel, our one-and-a-half-year-old brother, read about it in the newspapers and was moved by the tragedy of people dying inside their homes and no one caring or even knowing of them until it was too late. Upon our return, Mamma greeted all our excited conversations about Paris with an encouraging smile but once when she was alone with Papa in the kitchen and he waxed again about the many splendours of Paris, she cut him off with a, 'You know, a place where people die forgotten inside their own homes can't be that much of a paradise, nahi? Where were their families, their neighbours? Where was the entire—since she was not given to expletives, she did not actually say it, but her tone left me with no doubt about the intensity of her anger or about what was supposed to occupy the small hesitant silence between her flow of words. No Sir!—society?'

As I lay in the living room with my legs dangling over the side of the flower patterned couch in a way that Mamma disliked intensely, under the influence of the forbidden word that she had not allowed herself to utter but that had stayed in the air as an adult's small satisfying act of indiscretion, I had dreamily attributed my moments of melancholy in Paris to the dying old souls who had probably hung over the city, crushed by its treatment of them and yet, like jilted lovers, staying on for a moment longer for that one glimpse, that one glance, for that one chance of absolution.

I know better now, of course. There is no hovering after death. No lingering. One moment there is a person with definite ideas about what they can do, how they think, what they want to display. The next moment they are just a mass of chemicals strung together—a group of cells making a tissue, a group of tissues making an organ, a group of organs making a 'body'—for anybody to do whatever they want with it. Burn or bury them or even hang them out to feed the vultures. All the hovering happens before death, and if you are lucky, or unlucky, depending on how you look at it, by the people left behind *after* your death.

'We may not be perfect,' Mamma said. 'Our streets may be dirty, and we may go to potty in the open, but we take care of each other. Something like this can *never* happen in India.'

23 October 2014

1

The Multi-Hued Mummy

It is Diwali night. As the last of the sun's rays disappears on the western horizon, a bottle rocket lit by a young boy in his 6 x 5 feet concrete yard with its four mandatory potted plants—wilting plumeria, money plant, bougainvillea, and an undersized traveller palm—falls short, swerves and lands on the balcony of the apartment upstairs. It fortunately does not explode in fluorescent colours, unlike what the box it came in had claimed it would do, but the meagre sparks (still colourful) spewing out of its mangled remains set the pile of debris gathered there—dust, dry leaves, pieces of flying paper, twigs, the indeterminate particulates of smoggy urban living—on fire. The boy's mother sends him hurrying up to inform the residents of the house about the mishap. He rings the bell and knocks on the faded green door that is only partially visible in the glow of the row of tiny lotus-shaped bulbs strung by his father on the landing downstairs, for much longer than he normally would have because he does not want to return home and face his mother's wrath. He taps tunes on the door, he draws very light, impermanent graffiti with his fingertips blackened by charcoal, sulphur and saltpetre, and on an impulse, he picks up an empty mango wood packaging crate lying forgotten on one side of the landing, places it against the door and climbing on it, peeks into the house through the small hole that functions as an old-fashioned peephole. For a few moments, he sees nothing in the dark. But just as he is about to jump off the crate, the room lights up by the glow of another firecracker—the long burning, multi-coloured kind—that paints it pink and green and blue and yellow before turning it a deeper black than it had been before. And the boy stumbles back, nearly falling off the crate. In the room, he has seen two women. One tall and thin, moving or sitting close to the door, and another far behind her, lying so still and straight and dark and shrivelled that she could be the Egyptian mummy from the encyclopædia that he pores over often. And despite being only seven years old, the boy is sure that the woman is dead.

2

Death Comes Knocking. Life Arrives Unannounced. Or Is It the Other Way Round?

That isn't a knock, is it? It is probably just another firecracker. A new concoction of sounds cooked up by the evil cock brand firecracker manufacturing, child labour employing, blood sucking capitalists of Sivakasi. I like saying blood-sucking capitalist. Blood-sucking capitalist as opposed to the blood-sucked, perpetually gobsmacked working class. I know my twin sister, my clone, Layla, lying on the couch behind me, will like my acknowledging that people are pre-slotted according to their class, caste, wealth, gender, sexual orientation; all the ways devised to divide and discriminate that turn the wheels of the world. The pitching of 'us' against 'them'. Any opportune 'us' against any opportune 'them'. Yet the universality of cleaning of the butt after pooping. The method of cleaning may be different, some may use paper, others water, others just grass or leaves or even sand but everybody does it. Keep that thought in mind when somebody tries to bully you, picture them cleaning their butt after taking a dump and you will never be intimidated by anybody. This is one more irreverent, albeit Invaluable Layla Lesson (or ILL, as she likes calling them), among a series of life lessons that Layla had been prone to dispensing. I say it again. Blood-sucking capitalists of Sivakasi. Because Layla will like hearing it, because I like the sound of it. But mostly because I like how familiar, how much like her, I sound when I say it.

Although she has not really sounded like anything much for some time now, has she? For a long time now. I am not sure how long. There it is again. That sound. This one was definitely a knock and it came from our door. Or not. It could as easily have come from inside my head because why would anybody knock at our door? When was the last time someone had knocked—three months ago, four months ago? Probably since Layla and I have had almost nothing to eat. And we have not drunk any water for at least two or three . . . or more days. Time, time, time. Who knows how much time? It must have been a long time though because I am exhausted. All I can do is sit on this floor and look at this little grey-brown cockroach nymph wriggling in and out, in and out on its six spiny legs, of the low hole in the blue and green paisley-patterned wallpaper. But it is beginning to grow dark now and although there are flashes of light coming in from the fireworks outside, I am having trouble keeping track of the cockroach. Fortunately, all it has done for as long as I have been watching is go in and out as if not sure whether it can afford to leave the safety of its hole shaped sanctuary. An intrusion of cockroaches, I remember. It does not need a group, though, does it? Even one cockroach is enough of an intrusion. But this cockroach nymph is no intrusion. It is a welcome guest— somebody whom I would have ushered in had I had the strength—Namaste, Namaste, I would have said, putting my hands together and bowing my head low—because it is the *only* movement in our still, movementless house.

And now there are knocks, which should mean that there is somebody outside our door wanting to come in. But these knocks don't sound like that. They sound like a mistake. They are incessant enough and prolonged, but they feel unfocused. Ambiguous. As if whoever is knocking is looking away from the door, or as if they are knocking at the wrong door or are thinking of other things as they knock. *Thak thaka thak, thak thaka thak.* The knocks are melodic now, in tune. See, what did I tell you? Unfocused and ambiguous. The knocker seems to be using both hands and I *know* the tune. He is tapping *Bourrée in D Minor* on our door. I know the tunes. When memories start to leak out from the inside of your head, the last thing that goes are the songs and the tunes. Not that my memory is leaking. I remember everything. And I also know who it could be at the door playing *Bourrée in D Minor*. What is he doing here? And what does it even matter? I can easily ignore it.

The knocking is a new sound and it is soft. Soft. I can hear it only because it is so near, but it is not like I am not used to sounds. In Delhi, sounds are present everywhere, at all times of the day and night. On and on and on. Some sound, any sound. And the dirty air. And the unwarranted, unmitigated rudeness on the road. I have not been on a road for a long time and nobody has been rude or polite to me. Or said anything to me really. But the dirty air diffuses easily into our space, and the sounds have only grown bigger, more persistent. A long time ago, I had read that starvation makes hearing more acute. I don't remember why that happens, but in our lives, sounds have taken over as if to fill the void of our existence. Striding in pompously like a conquering army—*bang bang bang*—because there can be no vacuum in nature. No, not even two identical twenty-five or twenty-six-year-old blanks with two identical empty stomachs. Empty and festering.

Earlier, we could move, and we would see things too. Not just hear them. You remember that, Layla, don't you? When we would look out of our window. We would sometimes even talk about the people we saw—people with familiar faces, gestures and the oh so unmistakably familiar mindsets. Of course, we had hated all of them. Each one of them. You, you. *And* you.

When we stopped looking out of the window, we would still find people on our computer screen. Smiling people, shiny people, updating-statuses people, taking-holidays people, celebrating-birthdays people, commemorating-anniversaries people, having-children people, expressing-outrage people, eating-meals people. They were people we did not know, who we had never met, people with unpronounceable names living in places so far off the edge of our maps that we had not even known that those places existed and yet their lives, their children, their partners, their friends, *they* were available to us through a series of pictures, videos and location pinning. I AM HERE! Baffling us with their intention and their smugness. *I am here. I am here?* Of course, all that stopped too when our electricity went, or perhaps even before that. But the sounds have remained. Our sounds inside our house, when we had conversations about the invisible, apocryphal people. Papa. Mamma. Little Neel. Deepak. No. That is not true. Layla and I *never* spoke about Layla's boyfriend (he can be called that) or Layla's lover (he can be called that too), Deepak. How could we? Wouldn't speaking his name conjure him up like Candyman? Later Layla's words had fluttered, slowed down, and one day, they had stopped. But did I stop? No, Sir! I have continued talking. Wringing out every word available to me—one after another after another—speaking more and more as Layla fell more and more silent. I know that as long as I continue talking, she will follow the rhythms, the cadence of my words, and continue breathing.

And it isn't like I have been speaking in silence. When Layla's voice retreated from the melee, external sounds moved in as a kind of mismatched accompaniment to my hotchpotch of words—a macabre piano recital to accompany my equally bizarre vocals: the polished throttle of the new, increasingly expensive cars parked on the road in front of our building, the rough staccato bursts of the more utilitarian delivery vehicles: the Domino's scooters hurrying in with the pizza in thirty minutes, the Big Basket vans delivering groceries in two hours, the Amazon bikes couriering bulkily bubble-wrapped, tiny things in twenty-four hours; the persistent aggressive cooing of hundreds of pigeons expanding their territory at the expense of any other bird that happens to come in their way; the all-day whining of the dog tied in the balcony of a nearby building when its masters leave for their important daytime jobs; the shudder of mango trees holding out tenaciously against the perverse human instinct of converting every free living thing into an ostensibly easily-controlled, non-living one; the swish of the cleaner's swipe as she cleans the staircase at 12 six-days-a-week, or is it at 1? I am not so sure now that our watch has run out of battery. The cleaner lady is the only person who still comes up the stairs and I am used to the sounds she brings with her—the impatient clank of her steel bucket landing on the floor outside, the spill of dirty brown water that occasionally seeps in from beneath our door, the quiet swish of her swipe accompanied by tired mutterings on a bad day, and her soft humming on a presumably good one.

I had heard her the day she came up with a man. There was no swish of her swipe or the spill of water that day or the humming of the latest Hindi film song. Instead, there was the unaccustomed weight of two pairs of feet coming up the stairs for a clandestine rendezvous; the rustle of entangled clothes and bodies, the shy whispers and giggles of the first look, the suction of sweaty flesh meeting sweaty flesh, the rising of movements to an urgent, uninhibited crescendo, the barely smothered grunt of consummation and the sigh of contentment. There was complete stillness for a few moments after that. I could feel the man and the woman savour their bodies in that time. For those few seconds, they were as alone in the world outside our door as

Layla and I—staring at each other in the afternoon's orange light—were inside. But the quality of their aloneness was different from ours. Their aloneness was delicious. Ours, in the fourth month of our constricting, spiralling starvation, literally bereft of any taste, except as a kind of sick-smelling vacuum in our mouths and a clenched fist-like weight of guilt in our empty stomachs. They had hurried down after that and the man had never returned. Who could he have been? The cleaning woman continues to come though. Almost every day at 12. Or 1.

I can sometimes hear other conversations too, especially since a family moved downstairs a month or two ago. I have seen very little of the family and I can't quite delineate the words they speak, except once when one of them, a man who I presume is the dad, had shouted, 'Stop that!' But I can easily recognize the thrum and the timber of their voices. I can feel the scale of their ambitions, the level of their delusion. They are noisy people, this downstairs family of three. They have friends, they have parties and celebrations, and bits of music, laughter, and sounds of boisterous, if indistinguishable, conversations often wafts into our house, despite our tightly shut doors and windows and our thick, old concrete walls. They have a little boy. I think he is called Samar or Amar; I know the syllables of his name from his parents calling out to him often, but I am not certain of the alphabets contained within it. I have heard the loud *ting ting ting* of Samar or Amar practicing *Minuet in C* and the gentler melody of *Ode to Joy* on his piano. Sometimes his music is jaunty, full of the flushed excitement of a new-found love. At other times, there is the mechanical staleness of a love gone sour as if he is practising his music under duress.

I think the kid is a bit like Little Neel—all curly hair, wide eyes and a dimple or two. A face too sweet to put on a grown man. That is why Little Neel remains frozen in time. Our Peter Pan who never grows old. Or older. I am sure it is Samar or Amar who is knocking now because he is tapping his tune on our door with the same resolute petulance that has marked the *ting-ting-ting* of his *Bourrée in D Minor* for the last two days. *Ting ting ting* it had gone on and on and on as he had tried in vain to master the intricacies of the piece on his piano. And I have spent all that time *and* all the intervals in between his playing and probably even before that at the bottom of *this* very couch, in *this* very place; sleeping and waking and sleeping and waking through the darkness and the light within the thirty centimetre perimeter I have made for myself that keeps me always within a touching distance of Layla lying on the couch.

Layla. Despite all the noises from outside, I can feel every little sound and every movement that she makes, often even before she makes them. I know her connectome—every little strand of wiring in her brain. I know when her cerebral cortex initiates a thought. I can follow her neural signal as it travels down her spinal cord and spreads out to reach her motor nerves where the muscles of her right hand obediently raise her middle finger to show me exactly what she thinks of an ineffectual advice or a particularly stupid idea. I hear the shallow wisp of every breath that she takes. I follow the slow movement of her tiny asymmetrical lungs—the right, shorter and wider to make room for the liver and the left, narrow to create space for the heart. But we are mirrored twins so perhaps her heart is on the right side to mirror mine on the left. Why have I never thought of finding out? But I *have* tried to synchronize my breathing to hers, especially since she stopped talking—the lungs are on both sides, so mirroring does not matter there, does it? Breathe in, breathe out. Like in long-forgotten yoga positions. Breathe in, breathe out. Except our breathing in was sometimes so shallow that it could well be breathing out for all the oxygen that it got inside us. And in the last few days things have become worse. No matter how still I sit for however long thinking of nothing and speaking very quiet words, the sound of her breathing still remains shallower and much slower than mine. By today I have completely lost track of it.

Today is a bad day for sounds. As was yesterday but today is infinitely worse. The knocks have begun only now but the noises have been going on forever. The loud whistling *wheeeeeeze* of the rockets and the crackle, swoosh and sparkle of, I am sure I recognize the sound right, of the anars—the little fountains of light and shine but, as Layla puts it, a lot of noxious fumes of nitrites and sulphur and magnesium. That is the thing. There are two sides to everything. Yin and Yang, Layla says. Like us. But the question is who is the Yin and who is the Yang? There is the unending *splutter splutter* of hundreds of thousands of red crackers—little fingerlings of potassium chlorates (I think) encased in thin paper—on a string, bursting one after another—*splutterspluttersplutterer*—as if the sound will only end with the end of the world.

Vandana Singh-Lal

Look, now I have lost track of the cockroach, too. No, no, there it is. Only, unlike me, it has mustered the courage and the strength to crawl out of its hole and made its way to the print of *The Two Sisters* that hangs on our living room wall. Papa had bought the print in Paris for a princely sum of 40 euros. 'Don't laugh, Layla,' I say. Although no sound comes from her. 'Remember how much 40 euros had seemed at the time?' Our budget for Paris had been 100 euros per day and that amount had to cover our stay, food and 'any other expenses we may have,' Papa had told us (his tone implying that we should not have any other expenses) a week before our Paris trip, when I had stood intimidated by the smooth feel of the few crisp orange euros that the Forex guy had given us in exchange for the more weather-beaten, tempest-tossed (Layla's words, not mine) but larger wad of Indian rupee notes. I don't know why Papa had spent a precious 40 euros on one picture. Could it have been the intoxication of the Parisian air? I intoned 'intoxication' carefully. I know how important it is that words are used right. The right words. Spoken right. Always. Poshyshowy Miss LaylaTanya, our schoolmates would tease us in a sing-song. But Papa told us, use the best words you can find in the world at that moment. Even though it was the right words spoken with the right intonation that had brought Deepak into our lives and, later, it was the insistence on the right words that had triggered off the worst of his instincts, we still use the right words. I know I must be careful about what I say, when I say it and perhaps as critically, how I say it.

The sound at our door has stopped. Little Amar or Samar has left. No, he hasn't. He is still here. I can hear him again. He has begun tapping a tune I don't recognize— *Arrietta*? Perhaps I should open the door and ask him. But for the effort required, I might as well try to climb out unaided from a deep crevice off Hillary Step just short of the summit of Mount Everest! I think I am chuckling now. When I had been around nine or ten, I had read a low on style but rivetingly high on substance (at least to my mind) account of Tenzing and Hillary's climb to the Everest and I had decided that I was going to climb Mount Everest when I grew up. I had written down every little detail of Everest climbs that I could find—from the views and perils at various altitudes to the kind of clothes that are needed, to the signs of sickness to watch out for and the medicines to take if any of them manifested, but mostly I had read about and memorized the hazards at various places on the way to the top. Bits of those descriptions and names still remain lodged in my head. Or was it Layla who had decided that she wanted to climb Everest and had she drawn those columns and written down in her neat handwriting—Hillary Step, South Col, Khumbu Icefall?

I am so cold I could well be on the Khumbu Icefall. I am not sure where what part of my freezing body begins and where what part of my body ends. Or even where Layla begins and where I end. My voice too sounds strange. Am I speaking the words aloud, have I ever spoken the words out loud or has it all just been noises inside my head? Am I speaking different words or just repeating the same thoughts and words over and over and over again? There

are thirty-five steps to the door from where I sit. I had
counted the distance between every object in the house
when it had been too small to contain my restlessness.
That was perhaps only six months ago, but it could well
have been another life. Or a part of another person's life,
a remembered person. A woman who I know well but not
intimately; not inside out. A friend. A Facebook friend. A
prolifically status updating Facebook friend; every incident
in whose life and whose every relationship and every
heartbreak I can list; every meal that she ate (not too many
and not at all lately), everything that she liked (again not
too many things lately), everything that she read (too much
although not lately), and everything that she was outraged
by (far too many things for some time now). I know her life
story. She was born on 24 November 1988. Five minutes
after her twin sister, Layla. That would make them both
either twenty-five or twenty-six years old now. I am not
very sure because I have lost track. 'What month or day or
time is it now, Layla? This Facebook friend had another
sibling, a brother, Little Neel, born on 16 May 2002. She
has a master's degree in Economics and worked with an
NGO, while her sister is in the process of completing her
PhD in English Literature. But do I know how that woman
feels? Did I ever know how she felt? Do I even know what
feelings mean?

All *I* feel is pain. Unmitigated, unending pain. Like
a loud horrible *keeeeeeee* of a faulty microphone inside
my head. And cold. I am always so cold that I seem to
be discovering new parts of my body that are developing
little icicles inside them. My toes first, my head, my

roughly bitten, brittle fingernails that break at the slightest
of pressure. Here's another piece of fingernail off my left
index finger. The little hollow at the back of my knee where
a smidgen of dirt has encrusted, the dry scratched scabs on
my body, on the exposed part of the back of my neck, below
my roughly hacked hair . . . There are splotches of little
things in my mouth that I can feel grow larger each day—
little ridges on my palate that seem to be lined with fur.
Tiny crests of hardness inside my cheek that I can feel with
my tongue and small troughs of sticky wetness underneath
my tongue that I cannot; I have felt them with my fingers
though. There is the scratchy roughness that feels like a
two-day-old stubble growing *inside* the back of my throat.
It hurts to speak. It even hurts to swallow. But the longer
I speak, the longer Layla will continue to breathe. So, I sit,
and I speak, and I speak although I am beginning to get
very tired. If I get too tired to talk, will she stop breathing?
I know I need to get up. I need to walk the thirty-five paces
to the door. Samar or Amar will be gone soon and I will
never be able to muster the strength to walk down the two
flights of steps that separates us from the house downstairs,
and ask for help.

But what if I get up and I speak, and nobody
understands. Like the man in Bichsel's *A Table is a Table*;
'he could not understand what other people said which was
sad but what was much worse was that they were unable to
understand him any longer. And that is why he did not talk
anymore.' What if I am speaking gobbledegook now and I
am referring to the painting as wall, the couch as cockroach
and the door as floor? How do I know if I remember the

words right? No, no, no. I am sure I remember all the words but I can't get up quite just now and speak the words. Only the right words—Hello. I need help—I will say, but not quite now because first I need to keep track of the cockroach that sits very still on the print of the painting as if, like me, it too is waiting for something. What is it waiting for? I don't know, but I know it will disappear the minute it realizes the futility of it all. I lift my arm and try to touch Layla but now I can't reach her. She has shrunk into the couch and is out of reach even when I sit within the thirty-centimetre perimeter I have made for myself. I still don't turn around. Instead, I continue to stare so hard at the cockroach that like in that little sheet with a picture of two cats that ophthalmologists give you for your eye exercises where you are supposed to look so closely at the cats that they merge and become one, the cockroach blurs and disappears from my sight and all I am left with is the red of the painting on which it sits. I tilt back further to try to locate the cockroach and my fingers touch the skin of Layla's hand. It feels dry and crackling, and when I thoughtlessly pinch it between my thumb and forefinger, it comes up like parchment and just stays there. Unmoving. There is nothing holding it back, nothing to tether it to, nothing it needs to return to. The muscles underneath her skin have melted and there is no elasticity left to pull her skin back.

That's when I do it. I don't know how, but I crawl and I sit and I crawl and I sit. I move in very slow motion, determined to keep moving. Each movement takes hours or is it minutes or even seconds? I have lost all perspective of time. But I reach the door, lift myself up, unlatch the flimsy clasp and speak out the words. The right words. The necessary words—'My sister is sick,' I say, when I open the door and see a strangely skewed little boy dressed in shiny kurta-pyjama standing there. His feet—encased in golden mojris, I notice—are turned as if he is about to run down the stairs but he straightens up and pulls himself to his full height and says, 'Your balcony is on fire.'

Why is he saying that? I try to bend down to look closely at him. Have I not said the right words? 'You are the first person I have seen in four months,' I want to smile and tell him. Or five months. I want to reassure him. I want to show him Layla but he turns, and slipping slightly, flees down the stairs before I can say any more.

3

Feasting/Fasting

The TV cameras arrive at the complex before the ambulance. Almost immediately after the police. The scene in front of the apartment building would have been too clichéd to be a part of a respectable movie. But there it is. The rectangular, brilliant lights concentrated together like a congregation of monster eyes with their white hot threads of heat; the desperately young journalists who are on duty at the TV station on this night of Diwali festivities because of the lowliness of their status in the station's pecking order; the small clutch of hard-drinking, chain-smoking, old-school, outwardly laconic and inwardly anxious reporters who have moved from print media and despite lacking the preening, actor-like persona of true blue television journalists, stay on with the TV channels because they have bills to pay. They pretend they are above the forced joviality and commercial festiveness that Diwali has been reduced to. The jostling camerapersons each trying to get as close to the house of action (or inaction, as one reporter quips uneasily) as possible; the entangled wires; the hundreds of microphones being thrust at anybody who happens to fall in the range of the hail of questions—Do you know the sisters? How old are they? When did you last see them? Where is their family? What do you think happened to them and the ubiquitous—How do you *feel* about this?

Feel about what? About all the facts that have begun scuttling fatly out of the house one atop the other like overfed mice fleeing a flooded hole: that two sisters of indeterminate age—in their twenties or thirties—have been found starving to death in the beautifully-lit-up-for-Diwali upmarket residential complex full of beautifully-attired-for-Diwali upper middle class people who without exception, have more paraphernalia in their house and more food in their refrigerators than their parents had ever imagined. Particularly today, on a day of abject profligacy, of excessive drinking, of excessive eating, of excessive gambling, of excessive, excessive polluting. In a complex full of people who have travelled to more places, who unfailingly take yearly (preferably international) vacations and who pay little attention to the foul smelling, polluted Delhi air that embraces them enthusiastically like a smelly, homeless yet loving relative as soon as they step out of the sanitized confines of the airports or the artificial, air-conditioned, air purified insides of their luxury cars and houses, and even lesser attention to the ever increasing numbers of street children—sacrificed at the altar of televised Technicolor dreams or displaced in the acquisition of land for industries, for roads, for residential behemoths—

Vandana Singh-Lal

lining traffic junctions and selling chromium painted, lead filled, China-made plastic Supermans. About the fact that the house in which the women live, despite being twenty-nine years old, caught in the tailwind of the country's GDP growing at over 8 per cent per year, is already valued at more than two crore rupees because of its presence in a low-rise apartment complex (realtors' parlance for a complex where all buildings are only two-storeys high, as opposed to the burgeoning high-rises in the area) and for its location very close to an upcoming Hi-tech mini city whose tall grey unfinished concrete towers with interconnected walkways stand in a circle against the sky in the horizon like grotesque modern day Stonehenge trilithon. Or that although only a small open packet of salt has been found in the sisters' kitchen, there is gold jewellery in their cupboard and nearly five lakh rupees in their joint bank account (according to the passbook that the police discovered) and therefore poverty, obviously, is not what has starved the women. About the fact that the house stinks so much that the first four constables who arrive on the scene in a police Gypsy—its blue and red light flashing dramatically even against the shiny Diwali backdrop—corral two half-drunk cleaners to go inside the house before them to at least open the windows and are reprimanded thoroughly for the same by their senior in charge of the case, Assistant Commissioner of Police (ACP) Satya, (who arrives half an hour later) for defiling the crime scene. 'Crime scene? But surely no crime has been committed?' One of the constables mutters under his breath. Thankfully, they had the sense to not allow any TV cameras in, otherwise they would surely have been suspended, ACP Satya says before stepping into that cavern straight out of hell.

'I feel terrible, Sir,' the sixty-one-year-old perfunctory guard of the residential complex says, his mouth shamefacedly curved downwards. He wears a bright red gold lined vest—a concession to Diwali—over his dark blue uniform that hangs loosely on him because he has inherited it from the slightly more robust albeit much younger guard who is his nephew, and who left the complex to work in the upcoming hi-tech city where, as he puts it, in his CNBC Hindi parlance (of which he is an avid watcher), the prospects for growth are better. 'But I am new here', the old watchman says. 'I have only been here for three months and in that time, ma kasam, I never saw the women. I didn't see any light coming from there. I didn't see even a leaf move there. Sahebs did not tell me that anybody lived in the house.'

'We tried to talk to the sisters and wanted to ask them how they were, what they needed,' Mr Sanjay Deol, the president of the Krishna Colony Resident Welfare Association (who has tried renaming the complex but the name Krishna Colony has stuck despite the board outside proclaiming that this place is actually Bellevue Boulevard), who lives in Tower F, only one building away from Tower D, where the sisters live, reads carefully from a hurriedly prepared statement. 'But they always said no, so we could not do anything.' Mr Deol is a tall, balding seventy-five-year-old man whose broad weightlifter's shoulders turning to fat advertise the slackening of his life-long commitment to physical fitness. His late life gamble into a small sales-oriented call centre start-up paid off handsomely in the form of half-a-million dollar buy-out by the Hinduja Group eight years ago. Flushed with the late life luxury of time, money and self-confidence, he decided to contest for the position of the president of the complex, winning the hard-fought election by a narrow margin and holding on to the post since. But this tryst with power has taken a toll on his health, he complains sometimes, forcing him to undergo a heart bypass surgery five years ago (which was the only time he relinquished his position to his deputy for a month).

Mr Deol lists, among his many achievements, making the complex the first truly gated community in the city— nobody is allowed inside the complex unless expressly invited by one of the residents—and concretizing most of the complex parks into parking spaces to make them more in tune with the exponentially growing number of cars and, because of a successful selling of the DINKs (Double Income No Kids) and the DIOKs (Double Income One Kid) concept, the equally dramatically reducing number of children in the complex.

He had gagged upon entering the apartment and had thrown up his just eaten Diwali sweets at the sight of the sisters, under the very, albeit superbly indifferent, eyes of one of them, adding his bit to the putrid state of the house. And caught by surprise by the arrival of the television cameras when he had been waiting for the police outside the complex gate, away from the shadows cast by the lush old peepal tree, Mr Deol had agitatedly responded to the initial questions of the inquisitive reporters still dressed in the same green and black embroidered Nehru jacket that had held the colourful splatters of his recent disgorgement. But he has changed his clothes and found his bearings, as he said to his wife, while labouring over his carefully prepared statement at home from which he now reads.

'Last time I saw one sister, it was more than six months ago,' he says. 'They had a dog, I think. It was a street dog only—if you also want to know the breed, since you want to know everything.' He has watched enough TV and given enough speeches to know the value of casual banter and light-hearted asides irrespective of whether they are true or false in every, but especially in the direst of, situations.

'Two women were living alone after the death of their father and mother—very sad state it was. Par phir woh akeli auratein thi. How can I zabardasti make them talk to me if they don't want to?' he says self-righteously when he is asked the next day on television whether as the president of the resident welfare association he isn't supposed to be responsible for the *welfare* of the residents of the association during a TV Now debate on 'Who is Responsible for the Plight of the Women?', where the panellists sit in a straight line against the backdrop of the ubiquitous black and red picture of a woman covering her face in horror and shame that usually accompanies any television story that talks about the 'exploitation' of women. But nobody hears Mr Deol's answer, not even Mr Deol himself, because by now the decibel level of the routinely outraged argument among the routinely at hand studio panellists—who include a psychologist, a heart surgeon, a mandatory local politician and an elegant, articulate writer–social commentator whose books on relationships and dating are serialized in the *Cosmopolitan* and who is invited to every television studio discussion to comment on issues as wide-ranging as the role of politicians in the Indian society, to what women should wear and how principals of respected colleges should behave—is so high that only the anchor (with his microphone routinely adjusted for higher volume) can be heard, much to his own satisfaction.

The family of the dhobi in the complex is questioned. The neighbours, in their shimmering Diwali attires who have been lured out of their well-decorated, well-lit small domestic lairs by the arrival of the flashier television lights, are interviewed. Thin young girls from the dark, forested tracts of Jharkhand and Chhattisgarh, brought by opportunistic middlemen with promises of a better life, who end up working as 'full-time' maids in the houses of the neon lit complex, and who now stand huddled together, a little apart from the rest of the onlookers in the neighbourhood, are asked, 'Did you see anybody enter the house? Did the Sharma sisters ever talk to you?' and prompted by their employers, they all shake their heads in nos. The seven-year-old boy, Samar, whose breathless account to his mother of the goings-on in the apartment upstairs, had set the whole rigmarole in motion, is also questioned. But Samar, although startled by his celebrity status, like all children born in the intrusive age of unceasing news reporting, blogging, Instagraming, Facebooking and Twittering, is intuitively aware of its evanescence. He decides not to say anything to anybody anymore. Not a word. Not to the television reporters despite the increasingly anxious-for-recognition (until the narrative of the TV stories changes over the next few days and the neighbours go from being the saviours to the perpetrators to accomplices) coaxing by his parents. Not to the police, despite the strident questioning that evening by ACP Satya. And, with an obstinacy and a demonstration of will power never seen or perhaps never noticed in him before, not even to his curious classmates and teachers in school the next day. Or the day after.

Two identical stretchers come out of the building each bearing what looks like a little dishevelled heap of thick snot-coloured blanket with nothing in their fill or placement suggesting the presence of a human being underneath. But as the second stretcher is being loaded onto the ambulance, an orderly stumbles slightly and there is a gasp because there it is: a glimpse of close cropped dark hair for a few seconds until the doors swing shut and the ambulance makes its flashing, wailing way out of the crowd, driving through the mango tree-lined street and turning left out of the gate. The TV cameras pan slowly, following the fading red taillights of the ambulance. Reporters begin their competitively poignant wrapping-up commentary on the plight of the women. They have some footage of the house, they have a shot of the hair of one of the women, they have bites from a few people in the neighbourhood; their story is nearly complete and they are ready to pack up from the scene. All they now need is a little more coverage from the hospital; perhaps only a few stock shots of the hospital itself, a couple of bites from one of the doctors and they will be done. But Mrs Sunita Deol, wife of the

RWA president—a petite, confident woman in her own
right, whose job as a small time bureaucrat had allowed
her some domination of her family's matters only to see
her position undercut in her retirement year because of
the call centre (set up with the largesse provided by a rich
businessman who had needed information provided by her
to qualify for a government tender) windfall—is watching
the television crew closely and she has one more weapon in
her stockpile of information. She goes into her house and
comes out demurely flashing a seven-year-old photograph
taken at a Krishna Nagar society get together. The cameras
turn almost reluctantly to cover it, sure that it is one more
useless piece of information being peddled by somebody
seeking their little share of attention. But as they zoom in,
enlarging the photograph on their monitors, hush falls.
The photograph, taken against a generic setting, shows
two tall young women who stand far apart from each other
in a group. And even in the slightly indistinct photograph,
despite their dissimilar and not very flattering dresses and
expressions, it is clear that the two women are identical
twins and that they are distractingly striking looking.
Camera persons strain further in to get a better angle of
the picture as Mrs Deol stands still in her resplendent blue
and gold Diwali attire with a suitably downcast expression
holding up the photograph in front of her as if posing for a
police mugshot in an American wedding crime series; but
the journalists step back. They have begun making hurried
phone calls, asking for more senior journalists, more
melodramatic anchors, better cameras, better equipment
and the digging up of more, however remote, connections.

This, they know is the stuff of the long haul. The story of two beautiful starving women in an upmarket complex in Delhi is going to attract just the right kind of FMCG devouring audience, generating just the right kind of TRPs for all 823 news channels in the country that the promoters of those channels demand.

And they are right. One moment the house is shrouded in a cavernous half-curtained darkness and the very next moment all its accessible crevices, every available inch of the dust-thickened interior of elegant, old-fashioned furniture, strewn clothes, books and torn papers is laid luridly open to a voyeuristic populace craving a daily fix of outrageous news stories. Everything matters, everything is given meaning and no piece of information is allowed to go through without being churned endlessly as Breaking News. And, of course, it is all interspersed with advertisements peddling Lays Chips and Diet Colas.

25 October 2014

4

Covering the Starving Sisters' Story

Fortunately for Raman, he does not work for any of those TV channels and his phone did not ring that Diwali night. Not that he had been in any position to answer the phone, even if it had but that piece of information is immaterial to this story, as Raman himself would have said, had he been given the story to improve; squinting censoriously through his glasses at the rookie reporter for emphasizing the wrong aspects and slashing through the printout with a bold red pen the old-fashioned way.

No, it is two days later that the CEO of the magazine where Raman works knocks at his room door. By then, under the devouring gaze of hundreds of television cameras and 24x7 news coverage, every visible morsel of D332 Krishna Colony and its environs have been carved out and served up for public consumption and it has become the most famous residential address in the country (possibly second only to the Rashtrapati Bhavan) and the rather unusual names Layla and Tanya Sharma, after a few mispronunciations, have begun to roll smoothly off TV anchors' tongues. The CEO enters his room and tells Raman to write about the sisters for the next issue of his magazine. 'We need a short human interest piece and you are not covering any other story at the moment, right?' The CEO asks as he stands jumping up and down near Raman's desk—the CEO being a fitness banker (his words) who allows no possible cheque to improve his physique go uncashed. It is a rhetorical question anyway because he knows well that Raman is not working on any story, so Raman does not bother replying. But the CEO also knows that 'human interest' is the kind of story Raman would least like to work on; and if the CEO has any doubt about that, Raman makes it clear with his unapologetically unexcited expression at the suggestion. Raman is an investigative journalist who covers stories on arms deals, strategic policy, corruption in public places—not soft, human interest stories. And yet the CEO continues smiling as he jumps and talks to Raman because, pumped up on endorphins, he has no dour moments. He goes through life inputting carrots and cucumbers and outputting winning propositions. He has no place for negativity in his life, he says. Even when he is reprimanding somebody or firing somebody (which he, as far as possible, does not do in person) or when he is assigning the most maudlin story in the world to perhaps one of the most cynical journalists in the world, the beatific smile of a man in touch with every muscle and sinew of his body, never leaves the CEO's face.

Raman knows better than to ask 'why me?' and 'why now?' because he knows the answer to the former and does not really care to know the answer to the latter. He is not given to unnecessary modesty when it comes to calibrating his own worth (at least not inside his own mind) although he interacts with everyone from behind thick glasses, an even thicker curtain of exaggerated courtesy and with so much self-deprecating humour that only people very familiar with him can look past it and spot the disdain (or perhaps, fear) for the world in general lurking very close to the surface. He knows his assignment is a punishment, but also a challenge, a manifestation of the distrust that the CEO has for Raman's unpredictability, as well as straggling admiration that is a remnant of an earlier era (way before the current CEO's time). An admiration that stems from Raman's exposé of a top bureaucrat who had colluded with a local politician to siphon off large chunks of money from the relief package meant for flood-affected people of Bihar. The fact that the bureaucrat had graced the cover of illustrious magazines like *India Today* and had been decorated by the likes of the World Bank for 'exemplary work in the distribution of food aid' for the very aid package that he had been stealing from, meant that Raman had needed more gumption and even more evidence to persuade his editors to go with his story than he normally would have anyway needed to implicate a senior bureaucrat. It had also meant that when he had finally convinced his editors and they had devoted almost an entire issue of the magazine to Raman's detailed investigation, the accolades that came his way were superlative. He had been awarded the year's Ramnath Goenka Prize for investigative journalism for his exertions and had been warmly welcomed into the hallowed

pantheon of journalistic greatness with his story becoming
compulsory reading in some schools of journalism.

That had been the high point of his career. And it was
probably only befitting that since his ascent had come so
early, at twenty-one—when he had been a cocksure rookie
only six months into his journalistic career after having
dabbled in various vocations, including, at one point,
thinking of enlisting as a spy—the climb down should be
torturous and long drawn out. Reaching the point sixteen
years later when he has to cover the story of two pathetic
sisters starving themselves to death probably because of
some religious mumbo-jumbo; a story that nobody, except
perhaps tabloid magazines like *Manohar Kahaniya*, would
have paid any attention to in the pre 24x7 TV news era,
Raman thinks as he watches the CEO's perfectly sculpted
posterior retreat his messy room. His room has reams
of papers and books stacked and arranged in a way that
only Raman understands; never able to direct anybody to
manoeuvre through it correctly but always able to extract
the exact piece of information under piles of precariously
positioned parchments (or PPPPs as people in his office call
them). The room, too, is a remnant of a different era; a time
only sixteen years ago but Raman could be speaking about
when dinosaurs ruled the earth from the incredulous wide-
eyed look people, especially young journalism students,
give him on the few occasions he is forced to speak of
those times.

'Investigative journalism then involved swathes of hard
to clandestinely photocopy records and hundreds of deep
throat and not so deep throat interviews. Very little was

digitized. It was, obviously, a long time before the era of Wikileaks and Snowdens. The consequences then were immediate, to the point and quite physical. Your life or your death. But perhaps in a different way, that stands even more true today,' he says thoughtfully into the silence—sometimes awed but mostly sleepy—of his class.

Okay, to be fair, he still receives slack-jawed looks of admiration from the new intern. Her internship partner, her classmate, with his preening smile, his self-conscious poses, who has little knack for and even less inclination towards their kind of sedate print journalism where the reporter stays in the background reporting and not being a part of the news himself, and who has obviously joined the magazine only to be able to spend more time with her, stands no chance of winning her affection. At least not for the moment. For the moment it is Raman who is squarely the target of her adoration. Raman knows that the admiration is transitory. That the thin-boned, selfie-taking intern with her bright, freshly scrubbed face tightly bound by a long silky ponytail, is so much in love with herself, with her own idea of love that it does not matter where her idolization is tethered and that he just happens to be the prime candidate at the moment but it matters not a twat to him. Isn't love, he thinks grandiosely, anyway about being at the right place at the right time? The aligning of chemicals in the right order to form just the right compound? He knows that she does not know him at all and that any resemblance that her idea of him bears to the actual him is purely coincidental; he can be whatever comes into her head, whatever she is reading, whatever she is listening to or watching at this particular point in time but boy, does her admiration, however misplaced, feel good! Especially on bad days like today. Her hanging on to his every word, her faithfully noting down, in her flashy MacBook Air, every little piece of pontificating shit that comes out of his mouth. And her filtering his every expression through the superbly flattering lens of her admiration to find him to be a more handsome, a more intelligent, a better communicator, a better journalist, and most certainly a better person than he actually is. She had probably read about him in her journalism class and has no idea that in the sixteen years since that story, he has been systematically down beaten and bedraggled and alcohol-soaked until now, in what can be considered the lowest point in his career, he has been asked to do a story on starving sisters. Starving sisters—can it be any mushier than that? He is beginning to understand what keeps rock stars and matinee idols going. This type of blind adoration can be therapeutic. Or addictive. Or perhaps he is just getting old like his little office space; the plans for whose demolition—to make way for an airier, better-lit, open plan work area—are already in place. But SLASH SLASH in big bold lines of the red pen of the previous section. Again, entirely immaterial to the story at hand.

Raman sits at his computer and reads as many news reports and watches as much television coverage of the story as he is able to without going brain-dead, noting down in his little notepad, the few factoids that he is able to sieve from the unending dribble that is spewing forth. There are opinions, there are impressions, there is thundering condemnation, there is excessive sympathy, there is cloying empathy, there is outrage but there are surprisingly few actual facts being bandied about.

Twins. Age 25 years.
Weight 18 kg and 22 kg. 18 kg? Need to recheck.
Father: Irrigation Officer
Mother: Housewife or Teacher?
Brother: Younger. By how many years?
All three dead in an accident
The sisters living alone since?
What work did they do?
Money in the house and in the bank
No relatives or friends?
WHY?—religious cult, suicide pact, mental illness, stupidity?
ACP Satya
Mr Deol
Dr Vaidya

He double underlines 'stupidity', adds a bold line under ACP Satya's name, and when he looks up from his notepad, he sees that it is evening already and the narrow slice of his office that he can see through the half-open door of his room has filled up during the time he had spent looking through his material. Most of his colleagues seem to be in now and he can see that the two interns are in too. They are both dressed in white jeans and fitted shirts and stand apart like shining stars from the bedraggled state that defines his colleagues in the evenings. 'You will never make it as journalists,' he wants to tell them. 'If you do not allow your hands to get soiled and your nose to be muddied, and if this superficiality is all you care about, you will never be able to cover a story well.' But what does he know? One of them could very well return as his boss five years down the line and tell him what *he* is doing wrong and how *he* can no longer survive as a journalist because with his lanky frame, his earnest thick lens glasses that sit below a crop of very dark straw-coloured hair (the colouring, a slightly embarrassing feature, is the handiwork of a recessive gene that decided to manifest itself five generations later, of a British great great grandfather incongruously named or perhaps incongruously remembered as, Peter Patterson. Mr Patterson had tried to elope with Raman's great great grandmother but had been caught by her family on the way to the railway station. And after being confined in the spartan discomfort of her parents' home for three days during which he had felt the weight of hundreds of comings and goings and the buzz of scores of hours of consultation, he had been let out to be adopted by the childless staunchly Hindu family of the bride's distant relative, had been given a staunchly Hindu name of Praveen Parthasarthy and been allowed to marry Raman's great great grandmother) and his penchant for digging deep into a story, when all people want is the fast food equivalent of a story—attractively packaged and easily palatable—never mind how much it thickens the synapses of their brains afterwards, he does not have what it takes to be a journalist. Suitably chastised by this discomforting thought that puts him in just the kind of agitated state that he wants to be in, he sets out to seek the man who is in charge of the investigation but who, until now, is the only person who has not appeared before television cameras to tell the world about how he has rescued the two sisters or to espouse his elaborate, pat theories about what could have transpired or even to provide the usual favoured journalist with the obligatory, bite-sized TV-friendly 'exclusive' comments and is therefore, hopefully, a kindred spirit. Banishing the niggling doubt that it may not be his refusal to abide by the rules of television that makes ACP Satya behave like this but his inability to actually string his thoughts cogently that compels him to do so . . . even awareness of his own limitations is worth quite a lot in these days of illusions of grandeur, Raman reassures himself as he enters the police station, swinging his large backpack clumsily over his shoulders. The standard issue laptop backpack that he carries is meant for someone younger. A nerdy college boy perhaps. But it has so many useful little pockets that hold so many of the little essentials of his life in neat cloistered packages—perhaps the only place in his messily spilled life where things can be separated into neat little sections—that he is unwilling to let it go, despite its sagging bottom and its precariously worn out edges.

5

The Tarsier

ACP Satya is standing with his back towards the door when Raman comes in. He seems to be looking at the last light of the sun through the Ashoka trees encircling the police station that is located in Lutyens' Delhi. With its profusion of unkempt greenery and its ornate, dusty white pillars, the station looks more like a forgotten colonial haveli suffused with the indolence of hookahs and biryanis, than a buzzing, state of the art, crime solving centre.

'I don't know why you are here. I don't want to give interviews. I don't know anything more than what television channels have been showing since that night,' Satya says without turning around. 'Less, if you include all the theories that the TV guys are coming up with.'

He turns and Raman notices that he looks much more substantial in real life than he had looked in the few instances that television cameras had managed to catch him. It is usually the other way round with people. Even waiflike, wavering, inconsequential persons come across as solid and charismatic under strobe lights; many a movie star and many a president having been made under magic spell of the right light. Satya is tall with a head full of lush curly hair that shines like a halo, backlit by the fading sun and for someone whose job entails coming face to face with the basest of human instincts every day, he has surprisingly soft, long-lashed, almost feminine, eyes.

'But that's exactly why I am here,' Raman says, somewhat disconcerted. He is not used to interviewing soft-eyed young policemen. 'I want to print facts. Not bullshit theories.'

'Ha! Not a very long story then'.

'No. As short as possible. Preferably about 140 characters long,' Raman does not know what makes him say that. Satya's unexpected countenance seems to have demagnetized his mental compass. That and an afternoon spent watching tear-jerking melodrama on the sisters' plight on television. He knows exactly where the bitter sentiment comes from, though. No disoriented mental compasses there. Raman's Twitter account is nearly six months old, but he still needs to force tweets out of himself. Having to fit his expansive thoughts into 140 characters is the antithesis of everything he always stood for. But the well-packaged CEO of his magazine was categorical. In order to keep their jobs, every reporter must send out two tweets every day. Retweets, although useful for earning bonus points, are not included in the per day count. In their one-on-one meeting, the CEO had told him that Raman was young, and he should move with the times and that long reads were not what made magazines. 'Long reads?' Raman wanted to ask, but did not for fear of souring what was obviously a lovingly nurtured affair between the man and his number-crunched, algorithm-backed ideas. He should think of doing shorter pieces, the CEO told him; those that did not require the reader to turn the page, ones that could fully fit on one screen of their tablet or web browser. So long reads are essays, Raman had thought, nodding dutifully again. Tweeting is a very good way to learn to write short and pithy.

'Your tweets don't have to be about the story you are doing. That will be nice because it will make people interested but you could write about anything contemporary. The more sensational the better!' The CEO's beatific smile had not wavered in the face of Raman's deadpan acquiescence. And Raman is nothing if not a follower of the words of a dictate to the hilt. Especially the absurd, illogical ones. 179 days since the one-to-one. Exactly 358 tweets. All flimsy, all forced. None, unsurprisingly, re-tweeted or even liked.

'I am going to the hospital. You can come along. You can ask your questions on the way,' Satya softens. He has no interest in Raman's professional shenanigans and troubles, but he understands what Raman means and empathizes with him. He too is astounded by the slants and angles and the bizarre theories that have been circulating about the Starving Sisters or the macabre #SS under which their story is trending on social media.

'But our talk will be off the record.'

Raman does not think a drive is the best place to have the conversation but there is the possibility that he may get to see the sisters and because of that, he agrees. He knows from the TV coverage of the sisters that seeing them will be quite a scoop. No journalist has spoken to the sisters yet, no channel has even managed to get any shots of the sisters. All conversations about them hinge on second, third and fourth-hand interlocutors. And all the coverage of their physical appearance centres around one glimpse of shorn dark hair and one fading group photograph.

Satya instructs the orderly to sit at the back of the jeep and takes the wheels, motioning Raman to join him in the front.

'Ask away,' he says manoeuvring through the twinkling red taillights and the obligatory high beam head lights of a typical Delhi evening traffic.

'How old are the sisters?'

'Twenty-five years, eleven months and one day.'

That is almost too specific. Raman looks at Satya but he is staring ahead, his expression unchanged. Is this how involved Satya is with all his cases?

'How long have they been starving?'

'Doctors think they have not eaten anything for at least four or five weeks. And before that also very little for nearly six months.'

'How are they doing?'

'Not good. One of them is in the ICU. She is quite critical. The other is not in the ICU but she is only slightly better.'

'Do they really weigh 18 and 22 kgs?'

'Yes. No. They weigh even less now. They have lost weight since they came to the hospital. Dr Vaidya says that is natural. She is their attending physician. She says that they had fluid retention in their bodies because of edema, some kind of swelling of tissues caused by starvation. It is going away slowly but they have still not regained healthy tissue to replace the weight of the fluid. The doctor says that it may be not look like it but apparently it is a healthy sign. It shows that their bodies are trying to recover from starvation. But honestly, I have not seen any improvement since I saw them first.'

Raman considers asking him more about what happened when he first saw them first. What they were like. What their house was like. But he senses that Satya would then put him in the category of voyeuristic journalists that, from the little he has grasped from seeing him on TV, Satya has a particular disdain for. And Raman is not sure whether he wants to know the gory details anyway.

'Educated?' He asks instead.

'Yes. Yes. Very much. Master's in Economics and Master's in English Literature. Both from St. Stephen's. Seems like they always topped their class. One is even completing her PhD.'

This time Satya turns to look at Raman.

'Why?' Raman has to ask.

'You tell me, Sir. They are not saying anything. One can't and the other won't.'

Satya drives his jeep into the hospital's dark basement through the back entrance, away from the clamour of flashing lights and cameras and journalists camping in front. It has taken a lot of persuasion to convince the journalists to stay inside the makeshift enclosure that has been erected especially for them on one side of the hospital entrance to allow for the movement of ambulances and patients and visitors of patients, and perhaps he is being unfair in avoiding the journalists. But he knows that the doctors will be reading out their evening press statement in a short while that will provide them with enough fodder for another round of Breaking News to fill the next few hours of their reporting.

Satya walks straight towards the ICU but Raman hesitates. ICUs stand for everything that he keeps away from. The emotional swings, the hopes, the despairs, the goodbyes, the miracles. It is a world that communicates in a language that Raman has never been able to converse in. He is at home with the squalid, the tough, the uncomfortable questions, the dark alleys, the facts and the numbers but if he finds himself in a situation that needs him to be human (such a lame term, Raman scoffs, for all that it is meant to encompass), he flounders. He gets the bad guys. He understands how their minds work and he knows he can, to some extent, deal with whatever form their wickedness takes. But he cannot believe people can be good under all circumstances. Goodness requires a conducive atmosphere and given the right push, everybody can turn evil. 'I have a problem with the good guys', Raman says. 'Because I can't predict their actions. Or their motivations. Or the circumstances under which they will stop being so good.'

Good guys like Satya, who, Raman sees to his relief, takes off his shoes and carefully wears sanitized boot-covers before going in alone to see the sister who is being treated and monitored inside. Raman stands staring determinately into his phone to avoid having to look at the tired, dishevelled, shallow faced, bloodshot-eyed relatives of the ICU patients who mill around like quiet little zombies in order to stay below the radar of the hospital administration that has, precisely to discourage this kind of crowding near the ICU, placed no seats there.

Satya shakes his head when he returns.

'No improvement', he says and Raman sees he has tears in his eyes. Real, unadulterated, unforced tears. Tears in Satya's eyes are bad enough but what is even worse for Raman is that Satya makes no attempt to hide those tears. He does not avert his face or pretend that he has got something in his eyes. He just looks sorrowful and straight at Raman who panics and looks away quickly. Raman is *not* the touchy-feely, sympathetic type and he cannot handle emotions—not in little driblets and certainly not as an outpouring. The heart-to-hearts. The holding of hands. He, unsurprisingly, has no friends and he likes it and wants to keep it that way. He prides in having no emotional needs and the city of Delhi provides enough means to fulfil his physical ones. In order to avoid having to comment or react to the tears, Raman pretends to not see them and steps back a little to allow Satya to finish his crying. He continues to stay behind Satya who walks down the corridor, enters another room—this one a general room, not a part of the ICU—and he still stands hesitantly outside for a few seconds before following Satya in.

Stepping into Room 107 is like stepping close to a furnace. It is so hot that Raman's thin linen shirt sweatily sticks to his body almost immediately. Yet there are thick red blankets covering the sole occupant of the room who still seems to be shivering slightly on the bed. Surely that person is too small to be a full-grown woman? Raman stares at the tiny triangular face above the blanket and decides he has enough material for his article. He does not need to know more. His is not meant to be an investigative piece; he has to do a human-interest story. He begins forming the parameters of his magazine piece, how he will begin, the number of words, the angle, the tone, how he will describe what he is seeing . . . he has just about wrapped up almost the entire article in his head when the door behind him, moving slowly on its mechanical hinges, swings shut with a small click and the face opens her eyes and looks straight at him.

Raman finds himself staring at the most remarkable eyes he has ever seen in his life. Something inside him shifts. With her hair unevenly shorn close to her head, her ears jutting out and her overlarge eyes occupying almost her entire face, the woman on the bed reminds him of something delicate, vulnerable, endangered and not quite human. A tarsier, he remembers, the nocturnal primate of the jungles of Southeast Asia whose pictures he had seen quite recently in the *National Geographic*. Her eyes are fixed, unmoving exactly like a tarsier's but unlike a tarsier that has light brown or yellow cornea, hers are white, strikingly so, and lifeless. They look like they are made of unglazed porcelain with not a shred of red or a hint of life in them. The only sign of life comes from the monitor on the right that shows a waving green line and a lot of numbers among which the one number whose meaning Raman is sure of is the steady glowing '29' in green on the top right corner.

He knows that the number means that her heart is beating at a very low rate of 29 beats per minute as opposed to the normal 60–100 per minute. There are no feeding tubes attached to her but there is an IV drip that is probably administering glucose into her deprived, shrunken body, one drop at a time.

'Hello,' Raman hears Satya say softly. 'Can you hear me? Can you speak? What is your name?' He is bent close to her; so close, in fact, that he misses seeing her lips move but Raman sees it and he knows what she has said because he had learnt rudiments of lip reading when he was thirteen and had aspired to grow up to be a spy. A tough unemotional, unencumbered, womanizing spy a la James Bond of the 1970s. Not the humane/human James Bond of the 2010s who seems to have had a childhood and is sensitive enough to be tortured by the experiences of his childhood.

'Tanya,' Raman says. 'Her name is Tanya.'

And although Tanya does not move her head, or her eyes, or her lips, or any part of her body and nothing in her expression changes, Raman sees on the monitor that her heart rate increases to 35 for a few moments and he knows she has heard him. Perhaps she will speak to him too. Not today maybe. Maybe not even tomorrow but soon. She *has to*.

When they come out of the room, Raman patiently explains to Satya how he was able to understand what Tanya said, and later he dutifully takes notes while Dr Vaidya—a sharp, bespectacled woman in her early fifties wearing a block-printed cotton sari and thick buff-coloured shoes—briefs

Satya about the condition of the two women. 'Not good,' the doctor says echoing what Satya had said earlier. 'Not good,' Raman writes in his notebook. Dr Vaidya lists out a string of parameters and the sisters seem to be doing very badly on all of them. And Raman takes down every detail that she provides, from blood pressure to blood oxygen level to urea and uric acid level. Dr Vaidya calls the lack of redness in Tanya's eyes 'avascularity'—a condition of having almost no blood vessels (Raman writes a-v-a-s-c-u-l-a-r-i-t-y carefully in his notebook) and she tells him that it is an unexplained symptom of starvation. She smiles slightly and congratulates him on being able to communicate with Tanya, and Raman smiles in response, and nods in agreement when he hears Satya request the doctor to not include in her evening briefing the information that they now know which sister is who until they have had a chance to find out more. But all Raman can think about the entire time he is speaking with and listening to Dr Vaidya and Satya and taking down the notes and nodding in agreement, is the tiny tarsier face, the enormous tarsier eyes and the elongated tarsier fingers.

At night for the first time in his six-month old Twitter life, Raman tweets not to reach his obligatory quota of two tweets per day but because he cannot contain the magnitude of what he has encountered within himself. He tweets a picture of the two sisters. Not as they look now. Not as she had looked that evening. Not the shrunken skeleton of a person that she has become, although that would probably have been more dramatic. But the picture of the sisters as they looked earlier, as they are meant to look. Still with unusually large eyes that invite instinctive trust but with softly angled faces with the too small nose, the too wide lips, the too high forehead, all individually almost too strong to find a place in their small, triangular faces and yet fitting perfectly like a cleverly crafted jigsaw puzzle. Framed by very long, curly dark hair. Theirs is a remarkable face, even beautiful if you are not too fussed about proportions and crave symmetry. The picture is one that Satya had given him when he had asked Raman to come again with him the next day to decipher her words in case Tanya spoke again. Raman had tried to keep his expression neutral, but he was filled with an unfamiliar sensation that he almost belatedly recognized as excitement, and he felt alive in a way he hadn't for a very, very long time.

For all the training that professionals undergo, for all the qualifications that they acquire, what often distinguishes greatness from mere goodness is a kind of serendipitous proclivity for greatness to be at the right place at the right time. Of course, Raman has no delusions of greatness or even goodness but why Satya chose to talk to him and why he took Raman along with him to the hospital, Raman will never know. If he were the astrological type, he would attribute it to the right alignment of stars, but he isn't and before this evening he would have attributed it to dumb old luck. But, somehow, tonight he cannot.

For the first time, Raman's tweet is retweeted. Not once, not twice. It is the top trending tweet in the country and is trending among the top ten in the world, his CEO calls to exclaim.

'The picture has already been retweeted 1,80,459 times and there is a Twitterati war of sorts out there where opinions are divided equally and aggressively, almost violently, between people who think the sisters are beautiful and people who think they are not. But believe me everybody agrees that the twin sisters, by no stretch of imagination, can be called ordinary.'

'Nobody had got a picture of the sisters before! How did you . . .' the CEO continues but Raman disconnects the call before he can complete his sentence.

25 and 26 October 2014

6

Autophagy

I opened my door and let in a deluge. I don't know why I did it. No wait. I know why. I did it for Layla.

They say identical twins can read each other's thoughts. That they can feel each other's pain across distances and laugh at a joke that the other has heard. Universities conduct research on twinship and there are festivals that celebrate the magic of it. But for a long time, I did not think this was true for us. I could not read Layla. Not initially. Or perhaps never. Perhaps when I started to imagine that I could finally understand her was actually the time when I knew Layla the least.

Oh there were the usual squeals of delight at the pretty picture we made as little children. Our inner separateness camouflaged behind our identical dresses (that Mamma insisted on when we were very young, more out of functionality—one large piece of cloth to stitch two frocks—kind of functionality, than because she felt any need to showcase our cute sameness), our identical

limbs, our identical curly hair, our identical faces and
our identical smiles (one more hesitant than the other
but nobody had the time to notice that; people usually
moving to the next shiny trinket long before that). Those
were times when there was still some fascination with
twins. When the concept of artificially induced children
was too far out there to be a real thing and quadruplets and
quintuplets were so unique that their stories came out as
books abridged in *Reader's Digest*. But our twinship was
mostly practical and prosaic and as they would have put
it, if there were some superficially written article on our
lives, nothing in our early family life had suggested how
things were going to turn out for us in the future. But
does anybody's early family life suggest how things will
turn out in the future? Do artists know? Do industrialists
(unless it is their family business) do thieves (unless it is
their family business again), do terrorists? Do murderers?
Do murderees?

Layla and I were not brought up on stories of Pollux and
Castor, Romulus and Remus, and also the Ashwini twins
and although we had heard about Laxman and Shatrughan
and Luv and Kush, and Nakul and Sahadev, we knew them
only as characters in the Ramayan and the Mahabharat
and felt no particular affinity towards or understanding of
them. Of course, we read about many of the mythological
twins later, though it did not help that there were no stories
of female twins.

But even if there had been any, I don't think I
would have felt any kinship towards them either because

despite our near complete physical similarity, it had been difficult for me to think of Layla as my twin when we were young. Born out of the same fertilized egg that broke into two. Had the egg not broken, would I alone have been born with Layla's brain or would she alone have been born with mine? But the egg did break and two embryos were formed and two baby girls were born. And although the two baby girls were different from each other in all but the most superficial of ways, it did not seem to matter to anybody but us. We were the inversion of how Homo sapiens as a species are—all the men and women in the world who are almost the exact replica of each other in all but the most superficial of ways; the apparently insurmountable differences between races literally only skin deep; a result of very minor alterations in the genetic sequence, a quirk of a few codons.

It was the time before routine ultrasounds of children in the womb after every trimester and under any pretext, so there is no way to confirm this but had there been any pictures of us in Mamma's womb, I am sure it would have often shown us with our backs towards each other.

'The world still bridged us together, didn't it, Layla?' And our names, LaylaTanya were spoken unbroken in one breath by Mamma (who knew better) and Papa (who also knew better) and our teachers in school (who should have known better but never seemed to). And we were teased as Miss Showy, Miss Snobby, Miss Poshy—for the way we spoke—interchangeably too. I understand that these days schools split twins and put them in different sections of the same class to encourage individual ideas and thoughts and to facilitate the making of new friends. Our school didn't bother with all that and it didn't really matter because despite our close physical proximity in our school-going life, both at school and at home, we did not need any outside restriction or prompting to procreate individual thoughts. It was not for the lack of trying, though. At least not on my part. Only I had no real means of mentally plagiarising Layla's creativity. She read a lot but her reading provided no clues to her thoughts or tastes or ideas or ideology. At what age do we stop reading to form our beliefs and start reading only to reinforce what we believe in? At what age do we read not to get new ideas but to corroborate our existing ones? As far as I know, Layla never arrived at that age. That was also the time when information was not encapsulated to cater to individual palates and Layla hungrily and passionately read everything and anything that she could lay her eyes on. From billboards to envelopes made of newspapers to ingredients written on bread packets and composition of cosmetics, no written word ever passed by her without being devoured. But her eclectic reading meant that I could, for a long time, get no insight into what she stood for. Layla and I had different sets of friends too but I was close to nobody and I know she did not have any close friends either. Even as children, it was as if the magnetic field of our similarity repelled the advance of any outside force field. But we never thought each other alike, our physical similarity being of no consequence to our relationship for a very long time. That came much later.

'Although you kept me at arm's length, even you could not circumvent the biology of our twinship, could you, Layla?'

According to Mamma, as children, Layla and I reached all our physical milestones simultaneously, with Layla taking the lead and I tenaciously following her within the span of a few days and sometimes even a few hours to religiously take my place behind her. Our height and weight charts remained nearly identical. Our grades in school always matched (Layla sometimes scoring a mark or two extra) even though we were made to sit in different corners of the classroom to make sure we did not cheat, and we never studied together at home. And with our uteruses releasing their useless bloodied lining within a day of each other, our menarche, as they put it in the books that I read much later, happened together. And as far as I knew kept apace for as long as we had our periods, which wasn't for very long, if you really think about it—about thirteen years. Not very long at all.

I knew I had to open the door of our house to save Layla. If I didn't move soon, I would never reach the door. It would keep moving further and further away from me 35 feet, 40 feet, 45 feet. I knew also that Amar or Samar would soon realize that there were other roles assigned to him by the world. A world that keeps billions of people engaged in doing something. Billions of human beings toiling away in useless endeavours in a system set up to give some piece of work to everyone and to lull almost everybody into thinking that they mean something. They matter. That theirs is the only exalted species permitted to do whatever they want to do with everybody and everything else on earth.

Once the little boy outside our door realized there were other ways devised to keep him busy, he would be sucked away from the force field of our door. And if he lost interest in our door, Layla too would be lost forever, disappearing into a space that I would never be able to reach. I did not want that to happen. Some part of my brain always knew that one day we would come to this. That one day we would need to open the door that existed as a flimsy but oh-so-protective barrier between us and the world. The part of my brain that was still working.

With no food inside me, my body had been eating itself to stay alive. This phenomenon has a name but I cannot remember it now. I had read that the human brain takes up more than 20 per cent of all the energy that a body uses and there is something called the Blood Brain Barrier (BBB)— tiny vessels—that allow only a few nutrients to reach the neurons. These nutrients need to either fit themselves through the holes in the BBB or be carried through it by other substances or most interestingly they need to break down the BBB itself in order to reach the neurons that fire the brain. If my body had been eating itself to stay alive, did it mean that my brain too had been feeding on itself to fulfil its nutritional requirement? No, no. I remember. The brain accounts for only 2-3 per cent of the body weight. Had my brain used itself to fulfil its humongous, disproportionate energy needs, it would have eaten itself completely. And if that had really happened, what part of my brain would have given the instruction to its last remaining bit to take that last bite, finish that last morsel of itself? No. If my body was eating itself, my brain would get eaten almost in the end. Because if my brain died, I would die too. Was that what was happening to Layla? Was her brain dying slowly? Was her BBB breaking down and feeding itself to her neurons?

I could not let that happen. I had ushered in the noise and the lights and the human beings. Amar or Samar at first, and two and three and four and ten and many, many, many, human beings. Mostly men but women too who all seemed to be in such a hurry—zipping in and out of my line of vision making me dizzy, producing so much noise and talking so much—that it hurt to hear them. One man— whom I think I was supposed to recognize but I am not sure why—threw up in front of me. Was he sick too? There were lights outside that were blinding me. There were more lights than even human beings or perhaps it had just seemed that way. I had opened the door and let in a deluge that wanted to take over all my senses. So many parts of my brain were being targeted that none had seemed to be able to respond or even comprehend anything. I had felt somebody hold Layla. I had felt somebody hold me. It had felt horrible. Not poking touching perverted horrible. Just cold, clammy horrible. But the hands that were holding Layla and lifting her were assured, capable and I had begun to relax. They had asked me questions, I think. But my neurons and synapses had started to dislodge from their positions. The house had disappeared. The couch was gone, followed by the wallpaper and then the print of *The Two Sisters*. I could see nothing, hear nothing. I could feel nothing. No pain. No joy. No exhaustion. Only a glimmer of Layla's presence somewhere near me. Just beyond the reach of my shut eyes and my outstretched hand.

I am in a room with a white ceiling that has grey patches of a previously damp wall that had dried and is peeling off. My right arm is tethered to a drip.

'Tanya,' somebody says. There is a woman sitting next to me. She pulls her chair close to my bed and bends over my face.

'Tanya,' she says again.

How does she know?

'Are you awake? I am Doctor Anita. I am the Psychiatrist at the hospital and I am here to help you. Bachche, you have been through a terrible time. Can you hear me? Can you talk?'

She touches my palm hesitantly as if building up the courage to hold my hand. 'Don't touch me,' I want to say, but I see there is dried flour batter stuck at the corner of her right thumbnail. Just like Mamma. Mamma flitted from one chore to the next, from one person to the next, carrying little remnants of one job to another, the essence and viewpoints of one person to the next—binding us together.

Dr Anita smells of roasted peanuts. Roasted—R. We have not reached R in our alphabetical order of starvation. We have not even reached P. But peanut is protein and therefore contains amino acid. AA. I cannot eat it. In our alphabetical list of foods to avoid, A had obviously been the first. And one of the amino acids that peanut contains— Arginine—also begins with A. Peanut also contains potassium and magnesium and copper and manganese and iron and phosphorus. It is all coming back to me in little snippets of floating images like the mathematical formulae that float across the screen in movies that show math wizards making humongous calculations in their heads. Sine, cosine, tan, theta. It is probably all the salts they have been pumping in me through my arm that is making my brain go into overdrive.

'I can't understand anything that she is saying. She is not saying Layla or Tanya. What is their surname? No, no, no. I am sure she is not saying Sharma. But I really can't understand anything. Maybe she is talking nonsense. Gibberish.' Dr Anita is talking too loudly, addressing somebody in the dimly lit room whom I cannot see.

'I am not talking to you anyway, you loud maniac,' I want to shout. People in real life look so flawed. Their teeth don't match perfectly. Their skins are not as even-toned as they appear in their selfies. There are blotches on their faces and dark marks on their teeth. Even mirrors don't quite show you your true selves, do they? They either distort or enhance us depending on the quality of the mirror and the type of light. The last time I saw another person, if I don't count Layla and the little boy and all those people who had swarmed into our house who I can't count anyway because I had not really seen any of their faces, was as an image on my computer screen—Facebook faces—where everybody looked beautiful and well-lit and everybody seemed to perpetually be taking holidays, eating out and holding strong opinions. As Layla says, everybody has always played the lead role in the movie of own lives but now they can actually direct and see that movie online. Now they can put their best pictures, taken from their best angles, showing their best features. They can do things that they feel best doing or what is supposed to make them feel the best doing. They can literally build the narrative of their own lives according to how they want it or mostly as the way they want their lives to be seen by others. Mark Zuckerberg has taken fifteen minutes of fame and super-sized it!

But the side of Dr Anita that I can see is not particularly flattering. With little rolls of fat escaping her tight blouse, her printed polyester-blend sari, her hair pinned primly with what appears to be at least ten bobby pins on each side and her large bindi matching the pink and black colours of her sari, she looks nothing like our beautiful Mamma. How did I ever think that she reminds me of Mamma?

'Arrrre, I think she said "Mamma",' Dr Anita exclaims triumphantly.

Have I said that aloud? Had I shouted 'loud maniac' aloud too? Have I become so used to speaking all my thoughts out loud that I have lost the ability to curb that proclivity? I had used up every word to keep talking for Layla but am I now unable to distinguish between what I am only thinking of and what I am speaking out loud? I don't want to talk but I can't stop thinking, can I? And that probably means I can't stop talking either. Am I about to blurt out my entire life story to this woman without knowing and without her understanding even a little of what I am saying? This is scary. I don't want anybody to hear what I am thinking. I want everybody to go away so I can structure my thoughts. Construct my words. So I can think before I speak and not as I speak or sometimes even *after* I speak. 'Go away,' I say. 'Go away. Leave me alone.'

'We should get the journalist back. He can tell us what she is saying. But maybe he was just lying. He knows the two women are called Layla and Tanya and maybe he decided to call her Tanya to make his story sound better. How do we know that her name is Tanya?'

How do *I* know my name is Tanya? Maybe I am saying it to make *my* story better too. Maybe you are saying your name is Dr Anita to make your story better. I am certain I said this aloud too. But Dr Anita is so pleased with her line of thought that she is no longer paying any attention to me.

'You cannot trust these journalist types,' she is saying quite loudly again, obviously still not talking to me. 'You know, two TV people even came to my house yesterday with their big cameras. All because they found out that I worked in the hospital where the Starving Sisters had been brought. They scared my dog but you should have seen how excited Neha got. She wanted to do her own talent show. A private 'India's Got Talent'! Fortunately I was at home otherwise I am sure she would have started singing and dancing on *Poora London Thumakda*. She sings only that song all day long. She is eleven years old but already one thing is sure. She is not going to grow up to be stuck in a hospital like her mother.'

Dr Anita is laughing. Who is she even talking to? I can't see or hear anybody else in the room. Am I in a mad house? In one of those places they show in movies where a deluded inmate genuinely believes that she is herself a doctor? I try to turn my head to see if there is anybody

else in the room. But I can't. I try to lift my hand to
touch Layla. But my hand hurts. It hurts in a different way
than before. Whereas before, all of my body hurt, now
the pain seems to be duller and concentrated in different
parts. And Layla isn't here, is she? She is somewhere else.
Somewhere she is safe. Somewhere she is getting proper
help. Somewhere she is being looked after by real doctors.
Not a pretend-doctor.

I remember who had called me Tanya. The man whose
voice felt like it was cracked around the edges. As if it had
to scrape against his throat in order to come out. Like
speaking hurt his throat. Just the way mine used to when I
spoke at home. My throat doesn't hurt any more though.
Actually, I can't feel my throat at all. Have they cut it off?
Ha ha. Perhaps it doesn't hurt because I am not speaking.
Or am I speaking constantly even now but it doesn't hurt
because they are pumping all kinds of medicines into
me? Does the name of any of the chemicals in any of the
medicines begin with an A? Or B? Or any alphabet until
N? Would ingesting something intravenously that begins
with an A count as breaking the rules of our starvation?

But the alphabetical list of starvation has stopped
mattering, right? We could not find anything that did not
contain something with an A or B or any alphabet until N.
The only exception we had made had been for water. We
had not reached W, of course. But we had also ignored
its composition. Layla had suggested pretending to not
remember that water was hydrogen and oxygen and I had
played along. I wish Layla were here now. But maybe she
is better off where she is. With real doctors. Not inside this

mad house where inmates pretend to be doctors. I think I have said this before. 'Tanya,' the man had said. He sounded honest. I must be Tanya.

'She said "Tanya"!' Dr Anita has been able to decipher one more of my mutterings. 'Yes yes, I heard her say it. Call the journalist. I don't think he was making it up.'

Yes. Call the journalist, I think. Or say. I don't know. But don't call him now. I am tired and I want to sleep. I try to synchronize my breathing to Layla's wherever she is but I know without anybody telling me that hers is still much slower than mine. It is moving in fits and starts, like my talking. I wish Dr Anita and whoever is here with her would go away so I could calm myself and make my breathing slow down to match Layla's. I remember one more thing Dr Anita had said. Starving Sisters. LaylaTanya are obviously being bridged together again and now we are Starving Sisters. *Starving* Sisters. That is an interesting name. Has Dr Anita made that up? There is something else Dr Anita had just said that also sounds strange, incongruous. But I can't quite remember what it is.

I hear that gravelly voice again. But this time it is close to me and there is morning light in the room. And I can hear another voice. I have heard that voice before too. I open my eyes and there are two bodies towering over me and two faces staring at me. Two male faces about the same age, built similarly. Both are tall and lanky with a lush thatch of hair on their heads but that is where the similarity ends. One has soft, expressive eyes and the gentlest of smiles. I have seen him before. The other is scowling at me through his thick rimmed glasses that reflect patterns and numbers on the monitor above my head. I see that the man with the expressive eyes is wearing a policeman's uniform and I shut my eyes again.

Autophagy. I think the body eating its own self is called autophagy. Or maybe it isn't.

26 October 2014

7

The Incongruous *Fellowship of the Ring*

'ACP Satya!' Dr Vaidya calls out.

'This is ACP Satya,' she introduces Satya to another woman who stands next to her. 'This is Dr Anita. She is the psychiatrist who is handling the sisters' case. And this,' she says pointing to Raman, 'is the journalist I had told you about. I am sorry I didn't get your name yesterday,' she says to Raman.

'Would you two have the time to come into my chamber for a bit?'

'I am Raman,' Raman says to Dr Anita as they walk towards Dr Vaidya's chamber. Dr Anita smiles weakly in response.

'I heard you were able to understand what my patient said yesterday,' she says.

'My patient,' Raman notices. Not Tanya yet.

'Yes,' Raman says. He does not want to tell her any more. Her demeanour does not really inspire confiding in. Not a particularly helpful character trait if you are a psychiatrist.

'Come in. Come in.' Dr Vaidya is impatient. Both with the men and with Dr Anita, whose earlier suggestions about the line of treatment she wanted to take with Tanya has irritated Dr Vaidya. It is not how Dr Vaidya would ever approach her work, whatever the compulsion.

There is a long line of decrepit patients that goes far beyond the row of decrepit benches placed outside Dr Vaidya's chamber. 'I will examine them soon', Dr Vaidya tells the young nurse, who stands on her chamber door with a sheaf of papers in her hand shifting uncertainly from one foot to the other, before giving her a dismissive wave and shutting the door firmly on her face.

'Those are my spill-over OPD patients,' she explains to Raman and Satya. 'My two hours in the Outpatient Department are not enough to go through all my patients for the day. Most of them have made the long journey from Uttar Pradesh and Bihar to come and see me. I can't send them away without examining them. They have nowhere else to go in Delhi and they will end up sleeping on the road outside to come and see me tomorrow. That will only make them weaker than they already are. Chalo, we should hurry up.' Dr Vaidya motions all of them to sit down. 'Why we wanted to speak to you is because we are not able to talk to Tanya. And Dr Anita wants your help,' she says, looking at Raman.

'Yes, yes.' Dr Anita says. 'I cannot understand anything that she is saying.'

'Her mouth has fungal infection which is getting better with all the medicines. She is very weak like I told you yesterday but not so weak that she would not be able to speak at all,' Dr Vaidya says.

'She is probably suffering from extreme depression, or extreme depression underlined with some sort of psychotic element,' Dr Anita's attempt at psychiatric speak is limp and half-hearted.

'It will also help the sisters' physical treatment,' Dr Vaidya says. 'We have found no signs of toxicity in their blood streams but we haven't received the results of all the tests. If they have been exposed to any toxins or if they have taken any poisons, we should know about them as soon as possible. We can begin treatment immediately. The sister in the ICU is very critical.'

Dr Vaidya bends forward in her earnestness but she sounds tired. Raman knows she is one of the best cardiothoracic physicians in the country who is being wooed with offers of stupendous salaries by the swanky private hospitals mushrooming all over the city that are courting medical tourists. Is 'medical tourism' even a legit term? What diabolical mind had come up with it? Raman is doing his best to divert *his* diabolical mind from the proposition being put forward to lest his unseemly anticipation at the prospect of talking more with Tanya become evident to the doctors, making them suspicious of his motives and divest him of the opportunity altogether. Although even he is not quite sure what his motives are and where his eagerness stems from. Is it only because he is finally sensing the prospect of a good story? Or is there more to it?

'But all this has to be completely confidential till we have figured out the line of treatment and the sisters are on their way to recovery. I know you are a journalist and it is your job to write articles like it is ours to save lives. But you will have to wait a little. Afterwards you can write all the details in an "exclusive story", I think it is called in your language.'

Not really. In her position as a government doctor, she can't promise an 'exclusive', but Raman understands what she means. 'I can promise you my silence for some time. But I can't promise you any breakthroughs with Tanya. Tanya did not speak a word to us this morning.' Raman has to admit. If he does not say it, he knows Satya will.

Dr Vaidya and Dr Anita exchange a glance. Raman can see that co-opting him had been only one doctor's idea with the other going along because she does not have a better alternative.

'We will see how that goes.' Dr Anita looks straight at Raman.

Is she generally suspicious of journalists? Raman thinks, for which he can't really fault her. Or is it only this particular journalist that she is suspicious of, for which too she perhaps has a valid reason but since she does not have that information, he can certainly blame her.

'But can you come tomorrow morning to try to speak with my patient?' Raman hears Dr Anita say.

With Tanya, Raman wants to say. But stops short fearing that if he rubs her the wrong way, she may withdraw her largesse which she seems to be providing under duress because of the massive interest that *her* patient's case is generating. The Starving Sisters' case is on the front page of almost all newspapers this morning too, Raman had seen.

Today the story was accompanied by the picture tweeted by him. Even the pink papers seemed to have grabbed on to the story to serve as a kind of counterpoint to the buoyant post-Diwali mood. And judging by the presence of hordes of cameras and OB vans outside the hospital entrance, all kinds of news is probably still being broken about Tanya and Layla.

Raman is right. Dr Anita had not wanted anybody else involved in her case, but she had come to realize that she should use all the help she could get. As if the television cameras had not been enough, earlier in the morning she had been presented with another interlocutor who wanted to know even more concrete, cut and dried details about the Starving Sisters case and she wanted it all *in writing*. This kind of thing was easier for Dr Vaidya who had specific information to give. Blood pressure. Heart rate. Weight. Food and liquid input with enough delicate, oblique references to output of all kinds to keep everyone at least partially satiated from one bulletin to the next. In contrast, in the absence of any conversation with either of the sisters, all Dr Anita had been able to offer was 'acute depression with underlining psychotic elements' which was obviously neither here nor there. Fortunately, the Chief Medical Officer (CMO) of the hospital, who did not want to miss the opportunity of being in the limelight, had taken over media briefings from Dr Vaidya and since he was a man too self-important to really hear what anybody junior to him was saying, she had been able to get away for the last few bulletins with her 'acute depression with psychotic elements' theory. But this morning, there had been a knock at her chamber door and the CMO had walked in with the chairperson of the National Commission for Women in tow, who had not minced her words about how much attention she was paying to the case and how important it was for her to know *everything* about the sisters.

'It has already been three days and I have had *nothing* so far from you about the state of their mental health,' she had said. 'I have been answering all the questions on TV on the basis of nothing. Gulla. But now I need something. Winter session of the Parliament is going to begin in a week and some independent member will surely raise this question in Question Hour. Everyone wants to be on TV. You know how even small small Delhi issues become big national issues because of TV?' she had told the CMO who had nodded in commiseration. He had borne the brunt of and benefitted from many such cases in his long, circuitous rise to the top of the administrative hierarchy of his Delhi-based government hospital.

'So the Minister of State for Women & Child Development wants to be fully prepared. In four days you have to give a write-up to me that I will give to the Joint Secretary who will then brief the Secretary and the Minister,' she had told Dr Anita without a pause, and without waiting for her response, had walked out of the door leaving behind a faint trace of the red of her sari in the room and a rapidly diffusing residue of her heavy handedly worn perfume, changing the very character of her chamber. Dr Anita had been so flustered that she had immediately hurried to Tanya's room to see if she could, by some miracle, get all the answers she needed. But of course, that had not happened.

In fact today, unlike yesterday, Tanya had not even shown any sign of awareness of Dr Anita's presence, let alone react to her questions. There had been no tilting of the head, no flickering of the eyelids and not even the slightest movement of her lips. This complete lack of response had left Dr Anita in despair about the possibility of achieving any breakthrough before her report was due. Or ever.

Although Layla who was in the ICU continued to remain very critical, Tanya's vitals were improving slowly—her heartbeat was up, her oxygen intake was getting better, her kidney function was very slowly inching towards what it should have been, her liver was on the mend—so why was she not responding? As she improved physically, she almost seemed to be getting weaker mentally; the conscious part of her brain seemed to be shutting down. Perhaps she could give Tanya a Selective Serotonin Reuptake Inhibitor, an SSRI to re-activate her brain and get her to speak? But Tanya was primarily Dr Vaidya's patient and her consent would be needed before Dr Anita could add it to the cocktail of life-sustaining medicines that Tanya was being administered. With that thought in her mind, Dr Anita had rushed to catch Dr Vaidya while she was still on her rounds of the wards, before she went into her OPD. But even before Dr Anita had begun to state her reasons for administering the drug, Dr Vaidya had stopped her short with an incredulous, 'What are you saying? You know that Tanya's body is hardly in a position to tolerate SSRI,' she had said, barely able to keep her voice down despite being conscious of the retinue of resident doctors following in her wake.

Of course, Dr Anita knew that. She had been among the toppers in her MBBS course. She knew how strong the human body can be; how much people are able to tolerate. But she also knew the fragility of human beings, about what little it sometimes takes to push a living being over the edge. She had always been a very good student of medicine. She could recite the history of psychiatry in India backwards; from the Vedic times (the *Charaka Samhita* by Charaka, and the *Sushruta Samhita* by Sushruta) to the setting up of hospitals for treating mental patients during the reign of King Ashok, described in *Ashok Samhita* and the setting up of an All India Institute of Mental Health in 1954 and National Institute of Mental Health and Neurosciences in 1974—Dr Anita remembered it all. She knew the diseases. She knew the terms, she knew the practices, she knew the medicines and she could still regurgitate the lessons taught during her psychiatry post-graduation almost verbatim. But while she treated her patients competently, she had no interest in engaging too much with them. She already had too much that she had to engage with apart from her work. Her children, for instance. Fortunately, there had never been too many 'emergencies' associated with her work so she could always find time to attend to them. But that luxury had been taken away from her now with the Starving Sisters and the timing could not have been worse. Not only did she have to give the answers (in writing) as to why the sisters had done what they had, and provide a satisfactory roadmap of what could be done to avoid the recurrence of such a situation in future, she also had to return home early over the next few days because her son had his entrance exams of his engineering coaching this week that could get him enrolled into the premier engineering entrance coaching institute that would, hopefully, in turn, provide him with the wherewithal to do well in his engineering entrance exam so that he would be eligible to be admitted in one of the coveted Indian Institutes of Technology. She had the responsibility to ensure that he completed his preparation. She also had the responsibility to keep him well-fed and well-clothed and in good spirits. She marvelled at the long checklist of things that were all her responsibility; things to do and things to take care of, things that she had to ensure went well. She sometimes envied the women of her mother's generation. At least then their only responsibility lay in their homes.

'We have to take care of the house and of the kids, of course, but we also have to earn a living and contribute to the family's income. All the time saheb remains saheb whether or not he earns enough to put roti and sabzi on our plate. He is entitled to put his feet up and watch as much cricket as he is able to. There is always a cricket match on TV and there are always faithful watchers of all types of matches. So he impartially distributes his love between all the thousands of types of the games. He evenly appreciates the intricate techniques required to master every type. He is able to list the virtues of classic straight-bat batting of test cricket as well as the adrenalin-pumping hitting required in the T-20 version. I am sure this is not what feminists had in mind when they fought for women's empowerment!' Dr Anita tries to be wry about her position but this morning she had stood flushed in front of Dr Vaidya, looking so stricken by the thought that she had considered resorting to such a blatantly inappropriate, over-aggressive line of treatment with Tanya, that Dr Vaidya had curbed her reprobation and had suggested that they take Raman's help because he was the only one who seemed to understand what Tanya was saying. And Dr Anita had agreed because really what other choice did she have?

'Layla. That is an unusual name,' Raman begins when they get out of Dr Vaidya's chamber. But Satya is putting on the scrubs to go into the ICU and he does not respond. He has probably not even heard Raman. This is the second time today that Satya has gone into the ICU. The first time had been in the morning when he had donned the scrubs with the solemnity of a priest about to undertake a holy ritual and had entered the sanctum sanctorum of the hospital leaving Raman standing impatiently outside the ICU. Satya had, again almost ritualistically, come out of the ICU looking downcast. But, to Raman's relief, he had not cried and he was composed when he had entered Tanya's room after his visit to the ICU, followed closely by Raman.

'Can you talk?' Satya had asked Tanya.

'Do you remember anything of your time in the house?'

'How are you feeling today, Tanya?'

Tanya had opened her eyes at the first question, but she had shut them again and had not given any further indication to suggest that she could even hear Satya. Raman had noticed that although her heartbeat was marginally healthier today at 33, she looked paler and more worn out than she had looked yesterday. Satya had tried asking her every question that might elicit a response and provide them with the answers that he was seeking—details about the sisters and the reasons for their starvation—but he had given up after almost twenty minutes of inane questioning done in an arbitrary order; anything, he told Raman later, to get her to speak or at least to move her lips. If this is how Satya conducted his interrogations, he probably did not get too far, Raman had thought as he had stood back the entire time, hawkishly watching out for any response from Tanya. But there had been nothing. Her heartbeat had continued to be a steady 33 and her expression, except that one time when she opened her tarsier eyes, had remained unchanged.

When coming out of Tanya's room, Satya had said that he wanted to return to the ICU once again to check on the first sister, Raman had refrained from commenting on Satya's unusual interest in the sister struggling in the ICU because his own disappointment at Tanya's lack of response was so inordinately enormous that he had some trouble attributing it entirely to his professional frustration. After that lack of response from Tanya, Raman had not been sure whether Satya would allow him to accompany him to Tanya's room again because if she didn't move her lips at all, how would his lip-reading ability help? But when they were on their way to Satya's second visit to the ICU, Dr Vaidya had called them into her chamber and spelt out her exquisite proposition, allowing Raman to begin breathing normally again. Now he had the doctors' consent to come to the hospital to try to speak with Tanya even without Satya.

'Would you like to come for a drink at the Press Club this evening?' Raman suggests to Satya when he comes out of his second visit to the ICU, looking as despondent as he had looked after his previous visit in the morning. Raman is feeling generous. 'I don't think we will be breaching any professional boundaries,' Raman adds when there is no response from Satya.

'No,' Satya says, accepting the invitation. ACP Satya is not married. His parents, and most of his friends, are in faraway Hyderabad. He has hardly made any friends in Delhi and there is nothing worthwhile waiting for him in his very basic bachelor pad. Delhi to him is a strange confluence of sharp, generously lipsticked faces and perfectly buffed bodies spouting the most inelegant of words and displaying the rudest of sentiments. He misses the friendly, uneven cadence of the Hyderabadi tongue and the more natural, more polite, more unselfconscious edges of the Hyderabadi demeanour; and he can sense that for all his professed knowledge of the wheels that turn Delhi, Raman is as much, if not more, of an outsider in the city as he is. And he has his mobile phone so he can be reached wherever he is in case of any urgent work.

Raman is already at the Press Club when Satya arrives and conscientiously declines the subsidized Rs 36 Royal Challenge whisky on offer, opting instead for a glass of Tropicana orange juice that is priced much higher than the whisky and that the bartender has some difficulty locating amidst the haphazardly arranged bottles of more potent drinks. He brings his glass of orange juice to sit opposite Raman who is staring pensively into his own glass of a glittering light brown drink that he is rotating in his hand. The lights in the Press Club bar are dim and the magic evening light falling on the trees that stand outside the large glass windows are making even the concrete floor and the strictly utilitarian steel-backed chairs of the bar look elegant, full of possibilities. Raman orders cheese and garlic toast for Satya's strictly vegetarian palate but neither of the men is in the mood to eat.

'Dr Anita seems like a nice person,' Satya says after a few minutes of silence. Mostly to fill the blank space that has begun developing that is on the verge of turning awkward. It is as if his being in civilian clothes has changed something. Raman is still dressed in the same, by now rather crumpled, khadi-linen shirt that he had worn in the afternoon.

'Yes, a *nice* person.' Raman continues to look into his twirling glass where sparkly little ripples are appearing and disappearing. 'A perfect product of our wonderful middle-class education. If you do very well in your studies, it is almost obligatory that you aspire to be an engineer or a doctor. She never thought about why she wanted to be a doctor or even whether she wanted to be a doctor. She was adept at getting high scores in all her tests. She chose psychiatry as her specialization after her MBBS probably because she did not get gynaecology. It was a good second choice because it does not require long and unusual hours. She can go home to her family every evening at exactly the same time and dutifully raise sons and daughters who will appear for entrance exams and become doctors and engineers themselves. She probably has never read a book or a paper on psychiatry after she passed her exams and still employs fifty-year old psychiatry techniques and practices because that was when her textbooks had been written.' Raman knows he should not be too uncharitable towards Dr Anita because she is providing him with the opportunity to do what he wants to do almost more than anything else at the moment and yet, he can't help himself. Something about her weighs inside his mind, occupies a space that makes him react to her. As opposed to, for instance, someone like his CEO who he dislikes enormously too but indifferently. He pays only as much attention to his CEO as is absolutely needed because of his position as his boss. Raman can't think of him as a person. He has no interest in his motivations, aspirations or even his background, although he knows all about that. The CEO does not matter to Raman. But Dr Anita, somehow, does.

'Sir, what are you talking about?' Satya looks surprised. This is not the conversation he had intended to start. 'Did you know Dr Anita before?'

'I don't know her but I know her type,' Raman says. 'Her kind of uninspired stodginess percolates everywhere. Once you get a job that will provide you with a pension when you retire, you stop doing anything apart from what is absolutely minimally required of you. How can you live every day and come to work every day and do the same shit over and over again? The endless cycle of lowering the bar so much that even if you do the worst you can do, you still get by.'

'A psychiatrist can hardly be doing the same thing every day. She probably meets more interesting people than you and me. She has to deal with more than us. You can afford to be cynical. Everyone does not have that luxury.'

'All the more reason for her to push a little harder because she *does not* have that luxury. People come to her at their most vulnerable. She should aspire to do whatever possible to give the best treatment to her patients.'

'How do you know she does not?' Satya asks and Raman only looks back at him.

'OK.' Satya concedes. 'But doctors are human beings too, you know. They want the same things as merchant bankers. Fancy cars, big houses, holidays abroad.'

'What has that got to do with anything? Is that even an excuse? How does being bad at your job fulfil those aspirations? How does turgidity help provide for your needs? Acquisition of skills and knowledge should not only be a function of material rewards, should it? Isn't it among the most basic of human instincts to try to do better?'

'Actually, no. According to Machiavelli, the most basic of human instinct is self-preservation and the preservation of status quo,' One of ACP Satya's choice of subjects for his Civil Services exams had been Philosophy. Philosophy, with its limited syllabus, is considered a high scoring subject, likely to allow you to crack the exam and find a little slot to fit into the clanking steel frame that the British had meticulously put in place to administer the unruly natives and that has been even more meticulously preserved and strengthened by the natives in the sixty-eight years since the British left as one more means to delineate the 'elites' from the 'non-elites'. 'For somebody pretending to be a cynic, you are quite the idealist. Aren't you?'

'No Sir, I am as far from being an idealist as can be. But it is a kind of national malady. This inefficiency. Or perhaps it is an international malady. Maybe all people at work everywhere in the world at this very moment are slumped down on their desks and doing the very minimal they can to retain their jobs.'

'That is not a very pretty picture.' Satya smiles a little. 'OK. I take back all I said about you being an idealist. But people in my department are not sitting uselessly at their desk at this moment.'

'Are you sure? Not even metaphorically?'

'Not even metaphorically. *We* certainly do not have that luxury any more. In fact, that reminds me. We have to go to the sisters' flat very soon to check it properly. Maybe we will go tomorrow. Would you like to come?'

'Are you allowed to do that? Go through her stuff?' Raman asks almost vacuously. Of course, they are allowed to do that but now that he has met Tanya—however one-sided the interaction may have been—there is something intrusive, perverted about the thought of anybody going through her things without her express permission. Or even *with* her express permission.

'I have to do it. It is a part of our investigation. We have to rule out any foul play. The sisters have not told us anything. We already searched the whole house the first day but now I have to do it thoroughly. We have to look at each little bit. Otherwise tomorrow the media will say that we conducted the investigation like the Aarushi case.'

Of course, Raman knows of the Aarushi murder case. There is probably nobody in the country who does not.

The case of the young fourteen-year-old school girl who had been murdered at home at night while her parents had been asleep in the room next to hers, has churned yards and yards of newsprint, provided months of footage to television cameras, inspired two movies and sparked off at least one book. When Aarushi had been killed, the police had been quick to assign blame; almost immediately airing the theory, with smug confidence oozing out of the police spokesperson's face like pus, that the live-in servant who had gone missing from the house after Aarushi's death was responsible for the murder. They had fanned out men far and wide in search of the servant only to find out a day later that the servant had gone missing because he too had been killed along with Aarushi. But because his body had been left on the roof of the house, and because the police had not taken the trouble to search the house thoroughly, the body had not been discovered for more than twenty-six hours after the discovery of Aarushi's body. In fact, the police been so sure of their servant-has-committed-the-murder theory that they had not even bothered to secure the crime scene that had been touched, trodden, and trampled upon by the goings and comings of police, media, family, friends, and any bystander whose morbid curiosity had got the better of them, precluding any possibility of ever finding out or conclusively proving who had actually committed the murders.

'But this is a completely different kind of case, isn't it? Or do you know something that you have not told me yet?' Raman asks. He has stopped playing with his drink and is looking rather intently at Satya now.

'No, nothing. I honestly don't even think there is a third party involved.' Satya pauses for a moment. 'But there are similarities, can't you see?'

'Yes. Both cases come from the hallowed middle class. That badgering holier-than-thou custodian of a society's morality. Nothing can ever happen to them without it being somebody else's fault.'

'Don't you and I belong to the same middle class?'

'Yes. I have seen how it can hollow out people from the inside while everything seems to remain intact on the outside. The rules, the trampling of any possibility of creativity, the rigid notions of success and failure. Oh, yes and the *huge* importance given to what other people think. The dishonesty even with your own self. It does not matter if you are angry, just keep your voice down because "what will the neighbours think?" The veneer of respectability under any circumstances. "What will people think? What will people think?" As if people think beyond what their brains have been fed in a small colourful, sugar-coated, latest gizmo-administered doses.' It has been a long day filled with complicated emotions. It probably had not been a good idea for Raman to have taken that second drink while he had been waiting for Satya to arrive.

'I mean both cases are women-oriented,' Satya says quietly, taking the wind out of Raman's bluster. He is too thoughtful to be provoked into defending the middle class. 'Both are very high profile cases with media ready to use even small mistakes to hang us. But no, you don't have to go to the house if you don't want to. Actually you shouldn't go. It will not be proper.'

'No, you were right in asking me to come along in the first place. I should go. I may find something that will help me get through to Tanya. We have not had much success with that yet, have we?'

'And we cannot possibly let your friend, Dr Anita, who has reposed so much faith in our success, down.' Raman wants to add flippantly, but of course, he doesn't. In the face of Satya's still, thoughtful earnestness, he cannot.

'When did you say you were going there?' He asks instead.

'Maybe tomorrow, maybe the day after.'

Raman notices that Satya does not commit to a date or to taking him along, but he can think of nothing to say to make Satya decide in his favour. Perhaps, as Satya put it, it *would* be improper for him to be there. In fact, he is not entirely sure that he wants to be there. But he knows one place where he wants to be right then. He decides to go to Tanya's room in the hospital before going home. He does have the doctors' permission to do that.

8

I Begin to Speak and I Cannot Stop

I once again hear someone come into my room but I don't want to open my eyes. I am very sleepy. It is probably the nurse coming to prod me one more time to see whether or not I am still breathing although the monitor could do that job as adequately. Or perhaps she is coming in to search my body for one more non-existent vein to push one more painful needle in, or it can be one of the cleaning men but they carry an acrid, antiseptic smell so it can't be them. It can be the doctor or the TV repair guy who Dr Vaidya had shooed away this morning, saying that 'does this patient look like she wants to watch TV?' I had seen him give me a sideways stare even as he was leaving the room as if he wanted to convey something to me. But maybe not. What do I know? I know nothing about how people express themselves any more, if I ever knew at all.

The deluge that I had let into my home has followed me to the hospital, and although as far as I can tell the arrivals into, the hanging around and the departures out of my room are far less than the full-fledged flood that had entered my home, there are still too many people around me. I am so tired with my effort to keep my mouth resolutely shut since yesterday through the questions that come with the people—questions that are often vocalized but sometimes are silent too—that I have often not even opened my eyes, fearing that my thoughts would once again escape my brain and pour out through my eyes and my mouth.

'Why is your sister called Layla? That is a very unusual name.' I hear the gravelly-voiced man ask and I open my eyes. He stands so close to my bed that he is blocking out the diffused fluorescent white light that is the only illumination in my hospital room at that hour of the night.

'Papa named her,' I say.

I don't know why I say it. Perhaps I want to try out my voice on a real person. I look at the man, waiting for him to react but he stands silently. Have I not said the words? Have I said the wrong words or said the right words wrong? I am not sure and the silence of the man gives me no clue. It doesn't help that I can't see his face. I too had practised silence since I spoke with Dr Anita last night, I think. Or was it the day before? I don't know but I had also practised talking when the little digital clock on table next to me had read 02:00. There was nobody in the room and I had said 'Layla' and I had said 'Mamma', 'How are you doing, Layla?' I had asked aloud. There had been nobody in my room then but now the man stands over me looking like God or Einstein (perhaps they are the same anyway) with his thatch of hair silhouetted against the fluorescent light. The pain in my mouth is nearly gone and the IV drip has been removed from my arm. I remember why. This evening I think, I had taken little sips of the salty indeterminate broth that the nurse after noisily cranking my bed up had thrust into my mouth. I had not asked her what it was. I had not spoken at all. The monitors are there with their wires attached to my body still, but the removal of the drip has meant that I can now move my arms. And somehow it also seems to have unanchored my head and I am able to move it a tiny bit too.

I look around to see as much of the room as I can and, as far as I am able to see, the man is alone. There is no policeman with him or Dr Anita. Nothing in his demeanour or in the tone or volume of his voice suggests that he is speaking to anybody but me and that is probably why I speak. I decide to risk testing my voice on him. I could have tested talking to that nurse, she was real enough but there was so much animosity emanating from her—in her baleful disapproving looks and in the brisk efficient but cold way that she attended to my needs—either because of something that I had done or because of something that she had to do for me that I had not felt like saying a word to her. She had not said anything to me either. She had not even looked directly at me. When had *I* last looked directly at my face? I am not sure but then I had seen Layla every day until two or was it three days ago before they had wrapped her up and carried her away like a lumpy, unwieldy mattress with barely any filling.

I know my sister is beautiful. Well, mostly beautiful. But not always. Sometimes in moments of repose or introspection or at any random unguarded moments I have caught her with her face flaccid, her lips looped down and her bright eyes dull. At those moments, her nose shines too bright, her skin looks spotty and I know that is what I look like in my unguarded moments. Scrunched and completely undistinguished. Not the way I look in photographs with my smile and my expression in place or in the mirror with my mouth slightly puckered and my head held high. I looked away from my sister in those moments because she made me see the futility of my carefully constructed persona, shattering my illusions of grandeur. Of course, those illusions, any sense of my exceptionalism is long gone. In fact, I am probably only imagining that they ever even existed. It is difficult to feel unique when there is another person who looks exactly like you, mirroring your every expression, replicating your every action, even if the replicator is as good looking as Layla often is. I want to talk about Layla now. I want to ask the man how she is doing. But first I need to breathe out. I feel like I have been holding my breath for a very long time. I have been silent during all the questioning that I have been subjected to. The questions are random, arbitrary and sometimes even offhanded, as if the person was flinging out a variety of baits, not sure which one the fish would bite. And as far as I can remember this fish had not bitten anything. Or had I? Perhaps I had talked but had made no sense. Have I forgotten how to speak sensibly? I am suddenly panic stricken.

'Layla was the first English song whose lyrics Papa had been able to completely decipher and he wanted to name his first child that,' I say. 'Papa jokes that it is fortunate that his first child is a girl otherwise his son would have been stuck with the name Layla'.

I am not sure if I laugh after saying this but once I begin talking I cannot stop. I shut my eyes and continue to speak. Or not speak. I don't know.

'Papa takes care of visuals,' I think I am telling the man. Why am I using present tense? I know Papa is dead. Or isn't he? 'You can see he isn't handsome by almost any culture's definition of handsomeness, but he has not let that come in the way of his self-esteem. He compensates for the shortcomings in his physical appearance by dressing right for every occasion. His clothes, his hair, his shoes are always appropriate. His suits are cut and ironed just right. The cuffs of his shirts show just-so below his jacket sleeves. The length of his tie is always right, the puff in his hair always in place. There is a swagger about Papa despite the chubbiness of his cheeks and the roundness of his physique.'

I am sure I am smiling.

'Papa says his good taste comes from the aesthetics of the granite rock with its unmistakable and extraordinary flecks that abutted his house in his village. He was born in a picturesque high Himalayan village that had precisely eight houses and only one child interested in going to school. Papa's school was an arduous 12 kilometre hike up and down the mountains but that didn't stop him. He undertook that journey without fail every school day. He has never told us how he had learnt about school and how he decided to go to one. He does not speak much about his time in that village that lay between India and Pakistan, and all my knowledge of his background comes from Mamma.

But she speaks of those times in Papa's life in hushed reverential tones and tells such incredible stories of his childhood and his youth that I am sure a large proportion of those stories come more from Mamma's imagination than from Papa's actual life! I know that Papa has no brothers or sisters and his parents died when he was only thirteen in one of those senseless shellings and exchanges of fire that occurs ever so often between the Indian and the Pakistani armies that kill more civilians than soldiers. And although it is a bloody manifestation of the simmering, inane tension between our two countries that can barely afford it, it goes largely unreported except sometimes as a small news item on page six of newspapers.'

I don't know why I am saying all this. I don't know which part of my brain the words are coming from. But the part of my anatomy that I am using to spill out the words feels scrubbed and renewed and delicious. I don't remember when I had last used my mouth without any pain. I want to continue using it. To form clean, clear, crisp and important words. Little Neel, Layla, Mamma, Papa.

'Papa has never told us how he scraped past this calamity and found his way out of the valley into the flatlands of north India, got scholarships and after earning himself a degree in Engineering from Roorkee, joined the irrigation department where he thrived in managing big dams and even bigger political egos. But he has told us a little bit about how he made himself ground up, piecing himself together bit by bit, reading as much as he could, clandestinely skimming through fashion magazines in news-stands, polishing his Hindi vocabulary and diction

by listening to All India Radio, his English with BBC
World Radio Service, his Urdu with bootlegged copies of
Pakistani ghazals and shayari to become the well-dressed,
well-spoken, well-polished person who is our dad.'

I pause. My mouth is beginning to feel dry, but I want
to continue speaking. One word after another after another.

'In order to shape himself, he had to let go of pieces of
his life that was gangrenous, Papa told me once. Although
he has never told us what he meant, and he says that his life
went into an upswell of good fortune once he met Mamma.'

'You know, when I was twelve, I discovered some
pictures of Papa. He stood in front of a mirror in those
pictures, holding a largish box camera in his hands. It was
a pre-selfie, pre-digital, even pre-colour photography age
and the number of portraits of himself that Papa could
afford to take from what was probably a borrowed camera
was, I am sure quite limited. There are only eight pictures
of Papa in that set. In the first two pictures you can only see
the puffed top of his hair and the fan on the ceiling above.
In the next two pictures he stands googly eyed and it is
only in the remaining four that he got his camera straight
and his smile right. His smile in those pictures looks like
an obvious, although I have to admit, a very unsuccessful
imitation of his idol, Shashi Kapoor's smile. It is so fake
that only Papa could have believed that that is what his
actual smile looked like. He probably had never been
caught off guard on camera. But there is innocence in his
poses and I understood more about Papa looking at those
black and white pictures than I understood from all the
stories that Mamma told us. Papa is not self-conscious

about the slightly misplaced narcissism in his personality. The bar of his narcissism is low and generous, and he allows everybody the space to be at least a little narcissistic.'

I know I need to stop talking but I can't.

'Mamma on the other hand, has a careless take on beauty that only the really beautiful and the really ugly possess. And Mamma is really beautiful. Papa and Mamma's love for each other is so naked, so verging on the mushy that it sometimes leaves us exasperated. Why don't you guys ever argue, Layla asked them once and Mamma said they had settled all their arguments long before we were born! There is laughter in our house and Mamma and Papa are open to being labelled joru ka ghulam and pativrata nari. Even by Layla. Sometimes even by me. And I blame Papa for making us believe that our house is a microcosm of the world. Open to laughter.'

I stop.

'What is your name?' I ask the man.

Who am I speaking to? What am I saying? What is it about the assessing, intelligent eyes of the man whose name I don't even know that is making me say these things about Mamma and Papa.

'Raman,' he says. So I am not talking nonsense. That is a relief. Raman stands still, staring at me warily as if I am a bird who will fly away if he makes any sudden moves or sounds. And yet there is something about him—about his stance, about the way he looks at me from behind his glasses through half-closed eyes—that makes me want to raise my hand and touch him. After the miniaturization of

Layla, and the presence of mostly slightly built doctors and nurses in my room, Raman looks big, solid, and somehow reassuring, seeming to fill the low-roofed hospital room with his presence. He does not ask me any more questions. Perhaps he is in my room not to ask questions but to stand and look at me to 'monitor my progress' as Dr Vaidya puts it to the entourage of clean white coat clad young doctors who accompany her to my room. They carry themselves with gravitas and sincerity and although all their questions are about my condition, they are always staunchly directed at Dr Vaidya and none of them has ever actually talked to me. It is as if I am not in the room with them. But I don't mind that. I would not have answered even if they had asked me a question and perhaps they sense that in their studious wisdom.

'How is Layla?' I ask Raman.

'She is improving but she is still in the ICU.'

I turn my head and shut my eyes because suddenly I am too weary to look at anything anymore. I am not sure for how long, if at all, Raman stays on after that because I think I fall asleep almost immediately.

9

More Motives, More Motivations but with a Smattering of Absolution

Tanya's voice is scrappy. Like little driblets of sound coming from a faraway place but Raman can understand everything that she is saying. Whether it is because he can hear everything that she says or because he can read her lips, he is not sure. It is like watching a movie in a language that you half-understand with subtitles in another language that you only half-know. Sometimes the sounds and the words reinforce one another, at other times, they cancel each other out, but together they influence the experience of movie watching in an impactful and yet completely indescribable way. Raman is afraid to say anything, more afraid than he remembers being in his life. He is afraid to even nod in case he stems the flow of words that are coming out of her as if they are cracking open a shell and emerging from the carapace; separate from the sparsely furnished hospital room with its white walls and lowered lights that they are in, separate from the hospital that has quietened around them after the frenzied daytime activities, separate from the more brazen television lights and cameras camped outside the hospital that still sparkle occasionally despite the drawn thick grey indeterminately patterned curtains and the lateness of the hour; separate even from the curled up tarsier herself, the words seem to be coming out with a life of their own, in a world that they are creating even as they are being uttered.

Raman knows he has hundreds of questions to ask but he has not been able to think of any because they do not matter. He has the strangest of needs to cover her up and shut the door and not allow any of her words to escape into the world. Like some kind of mussed haired, giant-sized archangel, he wants to spread his wings and stand between her and the world, between her and whatever is out there that she is escaping from or whatever she has inside her shrunken body and mind that has compelled her to turn out the way she has. He stands between her and the door silently and watches as her words soften and fade and her large liquid eyes shut down. He would have stood there forever—looking at those long, knotted tarsier fingers that still clutch the end of her blanket and that occasionally shake suddenly as if she has been jolted in her dream—had the nurse not pushed open the door and stepped in. The practical nature of her ministrations inside the room— her dimming the light even further, her putting a stack of medicine in the drawer of the table by the bed, her shutting the en-suite bathroom door firmly—lends such an air of the absurd, even a hint of perversion, to his still, unrelenting gaze pinned on a practically unconscious woman that he reluctantly leaves the hospital room.

Raman has never been short of words in his life; they have been his companion, his saviour almost from the time he formulated his first words (at the ripe age of two) which were, according to his father, an emphatic, 'No Ma, I don't want to eat that', when his mother had been trying to force feed him the pumpkin and carrot broth that she insisted was good for him. He never spoke in less than full sentences after that and the fluency of his language had earned him high marks in school and college even when his grasp of the subject about which he was writing or speaking, had been shaky. And now, of course, his livelihood depends on the capacity of his words to 'take his readers on a revelatory journey with him' (as his previous editor described it) or 'remain hooked to his story' (as his new CEO puts it). But as Raman sits that night, dressed in his shorts and the faded yellow, red and blue estelada patterned T-shirt that he has owned for almost as long as he can remember, bathed in the white light coming from his laptop, in his otherwise dark room, no words come out. Even the mandatory vacuous 280 characters of the two-tweets-a-day that he is capable of churning out almost in his sleep elude him. He picks up the phone and decides to utilize the time that his lack of words allows him to make the obligatory phone call to his mother that he has made every night without fail, wherever he is in the world and however important the task that he is performing at that time been.

His mother's number rings, is picked up after the fourth ring and as usual there is silence at the other end. Despite him calling her every day, she has not spoken to him for the last two and a half years or 920 days to be

precise; since thirteen days after his father's death. And
tonight is no different. The withdrawal of her words is
her way of punishing him for keeping the severity of his
father's illness from her. Or perhaps of just punishing him.
Period. His mother has always traded freely in emotions.
Guilt in exchange of accusation, tears in return for slights
real or imagined, laughter in return for jokes small or
big, funny or unfunny. In that she has been diametrically
opposite to his father whose emotions, like everything
else in his life, were wielded sparsely, stingily, if at all. His
father had always been a small, spare man, leading such a
compact, compressed life that the loss of his appetite and
the shrinking of his body in the year before his death had
been taken as the natural progression of his life-long quest
for invisibility, and had elicited no queries or concern from
anybody about the state of his health. His job as a librarian
had compelled him, or perhaps more accurately allowed
him the luxury, to tiptoe his way through the cycles of days,
weeks, months and years within which he had found the
means to be as little of a husband and a father as it was
humanly possible without actually abandoning his family
altogether. There were only two things that he was ready
to shout out his affiliation for: his love for books which he
was never far from, not in his job obviously but not at home
either where he brought books that he borrowed from the
library for his evening and his Sunday readings; and two,
his attachment to the Communist Party. He was a card-
bearing member of the Party and he wore his allegiance
literally on his sleeve in the form of a small brass hammer
and sickle amulet on a red ribbon that he religiously wound

over his shirt sleeve like an armband every morning; the only accessory that, as far as Raman knew, he ever wore in his life.

He had been diagnosed with stage four metastatic pancreatic cancer at the age of sixty-three in a routine check-up that he had allowed himself to go for after years of Raman's urging who finally convinced him to go by saying that he had a job that allowed reimbursed annual executive check-up for his 'dependents' and therefore it would not cost him any money. Or perhaps he had been feeling sick for some time, although he would never admit to that for the fear of attracting too much attention to himself. 'Just my luck to be punished with cancer for undertaking the first bourgeois activity I have undertaken in my life,' his father had said to the doctor before refusing any treatment except the minimum required to ameliorate his pain. It was he who had told a stunned Raman to not let his mother know the nature of his illness.

'I have so little time left and I would like to live it going about my activities as usual. I want to go to the library for as long as possible. I don't want to spend the rest of my days in the shadow of hysterical emotions,' he had said and, after confirming the nature, intensity and the hopelessness of his father's ailment, Raman had agreed for the first time in his life to become his father's confidant, a keeper of his secret. A sharer of his pain.

Or that is what Raman would have liked to believe. He would have liked to say that he spoke more to his father during the five months that he lived after his diagnosis than in his entire life before that, and that he got to know his father better in the months when he struggled with the limitations and the indignities that the ailment begat, than he had ever before. He would have liked to believe that in the face of his impending mortality, knowing that he had only a few months to leave his mark on the planet that had supported his presence for sixty-three years, his father would do something to make his legacy count, to go out guns blazing, as it were. But none of that had happened. His father had neither opened up to him nor to the world. He had continued to remain the same taciturn man who he had always been; passing the phone almost immediately to his wife, if he ever picked it up when Raman called and whenever Raman met him, he saw that his father was living exactly the same life that he had always lived, except at a slightly decelerated pace. Still marking his presence as lightly and with as few strokes as possible, still getting up at the same time, having his frugal but long drawn out breakfast, still counting his money carefully before folding it into a dark brown wallet, still walking out of the house to reach the government library that lay just a short distance away; the only concession that he made to his illness was that instead of leaving at 9.45 am to reach the library at 10, he began to leave at 9.35 to allow for the sluggishness that the disease and the few medicines he took for his disease caused. Raman's father died in the library and, like in some kind of farcical tragi-comedy, nobody in the library— neither its frugal patrons, the old wifeless men who came to the air-conditioned library mostly to catch their breaths in their lives lived trying their best to synchronize their slowed down limbs with the busy, frenetic movements of the households that their sons and daughters-in-law ran, nor the underpaid staff of eight that Raman's father cursorily oversaw—realized he was dead as he sat behind his desk with his head lowered into Hobbes' *The Elements of Law, Natural and Politic*, that for some reason he had decided to start reading after years of tethering his thinking on the writings of Engels and Marx.

It made for a macabre, even a funny macabre story, when months later Raman was able to think of it objectively and he was able to retell it on drunken evenings without becoming emotional. But it had not been funny for Raman at that time. Not at all. He had been almost physically heartbroken by his father's death in a way that he had not anticipated when his father had been living. And it was not just a sense that Raman was 'the next in line', now that the last person who preceded him in the natural order of things had gone. Although that thought certainly existed, but what caught Raman totally by surprise was the strong sense of loneliness he felt. Like he had been left alone in the world with nobody to confide in. Which was absurd given that his father had never been somebody that Raman had confided in—neither was his mother for that matter— but perhaps deep inside, he had harboured the possibility that some day in the distant future, perhaps when he was as old as his father, he would be able to understand his father and share with him some of what he felt; tell him what a difference he had made in Raman's life. Maybe even write a Kafkaesque book on his father's life, dedicate it to him and find a place for it in his father's library. It was perhaps the closure of all those possibilities that made him bereft. Raman had tried to use logic to explain what was inexplicable to him but even as these thoughts were streaming through his head, even when he was trying to attribute such logical reasoning to the unreasonable emotions that he was experiencing as he watched his father's still, lifeless face disappear behind the last piece of the logs of wood used on the funeral pyre, he knew his loneliness was not rational or cerebral but physical, primal, and very painful. A knife twisting in the heart, a strong kick-in-the-balls degree of tearful, painful.

His own emotions at his father's death had taken him by surprise but it was his mother's response in the aftermath of his death that troubled him even more. His mother was distracted, almost rudely so, which he understood; her life had been arranged around his father, her timetable had been synchronized to his and although they did not talk much, she knew he heard every word of the long phone conversations she had with everybody because she insisted on carrying them within his earshot, firmly in the belief that even though her husband may never acknowledge it (which he never did), in her volubility, she spoke for both of them. The unravelling of the threads of marriage that she had looped in and out through trips and conversations and resolving of household and work problems; through the routine of everyday living; of getting up in the morning from a bed on one side of which he had lain almost every day for the last thirty-eight years; of sharing of the pot of tea with him in the evening after always adding a spoon of sugar extra in his cup to cater to his sweet tooth and as a tribute to his being 'underweight' on the BMI scale (of whose writ, she was a staunch believer) all his life; the discussions that evoked reassuringly monosyllabic responses from him—had left her flustered and almost perplexed as if she didn't know what to do with her days, her furniture, her tea, and, like a bad actress, quite what to do with her hands. This much Raman understood. He had stood by her side and done everything he could to help her and when after the thirteenth day, the final rituals of death had culminated and the crowds had dissipated, he had held her and rocked her gently, like the roles had been reversed and he had become the parent he always wanted to have and she had been become his child.

It was then that she spoke to him for the first time about her husband's death. Before this the long list of rituals associated with the dead and the living and the efforts required for procuring the even longer list of ingredients needed to carry out those rituals had precluded the possibility of any non-utilitarian conversation. But now she spoke into the crisp starchiness of the white kurta that Raman had to wear as the lead participant in the ceremonies of the day.

'He never told us about his illness, Raaaaman,' she said. 'You know, I would have taken more care of him. I would have taken him to more doctors, called all the relatives. How long do you think he knew of his illness? Do you think he thought we would love him less if we knew of it?' She said irrationally.

'How could he do this to us when we . . . ' she began again before she stiffened mid-sentence because she had, by now, sensed the difference in the way Raman held her.

She took a step back, looked up at his face.

'I knew,' Raman couldn't not tell her. But perhaps he shouldn't have because she turned around and walked off. She did not wail any more or shout at him—in fact, he did not remember her shouting at him ever in his life; she had never been capable of displaying honest emotions, any honest emotions. Perhaps that is one more reason why he missed his father. Now the only family he was left with was his mother, who had never been his family in any real sense of the term. Her emotions were so non-spontaneous, so practised that his father's honest disinterest had seemed more heart-warming than her tutored lines feigning interest in how he was and what he did, in any way that would not have a direct or indirect influence on her well-being or her own stature in the world. She did not cry now. She did not even accuse him of betrayal. She looked almost disinterested. Like it did not matter anymore. She did not want to know the details of her husband's illness either. She was not curious about how long her son had known or how they had found out or what the exact cause of his death was. But mostly she did not want to know why they had not told her. Perhaps she was too scared to know. She never liked anything, especially anything that did not fit into her idea of herself, spelt out to her. She did not even actually say that she did not want to know anything anymore. But with a tenacity that surprised him for its length, if not for its depth, for the last 920 days, she had snapped shut any exchange of words with him.

She did not speak *to* him but she spoke *of* him and got her messages across and she still expected him to be standing next to her in public and participating in some

of the larger family weddings and, most importantly, in
the yearly ceremony marking the death anniversary of her
husband. Even on those occasions she spoke not a word
to him but her non-verbalization was done so artfully that
none of their relatives had any inkling of the estrangement
between them. It was as if she spent days plotting and
calculating and carefully choreographing the rituals to
ensure that they went through everything without having
to exchange any word and without anybody sensing their
disagreement, Raman sometimes thought. She lived her
life based on other people's perceptions. Perhaps as a
reaction to that, he did not care what anybody thought of
him or how the society wanted him to look or behave or be.
And reflecting more deeply on his mother's reaction over
the long period of time that she had accorded to him to
ruminate upon her silence, Raman realized that he should
not have been surprised by his mother's reaction or even
by her tenacity. The proximity that we share with our
parents puts them smack up against our faces, closer than
the least distance of our distinct vision, often precluding
the possibility of our viewing them as anything but our
parents, blurring our eyesight and clouding our judgement
which otherwise works fine, even with admirable precision,
in the world outside the insides of our homes, Raman had
explained rather convolutedly to somebody once. Now his
distance from both his parents allowed him to look at them
as individuals and he recognized that his mother had stuck
to his father with the same kind of tenacity and with the
same one-eye-out-for-the-world's-reaction kind of way
that she was displaying after his death.

She had worked her marriage within the boundaries defined for her first by her mother, then by her husband's mother and then by her own idea of what constituted a marriage; living the role assigned to her without faltering despite being a competent artist and a scholar herself who had topped her graduating class and who knew there was a world beyond her marriage that she was more than well-equipped to explore. Yet she had put her blinkers on and worked at being the 'good' wife, an effort that she had continued until her husband had gone and died on her. She would still have been the good widow and would have remained the good mother too (another role that she partook with almost the same degree of enthusiasm but with as little a degree of emotion) but when she came to know that she had failed in the one exam that mattered; that of being her husband's conduit to the world, she gave up. It was as if she had rehearsed all her life for this leading role and on the big opening night, the day when she had to showcase her glorious performance in front everyone, she had been told that she had been practising the wrong lines, picking on the wrong cues and had been deemed unsuitable for the part. Well, she had decided, if she had failed in that primary role, she would give up on all the other affiliated roles that came with it and since the betrayer—the substitute who stole her part—had been her son, it justified her giving up on her role as a mother even more. But of course, she did all this only privately and never let anybody else get an inkling of her perceived betrayal or her exaggerated response to it.

Raman, for his part, had tried to break down her resistance. He had tried speaking to her. He had visited her every day, hoping that the sight of him would help her change her mind. But it hadn't. She would direct her old help, Savita didi, to give Raman a cup of tea, go into her bedroom, shut her door and not come out no matter how long Raman sat in the living room—even when he once stayed on the couch the entire night. This kind of emotional manipulation of his guilt drained Raman and perhaps because his mother knew it was this very guilt—arising out of his inability to do anything about her loneliness, and out of her perceived betrayal—that would tie him down and hold him back and allow her to manipulate him even more, she continued to feed it day after day, month after month, year after year. When his daily visits had not worked for an entire month, he had begun calling her every night about the same time he had visited her for the last one month. The phone too remained unanswered until on the eighth day of his persistent calling, it was picked up but by this time Raman was so used to hearing only the monotonic ringing at the other end that when his mother had picked up the phone he had almost disconnected the call in a bout of irrational panic reminiscent of his first phone call to the girl that he had a crush on in school. When he had called the girl's number after mustering courage for days and had disconnected the phone without saying a word when she had answered. The only saving grace in his mortification then had been that those were pre-mobile phone, pre-caller ID times and there was no way the girl from school would have known that it was the lanky pimple infested, mussed haired boy who sat in the last row of the class who had had the audacity to call her and therefore his ignobility had remained anonymous, albeit sitting like a hefty weight in his heart throughout his high school days; lasting infinitely longer than his ardour for the girl that had dissipated almost on the day he made the call because of how inadequate she had made him feel. Mercifully the object of his affection and his disaffection had remained as oblivious to his presence, except in the most perfunctory way, through the days of his disaffection as she had been during the days of his affection.

He had, of course, not disconnected his mother's call, but when she did not say a word after taking his call, he started talking about the behind-the-scene happenings of the news stories of the day and the latest gossip about an amorous industrialist, the way he had always talked to her. As if the death of his father and the month-long silence afterwards had never happened. He did not ask how she was. It was she who used to ask him about the state of his health and wellbeing. 'Fine,' he would always say, making no attempt to correspond his answer to the actual state of his mind, which more often than not, would not be so fine. But he knew her asking after his well-being was only ritualistic. She did not really want to know his state of mind. It panicked her to go below the level of the superficial world that she had built for herself. He remembered even as a child, she would turn away to do something or direct him towards doing something on the few occasions when he had felt particularly vulnerable and had wanted to share his hurt with somebody. If his hurt were physical, in a way that she could see, she would do the ministrations and give him all the medicines that he needed. She would give him food on time and take care of all his physical needs. But if the hurt or joy was not tethered to a physically visible pain or an overt public incident like India winning a cricket match, she did not know how to react to it. It was as if she had no use or place for abstract emotions in her practical, self-oriented life. He had learnt to clam up his feelings since childhood. Or perhaps he had stopped feeling altogether, as some women had accused him in the past. He knew his mother was proud of his achievements as a journalist and happy to be party to the accolades that came his way, publicly staking her claim as a mother on his capabilities but he was also sure that she had never actually read anything that he had ever written. All Raman had ever shared with her when he called her would be little titbits of gossip about famous people, particularly politicians; pieces of information that every journalist in Delhi had access to, but about which, adhering to a kind of unsaid code, nobody ever wrote. He dispensed such nuggets because he knew she took vicarious pleasure in these stories that he had become privy to when he took his job as a journalist, but also because it distracted her and satiated her hunger for information, blunting the onslaught of superficial enquiries about his work, his food and the amount, quality, timing and company of his drinking session the previous night. Questions whose answers she never heard properly but the formulation of those answers, whether honest or made up, exhausted him nevertheless. The phone monologue that he had with his mother after the month long silence was no different and that has set the pattern for every phone call that he has made to her every night for the last two and a half years.

But during all that time when he had spoken to her, he had always thought of saying things to her that would make her react with some, any words. Today, however, he does not make that attempt. In fact, he almost considers not calling her at all because he does not want to temper the strange kind of restless peace that he is experiencing. It is an oxymoron but he can think of no other way to describe the need for exhausting pacing up and down the house that he feels but in an exhilarating—trying to reach the summit of a mountain—kind of way. 'Words do not matter anymore Ma,' he wants to shout loudly, exuberantly. 'Your silence is acceptable. Your taking my call is enough.' But he does not. He speaks about the weather and how smoggy and polluted the air still is, three days after Diwali and he speaks about the Cricket World Cup and sprinkling little pieces of information and asides, hangs up the phone thinking that in these times of smart phones, hanging does not quite mean what it used to.

Hanging of a phone no longer means what it used to, does it?

He tweets and even this arbitrary tweet is re-tweeted thirty-five times because he seems to have got 25,000 followers since last evening and some of them are probably professional serial re-tweeters or automated re-tweet bots.

The last thing Raman does before snapping his laptop shut is look up 'tarsier'. Their eyeballs are apparently bigger than their brains, he finds out. They look as vulnerable and as intense as he remembered them with their large, almost

accusing eyes, but they, of course, don't look like Tanya.
And yet. Those fingers and those eyes and that expression.

He remembers what he needed to ask her. 'Aren't
your parents dead?' Raman needed to ask her, 'Or has
everybody got that wrong? And why did you starve
yourself?' But what he really wants to ask is 'What do you
think of me?' As if it is the most important question in
the world. Like his life depends on it. Inane. And yet so
important. Compelling almost. He has never felt this way
before and this alien feeling leaves him confused. Elated.
He knows the married colleague with whom he has an
easy non-committal and completely physical relationship,
will say that he is only attracted to Tanya because she is so
unattractive at the moment. Unattractive and vulnerable,
tied up with nowhere to go and no questions to ask. And
she will probably be right too.

*Why aren't there tales of men opting for starvation? Is it
because women have a conflicted relationship with food due to
societal pressures?*

Raman tweets the second tweet of that night. This is
not organic either. He is not interested in generalities. He
does not want to know about women in general. He wants
to know about one woman in particular but in a way that
is deeply unjournalistic and Raman is afraid that his story
is getting increasingly weak and subjective as his emotions
are becoming increasingly strong. 'But what does that
matter?' Raman says aloud into the darkened room after
shutting his laptop and going to his small kitchen to search
for some food because he realizes that, apart from a couple
of slices of garlic toast at the Press Club, he has not eaten

anything the entire day and he is suddenly very hungry. But as he stands slathering the bread with copious amounts of peanut butter, he thinks once again of Tanya and wonders what going without food for weeks and months would have felt like. And what magnitude of trauma had made Tanya and her sister subject themselves to that kind of torture. Whether it is because of that thought or because the slightly mouldy bread does not look that appetizing after all, Raman leaves the sandwich untouched on his plate and goes to bed, wishing suddenly like some callow lovelorn teenager that he would dream of Tanya that night.

26–27 October 2014

10

Fire, Fecklessness and Fury

I wake up in the dark with my insides on fire.

'Why did you shout?' A door opens and a woman stands on its threshold silhouetted against the light coming from the hallway.

Who is she? I don't recognize that voice. She steps into the room and switches on the light, casting a pale, sickly pallor over the room with white walls and pine wood patterned linoleum floor and I know I am still in the hospital and that she, in her slightly crumpled grey-white uniform, is a nurse.

'Are you all right? What's wrong?' The nurse is hurrying to my bed.

'My stomach hurts . . . ' I start to say but I only hear a loud, prolonged wail fill the room which I know comes from me but it is an entire separate being. There is nothing I can do with it. I have no means of controlling it, I cannot make it louder or softer and there is absolutely no way I can stop it. Aaaaaaaaah. The rest of the usually buzzing

hospital is quiet and my wail seems to echo, becoming the
only sound in the entire world. I look at the nurse who is
hovering over me. She is not my regular nurse. She looks
older, kinder and more concerned than my regular nurse
and a part of me wants to reassure her, tell her something
to make her stop worrying too much. 'It is my stomach,'
I want to say, 'just my stomach'. But my entire being is
concentrated on that centre of pain in the middle of my
stomach in a way that is so physical, so powerful that it
has ceased to remain just my stomach. It had become my
thoughts, actions, sensations, emotions, all of which are
being sucked in and grated into bits as if by a ruthless,
powerful, shuddering stone crusher. Aaaaaah. My pain
rises again and my wail rings out. I am reduced to just that
pinpoint of pain. Nothing else matters.

'What's wrong?' The nurse asks again. 'Should I get
you some water?' She is bending close to me and she sounds
unsure. Maybe she is not certain whether it is appropriate
to offer water to someone who has chosen not to eat or
drink anything for days. Maybe she is just unsure about
everything in life.

'Yes, yes, what are you waiting for?' I shout or I think I
shout although all I hear is a loud whimper. 'Do something.
Take away the pain. What is happening to me?' I arch my
back hard and wail once again.

'You will hurt yourself bending your back like this. Are
you in a lot of pain? Here, let me try to turn you a little on
your side. That might help,' the nurse says, perhaps fully
intending to make me comfortable but when she reaches for
me under my blankets, she recoils in horror. She probably

had not expected there to be so little of me for her to work with. She jerks her warm clammy hand off my shoulder and I can see that she no longer wants to touch me, much less hold me, or turn or lift or shift me. Her revulsion burns through my shroud of pain. I sit up and lunge out, curling my cold fingers around her wrist and pressing her palm hard on my stomach. 'IT HURTS HERE.' She loses her balance and falls on top of me with a startled whimper. She is a big woman and her weight makes me fall back into my bed, her darkness cutting off all my light. 'MAKE IT ALL GO AWAY!' I shout into that darkness and I bite into her ear that has landed very close to my mouth. She starts to scream trying to unshackle my fingers and tries to scramble to her feet but I hold on to her. I feel the saltiness of her blood on my palate, the tautness of her writhing wrist inside my palm, the weight of her body struggling against mine. Her breasts against my breasts, her stomach against the burning flames of mine. My insides heave and heave and I throw up on her face, on her dress, on her body and all over my bed. But even in the middle of my pain and her struggle, even as I am spewing out my insides, somewhere in the back of my head I am trying to remember the chemical composition of the first thing I have tasted in a very long time. The indeterminate broth that they had fed me did not count because I did not know what it was. But this I know—B–blood, H–Haemoglobin, P–Protein which included A–Albumin, G–Globulin and F–Fibrinogen.

When I wake up, I know by the texture of light sneaking into the room despite the carefully drawn curtains, that it is bright afternoon. There is nobody in the room with me. I smell clean and antiseptic and my stomach does not hurt anymore. I see that my arm is once again tethered to an IV drip and the point where the needle is stuck into my vein at the back of my left palm feels sore but it is such a gentle soreness after the wracking pain I had experienced last night that I do not mind it at all. 'I can live with this pain forever,' I whisper into the empty room. Perhaps last night's pain had just been a dream? I feel calm. I can even sense my sister breathing somewhere, not very close to me but not too far away either. And she seems to be breathing better than she had been at home. I breathe in deep in response and try to decipher some kind of pattern in the smudges of grey left on the white ceiling of my room by the seepage of water from some faulty pipe up there that seems to have dried out by now.

I hear the door of my room open once again and this time a man stands on the threshold, squinting at me.

'Would you like to watch some TV?' He steps into the room when he sees I am awake. 'It is working very nicely now. I have repaired it for you.'

I recognize him. He is the TV repair guy from the hospital who Dr Vaidya had shooed away a day, or was it two days, ago? But he looks different. Feverish. Excited. He is a thin man with dark greasy hair and eyes bulging with hypothyroidism. His slightly discoloured white shirt and grey trousers are so perfectly and insistently ironed that there are brown lines marking the creases. He does not wait for me to respond.

'You know you are on TV?' He says. 'Everyday. And now, see, see. I am on TV too!'

He beams and switches on the TV with a flamboyant forward thrust of the remote as if wielding a fencing sword.

'More sensational information on the Starving Sisters,' the gamine newsreader on screen in a baby pink jacket and short hair is saying. She is probably only a year or two younger than I am but she looks eons younger and very protected. She lives in a different century from me in a country where every period of time since the beginning of history stays smack up together, so tightly cloistered that the faces and the bodies squish, flatten and distort against each other like people in an over-packed train compartment, and it takes just a tiny shake, only a small puncture for one century to bleed into the other, infecting and poisoning and turning the world gangrenous. Which other country has a probe orbiting Mars looking for life and people looking for and killing a witch in a village at the same time, in the same year, in the same month, perhaps even on the same day? Ha, you don't know what awaits you, young news reader. Her father is probably a bureaucrat who had wanted to see and show his daughter off on television screen and the TV Channel had accommodated his wishes because of some licence that he had accorded to them without much fuss at some point during their nascent years when they had been growing exponentially and everything they had touched had turned into a shiny little profit-making nugget. All that changed with surprising alacrity with the explosion of television channels (many of whom are helmed by news anchors mentored by the pioneering channel) and an almost parallel increase in the number of ways news can be delivered. The pioneering news channel that we are watching has lost a lot of its lustre during this time and its stupendous profits has turned into almost equally humungous losses but the baba-log have remained and they continue to cover horrific events with the same well-dressed, well-made up, well-articulated, wide-eyed incredulity with which they cover the feel-good, lifestyle stories. The TV screen flickers off the newsreader and now it is the repairman's face that fills the screen.

'See, see!' He squeals—not on TV but next to me. 'I am there!'

On TV, the repairman is surrounded by scores of reporters and even though the unsteadily held camera is finding it difficult to focus properly on him through the thrusting microphones and inquisitive questions, I can see that the repairman is dressed in a brightly patterned green polyester shirt and his eyes look even more bulged out (if that were possible without them leaving their sockets altogether) on screen than they do in real life.

'Haan, I work in the hospital where the starving sisters are,' he is saying. 'My name is Shantaram. I worked in the hospital for ten years and baba, I have seen a lot in my time there but I have never seen a human being looking like this woman.'

I remember Dr Anita had called us Starving Sisters. So this is where she had got the name from.

'Like how?' A male reporter asks.

'What does she look like?'

'Can you show us anything?'

The repair guy looks confused. 'I am going to show you, na? Why are you here if I was not going to show you.'

A few reporters laugh.

'Go on. Show us!' One man shouts.

Next to me, Shantaram is mouthing the words silently. He has obviously watched the clip several times but he is still so engrossed in watching himself on screen that he seems to have forgotten that he is in my room where he has probably come to see *my* reaction to his revelation. I almost start to laugh. I am not interested in his information or his revelation and I am certainly not interested in the starving sisters. But I want to share what I am seeing with Layla. We seem to have become famous, I want to tell her. But she is not here with me. Instead there is only Shantaram in my room who stands by my bed with his mouth open in anticipation and his eyes narrowed in admiration of his brilliant TV-worthy self that is holding up his phone on screen. There is a small brown gravy mark on his white shirt, I notice. On TV, the cameras zoom into the picture on his phone and there it is—his big surprise, a shocking picture of Layla! I probably had expected it. I had probably known why the repairman is in my room but I am still stunned. More by the picture than by the fact that Shantaram has her picture. I had got so used to seeing Layla's face that I had seen nothing wrong or even remarkable about the way she looked. But now for the first time I am seeing her face in relation to all other 'normal' faces and she looks horrific, inhuman, like something conjured out of the bowels of earth that has ingested all the sins of the world. Her eyes are shut and it looks like all her flesh has been eaten away by worms from the inside leaving just a thin sheet of splotchy skin to cover everything that needs to be covered—that *has* to be covered—for her to keep breathing: Her brain, her kidneys, her lungs, her heart, her veins, her arteries, her capillaries, her tendons, her bones, her emotions. But the stretched skin is so fragile that it looks as if any moment it will crumble and all her insides will be scattered into the world like the contents of a particularly insidious Pandora's box. It is a face that everybody's worst nightmares are made of. I shut my eyes shaking, blocking the sight but the voices and the sounds do not stop.

'Is this the sister in the ICU?' Somebody is asking.

'No,' I hear the repairman say. 'This is the ward sister. You think there is TV in ICU? I cannot go to repair the TV in ICU and take pictures.'

He sounds irritated, amused and self-important in equal measure, I think. Trying desperately to fix my mind on the tone of his voice. Unable to fully process what I am hearing. Refusing to acknowledge his words that nevertheless begin to seep into my consciousness one at a time. No, he had said no. This isn't my sister in the ICU. This is me. I open my eyes again. This is what I look like. How many times have I wished to not look like my sister but never have I wished it more than today. So, this is what had repulsed the nurse. The cameras linger on the picture that show me dressed in the same chequered gray and blue hospital gown that I am wearing even now but unlike now when you can't see the gown because I am covered in thick red blankets and only my face and my left hand with its IV drip in place is visible, in Shantaram's picture the woman is uncovered—I am uncovered—with my gown falling around the near empty shell of my body and my blankets piled up untidily at the bottom of my bed. And there is more than one shot of me. The TV screen is streaming one picture after another all taken from different angles, all showing me in a state of repose or unconsciousness and all making me look like the embodiment of all the evil in the world. One picture shows my head with my hair in untidy little ringlets and the miniscule bald patches on my scalp highlighted because the camera has zoomed in on them—Layla and I had shorn each other's hair with the blunt kitchen scissors when we had run out of soap and the long thinning tangled mess of curly hair on our heads had started falling off in little tufts or were beginning to get stuck painfully to each other forming little ropes of matted hair that Layla said made us look like the naked ash-smeared naga sadhus who lived in the Himalayas and only came to take a bath in the Kumbh Mela every twelve years. Another picture is a top angle shot of my entire body taken with the repairman probably holding his camera aloft high above my bed. One shot is even focused on my shrunken, long monkey-like feet. Shantaram had probably had a lot of time to take my picture when one of the nurses had removed my covers to check my progress. Or had *he* removed my covers to take my picture when I had been asleep or unconscious. My breathing stops. The monitor by my bed begins to beep very loudly. I want to shout over the sound of the monitor, over the sound of the TV screen where a number of agitated, excited voices are still probably dissecting the contours of my disfigurement but I cannot say anything. My entire quota of wails seems to have been used up last night. I am choking and coughing and coughing.

I can feel Shantaram drag his eyes off the screen and turn to stare at me. He begins to come close. Is he going to take another picture? Is he going to touch me? The monitor lets out a prolonged high pitched beep and a nurse—my regular nurse—I think from what I can see through my liquid, floating eyes—comes in. She is breathing hard from the exertion of having to rush in.

'Why are you here?' She is angry at Shantaram but she is focused on me. 'Tum theek ho? Are you OK?' She asks.

I try to nod. I even try to smile. Never has the presence of such a garrulous person accorded me with so much relief.

'It is not good for you to be here,' this time she is speaking to Shantaram again.

'I am not doing any harm to her. I am only showing TV to keep her entertained.'

Through my bouts of coughing, and through the now lessening beep of the monitor, I can hear the smirk in his voice.

'I don't know whether you are doing her any harm or not. But Amma, she can certainly harm you. Do you know that she fractured sister Nirmala's wrist and almost ate her ear last night?'

So it had not been a dream.

'Really?' The repairman sounds very interested.

'Really. And now get out of the room before you get thrown out of the hospital by Dr Vaidya. She is very angry because of the photos that you took.'

'They are good photos, na? My camera takes very nice photos.'

'Did they pay you very much for them?'

'Arre nahi. Nothing. I should have asked money? Dhattt. Didn't think about that. But I looked very nice on TV. I should take two or three more photos now and ask money for them.'

'No. No way. Not on my shift. Get out of here. I don't want to lose my job because of you. Thank God I was not on duty when you took those photos.'

'Arre Dr Vaidya can't kick you out of the hospital. Or me. No doctor can. Our unions will fight for us. At the most, I will be suspended for three days after months and months of talking. That won't be so bad. I will get paid holiday. It has been a long time since I have visited my poor wife in the village.'

'I don't care. The doctor can have me transferred out of the ward and I don't want that. So out, out before this patient bites you or me.'

'I would not mind being bitten by her. Did you see the picture of the sisters before they turned into these monsters?'

I may have turned into a monster but I have not turned deaf or did he not notice that? Has nobody noticed that? Or because I no longer look human, I am no longer considered human? Is that why Dr Vaidya's resident doctors talk over me? Is this how animals feel when humans run roughshod over them? What if one day we discover that they could understand every word we said and seethed quietly at the way they were interpreted, represented and treated?

'I won't mind being bitten by you either. I saw you in the cinema hall in a red sari kal ya parso and I did not even recognize you. Why you didn't tell me you wanted to see *Bang Bang*? My friend has good connections in the picture hall. I would have taken you free.' The repairman has begun to flirt with the nurse who, after checking that my drip is working okay, is following him out of the door, leaving me alone once again in the room. But she forgets to switch off the TV and the remote still lies next to my head on the pillow where Shantaram has left it.

Carefully moving my right arm, I pick up the remote and begin to push one button after the other. I now remember what had been niggling at the back of my mind about Dr Anita's conversation. She had said that there were journalists stalking her house when they came to know that she worked at the hospital where the Sisters—we—had been brought. So this was what that had been all about. My picture is being shown on almost every news channel and we are being discussed in a number of them. I try to ignore the images and pause my surfing occasionally to hear what some of them are saying. The media narrative of us is one-dimensional. We are two stick figures who have got thinner and thinner still, like in the Stephen King book until we have ceased to exist as persons. But even in my thinned, brain-dulled state, I can make out that we are being treated like the cardboard doll that Layla and I shared as children where the doll had a number of paper dresses that could be hooked over her flat two dimensional body. It would allow Layla to turn her into a cowgirl at one moment and me to transform her into a beach comber in a tiny bikini and a colourful printed bandana the next. We are being similarly dressed up in any way that a channel wants us to dress, depending on the slant that they want to give to our story. We are being bent and curved to fit the narrative that they want to weave. We have been reduced to caricatures embodying horror, humiliation, passivity and stupidity. I think it will be our portrayal as stupid that will rankle Layla the most. Even more than humiliation. Even more than passivity. And certainly more than horror. Our starvation was not passive, impulsive. It was active, rational and well-thought out. Whatever the compulsions, however strong the driving force, Layla would not do anything that could ever be misconstrued as unintelligent.

The calm that I had felt when I woke up has long dissipated but the longing to see Layla has only increased. I desperately want to speak with her, to be with her. Somehow we can make sense of it all, somehow it will all fall into place if she is next to me. Somehow we can plan it all with each other and carefully chart our course forward. Not in this kind of hotchpotch confusing way that TV channels are building up stories and ideas but one step at one time or one type of food in one week.

May 2014

11

Planned Starvation

We did not do it haphazardly. Our starvation was not impulsive or illogical and it was not uneducated. It was systematic, scientific, and we had complete control over it. At least that is what we thought initially. Planned, systematic, scientific starvation. And it was not really starvation. It began as a game because that is what our lives had become—a game. But isn't that what all lives are? One long game. An assiduous game that occurs in the netherworld of wizards and witches whose noise occasionally grows so shrill that it pierces—all sound and fury—through the barriers of propriety and political correctness put in place by the Muggle world but mostly it remains quiet and invisible. The rules of the game get written and re-written and erased to favour a few and to leave all others out even as the games are being played. Yet everybody believes that they can figure out what is going on and if they make just the right moves—if they get admitted to the right college, if they have the right idea for a start-up, if they make the right amount of money, if they own a house in the right location, if they buy that right car or yacht or aeroplane, if they take that right vacation, if they marry the right person, if they send their children to the right schools—they will come out victorious at the end of the game. And although they witness the fall of one reigning deity after another, one illusionary victor after the other and know in their heart of hearts that victory is as fluid as the games themselves, it does not stop them from believing that they would ultimately be able to figure out the rules of the game and emerge whooping with victory, does it? In their eternal optimism, in their unshakable belief that they, their progeny, their species will live forever, every piece of good news shows them that they are on the right track, one more step closer to that ultimate victory and every bad news is brushed aside as an aberration, a result of being handed a faulty deck of cards, or a consequence of somebody else's inept moves. And the game continues one set of people after the next. One generation after another. One sweet chimera at one time.

'There are nearly 5 billion search results for "food" on Google, even more than "sex" which has only about 3.2 billion entries.' Layla had told me that morning—after it all began or ended, depending on your perspective—as soon as I entered the living room. She was seated in front of the computer. 'Of course, that does not mean as much as it should because a majority of sex related results are probably deemed too unkosher for Google and therefore not displayed at all.'

'Yes,' I said. I was distracted and restless. I had managed to fall asleep only in the wee hours of the morning and I had woken up abruptly in the middle of a horrible nightmare and although I did not remember the nightmare, its pieces remained lodged inside like clogged drain at the bottom of my stomach making me want to throw up. I wanted to sit in one place. I wanted to pace up and down but I did not want to talk or hear about food or sex or really about anything at all. I needed to get out.

'I am going out,' I said. And I walked down one flight of steps before I stopped. Where to? And what for? I returned, carefully shut the door, locked it from inside and counting the steps—thirty-five—to the couch, I sat down on it.

'So food rates higher than sex, higher than God and football and death. Here's something even more interesting. God, death and football all show results in the range of 1.7 to 1.4 billion and even taken together have fewer results than food.' Layla said.

She had not acknowledged my exit and she did not comment upon my immediate return. I too did not look at her. I sat staring at *The Two Sisters* on the wall. The older sister in the painting seemed to be clutching something in her right hand. I tried to look more closely at the print. Was she holding onto the arm of a chair for support as she posed for her portrait or did she hold some kind of macramé like rope art piece that she was in the middle of crafting and that she went back to whenever she had a moment to spare between her posing. (Her creation that had been relegated to the waste-bin of history while her brother's handiwork stood in the Louvre, lauded by millions and copied and printed by thousands.) Or was that a knife that she held in those curved fingers, concealed cleverly underneath her shawl. Was that why she had that tolerant, yet disdainful expression? Like she knew something that the artist painting the picture did not.

'Let me break that down.' Layla was continuing to speak. 'There are over 800 million results for recipe, 490 million results for nutrition, 850 million results on guns, 350 million results on knives.'

Guns, knives? What was she doing? Why was she talking like this? Why was she talking at all?

'What are you doing?' I asked Layla.

'Unravelling the world, as they put it. One Google search at a time.'

Now she looked up at me. She too wore the same tolerant yet disdainful expression of the sister in the painting but unlike the waiting kind of stillness that the woman in the painting projected like she was either biding her time to do something or waiting for something to happen, Layla's still gaze held frenzied maniacal activity inside it. Like she was viciously jabbing the air in front of her with a sharp pointed object and mentally drawing large concentric circles one after another so hard that she was tearing holes through the layers that stood between us and insanity. Breaking the barriers of propriety and humanness between the physical 'us'—with our identical eyes and identical noses, identical ears, identical mouths—and the floating world inside us and outside of us that sometimes submerged us together in a wave of same thoughts and same words and sometimes diverged us so far apart that for how much we understood each other, we could be strangers from different countries—speaking different languages, eating different foods and carrying the burden of different kind of memories—who only chanced to be seated next to each other on the plane and who could not even exchange a polite nod of acknowledgement. I looked at Layla. Was I too wearing the same look as her? Was I mirroring her expression of maniacal meaninglessness? I looked away.

'We need to get food,' I said. I don't know why I said it. Food was the last thing I wanted to have right now but Layla's harping on about food had made Mamma's ingrained practicality rise its head inside me and I remembered that we had finished the last of the eggs in last afternoon's meal. My mind had blanked out what happened after the meal but I remembered cracking the last egg for the scrambled eggs and bread that had served as our meal. Last afternoon's supper. The last supper. And Mamma too had been dead for a long time. Dead Mamma's dead practicalities.

'So order it or go out and get it.' Layla spoke loudly, artificially as if she was acting in a bombastic play in which she was the grandiloquent main character. I did not know how to respond to her or even whether I wanted to respond to her. I only wanted to sit on the couch and stare at the painting; looking closely, like an expert art authenticator, at every square inch of it. From the top of the gray-green wall faintly embossed with golden flowers to the last pleat on the younger sister's skirt. One square inch of red, gray, gold, black, blue, brown, white at a time—reducing the painting to its component parts. Blue paint, red paint, brown paint, white paint, stretched canvas, the women, Chassériau. Put the parts together and it is a painting of two sisters done by Chassériau. Go back in time and you have colours that Chassériau decided to mix and arrange in one way. Did he use oil paints in tubes that had then only recently been invented by artist John Goffe Rand or had he and his assistants ground each pigment by hand, carefully adding the right proportion of oil to achieve that exact shade of red of the shawls and the gray of the wall? If the same paints or pigments had been picked up by another person, the reds could have made the hue for sun-streaked horses or red painted barns or an early morning sun; it did not have to be a painting of two sisters. Did it? At what point was the fate of the colours decided? Did the colours have any choice? To not be bought by whoever bought them or to not be used by whoever used them? Did Chassériau have a choice? Could this Napoleon of painting not have continued to paint mythical figures, Shakespearean characters and Moorish life instead of making his sisters pose for him? Did the sisters have a choice? Do we sisters have a choice? Does anybody ever have a choice?

'Shall we play a game?' Layla looked calm now. As if things were beginning to settle inside her. One layer of wet cement after another.

'What game?'

'Let's break our food down to its components.'

Layla's words often became the extension and articulation of my thoughts. Or were my thoughts an extension of her words? The chicken or the egg?

'And let's not eat any food that begins with A this week. Next week we can go to B and C the next and so on.'

It somehow made sense. It made sense then. It makes sense now. With Layla everything made sense. I didn't ask

her where our elimination would end. There was no need
to. We started trialling and erroring. When we eliminated
all the A foods—apples, avocadoes, apricots, almonds—
from our diet, it made no difference. Because we never had
apricots and avocadoes anyway and we had not had apples
and almonds probably since Mamma and Papa had died.
We still had plenty to choose from. We decided to eliminate
all foods that contain ingredients that began with A. It
narrowed down the number of things we could eat but not
quite. Not enough. We then struck upon eliminating any
foods whose chemical composition included compounds
and elements that began with A. Food containing amino
acids went. That enormously reduced the types of food
we could eat. Foods containing Vitamin A went. Then
the Bs went and the Cs and Ds and we went on and on.
It was not starvation. It was a game that transmuted into
an experiment and we carefully discussed the effects for as
long as we could talk. For as long as we could eat. We
stopped eating when we reached N because we could not
find any food that did not contain an ingredient that began
with an N or any other alphabet before N. After that we
stopped thinking about it.

When you divide time into chunks, days, hours,
minutes, seconds, you need activities to fill it; you do
things, you strive for, you achieve. If you let time be the
large amorphous mass that it really is, differentiated only
by shades of darkness and light, you don't need to do much.
It progresses at its own pace, fast-slow, without you even
realizing its passage until you have to get up and switch on
a light or switch it off.

We did other things too. We decided to challenge the placement of objects. The pointlessness of picking up a plate from one place and putting it on another. The value judgement given to where things were put. A plate on the shelf: right. The same plate on the floor: wrong. A woman standing with another woman in the dark: wrong. A woman standing with a man related to her: right. A woman standing with a man not related to her in the way that the world defined relationships: very wrong. We rearranged the order of things. We placed objects in the wrong place and watched them turn into different things. Our chairs lay on their backs and their legs became the spikes of a torture chamber. The table became a shelf. The sofa often became our bed and the floor became our world—our dining table, our reading table, our chair, our bed and even our trash can. When Mamma used to harangue us to keep the house clean, she never told us that a neat house was a dead house. A house where nothing moved. We did not want a dead house, so we placed and arranged and displaced and rearranged.

We only left Mamma and Papa's bedroom as it was and we kept water out of our starvation game.

27 October 2014

12

The Weaves, the Wefts, the Strands That Make a Person

Raman walks straight up the unilluminated staircase, towards Tanya's room flashing the pass, that Dr Anita had issued to him when she had requested his help, at the perfunctory guard. He has entered the hospital through the back entrance and via the underground parking the way Satya had taken him and the way he had entered last night. That he does not have a car makes the entire process slightly slower and more than slightly disagreeable. He has to flatten his body against the wall of the narrow ramp that leads into the basement and breathe in the diesel fumes every time a car hurtles past; many more cars this morning than last night—but it is worth all the trouble because it allows him to evade the harried guard at the front gate who, daunted by the sweating, shoving masses desperate to enter the government hospital for one reason or another, would rather not allow *anybody* in than risk letting the wrong kind of people inside and be severely reprimanded by the hospital administration for doing so. Using the back entrance also means that Raman can slip in unseen by his fellow journalists who are camping up front. The unimpressive looking but surprisingly effective handwritten pass had helped him go unchallenged right up to Tanya's room last night and expecting an equally smooth entry this afternoon—after having spent a frustrating morning talking to an impeccably courteous but impossibly clueless bank executive to resolve an error that had reduced his bank balance to a precarious low—he stops short in irritation when the head nurse at the cluttered nursing station calls out to him just as he is about to reach Tanya's ward. The nurse asks him to go to Dr Vaidya's chamber instead. She looks severe and she does not offer any explanations when Raman, camouflaging his annoyance, very politely asks her why; other than saying that she has been directed to tell him to do so by the doctor. Raman has shaved carefully this morning, dressed neatly and has been rehearsing what he is going to say to Tanya in his head in order to get her to speak with him some more. Although, come to think of it, he did not seem to have done too badly despite saying only thirteen words to her last evening. He had been smiling almost inanely to himself at the thought to blunt the intensity of the anticipation with which he is looking forward to meeting Tanya. But the nurse has now interrupted his reverie and the intrusion means that he has to recalibrate his head quickly to carry out a conversation with Dr Vaidya instead of Tanya. He is not worried though; it surely is not going to be a particularly trying exchange. She may have heard of his meeting with Tanya last night and probably only wants an update on what had transpired, in which case he needs to use the few minutes available to him before he reaches her chamber to think about what and how much he wants to tell her. Or perhaps she has not heard of the meeting and she wants to give him another set of instructions before what she thinks is going to be his first meeting alone with Tanya. His assumption that she has called him for something to do with the state of Tanya's health seems accurate when he sees that Dr Anita too is present in Dr Vaidya's chamber. Dr Anita looks shiny-eyed with distress but he attributes that to her unease with her work being under such close and such unsympathetic scrutiny, and does not give it another thought. Although, come to think of it, if by any chance, they are here together to reconsider their decision to allow him access to Tanya, it would probably have augured better for him to have taken the trouble to transcribe his last night's conversation with Tanya, instead of only mulling over the implications and contours of it inside his head. If he could have produced a black and white evidence of the extent of the breakthrough he had achieved last evening, it would have made his case for continuing to see Tanya stronger. Well, he will see how it all goes.

'Is everything okay?' He asks without preamble. Neither his mood nor the atmosphere in the room is particularly conducive to exchanging pleasantries.

'Yes, by and large. Tanya had a very rough night. We had to sedate her to calm her down,' Dr Vaidya says.

'What happened?' Raman asks, trying his best to keep his voice neutral. Could it be something to do with his visit?

'She had a very severe stomach pain in the middle of last night.'

'But she is okay now?' Raman notes her use of past tense but particularly the substance of her message with a slightly shameful tinge of relief. He knows the thought of her in pain should disturb him and it does. But he is also relieved that he is not to be blamed for whatever has happened. And Dr Vaidya did say 'had'.

'Yes, she is all right. Her pain is under control. It *was* very severe but not very serious. Probably because of the abrupt change in her diet, she had acid reflux in her stomach which can sometimes be very painful. We have put her back on IV drip for some more time.'

'Is she asleep? Is that why you did not want me to go to her room yet?' Raman tries to sound calm. Dispassionate. Not like his life hangs in balance on the word yet.

Dr Vaidya's expression remains impassive and Raman is unable to read what she is thinking but Dr Anita is not as adept at camouflaging her feelings and he can almost see the battle between her instinct to not allow him to go anywhere near Tanya and her desperate need to get more information from Tanya for some reason which she has not confided in him but which does not seem to stem only from the necessity to keep the press satiated. Whatever her reason may be, it comes from something critical, something that probably could threaten her very job, a job which she does not seem to be particularly good at, but upon which Raman can sense that she relies to a large extent. Trying to get into Dr Anita's head is like trying to thrust a scalpel into a clogged artery or thrust whatever it is that they thrust into clogged arteries. He is not sure what compels him to do it despite his distaste for it and how he is so good at understanding her when he dislikes her so much. But perhaps he is just deluding himself that he understands her. Perhaps her life is entirely different from how he imagines it to be. Perhaps she goes out drinking and clubbing each evening and that is the reason she looks exhausted and seems so incompetent at her job, despite her professed intention of doing things right by all her patients. Raman's mind is wandering off the matter at hand. Living with his superbly self-involved mother has trained his brain to shut out all the outside noise and focus on what is essential in order to unshackle itself of the chains of guilt, pretence and need that she constantly clanks around him. But right now his mind is wandering off from the essential to the inessential. He wants to cram his mind with other thoughts to fill the silence that has descended in the room. The sounds of the hospital—the hurried footsteps, the clink of an unoiled wheelchair, the muted conversation of patients, the more boisterous laughter of ward boys—are very loud inside Dr Vaidya's chamber despite its closed doors otherwise he is sure he would have been able to hear the sound of the three people in Dr Vaidya's chamber breathing quietly, completely out of sync with each other and each unsure about what words to use next.

Raman hesitates because he has the most to lose if he uses the wrong words. He is troubled not just by the thought of Tanya in pain although that fact in itself is worrying but, he has to be honest, what is worse is that he may not be allowed to meet her—if only to ask her how she is doing—after spending the night and the morning anticipating the meeting with the kind of passion that nothing apart from his work (and not even that for a very long time now) has ever aroused in him. Although Tanya is related to his work, after last night he has given up the pretence, in his own mind at least, that his interest in Tanya is only professional.

Dr Vaidya is silent because it is Dr Anita who needs to answer Raman's question. It is Dr Anita who primarily needs Raman's help to assess Tanya's mental state. But Dr Anita continues to hesitate although she knows she really does not have that many options before her.

'I should warn you that her pain was not the only thing that happened last night,' Dr Vaidya senses Dr Anita's uncertainty and she decides to place the facts before Raman and let him take the decision rather than wait for Dr Anita to make up her mind; knowing whichever way she decides, it will cause her not an insubstantial amount of agitation. But Dr Vaidya hesitates once again and Raman waits for her to continue. He knows from her voice that whatever she is about to tell him is dramatic enough for her to lose some of her equanimity.

'Tanya looks very weak. And I am not saying she is not weak but she is not as weak as she looks. Last night she fractured a nurse's wrist.'

'What?' Whatever Raman had been expecting, it certainly had not even remotely resembled this. 'How did she manage that?'

'We are not sure but we think it was mainly because she caught Sister Nirmala by surprise. Although Sister Nirmala is a veteran at the hospital, this was the first time she was on duty with Tanya and she had not expected Tanya to be quite as strong.'

'Or as vicious. She also bit Sister Nirmala's ear.' Dr Anita finds her voice and begins to provide a detailed account of all that had happened at night. Raman wishes she would shut up. He does not want to hear any more. He wants to process what he has been presented with. He knows he should be aghast at the news, repulsed by the revelation but instead he feels elation that he knows he has to hide from the two doctors along with his every other emotion related to Tanya. Yes! He wants to exult. Yes, he knew there had to be more to Tanya than the narrative around the passive Starving Sisters seemed to suggest. To have his suspicion confirmed this way is exhilarating. Scary but exhilarating. In the account that has been built up about Tanya and Layla, they are two helpless, slightly stupid, very docile women who did not have the capacity to take on the world and had therefore stayed in and needed to be spoken of in a condescending, falsely sympathetic tone. But after meeting Tanya, her being a docile victim of circumstances did not sit squarely with Raman's assessment of her. Although he had spent relatively short time with her in person, he had devoted long hours to her mentally, analyzing the smallest of her gestures and the tiniest of inflictions in her voice ad-infinitum, and something in her had suggested a kind of depth that he was not used to encountering. Now he has been provided with some more clues about what exists behind her vulnerable tarsier eyes, and he is excited. This is a new challenge. And yet. Wouldn't it have been easier if she did not have this other side? If she could have been enfolded within the narrative that was furiously being woven about her with the help of disparate threads—some real, most imaginary—but all being accorded the same amount of space and value as if the difference between the fake and the real does not matter anymore as long as everything could be fitted into an easily explained, easily propagated, easily digested world.

'That was probably only a reaction to her intense pain.' Misconstruing his elation for apprehension, Dr Vaidya speaks into the silence that has descended once again after Dr Anita has concluded her tirade.

'But we will understand perfectly if you want to rethink your promise to help us.' After letting out her steam, Dr Anita almost wishes Raman would excuse himself and take the decision about whether or not he should be involved in the case, out of her hands. If Raman himself makes the decision . . .

'No,' Raman says and Dr Anita sighs. 'No, if she is awake, I will go and meet her now.' His voice is neutral.

Fortunately, because of the dramatic late night developments, the doctors do not remember, or perhaps nobody has had the time to inform them of, the meeting Raman had with Tanya last evening when everybody had left. This allows him more time to consider how he wants to fashion the information about her family and her feelings that she has given him that he would at some point need to present to the two venerable doctors and to the earnest police officer who is apparently too caught up today in other tasks to undertake his daily pilgrimage to the ICU.

Unless he had done it in the morning when *Raman* had been caught up elsewhere.

'You do know that Tanya's picture is on all TV channels, don't you? Not her older picture.' Dr Vaidya says when she sees Raman look at her quizzically. Wasn't he the one who had tweeted their picture? 'These are pictures that were taken yesterday by an employee of the hospital and they are generating, as you can imagine, the cruellest kind of chatter about Tanya's appearance. Which of course also means about Layla's appearance. This just adds another layer of complication to this entire sorry saga.' Dr Vaidya looks despondent when Raman rises to leave.

'Speaking of complications, just keep in mind that we will give sedatives to keep Tanya restrained if there is a repetition of her last night's conduct,' Dr Anita says. 'So if you see any sign of abnormal behaviour, you have to tell me. We cannot have any more drama.'

27 October 2014

13

Thick, Viscous Blood

The room is quiet. Somebody switched off the TV when I dozed off which could not have been too long ago because it is afternoon still. But something has woken me up. Something that is again happening in my body but unlike last night's searing pain, it is quiet, almost imperceptible, like something imagined. And yet unmistakable. Am I peeing without knowing? I had never had a loss of control over my bladder even during the direst time of our starvation. But then that is not really surprising considering how little of anything had been inside us at that time. No food certainly but barely any water either. Here, with the nurse thrusting some indeterminate fluid into my mouth yesterday at every chance she got and the IV filling me with fluids 24x7, I should not be surprised at my insides being so sodden that I have begun leaking out. I have no experience of this. What muscle should I employ to stem this flow that is not soft and continuous but intermittent and somehow intense? Should I clench

my gluteus maximus, as Layla calls the bum or scrunch my
pubococcygeus? No wait, it is a spurt of semi-solidity that
is meandering down. I know what *that* is. It is clotted blood.
I am bleeding. After months of going without my periods,
I have managed to keep this part of being the person that I
am—a woman—out of my mind but here I am back in that
world where I don't want to be. Stop it, I want to say to it.
Stop it. Stop it. Stop it.

How could have I not known what it was? I feel stupid.
Almost like the time I had my first period as a twelve-year
old, when after ignoring the sporadic bleeding for a few
hours thinking that it was something that I was imagining
that would go away on its own if I just pretended it was not
happening, I had finally gone to Mamma to solemnly tell
her that I was haemorrhaging internally and was likely to
be dead soon. That I was reading an old abridged version of
Christiaan Barnard's biography then—abridged carefully
by the editors at *Reader's Digest* to leave out any references
to his womanizing but letting plenty of gory details
about cutting open, bleeding out and dying remain in all
its graphic glory—may have influenced my rather grave
conclusion. I knew about mating, I knew somewhat about
how children were born, if not the actual details of it, at
least the general principles of it. The thing was that I knew
children were born and of course I was curious about how
that happened and I, therefore, had tried to find out about
it from whatever sources I could. But since I had not even
heard of menstruation, it was not very likely that I would
go looking for information about it, was it? Somehow I
even related the tampon and sanitary napkin ads that I saw

to women and children and nappies, possibly because they emphasized so much on their soaking capacity. God, am I still surprised at my naiveté? But to be fair to me, nobody had ever spoken about it. Our Catholic school that worked on the principle that if they ignored any references to sex and sexuality, it would somehow disappear forever from their world, had of course said nothing about it; I did not have any close friends who could have enlightened me, and Mamma too had never told me about the bizarreness of my insides beginning to spew out blood every twenty-eight days. Had anybody given me the slightest of hint, I would at least not have spent those scary hours trying to come to terms with my mortality at the ripe old age of twelve. Mamma told us that she had expected our periods to begin much later and she had thought she would have plenty of time to explain it all to us before they actually began. Like she thought she would have plenty of time to explain that our house was not a microcosm of the world and prepare us for it.

I tried to feel better when Mamma showed me the paraphernalia invented (so that is what all those ads were about) to make the entire uncomfortable experience bearable and told me that although due to the silence surrounding the subject I may feel I was the only girl who was undergoing it, almost every woman for nearly forty years of her life bleeds for about five days every month. So in forty years, each woman would menstruate for about 2400 days which would amount to bleeding for over six and a half years of their lives and since the number of women at that time who were above 13 years of age was about 2.2 billion that would approximately amount to about 14.5 billion bleeding women years, I had calculated. And I had not even taken into account the number of bleeding women years since the beginning of history or even the beginning of record keeping. Given the sheer enormity of those numbers, shouldn't somebody have explained menstruation in some detail somewhere—some literature, some stories, some articles? But I could sense from Mamma's expression it was an anathema, that there was stigma attached to it, which was probably the reason why it was not spoken about openly. Layla, whose periods, unknown to me, had begun only a day earlier, had acted all incredulous at my ignorance but I knew that she too was as disconcerted as I was by that sudden loss of control over her body that this unstaunchable bleeding evoked. And, of course, she had the questions.

'Shouldn't the onset of periods be celebrated?' Layla had asked Mamma. 'Isn't the fact that we have begun producing these eggs a powerful thing, implying that our species has still some chance of survival? That is ultimately the larger aim of all species, isn't it? The perpetuation of their existence? It means that the future of Homo sapiens is safe, at least for the moment, in our hands?'

'Yes, I am sure, we Homo sapiens feel very safe now,' Mamma had said impatiently. She did not have the time to engage with Layla's grand posturing because, as usual, she was trying to finish one task while also halfway into another. But then she had laughed. 'I don't know where you get your crazy ideas from,' she said.

When Mamma discovered she was almost three-months pregnant exactly five months after we began our periods,

Layla triumphantly proclaimed to me, out of Mamma's hearing, that we had reversed Mamma's menopause with the sheer power of our exploding oestrogen that obviously came in a double dose! And although Mamma spent the initial few days of the discovery of her pregnancy, moping around and wondering how she could have become pregnant after twelve years of giving birth (there is only one way, Layla had winked at me) to all the children she ever needed, she realized that after the long years of neglect, her pregnancy had brought the focus back on her body and there was a newness to that sensation along with all other sensations that came with having a growing human being inside her. This coincided with our beginning to come to terms with the changes that *our* adolescence was making in *our* bodies encircling us all in a tight-knit circle of womanhood that left Papa as a sympathetic but completely clueless outsider.

Mamma let go of her instinct to constantly be a mother to us and became a woman in her own right with her own needs and her own secrets. Her body became central to her existence as, to some extent for some time, ours became to ours. She became the Mamma of my dreams, a friend who shared jokes and banter that left Layla and me giggling helplessly. Little Neel was born exactly eleven months after our first period and I could feel Papa's relief when Neel was born a boy. Not because Papa wanted a boy to close the family's 'open bracket' as it tended to be in a large part of the country—a son to carry out the last rites kind of bracket (although the logic of it—like the logic of a lot of things people believe in unquestionably, almost ritualistically—defied me because what does anything matter after you are dead?)—but because by the time little Neel arrived, our home had become such a hot house of womanly smells, moods and whims that Papa needed an outlet. If Little Neel had not been born a boy, he said he would have built a room on our roof, somewhere he could hammer away at will. 'Chalo, I have at least saved you the trouble and the cost of the construction,' Mamma would laugh.

Once Little Neel was born, Mamma once again, almost overnight, assumed the mantle of a mother who needed to take care of three children but her breastfeeding, baby-nursing-self continued to remain aligned to our breast-growing, having-crushes impulses. We talked to her for hours. We shared our little stories with her. We told her about our impossible little infatuations. Or rather Layla told her about her impossible little crushes while Mamma fed Little Neel and I lay quietly listening to Layla's stories; gratified to be allowed for the first time to be an overhearer, an inconspicuous, inadvertent sharer of her confidences. Layla's crushes during those years ranged from Richard Feynman, whose brilliance and sense of humour she was deeply enamoured by and whom she quoted extensively— the only way to solve such a thing is patience, she said; to Vikram Seth almost as much for his *The Golden Gate* as for *A Suitable Boy*, because despite being completely enthralled by *A Suitable Boy*, she had been disappointed by its end. She understood the end, she said, but she still did not like it. She would have preferred Lata marrying Kabir. And Kevin Spacey, because of *The Usual Suspects*, why else? And after we returned from Paris, Layla also, for a short while, fell in love with Théodore Chassériau, the conflicted, prodigious artist who had painted *The Two Sisters* and who had died at young age of 37. 'Probably out of sheer exhaustion because of the stress of painting *The Two Sisters*, if the sisters were anything like we are,' Layla had said to Mamma. The two sisters in the picture were not, as I had almost guessed, twins at all and Chassériau had painted more pictures of them, most of which were of them individually. But *The Two Sisters* continued to symbolize Layla and I for me. The fact that they occupied such a large space in our living room probably helped to keep that thought lodged firmly in my brain. It was the best time of my life. I am smiling, I think.

'What about you? Who were your crushes?' Raman asks.

When did he come in? Was I speaking my thoughts aloud once again? How much had he heard? What did that even matter?

'I walked in when you were talking about your sharing stories with your mother.' I had not asked the question aloud so I guess he knew from my expression that I wanted to know how much he had heard. And since he has not asked me who I had been speaking to, I decide to answer his question.

'I followed Layla. I fell in love with everybody Layla loved. The reasons for her crushes were so well-articulated that I probably fell in love with those words as much as with the men, if that makes any sense.'

'Yes, it does.' Raman says and I look at him. He is definitely more voluble today than he had been yesterday. He stands at a distance, not hovering over me like he had done yesterday. I still cannot see his eyes behind his glasses but his hair looks neater and he smells very subtly of soap and shampoo. Somehow his endorsement pleases me. I had thought other people did not matter anymore. Their feelings, their thoughts were unimportant. In a world filled with images going viral and people giving out and counting 'Likes' like trophies, I had forgotten what genuine soft-spoken understanding feels like. What glow it imparts to your being. You don't need sympathy. All you need is one person who truly understands. Of course, you could argue that the accumulation of 'Likes' is one person's understanding following another person's following another person's but that will be like saying war is one person killing another person killing another person when we all knew that that definition of war has long gone obsolete. I am not even sure if it was ever relevant at any stage of human civilization.

And speaking of war, I can still feel my menstrual blood drip—a few drops at a time—after long intervals. I know I need to call the nurse and tell her to do whatever she has to do but wrapped in a reckless abandonment of letting go of norms of behaviour in the tightly structured hospital environment, I decide it can wait a while. The bleeding is very, very sporadic anyway. I can barely feel it. It is not enough to cause much damage or much staining, which was all the concern I had about my periods for a very long time of my having-periods life: that it should not be visible. After the initial few months, my periods had settled into a pattern and I had got used to having them. They did not cause much discomfort and unlike what I had read, they did not cause very painful cramps either but the flows themselves were crazy, erratic. One minute I would be cruising along smoothly with gentle drops of blood oozing out of my insides and being obediently contained within the pads that I used to contain them and the very next minute it would be as if a cloudburst had taken place inside me, torrentially bringing half the lining of my uterus out in one go. Nothing invented by humans, as far as I know, could then limit the boundaries of that gush which found its own path out of all the barriers put in to impede its flow and spilled forth into the world proudly in all its shiny redness. Of course, this meant that I became conscious about not leaving stains behind wherever I went or literally on my behind wherever I went.

How did my life go from only being concerned about a few stains to this? Or is it all just a continuum of shame and horror that has been a part of my life whether or not I had been aware of it? I know I am not speaking these thoughts aloud because Raman looks distracted, focused more on the monitor on my left than on me. At least, I need not worry about staining my bed sheets in a hospital. If there is one place that should have the mechanisms to deal with blood flows and blood stains, it would have to be a hospital. Isn't this what they do here? Staunch and cauterize much more copious amounts of blood spewing out of many more places. And I don't want Raman to go away. Not just yet. The nurse and the padding up can wait.

'Little Neel did not just prevent the need for an attic in our house, he filled gaps that we did not even know existed in our lives,' I say. Again I am not sure why. Raman does not know Little Neel and he had not heard my mutterings about his birth but once I start, like yesterday, I can't stop.

'He got appended to us and enhanced all our better qualities. He was a satisfied, happy baby who grew into an equally satisfied, happy child. As soon as he could walk, he began following us everywhere in the house like a little puppy, carrying his baby toys, his baby smells and his baby laughter along. His adoration was open and even-handed. He laughed at everything any of us did. Whatever we did. When we shaped paper into boats and aeroplanes, when we drew somewhat recognizable pictures of dogs and cats, when we fashioned ducks or elegantly gowned dancing girls out of silver chocolate wrapper linings, when we sang tunelessly for him, when we flayed our hands and feet to do funny dances for him, when we read out stories to him or later gave him books to read, when we allowed him to fetch our books from the shelves, when we gave him food, when we brought water for him or allowed him to bring a glass of water for us. He was so effusive in his glee that we were always doing things for him. Our house itself changed its character with Little Neel. Even Layla could not quite maintain her intellectual standoffishness in the face of his undiluted affection that was completely unperturbed by any lack of reciprocity. Not that there was any lack of reciprocity in our house. Our house was a happy place.'

'We played games, you know? Twenty Questions, Word Building but the game that Little Neel enjoyed the most was naming groups of animals. Did you know that a group of clams is called a 'bed' and a group of crows, murder? Neel's favourite was group of apes called shrewdness;

bloodhounds are called sute, it is a flutter of butterflies, a wake of buzzards, a clowder of cats, a coalition of cheetahs, a quiver of cobras, a gulp of cormorants, a cast of crabs, a bask of crocodiles, a convocation or aerie of eagles, a memory of elephants, a mob of emus, a charm of finches, a cackle of hyenas, a party of jays, a loveliness of ladybirds, an exaltation of larks, a leap of leopards, a lounge of lizards, a grin of opossum, a parliament of owls, a puddle of platypus, a prickle of porcupines, a rhumba of rattlesnakes, an unkindness of ravens, a purse of sand dollars, a surfeit of skunks, a scurry of squirrels, a fever of stingrays, a streak of tigers, a tumble of toddlers, a generation of vipers, a plump of waterfowls, a kettle of vultures, a destruction of wildcats, a descent of woodpeckers,' I am going through the list alphabetically the way Little Neel had taught me. I am laughing and I think I am crying.

'Here interlace the fingers of both your hands as tightly as you can with palm facing upwards. Like this. Can you see one small upside down triangle between two identical triangles? And these three triangles are bordered by two more triangles one slightly larger than the other who seem to hover on the margins of the three triangles. That is how we were. Our family. With Little Neel ensconced between Layla and I and our parents guarding all of us. We always called him Little Neel and he never did become Big Neel, did he?'

I want to speak more but I can't. I have begun to leak all over. Through my eyes, through my nose, through my body, through my brain . . .

'How much younger was he to both of you?' I hear Raman ask but I cannot answer him.

When the nurse comes in, I hear her too. I hear her admonish me for not letting her know sooner. Letting her know sooner about what? I think, confused. About Neel? About Raman? No, she is scolding me for not telling about something else but although I try to concentrate on her words and I can make out her tone and I can feel her pick me up, move me, change me, adjust me, I cannot understand anything that she is saying at all. Not a single word. I am trying to hear Layla. I am trying to find her breath. I want to synchronize my breathing to hers. 'How's my sister?' I ask the nurse when she finishes talking. But this time it is she who does not answer or who does not hear or perhaps I never ask. I don't know. Layla is so close. So close. As close as she had been to me when Mamma, Papa and Little Neel had died.

February 2013

14

Deaths—Plural, Pervasive, So So Painful

There are no 2-step, 3-step, 25-step, 500-step manuals on How to Deal with Death. Nobody tells you how death is different from even the longest of absences, the farthest of separations. There is hope in separation. The possibility of meeting sometime, somewhere. Nobody tells you how hopeless death is. How final. It is a termination. The End. No more Papa. No more Mamma. No more Little Neel. Ever. No one tells you that the brutality of the first shock at the news fades to nothing, *nothing*, when compared to the deep abiding bone-chilling sorrow that enters you and refuses to depart, leaving you shivering with cold forever. We only had each other left. Layla and I. And I have no recollection of Layla and I as separate persons in the first few days after the death of Papa and Mamma and Little Neel. I don't remember where her grief ended and where mine began. I don't remember which one of us got the news and told the other. I don't recollect any conversations or expressions of sorrow that we shared.

Not being able to tell Papa the thought that had come in my mind. Any thought. Not telling Mamma. Not seeing Mamma. How could I not see Mamma? She was always there. Where did she go? Where do people with so many thoughts and ideas, with *so much vitality* go? Never retelling the silly joke I had just read that I had tucked in my mind to recite to Little Neel because I knew how finely tuned his sense of humour was and how much he would laugh at it. His recently acquired permanent-teeth laughter. Nobody tells you about the games your mind plays in absences. The feeling of somebody being there and yet not. There should have been some preparation, some premonition, some things given away. Some goodbyes said. Some indication of what was about to happen. Some directives about how we were supposed to live if they went away from our lives. There wasn't.

I had barely looked up when they left. I knew Papa had dressed as usual, with care. For somebody who could not even go to the corner shop without carefully considering his attire, going to a friend's fifty-fifth birthday party had obviously required a lot of thought. He had eventually chosen the slightly rakish slate green corduroy jacket to wear over his more sedate light gray trousers and a silk shirt and Mamma had decided to wear her beautiful pink silk sari at the last minute after not being able to locate the earrings to go with the teal silk sari that she had initially chosen to wear to match with Papa's jacket. Layla and I had waved them off without looking up from our books for longer than a fraction of a second because we had expected to see them soon enough and I wasn't going to stop reading my book for even a minute longer than Layla stayed away from hers.

Should I have looked up? Should I have spoken out loud my reservation about Papa's decision to not wear a tie and a more formal jacket for what was bound to be a very decorous gathering from how Papa had described his friend? That would certainly have made Papa hesitate and would have delayed their departure from the house, and they would not have been at the intersection the moment the drunk driver of the speeding heavy duty truck had lost control of his large unwieldy vehicle and had literally driven over our little white car, inside which our still slightly flustered-by-her-late-motherhood Mamma was probably coaxing Little Neel to have his banana so that he would have something substantial in his stomach before being swept into the junk food junket that the party was going to be for children. And our always-abreast-with-the-latest-music Papa would have sat with his hands strumming on the steering wheel in tune probably with *Thrift Shop* on the billboard top twenty, as he waited patiently for the traffic light to turn green.

I know it sounds like a cliché but the days after the deaths did mostly pass in a blur for me. At first the words made no sense. No sense at all. What were we even supposed to do? Were we supposed to make all the decisions? Were we supposed to answer all questions? Pick up all the phones? Respond to all the doorbells? There were moments when suddenly, my breathing would stop being a function of my involuntary muscles and no neurological switch would turn on inside my head to activate my voluntary muscles. And try as I might, my next breath would not come until almost at the last minute just before I would be ready to pass out and I would come out of my paralysis gasping for breath like I had been underwater for a long, long time. Those moments seemed endless, so strongly etched out and so dark that being inside them was like being in a black hole; with the whole world sucked in and reduced to an invisible dot. But everything else was a blur. I do not even remember who rang the bell and stood at our door and gave us the news. At our door, on our threshold, ringing our bell. How could such ordinary commonplace things that stood quietly every day, doing their everyday things be a conduit for something so devastating. Or did somebody call to inform us of the 'fatal accident' as the newspapers put it. On our phone, in that voice, into my ear.

Unlike in the movies, nobody told us, as the next of kin, to identify Mamma and Papa and Little Neel. Nobody was even calling them that any more. No Mr Sharma and no Mrs Sharma and no Little Neel Sharma. They were long gone. They were bodies now. The bodies that never came home. We were kept away from what remained of the mutilated bodies but I did see a picture of our car in the newspaper many, many months later. It looked flattened and impersonal, like the cars they show in American movies that are being recycled for their metal. It could be any car. There were no white marks or insignia to indicate that it was our little white Fiat and no red marks to show that three members of my family had been crushed inside its mangled metallic body.

There were moments in the early days after the deaths that I would forget to grieve; like the deaths had happened in some other family, like I could discuss it over tea with Mamma and commiserate with the pain of the other family on their tragic loss. 'Three deaths,' Layla had said one time looking out of the window. 'Three deaths—that is really sad'. Like *she* was talking about it with Mamma. And I knew that for that moment, for those days, Layla was only an extension of me, and I of her. Our thoughts occurred contiguously and our actions were synchronized. We both knew the same things, we both heard the same things and it did not matter who spoke because the exact same words formed inside each of our heads at the exact same time. It was as if the mellifluous, good-natured confusion that everybody had always had about us—about who was who—had turned into an evil cold hardness after Mamma's death and Layla and I had become interchangeable. Changelings. Dr Jekyll and Mr Hyde. Layla and I worked as one. One 'egg' making all the decisions annulling the fact that it had split in two. Our neighbours had never been able to distinguish between us anyway and we could not distinguish between them either. We barely even remembered anybody's names. Our interaction with them had always been through the medium of our parents. With them gone there was no way to separate or disassemble and make sense of their proximity to us, both in terms of their physical distance from our house and in terms of the depth of our relationship with them, and therefore we had no way of knowing how to deal with them. Was Mamma closest to the aunty who hugged us quietly the longest and hardest or to the aunty whom I saw sat crying loudly in a corner, being consoled by everyone around her as if it was *her* parents who had died, I had thought almost absent-mindedly, envying her tears and her easy display of emotions. I had a feeling that more people had come to our house attracted by the drama of the deaths than by the tragedy of them and we probably had no relationship with a large number of grievers and consolers who ambled in and out of our house like the obscenely public death of the occupants of the house had made the house itself a public property. A prop in a tragic drama. A memorial to Mamma, Papa and Little Neel's existence. Like Sabarmati Ashram and Teen Murti Bhavan. This is where Gandhiji spun his cotton. This is where Nehru left his reading glasses. This is where Mrs Sharma cooked her last poha. And this is where Little Neel left his toy jeep.

People were drawn to the small array of pictures of us that had long hung ignored on our walls but beyond that, Layla and I did not provide them with any drama apart from our physical sameness which, to be very honest, was not that unique any longer with induced triplets and quadruplets. We had no screams. We had no tears. Tears were for tragic stories, for sad movies, for melodramatic endings. Our grief was unable to find recourse to them. How many drops of tears would we need to fill the hollow created by the absences? How much wailing would be needed to block the silences and blankness of empty rooms and unslept beds? Inside us there was the hardness of basaltic rocks from the core of the earth that millennia of constant battering by various elements of nature could not erode. There were so many decisions to make and we were so unsure about who was supposed to make them—Layla? Me? A friend of our parents?—that in the end, we made no decisions. We made no decisions about what to do with Papa's clothes, we did not try to find a pair of feet to be encased in the shoes that he loved. We did not need to sort Papa and put him away, or Mamma, or Little Neel, did we? Why would we need to do that and where would we put them away to make space for what?

Soon after that, flashes of Layla's thoughts began to pop up inside my head. I would look up to see Layla staring at me as if she had deliberately sent a stray thought across to test its strength or more likely, to test my receptiveness. And unlike what I may have led you to believe, I was not a complete doormat. I sent my own thoughts across to Layla too and although she never acknowledged their arrival, I did see her flinch when I wanted her to think about the time when Mamma had asked us to keep an eye on Little Neel and we had both with a book each in our hands and the usual obstinate one-upmanship in our heads, had ignored him until he had tripped and fallen inside the bathroom where he had wandered. The strange whimper that came out of his mouth that was followed by a shocked silence as he had encountered a frightening new reality in what had until now been his safe heaven, had Layla and I both running out of our room in panic. Fortunately, although Neel had subsequently bawled his tear ducts dry, his injuries had only been superficial. His name was Neel but we called him Little Neel because he had looked so tiny when he arrived that we could not imagine him as

Big Neel ever. He died at the age of ten squashed between two people who loved him most and two people we had loved the most in our lives, after adding only 36 more inches to the 20 inches frame that he had been born with.

You try to imagine the worse that could ever happen and the worse that could ever happen happens and yet you continue living. You continue breathing, you still get angry, you still laugh at things that you sometimes find funny, you continue feeling thirsty, you continue getting hungry. You continue eating. Day after day after day. You live. Contributing little to anything. Putting more burden on the earth. Exhausting more of its resources. Trawling its seas for food, drilling out billions of tonnes of oil that nature had carefully sequestered away to maintain the balance of oxygen and carbon dioxide. And yet what did it matter? It is not as if nature has ever been static. Earth's 3.5 billion year old history is pockmarked with stories of mass extinctions. Apparently 99 per cent of all the species that have ever lived on earth are now extinct. We are in the middle of the sixth extinction and Layla and I continued to add our bit to hasten the process.

With the apparent coldness of our responses providing little fodder for the curiosity of onlookers, the reams of people wandering in and out of our house began to thin down. 'You are young. You have to get on with your lives,' somebody, probably a genuine well-wisher, told us before leaving us as physically alone as we mentally had been since the news of our parents' death two weeks ago. 'You can't brood forever,' she said. Two days later Layla opened the fridge and found that there was no more food in our refrigerator left over by Mamma or provided by some or the other well-wisher. We had obviously exhausted our quota of sympathy and reached the end of the time allowed to us for grieving. Layla had let the door swing shut, making the fridge shudder in its emptiness and had declared that she was going to the University library. She had to do some research, she said. And as I watched her fit her tall frame into her trousers and T-shirt and pick up the bag that had laid forgotten for the past two weeks, I realized that the goal post for our 'normal' had shifted. This was our new normal. This getting up on time in the morning and leaving without saying goodbye to anybody and returning home in the evening. The practicalities: of buying vegetables, of washing our clothes, of paying our bills, of answering every time the door bell or the phone rang, we genuinely did try to get on with life or at least to get along with life. Layla and I. We entombed the pain of the absences and like little offerings left inside an Egyptian mummy's chamber, we left a large part of ourselves inside the tomb as our offering to Papa, Mamma and Little Neel, and went on living. From one day to the next to the next.

It was on one of the early days of our living when Mr Sinha arrived at our doorstep and told us there was one more thing we had to deal with. Mr Sinha was very tall but self-contained in a stodgy sort of a way. He moved his hands and legs with so much economy that I was not surprised when he said that he worked in the finance department at Papa's office. He did not look at either Layla or at me directly but told the large *The Two Sisters* print that hung in the living room that in order to access Papa's provident fund and Mamma and Papa's insurance money, we would need Death Certificates of our parents and our little brother.

'If it is only about money, we don't care,' Layla said. 'We don't want any money.'

But of course we needed the money and we carefully took down the address and directions to the local municipal office where those pieces of paper were issued. For the next one month, that was the office we went to nearly every day until we received the three certificates printed on hardened paper.

'What took you so long?' Mr Sinha had asked when we had handed the certificates to him. 'Didn't the officer ask for ten thousand rupees and issue you the certificates immediately?'

'Maybe he didn't ask for the bribe because you are women,' Mr Sinha had nodded and answered his own question without waiting for our response. We, in any case, had nothing left to say.

'Very nice painting. Very nice painting indeed,' Mr Sinha had nodded one final time at the painting and left.

27 October 2014

15

The Real World, the Reality of the Real World, Ambles in

Raman wants to stay. It doesn't matter where. Outside the room, inside the room, anywhere. He doesn't care as long as he is allowed to remain in the vicinity. Somewhere where he can see Tanya or hear her or even hear of her. The nurse had sternly shooed him off the room when Tanya had had, what appeared to be another breakdown, although this one was certainly not a violent one. It was a deeply inward-looking one. She had wept and cried and thrashed about but any violence it contained was directed towards her own self. Is that what their starvation had been? Violence directed towards themselves? But why? The more he hears the less he understands. What had happened? How had the Feynman-loving sisters turned into these freaks of nature to be gawked at? As the television, switched on in the room near the nurses' station where the nurse had finally relented and allowed him to sit, is calling them.

'But there are no guarantees that she will be willing or even be able to talk,' the nurse had warned Raman before she had left him alone to listen to the various ways in which Tanya is being looked at and described.

'I understand that and I would normally not have waited. But you know that Dr Anita wants more information about the patient to decide on her line of treatment, so if there is even the slightest possibility that she may talk, I want to make sure that I am around to record it to give the doctor some more insight,' Raman had said to her, not raising his voice, not making any sudden moves. Not allowing even the smallest hint of his desperation and his subjectivity to be apparent. He had dealt with enough junior clerks in government offices to know nothing raises their ingrained, almost institutionalized antennae towards secrecy more than a desperate man seeking information that is not backed by authority.

A freak of nature. That is how Tanya is being described. One particularly flamboyant journalist had come up with the term, as his channel repeatedly keeps reminding through a ticker that is kept running constantly at the bottom of the screen and now it seems to have become the legitimate way for all channels to describe the thing— no longer a person—whose images are being streamed in a loop. A freak? This woman of so much beauty that she has turned his world around? Raman tries to see how other people are seeing Tanya. One thing is certain. They are seeing more of her than he has ever seen. The top of her head, the shot of her long shrivelled feet—what sense had it made to shoot pictures of all that? And what sense is it making for people to be riveted viewing that? He looks at the images straight, he squints both his eyes, he shuts one eye and keeps the other open, he rises up and literally steps far back away from the TV to see if distance will make him see what other people are able to see in Tanya. And he is going 'loco' as the Columbian intern he had had some years back, who had tried to teach him Spanish, would have described it. *Completamente loco*.

His phone rings. It is his CEO. Raman toys with the urge to ignore the call, to pretend that he is deep undercover where there is no possibility of answering his phone without putting his and the CEO's life in danger. Definitely completamente loco.

'Yes,' he says answering the phone on its tenth ring.

'Hey Raman.' The CEO's cheery voice is loud enough to penetrate through the voices of TV anchors and sounds of TV reports that are crowding his head not as legitimate sounds full of words and sentences with sense and meaning but as distorted siren songs that are hypnotic but debilitating. 'Are you coming to the office? We need to discuss your story,' he says.

Raman wishes he could go back to the days, only about seven or eight months ago when his editor was the person who concerned himself with his stories not the CEO. But his new editor is just a figurehead, a name. The formula of rendering the editor immaterial to a publication and making everything entirely sales driven, that had been implemented with enormous success in one newspaper and is, like a carefully calibrated but utterly sham scientific experiment, being replicated across various publications, reached his magazine too after its ownership was transferred to an industrial group flushed with excessive cash but depleted on morals (according to Raman) . They did not want an opinionated (unless those opinions were seamlessly aligned with the party in power), principled (another word that was soon going to be labelled 'arch' or archaic in dictionaries, if it was not already) editor. His editor could have been anybody but the fact that he is a somewhat famous writer, who has the skills to improve at least the language of the magazine, if not anything else, but chooses to not even do that, is particularly irksome. As if like Wittengsten turned on its head, the right placement of words, of commas and the semicolons could resolve the moral conundrum of the sentences and the stories themselves and provide the right slant, the right viewpoint, and perhaps, if all went well, even the truth. But as it is, that question too is moot because all decisions, including perhaps the placement of commas and periods (there are no semicolons in his magazine anymore) are taken by the CEO in consultation with his 'Five Super Stars' as he calls his five member super-duper sales team.

'I will be in the office in about half an hour,' Raman says and he can feel the ripples of pleasure emanating from his CEO over the waves of mobile phone signals at his promptness. Raman's motives, though, are less sycophantic. He knows it will take him about twenty five to twenty eight minutes to reach his office if he leaves now and he calculates that after the meeting with the CEO which he is sure is going to be only a few minutes long, he can hurry back and reach the hospital just about the time when Tanya should have recovered from whatever is ailing her and should hopefully once again be ready to speak with him. The sooner he leaves the hospital the sooner will he be back. He knows, of course, that his calculations are based on a number of hopefullys, a series of fortuitous happenings—including traffic being just the way he wants it to be—but recently he seems to have discovered a reservoir of endless optimism within himself and he is going to allow nothing to affect his sanguinity. Not even if his CEO says that he should give up the story of the Starving Sisters and travel instead to Bhopal to do a story on the drying lakes in the city for the next issue of the magazine . . . which is exactly what his CEO tells him as he sits in his office with an untouched cup of coffee in front of him. And contrary to his professed pious intentions, despite digging deep into his reservoir of equanimity, Raman's sanguinity does get affected. It gets so affected, in fact, that he rises from his chair and almost shouts out a 'What?' at his CEO but remembering, just in time, that it is crucial that he keep his tone sensible and objective and even, he stops himself at the last minute, making his 'What-why?' come out like a strangled, slightly prolonged croak and his stance appear like he is in the middle of a half-controlled fart.

'Why?' He says quietly, sitting down. This time making sure that the CEO not only hears the word clearly, he also hears the disdain behind his word clearly. But the disdain part fails somewhere in its execution—it is probably unable to penetrate the CEO's endorphin strengthened hide—because he replies quite matter-of-factly, almost cheerfully.

'Because, you know, those sisters no longer need to be allowed space in our magazine. I am sure you can do the lakes story fairly quickly. In time to meet our printing deadline.'

What has changed between the day before yesterday when after the tweet, the CEO was purple-prosing with enthusiasm about the tale of two sisters and today? Nothing, as far as Raman knows, unless something *has* happened and he has missed out on picking the cues because his carefully honed journalistic instincts have been blunted by his intense, personal interest in the subject of the story—his story. Her patient. Perhaps he should not have been so uncharitable towards Dr Anita after all.

'Why?' He repeats. This time taking care to keep the disdain out of his voice, hoping that that will help inveigle a clearer response.

'Do you need to ask?' The CEO laughs. 'Because they do not make for an interesting story. They are too ugly.'

'What?' This time it is the CEO's words that almost do not penetrate Raman's hide. He cannot have heard right.

'You know what I mean. Did you see the pictures on TV? Do you think anybody cares if two sisters who look like that starve to their death? I am sure the interest in them has already begun to fade. By the time our story comes out, nobody will want to read about it.'

'Looks are not everything,' Raman says lamely, still unable to fully process the CEO's reasoning.

'No, they are not everything. There is Power that will beat Beauty any day and there is Titillation, Wealth and of course, perhaps the most important of all, there is Morality and Religion, but then religion is about Ultimate Power, isn't it? Ha ha! You will have to agree that this case checks none of these tags.'

Raman focuses on things that can calm him down. Things that he should be thankful for.

One, he should be grateful to the deity or force of nature or whoever prevented him from divulging to his CEO at any time that he has met one of the Starving Sisters. Two, the CEO's comments although outrageous sound more like a challenge than a *fait accompli*. Raman clutches on to that since it means there is still a possibility that he could change his mind. But for that he needs to finally focus on the CEO. Look at him straight and get into his head to find the right words and the right cues. His CEO is a textbook-liberal, Raman knows, one whose liberalism literally comes from books and textbooks. The CEO understands that it is cool to be a liberal in the intellectual circles that he wants to be a part of and he has trained himself rigorously for the role. He has read the right left-leaning books, he has meticulously memorized the right leftist jargon and he has mastered the usage of that jargon in almost all contexts. But inside his heart he still carries the seeds of conservatism and conformism that have been planted in him by his deeply conservative, strictly republican (members of Republican Hindu Coalition, no less) parents in the US. He is a man who carries an attitude which is liberal-left in his head, and conservative-right in his heart and Raman knows he needs to appeal to the appropriate part of him to obtain the desired result. The last thing he wants to do is to leave Delhi because despite the shroud of post-Diwali smog engulfing the city, despite the bad-tempered honking he had encountered on the road on his way to the meeting, for the first time, the city feels like home to him.

But Raman knows what the CEO is trying to say. As long as the sisters were beautiful, despite what they had done or what had been done to them, they could still be a part of the middle class moralistic narrative. The ugliness of the sisters reflects the ugliness of the society and nobody wants to come face to face with *that*.

'I am sure the TV cameras will soon be gone too.' Raman hears the last bit of the CEO's speech.

'All the more reason for us to be there. Once the cameras go, it will be time for more serious journalists to go in and write a deeper story.'

'Do you have material for your "deeper" story? *Is* there a deeper story?'

Yes. Raman wants to say. There is a deeper story, a much deeper story because Tanya has the kind of unfathomable depth that I have never encountered in a human being before. Whether that depth comes from her experiences and her choices or her choices are a reflection of her depth, I am not sure but I fully intend to find out. In this world of easy answers and instant fame and equally instant infamy, I want to spend days, months, years, a lifetime, trying to understand her.

'There seems to be more to their story than what is apparent, according to the police and the doctors. I have not yet been able to pinpoint quite what it is and how soon it will become apparent but if there is another angle, I think it will be good for our magazine to do a longer piece once all the brouhaha has faded. I know long reads

(Raman remembers the CEO's parlance just in time) are not fashionable but a reporter-at-large kind of longer piece should work very well here. People will still remember the sisters and they will appreciate our magazine for providing a different, a more insightful perspective.'

'And we have their beautiful picture also,' Raman adds.

The CEO looks at him closely.

'I had thought you would be happy to be taken off. You were not very enthusiastic about it.'

So he *had* noticed.

'I wasn't initially. But I don't like to leave things unfinished, especially if there is a bigger story waiting to be revealed.'

Raman pauses and waits for his allusion to the *New Yorker* to go through the plungers and the flippers and bumpers and hit the target. And after precisely seventy-five words and ten seconds of silence, it does.

'Okay' the CEO says. 'See if there is any meat in the story. If not, you go to Bhopal tomorrow evening to cover the drying lakes.'

'Remember Raman, you have twenty-eight hours.' Raman hears the CEO say behind him just as he quietly shuts the door to his room and steps into the dimly lit corridor connecting the CEO's room to the rest of the office. According to the new office plan, its walls are to be broken to be replaced with shatterproof glass to allow more natural light to come in but for the moment, it continues to be dark and dank and continues to hold the intoxicating smell of old newsprint. As Raman is walking out, he almost bumps into his intern standing with a printout in her hand waiting to show Raman the dummy story that he had apparently assigned to her and that she is supposed to hand in for his comments today. Shruti. Raman remembers her name suddenly. 'Shruti, not now,' he says. 'Not today.' And she steps back deferring to his mood immediately. How he wishes he could succumb to the uncomplicated, light-hearted flirtatious involvement that Shruti embodies but although he stares at her face longer than propriety allows, he finds nothing in her finely boned, perfectly unlined face attractive. It is a face that bears no markings of laughter or pain. And it carries no etchings of horror. A freak of nature. Perhaps *he* is the freak of nature who cannot distinguish between right and wrong, caught in the endless iteration of beauty and ugliness, good and bad, never able to separate one from the other. His phone rings before he can say any more. It is ACP Satya and he wants him to come with him to the sisters' house.

'We will be going there in two hours. Do you want to come?'

'Yes,' Raman says. He just has enough time to meet Tanya once more before he goes to her house, he calculates and hurries out without saying another word to Shruti who stays in the corridor long after Raman has left, leaning against the wall and holding on to the two sheets of paper that she had worked on for the last few days, staying up almost the whole of last night to perfect her phrases and deepen her context. She knows Raman thinks she is shallow, superficial and naïve. But despite all his years of experience, despite his all-knowing worldly wise cynicism, despite being her supervisor—who slashes impatiently through most of what she writes and who assigns her only the fluffy stories that he thinks is all she is capable of handling; stories that have no chance of ever finding a place in the magazine—she does not have to fit into the box that Raman has made for her, does she? And he can no more stop her from thinking what she thinks of him or from feeling how she feels about him and about the world in general than he can stop himself from being indifferent to her. And that is how things are, she remembers the phrase she had heard somewhere. *That is how things are.*

16

Of Twinship and Tangency

'You know they are conducting a study on identical twins at NASA. They are planning to send or perhaps they have already sent, one twin into space for a year where they will measure all his biological parameters and compare them to the biological and biomolecular parameters of his twin who will stay on Earth.'

Tanya looks calm. Her bed has been cranked up slightly and she is half-sitting. And if that isn't disconcerting enough, Tanya's first words to him are even more surprising. Raman was not prepared for this. He never seems to be prepared for whatever Tanya has to say. Every time he meets her it is like he is meeting her for the first time and he is almost always rendered speechless by what she has to say or what she has done. He is not able to slot her or anticipate her. Is this what interests him the most about her? Her unfathomable mind? Is this why he has failed to notice in any kind of conventional way what she really looks like. But it was her look that struck him the most when he first saw her. Her tarsier eyes and the expression in them was what he had been attracted to first. And every meeting shows him a new side of her, adding a whole new level to his fascination with her. Today her slightly upright position reveals her hollowed out collarbones covered by mottled, strange coloured skin. Will the novelty wear off with greater acquaintance or do shared experiences that come with spending more time with each other bring out more understanding and therefore a deeper kind of relationship? Who knows? He certainly doesn't and despite tomes of research and study on the art and the science of attraction and falling in love, he would be very surprised if anybody could pinpoint with any level of certainty who will fall in love with whom and how and for how long.

But despite his muddled mind and the fog of idiocy that his feelings for her surrounds him in, he is not deluded enough to not understand that most of what she says is not directed at him. Often she seems to be in a stream of consciousness kind of flow with little awareness of who she is speaking with, and perhaps even what she is speaking about. There is a practised flow to her speaking like she has spent days and months talking with no expectation of a comment or a response. However, on a more positive note for him, Tanya does not seem to have these bouts of stream of consciousness with anybody apart from him and therefore perhaps he does have a little more impact upon her than anybody else whom she has met in the hospital. This is of some consolation, albeit a small one, considering that she has more effect on him than anybody he has ever met in the whole world.

'They are doing it as a part of OMICS study which is a kind of all-encompassing study that includes all the –*ics* of molecular biology that you can imagine—genomics, transcriptomics, proteomics, epigenomics, metabolomics, microbiomics—you name it and it is included. They want to monitor the changes in the DNA, RNA, proteins and metabolites to form a full picture of the differences that will occur between the twin who travels to space and the twin who stays behind. They want to use these biological markers to test what impact space travel has on a human being. Because identical twins' DNAs are identical so this is the closest they think they can get to understanding the impact of space travel. The control subject is almost identical to the subject of experiment.'

'But you know, apparently even identical twin's DNA are not 100 per cent identical,' Tanya continues. 'A human genome consists of three billion letter codes. DNA tests analyse only a small fraction of these codes, which is enough to differentiate between ordinary people but it is not enough to find out the differences between identical twins. But if all the three billion letter codes are analysed, chances are that when one set of DNA was copied into the other twin, some typos may have crept in, making them not completely, not one hundred per cent identical. So Layla is probably not completely same as me. Scientists think that these typos are likely to be only about a dozen in the entire three billion code but they are enough to distinguish one twin from the other if the whole genome of both twins is analysed. Doesn't that sound absolutely crazy? Or perhaps absolutely brilliant. I have trouble distinguishing between the two.'

She smiles. Raman has tried to find out more about her family but has met with only limited success. He has not found any information about her father's family and the earliest record of her father's existence that he has been able to lay his hands upon is of the time when he had been admitted to the engineering college in Roorkee. He topped his Engineering class and was rewarded with a triangular trophy for his achievement which was what he held in his hand in the small indistinct black and white picture on the Roorkee alumni website that showed a short, slightly stocky young man with neatly puffed hair smiling widely for the camera. He seemed to have had a long, largely uneventful career with the public sector behemoth charged with providing irrigation to large swathes of north India and there are a smattering of black and white pictures of him on the internet with one minister or the other inaugurating one Russia supported dam or the other. Raman has had more success with her mother's side of the family. She seemed to have come from a prominent Rajput family in Rajasthan, and as far as he has been able to find out in the short time that had been available to him and from the not so high quality local stringers available to his magazine, they had severed all relationship with her when she had married their father who, whatever else he may or may not have been, was certainly not a pedigreed or any kind of Rajput and therefore had no place in the long line of prominent and wealthy Rajput men and women who constituted her erstwhile family. Raman had been surprised to discover that Layla and Tanya's cousins were the owners of the largest chain of luxury heritage hotels in Rajasthan.

What was even more surprising was that no newspaper or television channel had discovered their connection to Tanya and Layla. Either that or the few who had found out had been suitably compensated for their silence. He had, of course, also read about the deaths of her parents and her brother in the newspapers but those reports were perfunctory, small inserts in the city pages, mostly centred around a picture of a horribly flattened Fiat car.

'How do you know all this? I thought you studied economics.' He asks Tanya in spite of himself. Tanya was a student of economics and Layla of literature. Neither, as far as he knows, dealt with genetics and genomes.

'You know there is a thing called reading. You will be surprised how much you can get to know if you undertake this simple activity!'

Tanya is in a strange mood. But then every time he meets Tanya, she is in a different mood. Tanya's moods never seem to be tempered by niceties or rationality or politeness or context. There is no small talk with her.

'Why did you starve?' Raman asks. There is no opportune moment with her either, he decides. Every moment is as opportune or inopportune as any other. And he is running out of time.

'Because we couldn't find the food we liked. If we had found it, believe me, we would have stuffed ourselves like you or anyone else.'

Tanya's eyes shine with an animistic glitter in the near dark room. The Kafka quote accentuating the Kafkaesque bizarreness of a tarsier like human being sitting slightly up on a bed waving her reed thin arms about in a kind of bizarre yet strangely elegant skeletal dance, and a giant of a man standing darkly over her like an agent of death. Raman is beginning to feel helpless around her, incapable of reaching her. He no longer feels archangel-ish. He cannot be her protector against anything. He is more likely to be the harbinger of doom, he thinks morosely. Why had he ever thought he could protect her, he is not sure. Why had he even thought that she would want his protection in the first place? What ingrained chauvinism had made him think that? What stupidity? What delusions of grandeur?

'Why is her room always so dark?' He had asked the head nurse.

'Because Dr Vaidya wants it like that.' The nurse had replied abruptly before she had softened in the face of his unconscious expression of helpless confusion. 'She has extreme Vitamin A deficiency. Bright lights hurt her eyes.'

'Vitamin A. That was among the first things we had stopped eating.' Tanya says when he tells her about the dim light. 'Vitamin A. A. Although we did discuss whether we should consider Vitamin A as beginning with a V. But there was something poetic in starting our cleansing with Vitamin A (so, was that what the starvation was, Raman thinks, some kind of cleansing?) and going on alphabetically to B and C and D and E and K. We considered treating Vitamin A as retinol but we rejected that too. Oh and we broke Vitamin B into B1, B2, B3, B5, B6, B7, B9 and B12 and we eliminated one each day but we refused to treat them as thiamin, riboflavin, niacin, pantothenic acid, pyridoxine, biotin, folic acid or as cobalamin. We almost

gave in to the temptation when it came to Vitamin C—
ascorbic acid. We wanted to eliminate it in our first week
just to keep Vitamin A company, but we resisted that too.'

Tanya smiles her tarsier smile and everything that she
has said, every point that she makes seems perfectly logical.
Almost beautiful. But he cannot shake off the sensation
of impending doom that bears down on him. It is linked
partly to his conversation with his CEO but now appears
to be driven by much more than that. The CEO's words
seem to have dislodged an undercurrent of molten lava
that will soon flow out like ominous magma smothering
everything and everyone. He is beginning to feel he is
racing against something. That he is running hard—as
hard as he is capable of running—but he has no idea what
he is running towards or what he is racing against. All he
can think of is that as he runs, he is missing something,
something vital upon which everybody's fate depends;
something so obvious that it is invisible in plain sight. He
is not even making sense inside his own head. How is he
ever going to be able to make sense out of Tanya's words?
Yet somehow he feels that her answer will provide a way to
counter whatever he is going to encounter, whatever awaits
her. And him. Why did you starve? Why did you starve?
He wants to shake the answer out of her. But he is afraid
to touch her. What if she snaps between his fingers? Little
bits of her scattering like confetti all over the hospital floor.

'We were on a self-imposed action T4 program
of Nazi Germany. Our own little wild euthanasia. A
way to eliminate all the unwanted—the physically and
mentally weak, the people belonging to the wrong caste,

colour, creed, race, religion, sex, sexual appetite or sexual orientation—from the kingdom of the earth, from the face of the universe. If universe has a face.'

Raman stays looking at her. There is nothing he can say.

'Why do you want to know about our starvation? Why is it that everybody wants to know only about our starvation? Why are we only being defined by the six months in which we ate very little? We lived for twenty-five years before those six months.'

I want to know about the six months and I want to know about the other twenty-five and a half years and I want to know about every minute of every day that I am not with you, Raman thinks. But he is afraid to say anything. His desperation, his sense of urgency is almost physical, almost too strong for him to hold within himself.

'Probably because it is our defining characteristic— our MIP as Layla would put it, our Most Interesting Part, at the moment,' Tanya fortunately is answering her own question. 'The Starving Sisters. Like the fastest man on earth or the world number one in tennis, badminton, golf, squash, chess. Nobody would want to know their stories if they had not acquired those accolades. They get defined by that moment, that achievement. As if everything they did until then and everything they would do after that is of no consequence. And yet, they have wives and husbands and parents and children and they sleep almost every night and get up almost every morning, they eat every day, they cook, they take their dogs for walks, they get frustrated at traffic jams.'

'Life, when lived, is not a set of incidents, is it? It is a series of everydays. One repetitive day after the next, one repetitive moment after the next. Waking, shitting, eating, drinking, working at something arbitrary, designed to fill the spaces between eating and shitting and sleeping and procreating. The large incidents—an Olympic victory, an inauguration—take up 100 hours of a person's life? Or 500 hours or a 1000 hours, yet when autobiographies and biographies and life stories get written, those activities that take up most of a person's life gets forgotten and the focus is on the 100, 500, 1000 hours and not the rest of the 6,48,000 hours that an average seventy-five year old person lives. But it is only when the talk is about the other 6,48,000 hours that the true meaning or meaninglessness of life becomes apparent. And it is those meaningless hours, those conversations about nothing, those moments of doing the same things over and over again that we stretch and we strive and we do everything to preserve. When we want to live forever or failing that, when we want to cryogenically preserve our bodies for that time in the future when human beings will find some way of bringing people back from the dead, we do it not because there are goals that we want to achieve or unfinished tasks that we want to complete. Living endlessly—stupidly or intelligently or unthinkingly—is our only goal. Living on and on is the only task we want to complete. We try to prolong our meaningless lives because to each person those meaningless hours that seldom get written about are the times when they feel truly alive like every other organism on the planet. Each organism strives to preserve itself but each has only that much time on earth before its entire species become extinct. Very rarely, some species fall off the evolutionary map or literally go under the radar of evolutionary forces by hiding deep in the ocean or living submerged under piles of litter in a thick rain forest and are able to survive unchanged. But most species that survive through millions of years on earth do so by cleverly transmuting themselves into completely different, completely unrecognizable species and tricking Time into thinking that they are actually different and hence permitted to stay on earth just a tad while longer. The tiny land dwelling mouse deer like Indohyus becomes the gigantic aquatic whale through a series of changes and mutations over millions of years. Any species that is unable to do that becomes extinct. We humans with our chest-thumping proclamation of being the master of everything on earth and our heart-breaking pulverization of every natural thing can certainly not go under the evolutionary radar. And unless we transform ourselves into the science fiction android societies or become X-Men-like mutants or go out of reach of earth's evolutionary forces by moving to the moon or Mars, we are sure to become extinct at the blink of the earth's eye.'

'Oh we have our distractions, our gadgets, our parties, our races, our stock exchanges, our trading but the essential cycle of life remains the same, does it not? And we all know it despite pretending to be delusional. When we are feeling low or particularly unsuccessful, we like to hear the story of the mythical Wall Street millionaire and the even more mythical Greek fisherman, which lifts our spirits in a non-specific, non-threatening, indefinable kind of way.

The story in which the millionaire goes to a Greek village on a holiday and, impressed by the vast amounts and the excellent quality of fish that is available to the fisherman, tells him that he should buy some more boats to catch many more fish.

"What for?" The fisherman asks him.

"Well, you could then sell more fish to more people."

"What for?" The fisherman asks again.

"You could export the fish all over the world and become a millionaire like me."

"What for?" The fisherman asks again.

"You could do whatever you like with yourself then. You could live a life of luxury. You could go on holidays like me."

"You mean come to a place like this for a holiday? But I am already at this place, am I not?"

The same story would work for a Shanghai millionaire and a Taiwanese fisherman, or a Mumbai billionaire and a Kerala fisherman. But does a fisherman like that who is content being just where he is still exist or has he too been swept by the maelstrom of countable and accountable achievements? Does thinking of a life as a series of incidents make it less arbitrary than it would otherwise be? Like explaining a phenomenon through charts and graphs makes it instantly scientific and unquestionable. Or calling moments seconds or minutes or hours makes them quantifiable and concrete. Do you know what a collection of moments is called? Nothing. There is no name for it. Seconds, minutes, hours are transitory aren't they? Decided and defined by us. Time used to be the one fixed thing in life. "You cannot get back time. Time wasted never comes back," Mamma would say. You cannot turn back time. But you can, can't you? You can travel forward or backward in time. Did you hear about Sven Hagemeier from Germany who celebrated his birthday for 46 hours by flying from Auckland to Brisbane to Honolulu, spending most of his birthday eating plane food and probably trying to think himself out of the deep discomfort the hours of flying would have caused to his body? Not the best way to celebrate a birthday, I would say. But what does time mean then? And you don't even need to travel. All you have to do is turn every clock in the country forward by an hour in summer and every clock back by an hour in winter or it could be the other way round and voila, you are presented with one less or one extra hour. I was flabbergasted when I first came to know of this bringing of time forward and backward at will. We were in Paris then and came to know that on March 29 at exactly 2 am all the clocks of the country were brought forward and instantly from 2 am, the time became 3 am without traversing the 60 minutes or the 360 seconds that were needed for it to be 3. And on October 25, time would move back at 3 am to become 2 am again as if whatever was done in that one hour could be taken back. How would you account for whatever happened in that one hour? How would you account for babies born in that hour? How would you record a murder committed in that hour? If a murder was committed at 2.30 am according to the previous clock and it was discovered at 2.15 am according to the new clock, was the murder discovered before it was committed in a Minority Report kind of way? This arbitrary tilting of time shook the very foundation of everything that I had believed was intransigent, non-negotiable. Time was not meant to be something that you can turn back or bring forward. Where does that hour come from and where does it go away? There is no name for a collection of moments unfettered by man-made time, but it is precisely in those unnamed collection of moments that Layla and I had begun to live. The way every species on earth is supposed to live. The way every other species on earth *lives*. Moment by moment. As one undistinguished mass, unchained and unmarked and unchartered by man-made incidents or occurrences; separated from the shame and the humiliation and the guilt—from one sunrise to the next. Of course, we didn't quite understand it at the beginning and we certainly didn't start out quite like that. We started it all as an experiment, a game, a way to live away from a defined set of rules, a way to take control of our lives and here is where we have ended up. Although we could not articulate it then, I now think that that is what we were doing.'

Tanya pauses.

'Why isn't ordinariness celebrated? I think ordinariness is a very hard-earned virtue. What would I not give to be ordinary? To have a full ordinary set of parents, to live an ordinary life that nobody comments upon and you are asked polite questions like "how are you today" and you are expected to give polite answers like "I am great" or "I am fine" and move on.'

'We were not starving, you know. There is so much emphasis on food. So many magazines, so many blogs, so many websites devoted to food. So many ways of doing it: fast, mechanical, uniform, steadfast food, similar each day, every day, or slow-cooked long-drawn-out; food finding its way through the not-so-perfectly shaped, not-so-perfectly shined spuds and carrots and apples, or food that is picked up and eaten raw and unrefined in surroundings that are anything but raw and unrefined. What you should eat, how much you should eat, how often you should eat, what constitutes a good diet, what can be ethically consumed, how everything you cook or eat is linked to some or the other part of your body and mind—it is an endless series of permutations and combinations and variations. We wanted to see what would happen if we got rid of it. It was an experiment and we did not feel the deprivation initially. Or ever. We felt good. We were abolishing something and accomplishing something.'

'Didn't you crave any food?'

'Yes, I did initially. Chocolates. We eliminated chocolate by the third week. I wanted to cheat but we couldn't, could we? Even considering chocolate as cocoa would not allow us any reprieve. Nor considering its chemical composition cannabinoids, phenylethylamine or tryptophan or theobromine or epicatechin or gallic acid, anademide, serotonin.'

'Do you have a piece of paper?' Tanya asks.

Raman's backpack with its sequestered compartments holds everything that he needs in the world apart from one thing but that is in front of him anyway. Can it get sappier than this? He shakes his head, amazed at his newfound capacity to generate Hallmark card sentiments.

'Perhaps we could ask the nurse?' She misconstrues the shake of his head.

'No, no. I have it. Here.'

At least the object of his hallmark sappiness is as unhallmarkish as anybody can get. Will he still feel the same way about her if she returns to being the conventionally attractive woman that she obviously had been? Will that make her like any other attractive woman and therefore boring in his eyes? Yet how will her looks matter? She would still remain the same unpredictable Tanya, wouldn't she? Stop anticipating yourself, he tells himself. As they say in cheesy self-help guides: go with the flow. With the flow of her words, with the flow of circumstances, with the flow of whatever is in store for all of them. He has begun to feel better. What is it about this woman that takes him on a roller-coaster ride of ecstasy and agony almost at the same moment? Up and down, up and down. There is something so cathartic about discussing real thoughts after a lifetime of unreal conversations that he had with his parents, particularly his mother that the agony is almost as welcome as the ecstasy. Ok, perhaps not quite.

'Ah a fountain pen,' Tanya is saying. 'I love fountain pens.'

Tanya has begun to draw something. Holding the notebook he has handed her in her right hand and using her left hand, which until recently had been attached to an IV drip and is still quite red and a little swollen, she carefully makes the hexagon, the lines and the alphabets.

'This is Phenylethylamine, a component of chocolate and it supposedly works as an aphrodisiac.' She is laughing.

'Aphrodisiac was the last thing we wanted, didn't we, Layla?'

There is a glazed look in her eyes.

'You are lefthanded,' he says, hoping to bring her back to him from wherever she has gone.

'Yes,' she says. 'I am left-handed and she is right-handed. We are mirrored twins. Layla and I. Mirrored.'

Raman does not want to leave but he knows he needs to if he has to meet ACP Satya at Tanya's house. He hesitates. Should he tell her where he is going? Should he seek her permission, however inane that sounds because he knows it will not matter one way or the other? Satya will still go to the house, only Raman will not if she asks him not to. And Raman wants nobody to know more about Tanya than he does or at least before he does.

'Whatever the outcome of the OMICS study, whatever any or all of the –ics together may point towards, I can tell you right now with a certainty that has no statistical significance but an unshakable ingrained subjectivity, that physical distance will make very little difference to the mental proximity between twins. Whatever their biological markers say, it will provide no insight into their mental processes.'

Tanya speaks as if she is quoting from a textbook. She does not look at him when she speaks but just as he opens the door to leave her room, she looks straight at him.

'Distance and time do not matter,' she says. 'Whether the distance is a vertical 340 km or a horizontal 1340 km, and whether the time apart is one day or one year, we find a way to be with each other mentally.'

'How else would I know exactly how you met Deepak, Layla? How else do I know all the details of your relationship?' Tanya whispers but Raman does not hear this. He has left her room by then.

April 2013

17

Split

Eleven months. That was how much time I spent away from Layla. Only eleven months in our—how old are we now? Twenty-six?—in our twenty-six year old life. Our memories are so closely tethered that I am usually unable to disentangle the threads and assign individual stories to either of us. But we did have the nearly one year away from each other when I was in Rampachodva, a place so small that it is not marked on most maps and I am not sure whether it is now a part of Telangana or of Andhra Pradesh after the division of the state or even whether it exists at all anymore; it could perhaps have become a kind of *Toba Tek Singh* land and fallen between the cracks of two highly competitive, deeply ambitious newly minted entities one of which—Andhra Pradesh—dreams of building its vaunted capital city of Amravati ground up, embellished with the most modern of amenities and the latest of technologies while the other, Telangana, tries to use the same technology to shake off thousands of years of history

that seeps into its streets, its psyche, its cuisine and its
language. I had Rampachodva—a place that probably does
not exist anymore, and Layla had Deepak—who ironically
does not exist for us anymore either.

The letter offering the job at Rampachodva was
addressed to me and I had opened it and tried reading it
but I could well have been reading something written in
German for all the sense it made to me. I had pronounced
every alphabet very carefully but did not understand a
single word. What did the letter say? Why was it addressed
to me? What did it want of me? And how was I supposed
to react? I had handed the letter to Layla who had read it
aloud.

'Dear Ms Tanya Sharma,' she had read. 'We are
pleased to offer you the position of Programme Officer at
Shakhti Comprehensive Forest Development Programme
(SACFED) based at Rampachodva.'

Did they know that the person to whom they were
offering the job was no longer the person they had
interviewed? Would they still want me if they knew that in
the time between their interview and their offer letter, my
parents had died, leaving me an orphan at the age of twenty-
four? The word 'orphan' had an ominous ring to it. Could
an adult be called an orphan or was that term reserved for
little boys and girls who inhabited the hundreds of books
that I had read as a child? But even as a child, despite the
promise of exciting adventure that being an orphan held,
and despite being a stickler for adventure, I had not wanted
to be an orphan. I had wanted to go to a boarding school,
I had wanted to solve a murder, climb the Everest, I had

even wanted to be ship-wrecked on an isolated island but with my entire family like the Swiss family Robinson and not alone a la Robinson Crusoe. I categorically did not want to be an orphan. It never featured on my list of things to do but here I was with both my parents dead and with a letter being read by Layla that stated prosaic details like 'though the job offers a modest salary (as the organization is constrained by limited international and national donor support), your food, boarding, and conveyance will be well taken care of'—as if these words, these things still held any meaning for me.

It was a job with an NGO in Andhra Pradesh about which Mamma had been more excited than me. They are doing really good work in the area of afforestation, Mamma had said. And you will get to travel all over the beautiful forests of Andhra Pradesh. Layla had not applied for a job because she wanted to continue her studies, a decision given her proclivity and intellect, Papa and Mamma had completely endorsed. I had no such interest and I did not harbour any ambition of going to Oxford for a post-doctorate in English Literature. On the day of the interview, Mamma had carefully chosen her cream and brown silk sari (smart and dignified) for me to wear. Mamma and Papa had both accompanied me to the centre where more than thirty men and women of all ages dressed in clones of my brown and cream clothes (smart and dignified) waited patiently for their turns. Some were talking to each other, some sat in pensive silence, some were looking through the papers they held in their folders and all of them appeared older than I was although I am sure I stood taller than most of them. Even the men. As I sat between Mamma and Papa with a neat black folder that Papa had brought for me from his office in my hand, I was so sure of not getting the job that I was not even nervous. Papa too appeared more excited than nervous and I could sense that he was dying to complete the story of his first disastrous interview that he had begun with great aplomb in the car before he had been shushed shut by Mamma.

'You will make her nervous,' she had said. 'I don't think it is shubh to talk about bad interviews just before she has such an important one. Usko nazar lag jaegi and it will jinx her interview.' She had added impishly, knowing well that any talk of omens and jinxes was sure to set my non-believer of a Papa in a tangentially opposite direction with him insisting on continuing the conversation just to prove, when I succeeded in the interview, what claptrap this kind of belief was. And yet Papa became quiet when Mamma said this because his love for me and his need to make me feel confident before the interview won against his inclination to give in to his natural rationalist instinct. Mamma turned to look at me and we exchanged a glance so full of love for Papa that he almost seemed to sense it, taking his eyes off the road for a moment to ask Mamma what on earth was going on.

With perverse irony, the letter offering the job that Mamma had been more excited about than me was dated the exact day of Mamma's death although it had arrived a month and a half after that horrific Monday. Perhaps the postman had hesitated coming into a house struck with such an enormous tragedy with something so banal; perhaps they had forgotten to post the letter after they had typed it out or perhaps they were undecided whether or not to offer me the job and had set the letter aside until they had finally made up their minds. Whatever the reason, my date of joining was within two weeks of the arrival of the letter and I had stood shaking my head when I had understood the import of the letter after Layla had spelt it out to me. There was absolutely no way I was going to leave Layla so soon after our worlds had been hurtled and flattened and we had been left holding a misshapen, distorted entity that bore little resemblance to the life we had had before. A world that contained no recognizable signboards or landmarks or spaces for emotional refuge and yet it was a life we had to find a way to negotiate through. But I didn't want to be alone doing it and I didn't want Layla to be left alone to deal with it either.

'No,' I had said. 'No. No. No.'

But Layla insisted that I should join because that is what Mamma and Papa would have wanted, as if what they would have wanted mattered now. They are dead, Layla. They are all dead.

'We have to get on with our lives. You have to take this job. You have to move on.'

Move on to where? I wanted to ask but I called up the number given on the letter and dutifully told them that I would be taking up their offer. And ten days later I left for Rampachodva carrying a bag in which I had neatly folded the clothes that unambiguously belonged to me. In another life, Layla and I had fought hard to not allow the other to wear our clothes or negotiated a pair of earring for a pair of shoes or a top in exchange for another but those kind of quibbles seemed to have taken place between two different sisters, not between Layla and I. Never between this Layla and this I. I had taken a sweater of Papa's, Mamma's red dupatta and a small Lego car of Little Neel's too. Layla came to the station to drop me, looking forlorn and helpless, dressed in black shirt and jeans, waving her thin arm, standing tall and ramrod straight in a crowd of coolies clad in red, railway men clad in blue and variously slouched or furiously moving passengers dressed in different colours. I wanted to pull the chain and get off the train but for what purpose? I sat at my window seat and kept looking at her until she disappeared from view after which I turned to look around my crowded compartment where a family of thirteen occupied seats meant for seven people. The old man, the patriarch, began to ask me where I was going and why I was alone and how I should shift and make myself small in my own seat which although too short for me was wide enough, according to him, to easily adjust two of the youngest children in his group who both looked to be in their early teens. Upon getting no response from me, he made the children sit on my seat anyway after making it known loudly—much to the obvious discomfort of the two children who had squeezed themselves on to my seat at the old man's directive but were trying to take up as little of the space that legitimately belonged to me as was physically possible—to anybody who wanted to hear his opinion that stuck up single women travelling alone were usually up to no good and therefore not worth talking to.

It wasn't like I did not want to talk, I wanted to tell him. I did. I wanted to respond. I wanted to say 'it is okay, please feel free to use my space for your family.' In fact, I wanted to become *a part* of the large family, however temporarily, that was messily exchanging savouries and sweets across the seats and singing loud out-of-tune songs and getting into fights for space and on the rules of the games that they were playing on the train. But it was as if my mouth had been swept clean of words and emotions. I had nothing that I could give to them in exchange for their words and cries and laughters.

Only one train bothered to stop at the Ramachodva station and I knew why when I saw I was the only passenger who got out of even that one train that night onto a platform that was so bereft of life, it was as if I had stepped out of the train and stepped into my own self. Into my own dark inside. Nothing was alive there. There was not a single living thing on the platform. No human beings, no animals (not even the ubiquitous beautiful, brown Indian pariah dogs that make their home at almost every railway station in every place in the country) and no plants and trees either, at least none that I could see in the dark. I was sure there would have been a station master somewhere signalling the coming and going of trains from that little stretch of railway track that was the Rampachodva station whether or not a train chose to stop there and I knew that somebody from the NGO, SACFED, was meant to pick me up from the station and take me to the remote village that was to be my place of work where I would be documenting the impact of deforestation on tribal incomes but I could not see anybody on the platform. Not a soul. All I could see was a dull yellow naked bulb hanging from a wire somewhere at the edge of my consciousness. But I turned my back to it and stared at the pitch-dark desolation that lay ahead of me. For the first time in a long while, my inside and my outside matched perfectly. I could make out the outline of a small wrought iron bench and I sat down on it, placing my bag carefully at my feet and looking into the darkness for a very long time.

I was blessed with that night of complete darkness when I slept on a small wrought iron bench in a dark railway station defying everything that we had recently been told, everything that we had recently been shown about being a woman, about having a body and about being vulnerable in dark places both inside our bodies—between our legs—and outside. But it was not in lonely dark places where Layla and I had been handed those lessons on vulnerability and assault, had we?

18

Womanhood. Splat.

Layla, I know you will probably not agree with me because you loved him so much and you know that I loved him too, but I blame Papa for our predicament. For our unpreparedness. For the mismatch between the world that he told us about and the world he left us in. Did Papa think we would be spared the rites of passage that every woman in the country has to undergo? Or did he expect, like most other women, we would make ourselves smaller, less conspicuous, blank ourselves out into invisibility, not be available on streets and shops and public places and somehow get by? Or better still find ourselves a man—small, big, old, young, it did not matter—who could chaperone us and shield us from the hazards of unchartered, uncontrolled man filled spaces. Or did he believe he had made us strong enough to endure anything that came our way? Whatever he may have thought, however he had expected us to encounter the world, I am sure he did not expect us to be left to our own devices so early with such little preparation.

I blame Mamma a little too. Though unlike Papa, she did try to warn us sometimes. She would say that 'the world is not as easy as you may think' and although she always said it in the context of our studies, as in there is more competition out there than we can imagine and therefore we needed to do better, work harder, stay focused, if we wanted to achieve anything. Only sometimes and perhaps more often recently than before, there was a hint of the unsaid, an undercurrent of caution, a catch in her voice that would make me look up at her even though my expression of supremely indifferent resignation at another of her speeches would remain unchanged. At those times she said it like she didn't quite believe that working harder and focussing for longer and paying more attention would be enough. But perhaps paying more attention would have been, if not enough, at least better than what we were left with.

Don't get me wrong. We were not wide-eyed ingénues, naively looking at the world with the proverbial rose-tinted glasses. We were probably the most well read persons in our class, in school and in college. Our reading had been unrestrained, eclectic, uncensored and enormous—everything from *Famous Five* series to *Women in Love* to *The Art of War*—encompassing anything we could find. Nobody told us what good writing was or what age-appropriate reading entailed and we did not have unlimited access to books to enable us to pick and choose so we ploughed our way through anything that was accessible to us. I would sometimes leave a book unread or unfinished if I found my interest wandering after a few pages, but not Layla. Her insatiable appetite for the written word could not bear the prospect of leaving anything unread between one end—of a book, paper, brochure—and the other. And, of course, we understood the world. Or so we thought. But there is a vast difference between understanding and analyzing something and reacting instinctively, primaly to it when it crashes head-on onto you. With our carefully controlled outings with Mamma and Papa—shopping only at the malls, going to school in the school bus and to college in the University-special or U-special as they are called; never going to any religious festival or a fair or any place where there may be crowds and the potential for a stampede (which was almost every place in Delhi)—our experience of groping fingers and lascivious glances was almost non-existent and we entered the territory that came with being a woman in Delhi or perhaps anywhere in India, unprepared, naked and woefully unarmed.

When that touch, that sudden violent cupping of my left breast by a man who did not even stop long enough for me to see his face or for him to see my reaction to his assault came on the day I ventured into the busy market to buy vegetables for the first time in my life, two weeks after the deaths of Mamma, Papa and Little Neel, I felt the imprint of those splayed fingers upon my breast so strongly, so viciously that I actually looked down to see if his fingers had somehow X-Man-like burnt through the dark blue of my thick rib-knit T-shirt and the white of my utilitarian cotton bra and exposed my breast—with its dark concentric areola wrinkled like basalt formed by a *pahoehoe* lava flow—to the world. His hand had lain on my breast for a millisecond before giving it a hard vicious squeeze and my breast hurt like it had been cut open but not then. Not quite then. At that time it was only the inside of my head that had exploded. I felt slimy, dirty, guilty of being dressed wrong, of being at the wrong place, of being the wrong person—of wearing a T-shirt, of being on the road, of being the person who had breasts that could be touched and felt and squeezed by anybody. Even by the small spindle-legged man dressed in a muddy brown shirt, wearing cheap, sickly sweet hair oil and scuffed shoes. By any or all of the multitudes of strangers who were streaming around me, past me, into me on the road where I stood trapped and defined only by the protrusions and the caverns of my body. As if I had laid my wares on the street for anybody to gawk and have a feel of. Like the mangoes strewn outside profusely fruiting orchards on the highway to tempt motorists to stop and check and feel and cut open. Or for a dog to take, as a lawyer in a documentary that I later watched put it. 'Women were like a diamond,' he said. If you leave them on the street, a dog will take it. He had not explained why a dog would be interested in a diamond or who was supposed to make the decision about leaving or not leaving the diamond woman on the street, since it obviously could not be the woman herself—but he had looked confidently into the camera, sure that he had made his point quite eloquently.

I had turned around and had returned home without buying the vegetables, keeping my head down and my body compressed, the wind in my ear blocking out the sounds of the street, my downcast eyes not looking at anybody; afraid that there may have been witnesses to my humiliation, afraid that I carried the shameful aura of a woman who had been touched inappropriately because it was my fault, was it not? For being available, for arousing the lust, for being born the way I was? And what if the man came back? What if many men came? Wouldn't that be my fault too? I reached home, unlocked the door and leaving my jute bag—that in another version of my life, the other person that I was before I left the house had conscientiously carried, harbouring some notions of being environmentally friendly—outside, I locked the front door from inside, went into the bedroom that I still shared with Layla even though now we were the only ones left in the entire three bedroom, three bathroom house, locked that door, went into the bathroom and only once I had locked *that* door too that I began to shed my clothes on which I could still feel the touch of the rough hand and smell the burnt leaf smell of the herb infused oil that the man wore in his hair. I stood in the shower, turned away from the mirror because I could not bear to look at my face or my body. I wanted to shed my skin along with my clothes because it too bore the imprint and the smell. I stood under the shower and realized that this was the first time my breast had been touched by anybody apart from me. I scrubbed and I scrubbed and I scrubbed with hard pumice stone until the skin on my left breast peeled and scraped and bled and my breast become the open wound it had felt like ever since the man had touched it. My head burned, my brain became a frenzied mass of interlocked neurons. Like sparks flying out of a short-circuit, it spewed out stray thoughts that I had nobody to share with, pieces of conversations that I could not have, bits of passages that nobody was present to hear, tears of sympathetic neighbours that had no place inside me, whispers of curious onlookers that I could not hide away from, the buzzing and sparking and searing and the absolute emptiness of a house where every room was still filled with the paraphernalia of the living but where everything had died. One part of me—the part that Mamma had ingrained inside me, that part that focused on what needed to be done whatever the circumstances, however fraught the situation—wanted to be practical, wanted to order milk and bread and eggs from the shop outside our complex that home-delivered grocery because there was nothing for us to eat at home but that part of my brain was battered in and unable to do more than just harbour the thought; it was not able to articulate its intention clearly or direct the rest of me to obey its summons.

I don't know how long I stood naked under the shower in the cold bathroom, with a bruised and bleeding breast and with no coherent thought inside me, only bits of tempestuous feelings that I could not hold in but that I did not know how to let out. I could not shout, I could not cry and when I stepped out of the bathroom, I didn't know what to wear. Nothing looked appropriate. My jeans, my T-shirts, my dresses, my skirts, anything I picked, seemed too flimsy to cover the shame of my femininity. I went to my parent's bedroom for the first time naked without hesitation. Everybody who lived there was dead. Dead. Dead. DEAD. Nobody could stop me from picking up the red dupatta that Mamma had taken off and left on her bed. Certainly

not Mamma herself. She was dead. It was among the last
pieces of clothing that she had worn—it still carried her
smell that my mind shut itself against—before dressing
up in the beautiful pink silk sari and getting herself killed
on the road. I was suddenly very angry with Mamma and
with Papa and with myself and with Layla who was also
me with less than half a degree of separation. I wrapped
the dupatta tight around my breasts round and round till I
could no longer see or feel the blood or the breasts. I wore
Mamma's loose white nightgown that came only to my knees
with its long sleeves and faded yellow flowers and when I lay
down on the couch in the living room, I felt as if I was at
the edge of an abyss and could not move even a little bit for
the fear of falling over. I stayed precariously balanced at the
edge of the couch and I stared at *The Two Sisters* on the wall.
Were the sisters trying to tell me something about being a
woman? Did they, in that era too, have to endure this kind
of intrusion or did their voluminous clothing protect them
from the roving eyes and the wandering hands? Should I
stop wearing 'provocative' clothes like jeans and T-shirt that
was almost my uniform at that time and dress more modestly
in the one loose salwar-kamiz that I owned? I even tried
to think about what could have been going on inside that
man's mind to rationalize the assault somehow. What kind
of pleasure could he have derived from that contact? Would
that squeeze have appealed to his primal instinct of being in
control, if only for a very, very short period, of something
that he otherwise would not have had access to? Or was it
his way of punishing me for being what I was: a procreator,
a skill that he and his kind could never acquire and therefore

a skill that needed to be degraded and denigrated and made dirty, shameful. My breast and my womb epitomizing everything that he could not be and therefore most open to assault. Like spraying hundreds of bullets into a colourfully dressed young people filled, brightly lit open music concert by straight jacketed, black cloth wrapped members of rigidly indoctrinated religious cult. Intellectually I could unravel and disentangle and explain his action till heaven came but physically I still felt sick and humiliated and very, very tired. I had not looked at myself since I had returned from the vegetable market but when Layla came home in the evening, I could not avoid seeing myself in her. In her slightly flushed face because of her exertion of carrying the heavy bag filled with books up the stairs, in her eyes that looked sad and tired but mostly in the way the swell of her breast showed underneath the pink and white striped shirt that she wore over the loose fitting beige trousers. I hated her too, then. Why was she so much like me? Why must I keep seeing myself over and over and over again when all I wanted was to obliterate my body?

'Why did you leave your bag outside?' Layla asked. But I did not want Layla in the room with me. I did not want anyone in the room with me but mostly I did not want Layla. I shut my eyes and felt her breathe softly above me before she stepped back and went away quietly so as not to wake me up and I heard her order the milk and bread and the eggs that I had been unable to call for, speaking in a very low tone at first and then loudly because the man at the other end was probably not able to hear her in the din of his shop. I heard her add two more cartons of milk to the list probably because the man at the other end refused to send somebody all the way to our house for so small a sale. By the time the knock came at our door, I had drifted into a hot, sensation filled dream but I woke up to the smell of eggs frying and before I could fully comprehend what the churning in my stomach indicated, I felt a giant blob of bile rise in my stomach and I threw up while still lying down on the couch. I soiled Mamma's gown and the dupatta and even the breast that despite being squashed under the rolls of red cloth was still available and open to assault.

I had high fever that night, Layla told me later. She said she had let me sleep on the couch because I had refused to sleep in the bedroom that we shared, but I had screamed so loudly in the middle of the night that I had woken her in the next room and she had ended up spending the rest of the night with me in the living room, sitting on a chair and making sure that I was alright.

I had no recollection of my disturbed night and except for the dark, throbbing, bruised left breast, I bore no visible scars of the events of the previous day either. I resolved never to tell Layla about what had happened. But, of course, she knew. And if she didn't then, she knew soon enough. The lessons of that morning were repeated again and again, almost each day every day, in some form or the other over the next month. Again not in the dark but in the well-lit albeit squalid office with its small windows, paan and rainwater streaked walls, mismatched tables and chairs and teeming populace where we had had to go for a month to fulfil one formality or the other—one more form to fill, one more document to attach, one more signature to be had—to

get the death certificate of Papa and Mamma as if dying
was a particularly difficult to attain credit that needed to be
certified by multiple people to be deemed credible. We were
poked and touched in there. We were made to feel as if
our presence in that office teeming with men permitted our
body parts to be examined and assessed and felt and touched
by anybody who was curious about the female form. It was
there that we learnt to walk with our elbows jutted out to
create a small perimeter of personal space and to bend our
bodies inwards and outwards and sideways to avoid being
touched by perverted fingers and palms and hips and dicks.
Layla and I did not speak to each other in those days, we
could not even bear to look at each other properly. And it
was in that office that the well-meaning old clerk, his eyes
encircled in sympathetic round steel framed Gandhi glasses
had, in all honesty and brimming with good intention, said,
'Why do you girls have to come here? Can't you send a man
instead?' Send-a-man not to the dark lonely place with its
dark wrought iron bench open to the elements of nature
but to a place teeming with people where birth and death
were both reduced to rectangular pieces of paper bordered
in gold and emblazoned with dozens of seals of unknown,
unknowable authority and where the small teller's windows
dishing out these all important pieces of hardened paper
opened only for a short, arbitrarily decided time each
day and sent everybody into a shoving, pushing, poking,
touching frenzy when it did.

Why hadn't we been prepared for it? Why had we
needed to be prepared for it? Why did we need to protect
our faces, our curves, our protrusions, our caverns?

I think about what I had looked like on the TV screen and I try to smile. There are no curves on us now, are there? No bodies. No faces. Just two freaks of nature. And yet, somehow I know it wouldn't matter because we are still women, aren't we?

'I never told you this Layla but I slept the whole night on that small wrought iron bench in the railway station at Rampachodva.'

In the morning there was shock, commiseration and apologies by the director of the NGO for his driver's inaptitude and impatience. The driver had apparently waited for nearly three hours for a train that was late by over five hours (for reasons not disclosed to us, the lowest rung and the least important part of the railway behemoth: the passengers) and had then left assuming that I had decided to not come after all, without bothering to check the timing of the train or perhaps not finding anybody on the station who he could check it with.

'He had thought why would a Delhi girl like you come to our remote village? And you know, I can't completely blame him for thinking that. Can you?' The director had smiled.

And I had smiled back because, despite my dew-soaked hair, my crumpled clothes and the stale taste in my mouth, I had had the best sleep in a long, long time.

Would a night sleeping alone under the stars have saved Layla? Was it because she was denied that night that Layla needed Deepak? I will never know but when I returned to Delhi eleven and a half months later, Deepak had penetrated deep into Layla's and, by extension, my life.

27 October 2014

19

D for Darkness. D for Dysfunction.
D for Despair.

It is beginning to turn dark already at four in the afternoon when Raman reaches Krishna Colony. Although the sky above is still a clear crystalline blue, deep black clouds have congregated on the horizon, producing wafts of cool breeze that is clashing with the tepid air that has lingered over the city over the last few days, turning the place warm or cool in quick succession.

It is a strange weather probably appropriate for the strange times that the old guard at Krishna Colony is living in at the moment. He is harried. His world of small one-room hutment in the illegal settlement where he moved recently with his wife and three grown children is not meant to be mixed up with the world of Krishna Colony residents except in the most perfunctory of ways. He is supposed to provide a service, be paid miserly for it and to shut his eyes and ears to any thoughts or feelings beyond that. For instance, he is not supposed to notice that the group of people who haggle about increasing his salary by even Rs 500 in a month, spend five times that amount on one meal every time they order pizza with and garlic breadsticks and cheesy dip. So why is he being questioned as if he should know something about this world where women with lakhs of rupees in their bank would starve nearly to their death like the beggar on the street he had seen a month back who had died of a combination of heat stroke and starvation and who had hundreds of flies hovering over him—the first set of creatures to feast over the largesse provided by the prone, unmoving body. Other creatures would come next—saprophytes, distant relatives, questioning NGOs and quick and dirty last-rites providers. How is he supposed to have answers for the unending stream of questioning people—policemen and journalists and camerapersons but also curious onlookers and that team of sweet-smelling but extremely rude women from the National Commission for Women, who had asked their questions so persistently and had looked so incredulous at his lack of knowledge it was as if they thought *he* had lived in D332. Going into every house is not my job, he wanted to tell them. I cannot go far from this makeshift shelter with an asbestos ceiling near the gate, which does not have a cooler or even a fan. Each visitor has to be treated differently otherwise he would face the wrath of the president of the Resident Welfare Association for being too polite, too rude, too helpful, not helpful enough. This is not what he had signed up for after retiring from the post office where he had spent the last thirty-five years. He took over the job from his nephew only because he had been told by that very nephew that being a guard at Krishna Colony was an easy four step process: 1. Stay near the gate and salute every man 2. Write down the name of the guest if any come to the colony 3. Call the house where the guest wants to go to on the intercom 4. If the saheb or memsaheb tell you to send the guest inside, let them go in otherwise send them off. 'It is very easy, Chacha.' He had said. 'And you don't have to walk around or anything. It is just like your previous job. You don't have to actually guard the complex even though you are called the guard. You have to stand at the gate from where everyone comes inside and you don't have to worry about anybody entering from anywhere else. That is not your repertoire of responsibilities.' His nephew had used 'repertoire' carefully. Borrowing one of Mr Deol's words, as the guard soon discovered—other important words in Mr Deol's repertoire being abdication of responsibility, honoured guest, scum of the streets. But his nephew had not told him about Mr Deol's lexicon of approbation. Instead he had said that people were normally quite decent and not too many people come visiting anyway.

'We could use the income,' his wife had said, using a word out of *her* lexicon of approbation. It was that word that had done it for him and so after years of going to work every day, just when he had thought that he would finally get to savour some free time, here he is in a job that has, in the last four days, turned out to be more taxing than the thirty-five years he had spent working for the government. The constant movement of people, of cameras and microphones, the interviews, the covertly hostile questions, the overtly hostile reactions when he denies somebody entry under the RWA president's directive. He can't even quit his job because who knows what motive will be ascribed to that and who knows what part of the blame for the entire sorry saga will be apportioned to him. And as if that is not bad enough, he gets no sympathy for his plight or his difficulties at home. You are always on TV, his nephew says. Everybody knows your name. Why are you complaining? What more do you want? He can see the envy in his nephew's eyes for his ill-gotten, unwanted, extremely transient infamy. You should have stayed on the job, he wants to tell his nephew. But he keeps quiet. The more he complains, the more his nephew, his wife and even his children think he wants more attention for his good luck. So he is stuck here with no sympathy or appreciation (which he had never got anyway and he wouldn't know what to do with if it comes crashing on his head, so that didn't really matter) but with so much attention (which is also something that he had never encountered and definitely never ever wanted; content to be the stamper of letters who almost nobody noticed but whose proud handiwork was present in every envelope and postcard that passed through his post office) that he has to literally be on his guard all the time.

He isn't sure what category to place Raman in when he shows up at the gate with a worn out bag on his back and a distracted frown on his face. Raman, for his part, stands patiently by the enormous wrought iron gate that shakes every time a gust of wind blows while the old guard, after carefully appraising him and noting down his name, picks up the intercom and makes the call to Mr Deol, who probably asks the guard to let him in but perhaps in not the politest of terms because although the guard tells Raman to come in immediately after the call, he does so with his eyes downcast, as if he does not want Raman to see the remnants of his mortification at Mr Deol's tone in his eyes. Raman understands that despite being old, the guard is probably new to the humiliation that comes with being among the lowest rung in whatever whimsical hierarchy that exists in a housing society or in the city and at the mercy of whoever wields power at that particular time. Once he gets used to the treatment meted out to him from those above him, he will still be hurt and angry but he will take his anger out on the visitors by being brusque and impolite with them in a kind of negative pay-it-forward way on which the city's notorious bad temper thrives. But he is probably new to the job and perhaps to the city as well and he bears his humiliation with lowered eyes and a slight quiver in his voice as he gives precise direction to D332 to Raman without looking at him even once after his intercom conversation. Although he does manage a downcast smile at Raman's profusely vocal thankfulness which, those who know Raman would recognise as the manifestation of his guilt at being a part of the world that is so vehemently, so hierarchically, so unapologetically divided into those that dish out and those that take it.

But all thoughts of the guard and his travails fly out of Raman's mind at the sight of the squat-gray soviet style concrete building that he spots instantly as he obediently takes the first left turn off the gate. He has seen images of the building so often and so persistently everywhere he

has looked in the past few days that he is sure he is inured
to the sight of it. And yet in a Taj Mahalesque kind of
way where you have seen the pictures of that magnificent
monument so many times that you are sure that the sight
of it will be clichéd and will leave you underwhelmed, but
when you actually see the Taj Mahal for the first time,
the otherworldly splendour of it amidst all the worldly
cackle of hustling photographers and craning, posing
selfie-taking crowd, still makes you catch your breath,
the sight of Tanya's building amidst similar monolithic
concrete blocks that make up Krishna Colony, leaves him
standing absolutely still on the road. The road is lined by
old mango trees that shiver intermittently every time a gust
hits them because although they have withstood many a
Delhi storms, they were weakened recently by the concrete
poured around their roots to make the cemented walkway,
and have therefore become prone to being toppled over
whenever the first big squall hits the city—which could
well be today.

Tanya's building is like all other buildings around it—the
same size, the same bulk—except unlike the other buildings
where the houses on both levels have been repainted or
redone in small and big ways to make them stand shiny and
refreshed and a proud part of the new myth of economic
boom that is being perpetuated about old India, Tanya and
Layla's house stands above its freshly painted ground floor,
paint-peeled and dirt-encrusted like a rectangular piece of
forgotten time. 'The apartment that the Sharmas inhabited
was a gaping hole in this upmarket neighbourhood,' Raman
remembers the description given by one of the news stories.

How had this gaping hole not been noticed? How had it stood for so long amidst all the painting and scrubbing and banister-fitting and tile-replacing without anybody commenting on its lone grimness and its griminess? Was it too close, too messy, too touchy-feely, too knotted to be disentangled, and resolved by words alone and therefore not worth the time? If something has not been reported in the newspapers and television or posted on Facebook, has it even taken place? Can you be outraged about anything unless there are cameras to cover it, selfies to make it worthwhile, Twitter to start trending it, Instagram to flaunt it or Facebook to express it? Has the social media made us sympathize with the plight of people flung all across the world but made us forget good old-fashioned kindness to our neighbours? Has the 'personal' become too small to be valued and yet big enough to be advertised? Or was there something else that lay behind the forgotten house with its starving inhabitants?

Achha, there you are! I was wondering whether you have been sent somewhere else by that old fool of a guard.' A big Punjabi man with stringy muscles-imbrued-with recent deposition of fat, old wrestler's physique, who Raman recognizes as the venerable Mr Deol, is boisterously coming towards him. 'ACP Satya has asked me to send you to D332 as soon as you arrive. Of course, I am allowed to go only up to the door. A bit strange, if you ask me, since I was the first person to step into that house. I was the one who got the sisters out.'

But Raman is not asking him. In fact, he is barely registering what Mr Deol is saying. As he follows

Mr Deol up the dark old-fashioned staircase made of solid concrete slabs, he wants to stop at each step, breathe in the air and prepare himself for entering Tanya's house. All his intellectual and philosophical rationale and beliefs are being smothered under the sheer physical sensation of walking up the stairs towards the house that may hold the secret to Tanya and Layla's self-imposed incarceration and provide at least a partial insight into Tanya's unfathomable mind. He hesitates at the lone faded green door on the landing not sure whether he needs to knock. Mr Deol, however, has no such qualms. He steps forward, turns the plain brass latch of the door and pushes it open. He says something about preparing Raman for the sight of . . . but the police constable posted just inside the door turns around and shuts and bolts the door on Mr Deol's face, pointedly cutting him off mid-sentence. Raman, in any case, has not heard a word of what Mr Deol had been saying, nor does he notice the door being shut. He does not even see ACP Satya who is carefully dusting a small photo frame that stands bang at the centre of the living room floor. Raman is staring at the larger than life print of a painting depicting two women dressed in identical clothes that almost covers an entire wall of the room but seems to be—both literally and figuratively above everything—detached from, and mildly judgemental about, the squalor of the rest of the room. The uneven film of dust on it only serving to enhance the painting's texture, giving it a strangely three-dimensional aura. He is sure he has never seen the painting before but it looks strangely familiar like its image has been implanted inside his head on a chip without him being aware of it.

It stands opposite the front door and the women in the painting seem to be looking at him, one sideways and one straight but both their gazes hold secrets that he is allowed no access to. And yet, there is challenge in their eyes as if they are saying if he digs hard enough and is sincere enough, they may let him into their world and allow him to see them in all their spectral glory. There is a sudden flash of lightning that casts a bright glow in the room before all the lights go off and because of after-image (Raman tells himself sternly) it almost feels as if the women in the painting moved a little from their previous positions.

Nobody says anything for the briefest of seconds in the dark until the proverbial other shoe drops in the form of a loud clap of thunder signalling that the lightening had occurred quite close by and Satya says he sometimes wishes smoking was not so much of an anathema these days that nobody seems to carry any matches or lighters. Before anybody can reply, they hear the sound of heavy footsteps above the lashing wind and somebody, presumably one of the constables stationed to man the door, opens it. Mr Deol stands on the threshold with a large torch in his hand as if he had been waiting all this while down the stairs anticipating this very moment, to perform this very task. He shines the torch directly on Satya's face before saying 'sorry, sorry, sorry' and stepping into the room without waiting for Satya's permission to enter. 'I am helping you,' he says importantly by way of explanation as he heavily turns the thick red lever that is attached to the right wall of the room on the side of the door where Raman still stands. *Khat* once. *Khat* twice. 'Wait it should be here . . . there!' he says

triumphantly as the lights in the room come on. 'We have
all contributed as a society to pay all the sisters' maintenance
dues,' he says piously. 'That is why there is electricity in
the house now and water and even the power back-up.
You know the diesel generators that we use because the
electricity supply that we get is so unreliable. That is also
working in the flat.'

The power-backed lights look brighter than the erratic
supply lights, Raman thinks. Or perhaps it is just an illusion
created by the contrasting pitch-darkness that had preceded
it. Raman knows he is thinking these irrelevant thoughts to
allow his mind to process the information that Tanya and
Layla had lived in the dark and the heat with no electricity
and at least for some time, with no water, before they had
been taken to the hospital; as well as to take in the spectacle
in front of him slowly—one section of the room at a time—
in order to inure himself against missing something vital
but mostly to protect against over-stimulating his senses
which he knows may make him act rashly and foolishly
and, in all likelihood, disastrously. Like allow him to give
in to the intense urge to push everybody physically out
of the room. Out, out, out. NOW. Mr Deol, who after
being thanked, is fortunately being led away firmly by his
elbow by Satya—'you cannot enter without the gloves and
the shoe covers,' Satya says. 'In any case, you cannot come
in until we have gone through the house completely'; the
two constables, one of whom is holding out a pair of shoe
covers and gloves for Raman to wear and even Satya who,
despite his earnestness and his obvious, more than purely
professional interest in Layla, is still an intruder in this

space which belongs to Tanya and Layla alone and that
nobody, not even Raman, has the right to poke and judge
and sacrilege. But, of course, he cannot send everybody
away and he cannot cover up the house and hide it away
from all eyes until Tanya is ready to open herself and
her spaces to anybody or nobody as she chooses. And he
cannot not prevent the world from saying whatever they
like and form whatever opinion they want about Layla and
Tanya either.

'There was a very bad odour coming from the sisters'
house.' Raman remembers another bit of description
given by one of the neighbours who had first come
into the house. He had heard it during his afternoon of
concentrated television-watching when he had been
reluctantly researching the sisters' story (which was only
two days ago but feels like years ago from the person he has
become since then after meeting Tanya). 'One of the sisters
was half-nude and I think bleeding from the mouth, the
other sister was wearing woollen clothes even in this warm
weather,' the same neighbour had also said. But Raman
can smell no bad odour in the room. Instead the house
emanates the petrichor from the first drops of rain landing
on its dust-strewn balconies and windowpanes. And as
thunder rages outside, Raman stands inside the door and
tries to assimilate each bit of the room slowly.

He has covered many tragedies, many a storms and
earthquakes and displacements and squalor but he has never
seen any place that looks even remotely like this. Just as it
was rumoured, just as everybody who had stepped into it
had described it, the room is a mess yet there is something

deliberate, something vicious, something debilitating about
the mess. Absolutely nothing, apart from the painting, is in
its right place but it is as if the displacement of every piece
of tasteful old-fashioned furniture, furnishings and knick-
knacks that made up the happy home that Tanya had
described, has been carefully choreographed to let nothing
remain in its conventional, pre-defined, rightful place. The
backless couch stands in the middle of the room facing
away from the door and towards the painting, the centre
table is on one side and a large dining table on the other.
All the chairs are toppled over but they lie in a straight
line with the tops of their high backs touching the wall
and their legs splayed almost grotesquely forward, showing
the underside of their seats. There is a dirt-encrusted,
presumably non-functioning gray telephone on the floor,
there is a large desktop computer with its monitor facing the
wall. There are cushions and carpets and plates and glasses
and boxes and clothes, there are books—scores of them
and then there are papers. Everywhere. On the floor, on
the cushions, beside the chairs, between the chairs, on the
tables. A coat of dust covers almost everything except the
couch and a few other objects where the dust is thinner as if
those objects have been touched more recently, perhaps by
Tanya and Layla but perhaps also by the orderlies from the
hospital who had picked them up or by people like Mr Deol
and the lady who had found the room and the sisters foul
smelling—the scores of footsteps on the dust-covered floor
a testimony to the multitude of arrivals and departures that
this place has recently witnessed. The constable shuts the
door behind Raman, muffling the sound of the rain that is

pouring down torrentially by now and Raman bends down to wear the shoe covers and the gloves that the constable has given him, before he steps fully into Tanya and Layla's home.

October 2013

20

The Perfect Lover

Why did Deepak have to come into their home? Why did there have to be a relationship? Couldn't the exploration of bodies, the satiation of desires happen without allowing Deepak access to their homes and their minds? But I guess it had to happen that way. In a country where everything takes place outside in the open, where people bathe, eat, pray, sleep, shit, fight, play, kill and die on the road, the only thing that does not and that cannot happen on the road is love; the making of it, the display of it, or even the allusion to it, except in the larger than life film posters. But the posters too remain coy, allegorical, metaphorical. No kissing is allowed on the roads of the country, no holding of hands, no looking for too long into each others' eyes either. So Layla had to find a place for them to meet and a relationship; a veneer however thin or translucent or unconvincing. Which was tragic. Deepak would have been perfect as a lover. Deepak *was* a perfect lover. The long hours he had put into the task of mastering this art, the vast and quite literally varied body of experience that he had, the way his mind and all his senses worked in tandem to mine every piece of information for anything that he could use in the future, meant that Deepak knew exactly what he was doing when he touched Layla in the small of her back outside the library; the fingertips of his right hand applying the gentlest of pressures, just enough to allow her to feel their presence on her body through the thickness of her shirt and enough to give her a primal hint of everything that those fingers were capable of doing, making her involuntarily lean back into that hand to amplify and prolong the sensation.

It was a beautiful evening in October, that time of the year when, for once, the skies of Delhi clear up and the clean, crisp evening air begins to carry traces of the cold that November will bring but not of the smog—created by the mix of the still Northern depression and the bellowing smoke from the burning kharif crop residues in Punjab and Haryana farms—that will shroud the city for the entire duration of its four-month long winter, graying its sun and injecting poison into its inhabitants' lungs. Layla stepped into the fading evening light and shivered slightly in the cold. Although the khaki shirt that she wore was made of thick cotton, the difference in temperature between the inside and the outside of the library was too much for the shirt to adequately mitigate. She should have got her thin shawl, Layla thought but not with any sort of conviction. She was too far away from her immediate surroundings to register it fully because although the outside of the library was drastically different from its inside, Layla's mood was still on the same wavelength outside as it had been inside. Her mind was still in fourteenth century Italy and her body still languid in the throes of the poet Petrarca's unrequited love, the outpourings of which she had been blissfully reading through.

Io canterei d'amor sí novamente
ch'al duro fiancho il dí mille sospiri
trarrei per forza, et mille alti desiri
raccenderei ne la gelata mente

I would sing of love in such a novel way
I'd draw a thousand sighs
And I'd force a thousand desires
Out of that icy cold mind

She had spent the last seven hours cocooned in Petrarca's world of longing which, in Delhi, was located in the very familiar and the very comforting womb of the Delhi University Arts Library. The books lined there were reliable friends who emanated the dusty, mothy smell of untouched old paper and held within them the secrets of a long forgotten world of iambic sonnets and lovelorn humanists. Since spending a lifetime writing nearly four hundred poems for a love not reciprocated was an antithesis of contemporary self-appeasing thought processes and hence considered extremely unfashionable, the section of the library where Layla sat was seldom used and she had been left practically alone for the entire seven-hour duration to work on her thesis that, among other things, entailed deciphering how many of Petrarca's similes that included 'burning like a fire' and 'freezing like ice' had found their way into the sonnets of Elizabethan England and subsequently into the cliché of the English language. Had it been possible, she wouldn't have minded staying in the library forever despite its utilitarian blue-gray painted iron shelves, its dusty-brown walls, its shabby tables slinked shiny by overuse and its hard wooden chairs with rounded butt outlines that made absolutely no concessions for the vulnerable bottoms and backs of long-term scholars and researchers. But she knew that the library would shut at seven and she did not want to negotiate the streets of Delhi after dark. Also the last U-special bus that would take her home was scheduled to arrive at 6.35 pm so she had shut her books and walked out of the library. But reluctant to leave the gentleness of that world quite yet, and knowing she still had ten minutes to reach the bus stop that was only a brisk five-minute walk away, she had stood outside the exposed brick facade of the library, looking into the tree-lined vistas of this part of the sprawling Delhi University campus that was far away from any college and, probably as a testimony to the quality of and the attention paid to liberal arts education in the university or in the country for that matter, was completely deserted at this hour.

'You looked like a stranded owl with your large stricken eyes and in your khaki-brown and black attire,' Deepak had told her later.

'And my rotund figure!' Layla had said although she was not rotund and she knew not all owls were rotund. But by then she also knew that Deepak, with his very limited, almost non-existent, reading and even more limited interests, was not likely to have that kind of information that did not figure in the usual small talk in polished diction that he liked to be a dominant, suave part of. When Deepak had seen her in front of the library, she had looked stricken because she had been yanked out of the sublime passions of fourteenth century Italy and had been placed plonk in the middle of the grating mechanics of twenty-first century India, having just remembered that there was a DTC bus workers' strike that day which meant that there would be no U-special at 6.35 and she would therefore need to figure out some other way to reach home before it got too dark. And accompanying that thought had come the realization that spending seven hours bent over books, reading and writing without stopping for any food or drink was very bad for her lower back and her shoulders which had both begun to ache and all she had felt capable of doing, when Deepak had seen her, was slump down and cry her heart out because of her tiredness but more out of the sudden loneliness that had enveloped her. She really had *nobody* whom she could tell even her small inconveniences to, let alone share her bigger, huge, *humungous*, troubles.

That had been the perfect moment for Deepak to swoop in. He had razor-sharp instincts in recognizing an opportunity, he told the transient friends of all ilk and varieties he made as he went through thirty-nine years of his life moving from one moment to the next, from one place to another, from one precarious circumstance to the next. And it was not an entirely idle boast either. He did have that instinct. He had to have those instincts; his life—

the quality and perhaps even the duration of it—depended on his ability to quickly assess a situation and use it to get the best for himself and sometimes, when cornered, even try to mould the situation to his advantage. Although as far as possible, he preferred not to do any moulding. One, because he was too lazy to put in too much effort when there were enough gullible men and women in the world who wanted to spend their kind of freshly acquired new money on his kind of freshly squandered old money entitlement. And two, because he went into such a frenzy of single-minded, obsessive behaviour in such a circumstance that, in addition to losing his moral compass (for which he never had much use anyway), he tended to lose his legal compass too and even worse, he sometimes lost all instincts of self-preservation, with predictably disastrous consequences. He became reckless and stupid in such situations, once even narrowly missing bleeding to death when that had happened. So he invested as little of himself in any situation as possible, taking advantage of moments of weaknesses and chinks in people's armours but usually not bothering to actually work anything to his advantage. If the situation required too much work, he, using his entirely superficial, and yet no less devastatingly effective for being so, charm, moved on to his next adventure or his next target depending on how you looked at it. It was critical for him therefore to meet people at their most vulnerable. The next steps became easy then. Of course, he never disclosed this part of his mind to his friends or to Layla, even when the gloves were off and even when he knew he had her pinned and did not need to pretend to be anything or anybody

other than who he really was. He did confess many a sins to
Layla though; things he had never told anybody, perhaps
because he was aware—mistakenly as it turned out—that
she was incapable of using that knowledge to cause him
any harm. But all this came later.

On the evening that they met, Deepak was driving
another of his transient friend's car, a sleek, black BMW.
The friend this time was a small-time trader who had made
it big. He had reached the next level of Maslow's triangle
and was looking for a higher level of respectability than
he was able to commandeer with money alone. And he
also wanted to have some better-talking, better-pedigreed
friends of his own to take on the overly cocky, overly
condescending, overly smooth-talking so-called wealth
managers who, spinning their web of numbers and taxes and
profits, probably made more money out of *his* money than
he did. There were many of the businessman's ilk found
scattered in many a big and small cities of an economically
booming India. Men whose ancestral land, because of its
proximity to an upcoming residential or industrial hub and
particularly if close to a Special Economic Zone, or men
with ancestral business with a base of loyal clientele whose
enhanced spending power every multinational corporation
in the world wanted to have access to, were suddenly worth
a lot of money. The trader with the BMW wore Tom Ford
suits that didn't quite sit comfortably on his wide shoulders,
hamstrung as they were by an even bigger stomach. He
was the kind of person who could afford the swankiest of
cars but would not use the most basic of its accessories like
its indicator, mostly because he came from the school of

thought, held by many in North India, that believes that all you really need to know in order to drive a car is how to use the brake and the accelerator and also because instruments like indicators are only meant to help other drivers in other cars and have no role to play in enhancing the comfort or the swag of your own car and therefore entirely expendable in the same way as waiting behind people for your turn in a queue or apologizing for anything that you have done is. Indicating which direction your car was about to turn, in other words, was for sissies.

Of course, Deepak had spotted this man unerringly from afar. Although older to Deepak, he was the new age, newly wealthy equivalent of Deepak. Or perhaps the trader had spotted him, the scion of a former miniscule princely state, one of the hundreds that had thrived in pre-British and British India but whose relevance (if there ever was any) as well as whose wealth had trickled from one generation of supremely entitled individuals to the next, waning and waxing through the transgressions and acumen of each generation and the policies of each set of government until finally disappearing completely before Deepak came of age. Deepak's pedigreed body still carried the wide forehead and thick sword-wielding forearms of those ancestors but his arms were pockmarked and hollowed from the inside by the injections of a concoction of drugs that he took in his misguided days before he discovered pleasures of other, if not less damaging, at least less expensive and more exhilarating kind. His thin body swooped slightly but he continued to have the bearing and the lingo of a prince. He still had two Valentino jackets that he had inherited from his father but he had nothing else—no place of his own to live in, no knowledge except the most perfunctory required to navigate through drawing room, cocktail party and the occasional high table conversations, no education except the little he had been taught in the founded-a-long-time-ago-by-his-family-therefore-somewhat-tolerant-towards-his-misdemeanours kind of schools, no skills except the ability to accurately say almost exactly what his interlocutor wanted to hear, no sense of loyalty towards anything under any circumstances and of course absolutely no money—below the vacuous, superficial level at which he operated in the world.

All this was of course not evident to Layla in her state of abject tiredness that October evening, although she had stiffened a moment later and moved away from the hand on her back and turned to see a thin, fair-skinned man in his late thirties who too stepped back respectfully with an apologetic expression on his face.

'I am sorry. I thought you were about to fall down,' he said and looked away from her for a second before turning to her once again.

'Look, I don't mean to sound retrograde,' he said. 'But are you sure it is a good idea for you to stand here alone at this time with Delhi being the way it is? I have no intention to play prince charming to your damsel-in-distress but really, isn't there somewhere I could drop you? I do have a large car and it seems ecologically callous to use it for transporting only one person around.'

There. He had used all the words that he thought a woman standing with a bag of books in front of a liberal arts library would want to hear. It would have made things easier if she had a book in her hand whose title he could read but perhaps it was better this way. His sprouting words that emanated from the subject of her obvious interest may have made her suspicious. Instead, like a soothsayer, he had hedged his bets. She, who stood in front of a liberal arts library, had to be into environment and classics at some level, perhaps even into philosophy or history or literature. And, of course, he was right. He *had* used the right words and he *had* said them right and Layla was tired and very lonely and yet she hesitated. After her recent experiences with strangers, she was not sure if she wanted to sit in this stranger's car.

'I'll keep my windows down, if that will make you feel safer.' Deepak said.

And when Layla still did not reply, he said, 'Theek hai, if you'd rather not, I will leave you to it,' and turned away.

Layla continued to look at his back as he walked towards his car parked a little away; its windscreen catching the last light of the evening sun and shining like a large reflector. She knew she should let him go.

'What are you doing here at the university at this time?' She asked him, instead. Her need for human contact, any sensible human contact, outweighing, for the moment, her new found fear of strangers in this city chock-a-block with strangers.

'Would you believe, taking a shortcut to Ajmeri Gate! But I got horribly lost because my phone ran out of charge and there's a problem with the car's GPS. I had stopped here hoping that there would be more people in the library. I guess I should have known better.' He gave her a rueful smile, 'So yes, you are right in being suspicious of my motives. My offering you a lift is not for purely altruistic reasons. I am hoping that you will help me find my way out of this quagmire of university roads even if you have to go in the opposite direction for me.'

She noticed that his full lips that stood out slightly petulantly on his thin face, arranged themselves around his small even teeth in a perfect arc when he smiled and strangely, instead of making him look feminine, it made him appear utterly, insincerely, rakishly masculine. She didn't believe a word of what he was saying but she was barely listening to him anyway. She was instead remembering the fingers on her back and was wondering what having those fleshy lips around her mouth would feel like. She should probably have just voiced her thoughts aloud and they would have gone somewhere and she would have satiated whatever physical need, whatever curiosities his presence and his fingers and the sight of those lips evoked. But the society in which she was brought up was not the society where such thoughts could be spoken aloud. She was not even allowed to feel these sensations. The stories of forthright femininity and reckless desire that she read of in books were just that to her: stories. Her own femininity had become increasingly transcribed with reference to its effect on the men around her, the desires that her presence evoked in them and the bestiality that the sight of her even slightly exposed flesh brought out. All she was left with were the inconveniences that her femininity caused her—the blood-soaked days, the struggle to decide how long her skirt should be, how tight her jeans could be, how deep a neck was she allowed to have in her blouse before she would be accused of provoking the intrusive attention that she would still get. But if her skirt was long enough and her blouse frumpy enough, they would provide her with some, however-ineffectual, however-insubstantial, however-useless, right to defend herself. The world that the books or even the Facebook posts created was completely different from the world that she encountered around her. So many women were groped and molested and harassed each day that everyday thousands of statuses should reflect that but nobody said, 'Feeling outraged because I was touched inappropriately today.' Instead Facebook lives were an endless saga of trips and food and high marks and high achievements. Which was not such a bad thing in itself perhaps but it blinded people to the happenings around them; that quest for a perfect selfie, that placing of themselves squarely in the middle of every thing of beauty was the narrowing down of the already narrow anthropomorphism into self-morphism. No, she was not allowed to put out her hand, hold his fingers and press them to her body although that was all she wanted to do—just a few moments of physical satiation. Instead when she stepped forward and Deepak hurriedly moved to open the passenger door with an exaggerated comical bow, she forced a smile out of herself and asked him his name before settling into the plush cream leather seat that seemed to fluff and lift and sensuously mould itself to hold the contours of her body perfectly.

'Yes, that is a good idea. Let's begin afresh and start at the beginning. Hi, I am Deepak,' he said, a little facetiously. His voice was teasing but a little hesitant, a little distant as if his heart was not quite into the banter. On any other day Layla would have heard his tone and stiffened in response. On any other occasion, she would have tried to interpret his hesitation. At any other time she would have been conscious of the incongruity of placing her well-worn, discoloured jute bag bulged shapeless with books on the impeccably lined spotless back seat of the car. But not today. Not at this hour.

'Turn left from up ahead, Deepak,' she said. 'Then take the first right and drive straight for about 3 kilometres until you reach a T-junction from where another right will take you out of the university gates,' she said, giving him the directions that he had asked for. After the exhausting mental calisthenics of the past seven hours, the sheer physical gratification provided by the luxurious seat, the presence of a strong forearm covered with a smattering of dark hair expertly manoeuvring the wheel to almost magically devour the distance that she had been dreading to trudge across in her tired, hungry state; the low imperceptible hum of the near perfectly engineered contraption beneath her feet; the pervasive smell of Deepak's unsmothered-by-expensive-perfume masculinity in the narrow confines of the car; the fading magic light filtering through the trees onto the near-empty roads inside the campus, were enough to smoothen out the convoluted lines of her non-retractable, arduous everyday living, if only temporarily, making her turn to him and say, 'I am Layla', with a smile of so much sincerity, that had Deepak not been so circumstances hardened, he would have dropped her at the bus stop and would have left her alone after that. Or so he said to Layla later. But he was what he was and the sight of a particularly easy target only made him crueller, more sadistic. He let go of his hesitation and ratcheted up his charm so high that even the usually sceptical, the almost always level-headed, and lately the always, always cynical, Layla, allowed herself to be blinded by the shiny potent mix of protectiveness, caring and playfulness that he decided to flash.

Layla gave him her address and settled back in the car. The conversation was light, filled with easy companionable silences that Deepak encouraged every time he thought her energy was waning and later Layla would remember very little even of what little they spoke about during their longish ride. But she remembered marvelling at the almost forgotten sensation of being inside a little bubble of tranquillity and luxury and soft music, untouched, unlooked and unmolested in the streets of Delhi. She gave him her phone number almost without his asking and she willed that he call because her prickliness, her constant struggle to protect herself from unrelenting, unwanted physical intrusion of strangers, her aloneness without her parents, without Little Neel, without *Tanya* had become so immense that she had begun resorting to having useless conversations with her taciturn PhD guide whose credo was to provide the few PhD students that he chose to take on with a list of references and then let them flounder their way almost blindly into their doctoral thesis, the drafts of which he would then rip through until after about a hundredth iteration, the thesis that would finally emerge would be almost identical to the initial draft except that it would now contain those four extra lines that he had been looking for through the years of unrelenting redrafts and unapologetic ripping-aparts.

When her phone left at night near the picture of *The Two Sisters* in the living room, rang in the emptiness of her house the next morning just as she stepped out of her shower, she walked across the length of her bedroom to answer it and with the cold water passing deliciously through the crevices of the body before dripping on to the concrete and stone floor, she agreed to a meeting in the evening with the soft-spoken owner of the beautifully polite voice on the other end. That day in the library, Petraca's world of longing acquired a new nuance for Layla and by the time she stepped out at 6.30, her long unruly hair whipping in one of those sudden dusty Delhi squalls that go away as quickly as they come, making mouths gritty and leaving behind a film of dust over everything or, if lucky, followed by a sprinkling of light rain that washes out some of the accumulated dirt, she was primed to allow Deepak access to much more of herself than she, and perhaps even he, had thought possible. Today was one of those lucky days, at least as far as the weather was concerned, when light shower fell on Deepak's tightly shut windows. Layla leaned her head on it and watched little droplets form outside and slide down on the smooth surface of the window pane, leaving thin shiny tails that sparkled one last time in the newly washed sunlight, before they fell down and disappeared forever into the concrete road, blackened by the rain.

27 October 2014

21

Piecing It Together and Turning Away?

'This is where we found Layla.' Satya is pointing to the blue-green paisley patterned backless couch directly below the painting of the two women.

'She was conscious then and she tried saying something but I couldn't understand it. After that there has been nothing. Not even one word. Like I had dreamed that she said something to me. But she *had* said something. Proper sentences. Not just sounds or any arbitrary string of words but actual sentences.'

Layla had begun bleeding from her mouth almost immediately after that and all those sentences and sentiments and whatever else she may have been trying to convey to him had got lost in the maelstrom. She had become unconscious soon afterwards.

'And bas, that is it. After that, nothing. She has not become conscious ever after that. In all the time I have been with her at the hospital, she has never responded to me. Not once.' Satya pauses. 'Yet I think she can sense my presence. I feel she waits for me and she was disappointed that day when I did not go to the hospital.'

Or maybe it is you who feels the disappointment and it is you who waits for the opportunity to visit her, Raman wants to say. But that will be akin to self-flagellation.

'If only I had understood what she was trying to tell me . . . I could have used your lip-reading skills then.' ACP Satya sounds tired and wistful—his emotions, as usual, so naked, so unselfconscious that it almost feels like an affront to keep looking at him. Like taking pictures of a little boy from a remote tribe who comes to you all trust and joy and curiosity only in order to sell his pictures set against the spectacular mountainous backdrop of his home for a hefty sum of money to a leading travel publication, thereby opening up the area for prospectors who immediately draw up the blueprints and build the hotels and employ the little boy to dance for money (of whose importance 'in the larger scheme of things' he is educated soon enough) to entertain the string of people with high economic and low ecological sensitivity. They come there to spend their weekends and their vacations and leave behind their droppings of toilet paper and empty whisky bottles in the pristine mountainside, turning everything into a traded, tradable commodity—the boy, the mountains, the skies, the streams, the trees, the rocks. Raman turns away. He does not want to look at Satya, anyway. He wants to see the house where Tanya lived.

'There are four ground rules you have to agree to before you start,' Satya says. Sounding professional now. 'One, under no condition are you allowed to take off your gloves or your shoe covers. You can touch nothing without your gloves. Two, if you pick anything up, you have to put it back exactly in the place where you found it. Three, you have to show everything of interest to me. To me alone. Not to any of my subordinates who are here with me. And four, this entire search is off the record. You can write nothing about how we went about the search and what we or even you found here. Do you agree? If not, *I* will do all the searching and you can wait at the door, Sir. I will show you anything that I think you may be able to use for your conversations with Tanya but I will not let you enter this house.'

Of course, Raman agrees to everything. He does not want the search to take place at all but since that option is not on the table, he is not going to be prevented from entering Tanya's house. He wants to access only those bits of her home and her mind that she wants him to have access to because somehow, it is beginning to seem even more imperative that he not go any further than she wants him to. That nobody goes any further than she wants them to. That her boundaries not be breached.

'Yes,' he tells Satya solemnly. Yes. Knowing no other answer is possible. He also knows that no other tone will satisfy his earnest, strangely trusting friend. And Satya somehow does seem like a friend despite the short duration of their acquaintance and despite his personality being an antithesis of Raman's. Perhaps because of the identical intensity of their feelings for the two identical inhabitants of this house. Perhaps also because somehow Raman's usual cynicism seems to suddenly have gone in short supply in the last few days.

Raman can see that the constables who accompanied Satya have not stepped too far into the house. They stand by the door ensuring nobody comes in but otherwise continue chatting with each other and barely pay any attention to the goings-on. If they are able to hear the conversation between Satya and Raman, they give no indication of any interest in that either. Perhaps they are too battle-weary to be interested in the case that is generating so much interest elsewhere or perhaps they are just superb actors.

'Surinder and Parminder are very loyal but they are not very curious or very ambitious people,' Satya says quietly as if reading Raman's train of thoughts. 'I took them out of VIP duty when I joined service here in Delhi. So obviously they will not do anything against my command.'

Raman knows how demeaning the work and how unpredictable the work hours of policemen assigned to VIP duty—that of guarding one of the umpteen ministers, members of parliament and sundry men and women who are deemed (at least in some bureaucrat's mind) to have a threat to their lives or who pull strings to be thought of as having a threat to their lives because it lends gravitas to them and because having an entourage of policemen following them whenever they are in public enhances their fragile prestige—could be, yet he is not as convinced of their loyalty as Satya is. But they are positioned at the door of the house and they are not looking for or even touching anything and therefore, they can't do much harm, wherever their loyalties lay. At the most they will become anonymous sources for eponymous television channels but those multiple television channels do not really matter, do they? If they do not have access to Surinder and Parminder, they will still make up stories. So perhaps it would be better if these constables were stooges who would provide them with some of the titbits. At least then there could be a some truth, however beaten up, however deeply buried, in the flamboyant stories that the channels would come up with. And yet, Raman is sure, nothing that the TV channels can conjure up would match the spectacle that lies in front of him.

There are scattered bits of smothered, dystopian life wherever he can see in the room. Everything has been displaced from its designated position but everything still seems to resonate with a kind of intensity that carries remnants of disturbing experiences not yet purged. Like you have stumbled into that part of the museum where objects from the estate of its recently murdered owner have been kept. Objects that have been bequeathed to the museum in her will and that despite their placement in the alien museum setting, still carry all the memories and all the smells of the generations of lives that were created and destroyed in and around them. Those objects will soon be stripped off those feelings; any memories, any ghosts that lay hidden will be purged as they will be cleaned, shined, curated and displayed for the benefit of hordes of people who will admire their lines, their curves, their colour, their beauty or their ornate ugliness but who will remain oblivious to the emotions that had swirled around them in the halfway home of the room where they had been stacked up for some time.

Raman shakes his head. This is bizarre. He is not used to thinking this way. Perhaps it is the strange deep darkness in the afternoon and the quiet patter of a tamer but still intense rain that is heightening the sensation of being inside a box and making him feel that the world outside no longer remains in the form that he knew it. That nothing recognizable now exists beyond these walls and that all rules that define how lives are supposed to be organized and lived can be turned on their heads in here. Is this how the sisters felt inside the house? Locking themselves away from everyone and everything and deciding their own statute of deprivation? He needs to concentrate. He needs to examine each object, see the patterns, find the tell-tale signs left behind that will fill the vacuums that have remained open and festering like gaping wounds in Tanya's convoluted tapestry of a story.

He begins to look at the books hoping that they will provide some, however tangential, insight into Tanya's mind, but the books too prove to be as translucent and unyielding as Tanya's answers. Dazzling in their brilliance but providing little clarity or understanding. They are an esoteric collection of titles that show no particular affinity and fit no patterns that Raman can discern except to show that the sisters and/or their parents had read a lot. There is *The Little Book of War* and there is *Age of Greed* and *The Triple Agent*, the scattered bits of fiction too encompass multiple genres—from crime to literary to high adventure and Science fiction—and give nothing away about their readers' proclivity. A few of the books have been borrowed from the Delhi University Library and Raman feels a tinge of disquiet that is a legacy from his librarian father on seeing that they are long overdue. Those books are mostly academic titles related to literature, society, economy, environment and anthropology. Raman flips through the pages. He has read some of the books and knows about most of them and he is not curious about their contents but these are the same pages that Tanya has probably touched and he feels an inane thrill at going through them. For a thirty-seven old man who took some, and not completely unjustified (he would like to believe) pride in his judgement, his intellect and his ability to eschew emotional claptrap in his life and in his writing, it is disconcerting to, like a star-struck fan, be grateful just to be able to touch the same things that another person has touched and to try and imagine the feel of and the thoughts that lay behind those fingers. Is he losing his mind? A folded sheet of paper drops out of *In the Garden of Beasts*. And somehow, even in the midst of his most unjournalistic emotions, his journalistic instinct kicks in, and he, almost without thinking about it, folds the piece of paper and puts it in his pocket.

Satya has gone back to looking at the photographs but Raman is not particularly interested in them. Photographs capture moments of time that hold meaning only if you remember or know what happened before or after the picture was taken. Bereft of the knowledge or an understanding of those experiences, photographs do not really matter. At the most, they tell you where the people in the photographs had been, how happy they were or how happy they pretended to be when the photograph was taken, or how tall, short, thin, fat they were mostly in relation to persons around them. But not much more. Even judgements about their looks cannot be made without the filter of the tutored aesthetics bombarded into your head by the ever-present societal images; your own prejudice being the primary component of anything's beauty or ugliness. Raman has stopped being curious about the sisters' physical appearance. He is not sure if he can trust himself to judge how they look anymore but he knows he needs to do that, he needs to be objective when he writes his article. He cannot stray too far from accepted norms of being and of behaviour in that. He is trying not to think about his article but it lies like a sharp, uneasy sensation at the back of his head because of his CEO and Dr Anita's timelines. For the first time in his life, his work and his emotions are entangled in such a way that it is impossible to extricate one from the other and Raman is not sure if he is comfortable with that. Does he really want it? Is he willing to stake all that he had built in the sixteen years of his working life for the sake of feelings that he can barely articulate, let alone rely upon?

There is a sound from downstairs.

'Who lives there?' Raman asks. 'Don't they know something?'

'Not really. It was their seven-year old son who discovered the sisters but that was only because he had set the debris on the balcony on a small fire with his Diwali rocket. That family moved in only about a month and a half ago. The sisters had shut themselves in long back. They said they never heard any noises from upstairs and they were not sure if anybody even lived there. Of course, they never tried to find out. But I guess this is what Delhi is all about. So, to answer your question, no. They don't know anything.'

Satya begins to heave up the computer which he carefully places on the table before connecting it to a socket and switching it on.

'There is no password,' he says.

He straightens a chair, sits down on it and Raman positions himself behind him to look into the contents of the computer over Satya's shoulder. Satya begins going through the contents very slowly, one careful step after another. Only there is not that much to go through. It is a curiously austere contraption, bereft of any extraneous, any non-essential programmes or files. There are no other programmes except Microsoft Office and Internet Explorer. There are no pictures in it. No music and the few documents that are saved on it form, judging from the turgid, highfalutin, minutely referenced academic lingo used in them, parts of some kind of academic paper on literature—probably Layla's PhD thesis, Raman remembers Satya had told him about it. Satya opens Internet Explorer next and begins looking at the history of searches. There is nothing in the last two months but before that there is a long list of websites that the sisters seemed to have visited that are all related to food: its paraphernalia, its composition, the recipes and even the science of food. There is also a range of information on starvation where the descriptions and the pictures have a hauntingly familiar quality. The same shrunken faces and bodies, the white, vacant looking eyes . . . Satya stops. His shoulders look slumped.

'Should I do this?' Raman asks him.

'No. No. Thanks but no. I am okay. There has been no crime here, has there? Except what the sisters have committed against themselves. Perhaps we should just leave now?'

Raman knows from Satya's tone that the question is not directed at him.

'You have not been to the rest of the house but once you go in you will see that their parents' and their brother's things have been left in the house. There is dust everywhere but I don't think they have touched anything from those rooms. Even their father's slippers are still under the bed of the master bedroom. Maybe exactly where he left them before he went on that drive. It looks like the sisters used only one bedroom, this living area and the kitchen. Whatever little they used that for. You know it has been more than a year and a half since their parents and brother died but everything is kept like they expect their family to come back and start using them again.' Satya stops. 'Okay. I think you should take over now. If you find anything on the computer, tell me. But you don't have to spend too much time on it. We can send the computer to our cyber cell. Although I don't think that will be needed.'

As soon as Raman sits on the chair vacated by Satya, he regrets having offered to help. There is something creepy about going through Tanya's computer. Although he has clandestinely hacked many a computers and has accessed many off limit files, it had always been because he was investigating a crime and trying to assign culpability. Now because of his tangled sentiments, it feels voyeuristic to look into what Tanya and Layla had looked at. Following the links one after another feels like following their train of thought from months ago. There were more sites on food that they

had visited, sites that spoke about the contents of various
types of food items, the chemical composition of everything
and even the science of digestion and fasting. They had
read the paper on the psychology of human starvation by
Josef Brozek, they had read about the starvation experiment
undertaken during the Second World War by Dr Ancel
Keys. And they had also spent time on Facebook where they
seem to be registered as TLS, which Raman assumes stands
for Tanya Layla Sharma. There is nothing posted on that
Facebook page, and no profile information provided. There
is no profile picture and no photographs in which they have
been tagged. They/She probably had registered themselves
on Facebook not to share anything but to watch other
people and other lives. From what Raman can see, there is
no pattern to their Facebook searches either. They seemed
to have spent their time looking at random people's lives
from all across the world, following nobody, befriending
nobody and responding to nothing. Raman looks at Satya
and shakes his head. Nothing. But he keeps searching
further and further back. It is like travelling back in time.
Still nothing except random Facebook searches and food
related sites. And then there *is* something different. They
had searched for football, God, sex, death and how quickly
cement hardened. How quickly cement hardened? That is
not a philosophical question, is it? Was there a point in all
this that he is missing?

'Found something?' Satya notices the change in
Raman's expression.

'Not really. Some of these searches do not quite fit the
patterns that we have been observing. But there are usually

no patterns in searches, are there? They are like stream of consciousness with one link leading to another until we forget what we had been looking for in the first place.'

Satya smiles slightly but comes to Raman anyway.

'What is it? "How quickly cement hardens?" Actually there *is* some strange cement in this house. I had noticed it before. Their bathtub is filled with hardened cement. I had thought they might have done it to prevent their little brother from accidently drowning in it. People board bathtubs for similar purposes. I thought that this was a more aggressive form of that same precaution. But if they searched for it only about five months back by then the brother was long dead. Do you think there may be something to it?'

Satya's phone rings before Raman can answer him.

'Theek hai.' Satya says on his phone before he addresses Raman once again.

'I have to go now for a meeting in the office. We will come here again later tonight or perhaps early tomorrow morning,' Satya says, as he begins walking towards the door. 'Wait. Perhaps we should take the computer along to our cyber cell. Yes.' Satya directs one of the constables to pick up the computer and as they head down the stairs, he asks Raman if he could drop him somewhere.

The rain has stopped and the newly washed leaves of the mango trees that have managed to live at least through this storm glow a little sinisterly red in the last shiny rays of the setting sun amidst floating lightweight wisps of cloud, as if it is a deal with Mephistopheles that has ensured their survival.

'No, I will find my way out,' Raman says, walking slowly behind Satya.

'Okay. See you later then. I will call you when we return to the house.' Satya says and Raman manages a short wave in reply.

Perhaps there is no story. Perhaps his emotions are completely misplaced. Perhaps they are just stupid, sentimental sisters after all. Perhaps, like Satya, he is projecting whatever he wants on Tanya. How pathetic is that?

Raman's phone rings. It is the Admin assistant from his office.

'Sir, CEO sir has asked me to check with you to book your flight tickets to Bhopal for tomorrow evening. Shall I send you flight options?'

'No,' Raman says. 'You don't need to send me the options.' He has made up his mind. 'Just book any flight after 9 pm. I will wrap up whatever needs to be done here by then.' He will call his mother tonight once he reaches home, he decides. And tomorrow he will call her from the airport and the day after tomorrow from Bhopal and the day after that from back in Delhi and perhaps that evening he will also check whether his colleague from work will be available for a pre-dinner rendezvous. She would be, if her husband is out of town or if she is feeling particularly horny even when he is in town. Her husband apparently never asked. Like she never asked him about his whereabouts, she said. It was a comfortable marriage. The kind of marriage that works because everybody's intellectual and physical interest is taken care of in an immediate, non-obtrusive, unquestioned kind of way.

'Why continue with the marriage at all?' Raman had asked her once.

'Why not?' She had said before she had added. 'Perhaps because I don't like the way divorced women are looked at, the kind of interest they generate, the kind of attention— sometimes even cloyingly well-meaning ones—they have to fend off, and the stories that they have to make to rent a house, to book a ticket or to get their passports renewed. Or perhaps I just couldn't be bothered. But let's not talk about that,' she had said and Raman had not talked about it after that day.

22

Of Entitlement and Disenfranchisement

Raman walks to the gate of Krishna Colony where a thin young man stands. He looks so much like the old watchman who he had met when he had come in a couple of hours ago that for a crazy moment Raman thinks that he had been tricked earlier by the afternoon's darkness into believing that the watchman was old when in reality he was only in his late twenties as the young man standing in front of him, his outlines softened by the red-yellow sunlight, obviously is.

'I am standing in my uncle's place. He has gone to the toilet,' the young man tells Raman perhaps sensing his confusion or perhaps only because he does not want his uncle to get into trouble for dereliction of duty. 'There is no toilet here for him so he needs to use the Sulabh Shuachalaya. It is a little far.'

'Which house did you go to?' He asks Raman, opening the register. The entry and exit of every visitor has to be registered.

'D322.'

'Are you from a newspaper?' The young man's interest is piqued.

'No.' Raman shakes his head. 'From a magazine.' He is not sure whether he wants to have this conversation. But every potential source, however perfunctory, is worth pursuing.

'Do you often take your uncle's place when he is unavailable?'

The young man's expressive dark brown eyes practically glitter with excitement.

'No. Not that much. This is first time I came to Krishna Colony. After a long time. Myself Raju, Senior Guard Hi-tech city—woh samne wala.'

Raman nods and turns to go out. Obviously nothing is going to come of this conversation.

'But I was a guard in Krishna Colony for nine years. I gave the job to my uncle about three months ago when I got a job in Hi-tech city. The prospects of growth are much better there. I am senior guard now. I am the supervisor of three other guards.'

The young man is obviously well-versed with the lexicon of enterprise which is promising but is he worth talking to?

'Sir, I am a guard but I am smart, even my manager thinks that. He made me senior guard in three months because of that only. People like me are not supposed to know what all happens in the lives of people in the complex. But I can tell you that they are all speaking very nicely now about the sisters. But they were singing a different tune six or seven months ago.'

'What?'

'Everybody here knows the story but nobody will talk about it on TV. They are afraid of Deol Sir and RWA. They will not say anything. There was a man living in that house when only one sister was there. I don't know which sister but one sister had gone somewhere else. That man was like a raja, Sir. He knew how to rule. And that is okay. Not like upstarts here who don't know whether they want to rule over us or be our best friend. Tell us what to do, we will do it and you give us money. We don't want to be your friend because the glass in which you will give us water is separate from other utensils. You will never let us use any toilet here and when we will be weak, you will throw us out without thinking. But that man was some kind of a king, Sir. Every day he would come in new car. I and all the drivers had bets on which car he will bring. One time I won two hundred and twenty rupees for guessing that a Honda Civic will come. I even told it would be a red Honda Civic.'

'But I thought you said he lived here?'

'Yes, later. Deol Sir was very angry when he used to come here. He would check the register and see what time the man came and when he went away.'

'So that man used to register his entry and exit. Is the register still here?'

'No, No. We finish one register per month. Old registers are not here. They are at Deol Sir's house. He sells them to the raddiwala.'

'Do you know the man's name?'

'I don't remember clearly par shayad Deepak, I think. Deepak something. He was gentleman, Sir. Very nice clothes. And the sisters looked very nice too. I saw the scary pictures on TV. Are you sure sir that they are pictures of the same girls? Is it something they did to them in the hospital? Because they used to look nothing like that.'

The young man is beginning to lose some of his initial enthusiasm.

'I saw them since they were very young, Sir, and it was such a sad thing about their family. They were left all alone after that. Nobody came to live with them, Sir. No relatives. People said they did not belong to any caste. How is that possible, Sir? But hardly anybody visited them till this man came. There was talk among the drivers about the man, Sir, but we understood. We are also human beings. How can any girl live alone like that? Her sister had also left. They also should have understood. She used to go to college sometimes and she looked sad, Sir.'

So, Tanya had left. To do what and for how long? And it was Layla who had the relationship. Not Tanya. Can he acknowledge now that what he had felt just a short while ago was very much like jealousy? Is he allowed the slight uplifting of spirits that the guard's words have evoked? Is it callow and very, very selfish to be just a little bit happy to know that Tanya had not been in a live-in relationship six or seven months ago?

'Who should have also understood?' He asks the stand-in watchman.

'RWA, Sir.'

'Why, what happened?'

'There was big meeting, Sir, when the man was living here. We don't know what happened in the meeting but after that they put up a notice about how everybody should behave in the colony.'

'Notice?'

'Yes, Sir. It was put here also. It is probably still there under all the new notices about car parking and Diwali celebration and about tambola that happens here every Thursday.'

'What did it say? Can you show it to me?'

'It was in English but it was about till how late at night guests could stay if there are no men in the house. There was also a rule about any man who did not come with family and stayed for more than one night in any house. They had to tell the RWA and had to give copy of ID proof. They had to write a letter to RWA to tell how they were related to people in the house. Deol Sir went personally to give the notice to the Sharma house and to give a warning. His driver told me. Deol Sir never sent anybody to ask if she needed anything when she was alone but now he was interested in what she was doing just because there was man in their house. Sometimes, Sir, it is better to not live in houses like this where all the rules are decided by people who have nothing better to do with their time. It is better in our houses where we don't have light and water and no guard and no gate but in our house everybody takes care of everybody and we understand.'

'Do you think Deepak's ID would be at the RWA office?'

'I don't know, Sir. I don't know if the sister did what Deol Sir asked them to. Sir, I am not saying this because I want to get anybody in trouble but everybody is calling the sisters all kinds of names on TV. They are not like this, Sir. The family used to go out together in their car and they looked very happy. I never talked to the sisters but madam and sir were very nice. Their little boy would cycle around the colony every day. It is a very bad thing that has happened to the sisters, Sir.'

He has begun to look dejected. He had waited for this moment to speak to somebody for a long time, to grab his share of the limelight but now that he has been presented with that opportunity, the full implication of all that he has become a party to is beginning to bear down upon him. Away from the hypnotizing, mind-numbing web of words spun by the haranguing TV presenters and opinion spinners, in the quiet of the fading evening light, he has begun see the gossamer of moral conundrums through which he has to find his way and he is not sure any longer that he wants to put his lot with the people who have the most glittering of set-ups, the loudest of voices and the highest of TRPs.

'Sir, please don't say what I told you to my uncle or anybody. My uncle will lose his job that his family needs. He does not know any of this.'

'Can you show me the notice?'

'What notice?' The old watchman asks. He is back. His nephew had probably spotted him coming before Raman saw him.

'Nothing, Chacha. A notice that had been put in the colony by Deol Sir seven or eight months ago. But I don't think it is here anymore, Sir.'

'Hum check karte hain,' the old watchman says. Apart from the paid toilet, Sulabh Shuachalaya, the DDA market complex that the watchman had had to go to, also held an electronic and electrical goods shop, a sweets' shop, a grocery store and a Mother Dairy booth. It was at the electronic store where, on his way back, he had seen the images of the sister that were being played and replayed in HD with a ticker tape explaining whose picture it was on all three TV screens on display. Because the TVs were muted, he could not hear the words that the presenters and the gleeful man from the hospital were mouthing and he was able to form his own opinion of that face and those images. There was something sinister, something demonic, something tragic, something that made him aghast, almost disconsolate about the saga that was unfolding before him. No human should look like that. He knows the girls are about his daughter's age. If Deol is complicit in that horror in any way, his karma will mete out his punishment but if the watchman can do anything to make Deol pay for some of his sins in this world, he is ready to do it.

'What happened, then?' Raman asks.

'I don't know, Sir. I think the other sister also came back. The man probably went away also. I have not seen him since then. That is why I am not sure if the RWA will have his pehchan patra.'

Could the breakup have been the reason for their starvation?

'I didn't see the sisters also but then nobody really sees anybody here. People just stay in their houses and their cars until they don't and we can't ask any questions. We are not even supposed to be aware of what is happening. Although often we know, even though nobody here tells us anything, this time we all missed it. I thought they both went away. We did not know that the sisters were still inside the house, Sir, but nothing else was entering or coming out of their house. They said on TV that the sisters had been starving for two or three months. How can anybody do that, Sir?'

'I don't know,' Raman replies.

The old watchman is determinedly taking out one printout after another that are pinned one atop the other on the large board in front of his small makeshift excuse of a room.

'This?' He asks taking one out.

No. It is a notice stating that dogs needed to be taken out of the complex on to the road for their 'business'. So it was okay to use the road outside the complex as a toilet as long as the complex remained clean.

'No it isn't,' Raman says. 'It is about . . . ' he starts to say but what would be the point?

'This?'

It is a notice fixing the wage of maids and drivers who aspire to work in the complex. Fruits of free market economies obviously do not trickle down.

'What about this?' The watchman has taken out another notice stating that the few young children remaining in the complex are not allowed to play in the three small patches of green grass in the complex because it will spoil the look of the complex.

'No.' Raman replies. Dogs, maids, children. The next one has to be for women. And it is.

'Yeh hoga.' The watchman triumphantly takes out a sheet of discoloured white paper.

'Haan, it is.' His nephew hands the fragile paper over to Raman.

Rules for Safe and Virtuous Living in Bellevue Boulevard, Raman reads the title of the notice written in big, bold letters. The paper is wavy and crackly like it has got wet a few times in the rain. Most of the smaller text has faded in the sun but some of the big words still remain. There is sanctimonious and sanctity in two places. There is upright and dissolute and debauched and moral and moralistic. There is not much more that he can read or understand from the faded letters of rule numbers one to nine. The last rule—rule number ten—has, however, been preserved in all its detailed glory. It has probably been saved by another notice put on top of it because below the yellowing paper of the rest of the notice is a neat border of white within which the words of rule number ten can be seen clearly.

Since the rules above deal with our culture and the moral fibre of our society, non-compliance would lead to the immediate withdrawal of all common facilities and privileges, including access to electricity, water and the services of the society's plumber and electrician.

'The errant household will not even be allowed to avail of the complex's waste disposal provisions,' it also said. Raman knows it means that nobody would come to collect the garbage from the house's doorstep. Garbage that would all go unsegregated into Ghaziabad, where it would add its bit towards the landfill mountain range there, increasing its height much quicker than the rate at which the literally earth-shaking thrust of Gondwana plate can ever manage to lift up the mighty Himalayas. And in those landfill mountains the little and big scavenger children would compete with the soaring and swooping multitudes of eagles and the few remaining vultures of Delhi to rake through the wet, the dry and the toxic sludge to access that small amount of the mercury of the CFL light, that small piece of a battery pack or bits of the motherboard of computer peripherals that they would sell in Seelampur where it would be added to the waste brought in on overloaded ships from other parts of the world where waste occurs two or three stages earlier in the chain of consumption. Everything—the imported and the scavenged waste—would be reformed into 'lesser' things but not before leaching bits of their bleeding little chemical hearts into the air, the land and the water, forming compounds so hazardous that they cannot be named—like Voldemort—for to name them would be to admit their existence. So they remain in the netherworld between being and not being, manifesting themselves as cancerous cells within organisms or as discoloured rocks at the bottom of hills or as giant soap bubbles on riversides.

'May I keep this notice?' Raman asks.

'Yes, nobody will ask for it.' The watchman is sure.

'Sir, I am not saying all this because I want to get anybody in trouble,' the watchman's nephew says again. 'Who is blameless in this world? Hamaam mein sab nange hai. But Sir, it is not good what happened to the sisters.'

'Yes,' Raman says. And deciding that the fragile notice will not survive being folded into his pocket, he opens his bag and puts it inside. But even as he is smoothing and laying the paper carefully against his laptop to prevent any further damage, he is not sure why he is bothering to keep it. There are probably variations of the same sentiments being expressed and communicated in various places—in other apartment complexes, in colleges, in universities, in entire villages and towns, perhaps soon in the entire country—the paper is not unusual and putting it inside his bag serves no purpose whatsoever except to ease the conscience of the younger and the older version of what look like the same man standing before him with the same eyes, who are both looking at him with the same expression of undisguised hope. But perhaps serving this purpose makes more sense than a lot of other things that he has done in his life which, although more lucrative monetarily, were infinitely more pointless morally.

Raman thanks the uncle and the nephew and gives them his number in case they remember anything else that they think could be significant before turning back and for the second time today walks away from the Krishna Colony's wrought iron gates into the complex. This time, however, he is going to F331 that is Mr Deol's house according to the watchman, Hariram. That is his name Hariram and his nephew's name is Raju. Myself Raju.

Mr Deol is a puffed up peacock of a man within his fiefdom of Krishna Colony, Raman decides as he sits on the Rs 6,00,000 (Raman knows its exact price because his magazine had done a feature on the exorbitantly priced imported furniture that a certain category of Indians have begun to favour) zebra-printed Italian sofa with sleek steel legs that vies with the hundred-light colonial-style chandelier to form the centre point of the knick-knack stuffed modestly sized living room that had been built at a time in Delhi when ambitions, emotions and windows were smaller and less ostentatious, and listens to Mr Deol's, smoothened by a glass of whisky and polished by regular use, monologue on how thanks to his efforts, Krishna Colony has become one of the prime real estate destinations of Delhi's upper middle class. 'Can you see that?' Raman can see the 'that' that Mr Deol is pointing towards—a freshly painted white structure—but he is not sure what he is supposed to 'see' in that. 'That is the new RO plant we have put up so the entire colony now gets soft, filtered water.'

'Even D332?' Raman asks.

'Yes, of course. Didn't you hear me tell ACP Satya earlier that we divided the cost of D332's outstanding maintenance dues among all the residents of the complex so each of us had to pay a little more maintenance fee this month but now D332 has water and electricity?'

'But the Society was not as magnanimous with the sisters earlier. Was it?'

'What?' Mr Deol smiles.

'Wasn't there a man living in their house that you had objected to?'

'I don't know who you have been talking to but it is a simple story, yaar,' Mr Deol says losing none of his bonhomie. 'The sisters or sister, who knows which is which and who does what—were living amorally. If women lose their morality, society loses its morality. We could not let them continue like that could we? It is different for a man, yaar. Nobody asks which vessels he has eaten from and who he brings home when his wife is not around, hain-ji?' Mr Deol winks and guffaws. He is the kind of man, like many of the same status-quoist ilk, who is so sure of his place in the sun, so puffed up with his sense of entitlement that he does not have even a smidgeon of doubt about anything. Raman sometimes almost wishes he could live like that. Live without the hairshirt of doubts and questions and suspicions and guilt about the way things are, about the way the world is, about the very basis of life that pricking his insides, never allows him complete, unmitigated respite, even when he drinks himself out of his mind. But no, he will kill himself the day he thinks he is becoming anything like the venerated, vociferous, vile Mr Deol.

'Who was the man?'

'Arre, some well-dressed lout, yaar. We had asked them to submit his identity document but we never found out much about him. We made the rule that we could not allow any overnight male visitor in any all-women household until they handed over his passport copy and gave us in writing what relationship they had with the man. I personally went to tell the sister that and to give them a copy of the notice. You know, the sister had looked at me very strangely then.'

For the first time in the entire conversation, Mr Deol begins to look slightly uncomfortable. 'They are strange sisters. I am not surprised that they have ended up in the state they are in. Two identical women living all alone is in itself amoral without the additional immorality of having a strange man living with them. It is not natural. They *are* probably the freaks of nature that the TV people are calling them. Who knows what has been going on in that household? How could these sisters have survived without food? I am an educated, rational man and therefore I did not say these things on TV but some things can't be explained. Two identical women living alone were, like my astrologer told me, probably involved in some kind of black magic that went wrong. Did you see their hair?' Mr Deol has regained his self-possession and self-assurance and Raman has regained his urge to plummet Mr Deol's face into smithereens.

'But haven't you known the family for a long time?' Raman says carefully instead. Concentrating on forming each word separately with the vowels articulated just right and the consonants emphasized on as perfectly as possible. Family, long time, known. Divesting, diverting, demystifying, detailing, demonising, dehumanising, decanting, decocting, debriefing, debating.

'I did. We all did. But yaar, who knows anybody in this day and age? Sharma had opposed my candidature when I had first stood for the post of the President of RWA. That was a long time ago and I don't hold any grudges. But do we know anything about their family? Nahi, bhai. Which Sharma clan did he belong to? Nobody knows. Anybody can call themselves anything these days. I know theirs was at least an inter-caste marriage, if not an inter-religious one because once Mrs Sharma accidently told my wife that she was a Rajput. No relatives ever visited them. Don't you think that is very strange? But why are you getting into all this yaar? Are you sure you don't want a drink? I can offer you something very special. I have a bottle of world's finest whisky that comes from guess . . . guess . . . can you believe it? Japan!'

Mr Deol guffaws again. There is no other way to describe the sound that comes out of Mr Deol. The word was probably coined only to describe Mr Deol's laughter, Raman thinks.

'I certainly did not believe it until my friend bought and sent me a bottle of the Yamazaki Single Malt Sherry Casket 2013 from Japan and yaar sach mein, it is like tasting heaven.'

It has begun to drizzle lightly again when Raman leaves Krishna Colony and he can see thin gossamer like lines of water against the street lights before they disappear in the chaotic clamour of traffic and pedestrians of a typical workday evening of the city. Despite the additional traffic snarls that rains cause, Raman usually loves Delhi rains. It transforms the character of the dust bowl of a city, washing away months of accumulated dirt and cleansing its acrid air temporarily of pollutants. But today it is not the love of the rain that has made him decide to walk the three kilometres to his house through the soaked pavements of Delhi whose puddle filled holes cause his shoes to become wetter than the rest of his body, it is his need to clear his head and cleanse himself of exhausting emotions of the day.

Halfway to his house, he remembers the paper from Tanya's house and immediately feels its reassuring presence in his pocket, now that he has remembered it is there. Since he is carrying his backpack strung across his chest and not to his back, to prevent his laptop from getting wet, the paper is safe from the rain. He knows that he should have handed it over to Satya but he has done very few right things in his life. And, in any case, it is probably just a grocery list or a receipt for something else that the sisters might have bought that anyway does not merit Satya's attention and he should not have any expectations that it will reveal anything that he does not know already. He is finding it so difficult to process what he already knows that he is not sure whether he wants there to be anything revelatory there. Where will he find the place to fit in any new information that the paper may contain? He will know soon enough. But showing the kind of restraint that he is not particularly known for, Raman reaches his house, changes his clothes, puts some fried peanuts that he finds lying on one of the shelves into a bowl thinking about the one of the only 18,000 bottles of Yamazaki whisky that he had declined as he pours himself a small glass of cheap whisky, and telling himself that it would serve him right if he dies of aflatoxin poisoning from the rancid peanuts as a punishment for all the phone calls (seven!) from the CEO's assistant that he has ignored who was, in all likelihood, calling to tell him that she had booked his ticket for Bhopal. But he knows there is no way he is going to be on that flight so it does not matter whether or not he answered the call. There is another niggling thought that he cannot not quite place about another phone call but he forgets all about the niggling call and the calls of the CEO's assistant and even his daily dose of two tweets when he unfolds the A-4 size sheet and sees that it is a handwritten note. *A City without Women*. By LS, it says. Raman sits down and begins to read.

23

A City without Women

A City without Women
By LS

Women have begun to disappear from the streets of Delhi. It sounds like a new Agatha Christie story. 'The Mystery of the Disappearing Women'—the latest whodunit from the queen of crime. Where shall we look for them? Are they there? Were they ever there? They are certainly present as numbers and statistics in the now digitized but previously painstakingly analogue records of the census organization. The numbers that say that there are 7.8 million women in Delhi, and that they have actually increased by 1.6 million from the 6.2 million who were present in 2001. OK, to be fair, they are occasionally spotted. As glass faces in high rise buildings; as a swish of a sari or salwar or skirt in a mall; as the vegetable seller who leaves the market before the sun sets whether or not all her vegetables are sold; as the beautiful, heartbreakingly young beggar with an incongruously small baby in her arms on the traffic light dressed in a lehenga whose intricate embroidery even the dust-coated, diesel-fume reeked hopelessness of her setting cannot quite camouflage; as the student walking past hurriedly to catch that U-special bus. But for a category of persons who form 43 per cent of the population of the city, the sightings are ephemeral and erratic and mostly as one part of a couple or a third or fourth part of a family. The few single women on the streets are purposeful, intent, unwilling to attract attention, even less willing to catch anyone's eye. There are no women loitering about on the street corners, no women enjoying the sludge in the ridge greens after an unusually intense Delhi rain, no women relishing the tapestry of aroma in the Old Delhi spice market, no women lying down in the grass to soak in the winter sun in Nehru Park, no women playing cards to prolong their lunch hour in the spotty grass enclosures near the squat-gray Soviet era central government buildings. No woman out on the streets of Delhi just because she feels like it.

The other day while watching a scene in a movie where the hero and his friend return very late at night from a party in a taxi, I told Tanya that that can never happen with two women. This kind of casual returning very late at night. Not without there being multiple questions about the safety, the probity, the appropriateness of two women being out alone at night. What was she doing out that late? The top-notch lawyer on TV had asked of a high society daughter-in-law of a senior government minister, who had jumped off the roof of a five star hotel and killed herself. Not why she jumped. Not who was responsible for her suicide. No, those were secondary questions in his eyes. Why was she out that late? Wasn't her being out alone that late enough of a cause for her to commit suicide? Perhaps only call centre women—back-ending in another country's daytime and calling themselves *Ann* and *Beth* and *Sally* to fit more easily into the irritated mouths of those irate customers who want to know why their refrigerator or their Xbox or their holiday vouchers have not been delivered yet—and to use that old-fashioned term, 'call girls'—working for the pleasure of the other sex and calling themselves *Dolly* and *Mona* and *Lily* to fit into the fantasy of their paying clients—are permitted to stay out late.

The spaces for women have been systematically, methodically truncated. Not by any dictate. That would be too obvious. There are no boards outside buildings or on roadsides stating—like the infamous boards from colonial times that raise our heckles every time we see them in our movies or our books—'Dogs and Indians not Allowed'. No, there no boards saying 'Women not Allowed'. But open a map of Delhi and there they are. The many, many places where no woman can go and the many, many more places where no woman can go after sundown. A temporal and areal-shrinking of their boundaries. They make themselves small, dowdy, inconspicuous and yet they are spotted and targeted. The violations are not always large, something that they can specifically touch. Not with their fingers and sometimes not even with their imagination—did he really rub himself standing against you when you sat on the corner seat in the bus or did he keep swaying against you because of the bus driver's erratic, whimsical overtaking through the crowded Delhi traffic?—but they remain in there like the rotten core you find inside a perfectly formed walnut shell. The insidious knocking down, of the body, of the self, one day after another; the odd, sometimes seemingly accidental and sometimes brazen touch, the long, leering stare; the comments about sizes and shapes *and the texture of any body part, even the knees. Sometimes you can't even mention the intrusions without sounding paranoid. Rotten core inside a perfectly formed shell? How do you <u>know</u> it is rotten then? How do <u>you</u> know it is rotten then?*

But sit down, breathe deep and ask a woman. Any woman. They are there. Subtly and brazenly diminishing them. Breaking them down little by little. With their words, with their actions, with their policies. The women may not actually be raped on the street. Although that happens too and that happens too often. Rape Capital. And that is not really surprising is it? Considering that for a long, long time, although no kissing between two adults was allowed on screen, and no men and women were allowed to openly express or even acknowledge their love for each other except in a mostly paternalistic—worshipping the flowers at your feet—kind of way, at least one attempted rape or a full-fledged rape was a mandatory part of almost every Hindi movie. Somehow the script, whether set in an urban bungalow with a large central stairway and manicured gardens or in the rolling rural greens with snow-capped peaks as the backdrop, always managed to spread out to accommodate a graphic rape with evilly contorted lips and grasping hands. And in every movie the raped woman—her bindi askew, her blouse sleeve torn, her sari missing or mussed up—had to kill herself because no woman could continue to live after that kind of assault, could she? As if like the boy about whom I had read years ago in Reader's Digest, who lived inside a spaceman bubble and would die of infection if there is a breach in his bubble, her entire being is hymen-wrapped whose rupture would end her existence, her right, her very potential to stay alive.

Even today it is the rape victim's face and the rape victim's name that is pixelated, blotted out, fictionalized like it is she who has committed the crime and it is she who should be ashamed for carrying the body, for being the body that was assaulted. The much-touted fund set up by the government after the horrifying rape of 2012, ostensibly in the name of the victim, to help other victims of her kind of assault, does not even bear her real name. Her name Jyoti that means light cannot not be allowed to glow after being a victim of the darkness that a rape is, can it? Instead the fund is called Nirbhaya—fearless. But who is fearless? The raped or the rapist?

Deepak said this morning not leeringly, not sarcastically but straight, matter-of-fact, 'Women have an extra opening that, like a hole at the bottom of a safe makes all the locks useless and all their insides available for the taking.'

Making them worry more about the length of their skirt than the expanse of their minds, issuing the diktat that women should not be allowed mobile phones because that will give them the freedom to talk and to plot at will, deciding what dress they can wear and how, what places they can worship in and how, deeming them impure for six days each month and nearly twenty per cent of time in an entire year, making them scale the crevasse of propriety, probity, honour and responsibility before they make any decision, using the lexicon of shame when speaking about the life-giving elements of their powerful life-giving bodies, fettering the bodies to chain the minds that want to soar . . . and they have succeeded have they not? The chains hang large and thick inside and

It ended there. Layla seemed to have run out of time or motivation or ink. The note was written the old-fashioned way with a fountain pen. Raman could recognize the fountain pen script almost immediately. Both sisters seem to like writing with a fountain pen and if he remembers right, their handwritings too are almost identical. There is no date on the note. No hint of when it was written, under what circumstances, who it was addressed to or what purpose it was meant to serve. Then, there is Deepak. Who is he? Raman wants to go back to the hospital to check on Tanya and to talk to her to ask her why Layla has written what she has. And to speak with Layla too, if possible. But no, that is impossible unless she has miraculously regained her consciousness in the few hours since he has left Satya. There is something raw about the unfinished note, something peeled and exposed and bleeding like a brain when the cranium is cut open. That curiously compact and yet squishy lump of material that looks like nothing else in the world and yet contains the entire world within itself.

He remembers reading in one of the pieces among the sisters' web searches on articles and books about starvation that consuming food is perhaps our most tangible link to the physical world and that most of the world's religions have, at some point of time, seen the denial of food as a step towards breaking the bonds of the physical world. Among the reasons why monks advocate fasting, apart from as an act of penance, he had read, is because it reduces sexual desires, another tie to the wicked, physical world. What had happened to Tanya and Layla? Raman is suddenly so tired that he puts his head on the table and sleeps.

His phone rings.

'Why have you not called?' For a few seconds Raman
is assailed by a bizarre panic attack like he has fallen off a
cliff in his sleep.

'Who is it?' He begins to say before he remembers.
'Ma? Ma.' He has not heard her speak over the phone for
so long that that he is not sure whether or not he is still
asleep and still dreaming.

'Yes, who else will call you?' His mother answers. 'Why
did you not call me last night? Are you unwell?'

'No, I am not unwell. Just very busy.'

'Very busy or very drunk?'

Raman does not reply. He does not know how to reply.
He wishes he has the gumption to disconnect the call or
tell her exactly what he is feeling at the moment. What is it
about his mother that leaves him speechless and spluttering?
He remembers that everything bad that happens to his
mother has always been somebody else's fault and anything
that any of their acquaintance achieves—however distant
her connection to them may be—is always, in some part,
due to her own quality or skill or advice or the chance
meeting she had with that person at some point in her life.

'Where are you? Are you okay?' He manages to find
his voice.

'I am at home. Where will I go? It is not like you take
me with you on your trips.'

They are work trips, Ma, Raman wants to say. He has
the nightmarish vision of his mother asking for tea (that
she had to have at five every evening come rain or shine)
in the middle of his journey through the mountains of
Kashmir where he had once gone to interview the suave

and extremely hard to pin down Sheikh Mustafa, who was on almost every government's terrorist list.

'And what will ever happen to me?' He hears his mother continue. 'It is my destiny to live a long and lonely life, so I will do so.'

She says it like it is he who has not spoken to her for all those days. He is already beginning to get nostalgic for her days of silence. Had he ever wanted her to speak with him? What had he been smoking?

'Ma, is there something you want me to do?'

'Yes. I want you to take me today to the bank for Dad's pension. I need to show them that I am alive before they can give the money to me.'

'Today is a very busy day for me, Ma. Why don't you go with Savita didi?'

'When are you not busy? Can you not spare one hour for my work?'

Why is she asking him to come along this time? Before this, she had always sent her loyal maid, Savita didi, with the papers—those that he needed to sign to relinquish his right in favour of his mother to any property or bank accounts that his father had held, because under the Hindu Undivided Family Act, he has as much right over his father's wealth as his mother does; those that committed him to paying her for any additional expenses that his father's pension may not be able to cover (that he had signed although he was not sure any commitment like that would hold in court should he ever decide to challenge it. Not that he had any intention of doing so but the logic of getting him to sign something like that defied his otherwise adequately fertile imagination). He remembers he had forgotten to call her last night for the first time in two and a half years. Has she called because she has begun to sense in his failure to undertake his daily telephonic ritual that his emotions and his attention is shifting elsewhere and she wants to get her grip back on him?

'Okay,' Raman says, giving in as usual and cursing himself for his weakness even as he says. 'I will pick you up at 8 tomorrow. Or today?'

Is it today already? Raman remembers one of the drunken games he had played with his friends in college where each had to imagine the worst way to be woken up and his friends had spoken of situations like being woken up with their mattress on fire, or with the ceiling fan falling on their heads or finding themselves stranded on a remote treeless atoll with nothing but a vast ocean all around them but he had said that the worst way for him would be to be woken by his mother calling out to him. It had made everybody laugh but that was truly how he had felt then and it seems even after all these years, he has not completely outgrown that emotion. To say that he feels horrible right now would be an understatement. He feels like a beetle crushed within a centimetre of its life under the weight of a stinky, flatulent bum. His mouth is bitter from all the bacteria that are having a field day feasting on the concoction of bad whisky and stale peanuts inside his mouth; his neck and back are stiff solid from having slept so deeply at such a bad angle on a chair that is not even ergonomically suitable for sitting for more than a couple of hours at a stretch, let alone sleeping on for an entire night. But it is his mind, unable to fully process everything that he is trying to come to terms with, that is worst off. Had that conversation that he had just had been a part of a horrific nightmare or had it really happened? Is he asleep or awake? Is it night or morning? The drawn curtains and all the lights that had remained switched on while he had slept are giving him the feeling of being in the midst of excruciatingly painful timelessness, suspended between night and day, between heaven and hell with no possibility of being taken into either place anytime soon. What *is* the time anyway? He squints into his phone. 0450, it says. So it is 4.50 in the morning. What on earth or in the sky had compelled his mother to call him at this crazy hour? Oh yes, he remembers. She has her morning tea at 4.30 am every day. It is probably when she sat sipping her tea this morning that all the affronts that had been committed against her, everything that the world, but particularly Raman, owed to her had come flooding into her and she had picked up the phone to call him and perhaps some other people too without bothering to remember that everybody does not adhere to the same inhuman cycle of waking and sleeping that she sticks to.

Well, 4.50 or 5.50. There is no way he can get into bed and go back to sleep. He stands up, making Layla's note that, unknown to him, had last night become lodged somewhere between his body and the table, fall off. It is not a suicide note but it could well be, he thinks, picking up the paper. A suicide note for the entire womankind . . . gosh, what is happening? Has his mind swelled into becoming a blunt amorphous mush incapable of holding any rational, sensible, insightful thought? But as he stands under the shower that sprays him with ice-cold water, among the first signs that the Delhi weather is beginning to turn, he remembers bits of phrases from the note. Is that what being a woman is like? He is no male chauvinist. And although he knows women are as fallible and as capable of evil as any man any day, he prides himself in having deep respect for women, never speaking to or even of them lecherously, never in his wildest dream thinking that they are any less than any man; on the contrary thinking in the little time he gives to such thoughts that they, as an entity, if not individually, are capable of doing much more than men and not just biologically, where because of the dint of their reproductive abilities, they are in any case far superior to any man, but in every way possible. But all these sentiments, these pious thoughts and lofty ideas that he had been proud to have, now seem facetious and condescending. He had never thought of the everyday lives of every woman, the burden of each moment being under scrutiny for every woman. Any woman, as Layla had put it. Is that what it is like? Is the world really different for women? Even for the modern woman of today? The everyday world of everyday things that he has always taken for granted? There is something else about the note too that had stuck in his mind when he was reading it. Something that was important and although he cannot remember it right now, he is sure it will come back to him as the various strands in the saga disentangle themselves in his mind and smoothen down in neat lines to show their myriad patterns. What he is not sure of, though, is whether he is ready for the strands to be displayed in the right order and whether he really wants, whether he can really bear, to see the full picture.

Raman's phone rings again at 7.27 just as he is finally having his long overdue cup of coffee and steeling himself to spending an hour and a half, or maybe even more, in his mother's company.

It is Satya on the phone this time. 'We are on our way to the house again,' he says without preamble. 'We will reach in about twenty-twenty five minutes if you want to join us.'

'Absolutely,' Raman says and unwilling to talk to his mother, calls her maid instead to tell her to inform his mother of the cancellation of their appointment. 'Something really urgent has come up,' he tells Savita didi, knowing that she is likely to understand, much more than his mother has ever been able to, the fact that other people also have important things to do that they cannot very well abandon at the drop of the hat or in his mother's case, at the first words of her dictate. Thinking as he does so that there are so many little negotiations and trickery and convoluted choices that each person has to make every day that it is not surprising that most people live their entire lives negotiating through the minefields of every day decisions and find no time to attain anything tangible and permanent and of value to anybody besides themselves, if even that. Although how permanent 'permanence' is also open to debate.

Satya's jeep is still at the gate of Krishna Colony when Raman reaches it. Satya tells Raman to get into the jeep with him and he drives past the gate without obviously stopping to register his entry, giving Raman no chance

to acknowledge, the guard, Hariram, except with a slight
wave and a nod which is duly ignored by old Hariram who
knows better than Raman the repercussions of showing
more than a passing familiarity with a journalist.

Raman wants to show Layla's note to Satya but not just
yet. He can, however, begin talking about the RWA notice
and about his conversation with Deol immediately.

'Yes', Satya replies, looking less surprised than Raman
had expected. 'We too have received some hints about
there being a man and we have been trying to locate him
but we have not had much success. Nobody seems to
know who he is and there are no further leads to go on.
In any case, I am not sure I can justify putting any more
of my department's resources into this case. There is the
whole media brouhaha around it but it does not look like
something that the police needs to handle. It does not
look like a case about any individuals. Deol or Deepak
whom nobody seems to know.'

'You are probably right.' Raman says, handing
Layla's note to Satya. 'I found this yesterday in one of
the books.'

Satya again surprisingly does not comment on Raman's
transgression and begins reading the note. He seems more
distracted and pensive today than yesterday.

He sighs slightly when he hands the note back to
Raman. 'You can keep it if you want or put it back in the
book where you found it.'

'But make sure you remember where you keep it,' Satya
says almost as an afterthought. 'I may need it later.'

'Is everything okay?' Raman asks Satya.

'Yes, as okay as things can be, I suppose. I went to the hospital before I came here. Layla is not getting better. The doctors can't do anything but wait and watch and keep her on life support.'

They have entered D332 and fortunately, the ubiquitous Mr Deol is nowhere in sight. Raman is in no mood to tackle the misguided cocksure certainty about life that he embodies. Like he knows all the answers to any questions that anybody may ever have although he cannot imagine why, in the first place, anybody will have any questions about the perfect way the world works.

Layla and Tanya's living room is the same as it was yesterday but the broad rays of sunlight, filtered by the newly washed mango leaves coming in through one window, are highlighting little particles of swirling dust in the air inside and giving the entire room a sepia tone, making it look like the set of an angst-ridden desolate Guru Dutt movie. The painting of the two women is in the shadows, beyond the reach of the tempered light and Raman is almost glad that he cannot see the watchful eyes of the two women in the painting on him as he goes about looking at and touching things that he has no business looking at or touching. And although it feels frivolous to think about these things right now, he cannot completely ignore his back and his head both of which hurt. It is obviously going to be one of those days.

October 2013–April 2014

24

The Not-So-Perfect, Not-Even-Much of a Lover

Layla's loneliness ensured that Deepak became an integral part of her life very soon. He began picking her up every other evening—not often enough for her to take him for granted but often enough to make her become increasingly familiar with his presence and his smell and enough to make her miss him when he did not come. And although—beyond that first day that she recalled vividly—there were not many specific circumstances or conversations with him of those early days that she remembered precise details of, she did remember that their initial outings centred around food. He took her to obscure places to eat—the Bengali restaurant tucked in one corner of the bustling Dilli Haat that made the most spectacular but the most underappreciated fish kalia, the shop at Majnu-ka-Tila that made the best pork momos, the keema parathawala near the IIT flyover, Ghalib Kebab at Nizamuddin for the bakarkhanis, Kashmir House for rogan josh. Most places that, to his very vocal surprise, she had never visited.

'Maybe because they are secret places,' he said. 'Available only to a true Delhi insider.'

'Which obviously I am not, although I have lived here my entire life,' she said.

'No, you are not, are you? Not many single women are. And here I am as a single man—an insider in every city that I have ever lived in.'

'How many cities would that be?'

'Infinite.' He had laughed. His laughter was controlled and practised and pleasant. This was much before she saw that hint of sadism that even his rehearsed laughter could not camouflage or perhaps by that time, he had stopped bothering to camouflage it. His laughter never reached his eyes properly (she saw that too although again much too late) except when he was laughing at her discomfort. Or when he regaled her with stories of something horrible that he had done to somebody or something horrible that he wanted to do to her. His entire thin, slightly curved body was in synchrony then like a taut perfectly tuned violin string, alive and strumming to the pleasure that he got out of it.

All this came later but even during those initial days, she had understood that the obscure places that he took her to were perhaps also the only places where they were allowed (without having to pay exorbitantly or having to order food constantly) to be on their own for some time with no waiters and managers (who all seem to have a sixth sense when it comes to targeting couples who did not have a biologically or socially legitimized relationship—father–daughter,

brother–sister, wife–husband) hovering over their heads.
Deepak, during the early days, almost always spoke the right
words and she revelled in their conversations although she
began to sense soon enough that a lot of what he said was
not because he meant those words but because he knew she
would be happy hearing them. And she *was* happy hearing
them. They may not have been sincere words but they
were interesting words—bits about literature and current
affairs, profuse compliments about her sharp, focused mind,
frequent but oblique and understated praise for her looks—
they were words that she had longed to hear for so long
after the intrusive, insensitive attention that strangers had
been showering upon her that she took them in and found
a special place for them inside her head where her usual
questions were toned down and her cynicism was absent.

Perhaps this is how courtships are supposed to be,
she thought. This sprinkling of insincere but flattering,
interesting and often intense words around meals and
meetings and this is how attraction between people begins.
Like expertly applied make-up that highlights the positives
and covers all the flaws. She once thought of speaking
about it to Tanya but she knew doing so would give her
meetings with Deepak a shape and tangibility that she was
not sure she was willing to confer upon them. Not yet.
Perhaps never but that was not the kind of thought that
she was able to harbour without feeling so guilty that she
had to give up on it before it even began to form properly
inside her own head. Because what was she doing with
Deepak if she did not think that it would lead to tangibility
and legitimacy—to engagement and marriage and children

and living happily ever after? In the middle class Delhi
society that she lived in, dating is a word from American
movies and sitcoms, any relationship between a man and
a woman not related to each other is considered bad. Any
relationship if not headed towards the holy matrimony, is
immoral. And any physical relationship between a man and
a woman without the holy matrimony is utter sin (albeit
only for a woman).

Yet, even though she deluded herself, even bound by
the notions of the society that she had been brought up
in, the society that she continued to live in, in her heart of
hearts she knew that her relationship with Deepak could
not be about words and feelings and legitimizing and
happily-ever-afters. Despite her not quite up to the mark,
bookish knowledge of relationships, even though she was
not able to articulate it properly, she understood that it was
not conversations that she wanted from Deepak. What she
felt for Deepak, at its most basic, was purely physical. His
presence arousing the kind of physicality in her that she
was not sure she could find the words to acknowledge, or
even whether she wanted to find the words to acknowledge.
She knew the emotions that she read about in books were
mostly cut and dried. There were the good emotions, there
were the bad emotions and there were the mixed, complex
emotions. There were good characters and there were bad
characters and there were the mixed complex characters but
all those feelings and people could be put into words, some
words, any words. How was it then that her emotions in real
life were so convoluted that they were almost impossible to
speak about? For instance, what could she say to Tanya?

That when listening to Deepak, she was more focused on the way his lips moved, wanting to know the feel of those lips that spoke those words against hers, than on the actual words? That she wanted Deepak's body against hers? That she wished he would stay touching her longer than the fraction of minute that he did when he guided her to his car with his palm on her lower back, or when he almost absently held her hand when crossing the road, or when the heel of his palm touched her cheek as he removed the piece of lint from her eye or when his fingertips wiped the leftover ice cream from her upper lip?

She never said those words. She never expressed those emotions. Not to Tanya. Not to Deepak and not even to herself except much much later, when she had the long, stretched out days to analyse everything. But her relationship with Deepak did begin to change. The fingers did begin to linger a little longer. The palm stayed in place and the hand continued to be held even when the road had been crossed. But not for too long, not long enough to attract attention. Well, at least not too much attention because they could not completely avoid the attention that came their way anyway because of what they were, because of what they exuded when they were together. They stopped going to the same restaurants too because by now they had begun to get leering, knowing looks from the more 'legitimate' patrons of those places. They could not go to one of the many parks that held on tremulously between the high and low rises of a boisterously expanding Delhi's 'residential and office spaces' that were so enthusiastically celebrated by real estate agents and developers, because once, only once, Deepak drove her to the beautiful Buddha Jayanti park, lush with February flowers. And it was there that for the first time, he held out his hand and held hers deliberately. One finger lingering against the other. But they could find no secluded place to sit in that park. Every alcove, every tree, every bush was taken by couples mostly younger, some older but all probably more desperate than they were. There should have been beauty in those couples' need, in their obliviousness to their surroundings as they held each other or kissed each other. There should have been joy in the promise of fulfilment of one of the most primal, one of the most deeply held of longings. Instead there was such a pervasive sense of illegitimacy and putrid smell of dishonour surrounding the neatly lined hedges and the blooming poppies of the park that it had shocked Layla. The vulnerability of those couples was exacerbated by the arrival of two constables, out to make easy money, who tapped on the shoulders of one oblivious couple after the other, making them rise scrambling up for clothes and phones and money to escape the clutches of law that forbade couples being in a secluded place together, according to one paan-chewing constable who thoughtfully looked up and down assessing the maximum paying capacity of each couple before demanding a suitable amount to compensate for his magnanimity of not booking them for solicitation or for vulgarity in public. Layla never returned to Buddha Jayanti park or any other park with Deepak after that and soon she and Deepak ran out of places to meet. Soon there was nowhere they could sit and talk in peace, nowhere they could hold hands, nowhere left to go but to D332, Krishna Colony.

'You brought me home, darling,' Deepak told her later, when she wanted him to go away from her life. 'I did not force you to bring me here, did I? It was you who could not live without me. Now I cannot live without all these comforts and you can't simply tell me to leave because you don't want me anymore.'

She looked at him steadily. What he said was true. She *had* brought him home. At first only so that they could be together without having to face the leering glances of strangers, soon because there was no other place where they could even kiss each other and very soon because where else could they make love in the city of Delhi? But Deepak began to stay on for longer and longer each time until one rainy night, looking at the water-logging on the streets that, as frequently as it occurs after a heavy downpour in Delhi still manages to catch almost everybody—from municipal workers to the multiple administrators of the city, to commuters—by surprise, he asked her if he could stay the night. 'I will probably get only as far as your society gate if I attempt to cross this vast overflowing river of sewage that the roads have become right now,' he had smiled ruefully as he said it. And she could not say no, could she? There was no reason for her to say no. God knows she had enough empty space that she did not know how to fill, so without realizing the implications of it fully, she agreed. And that night changed everything. Somehow, somewhere her assent spread out to allow him to not leave her or her house at all after that. Slowly, unobtrusively, his few belongings moved into her house and she noticed that she had begun to provide for his food and his drinks and his recreation.

She did not even mind that at first. At first it was nice to come home to somebody after the months of loneliness. But more than that it was the deep physical satisfaction that he provided her that she looked forward to; the way he made her feel when he touched her, the way those expert fingers moved up and down her body completely in tune with how she wanted them to move. Hard on some days, and at some times, soft and fleeting on other days, at other times. Always saying the words that she wanted to hear, grunting softly when she wanted *him* to react to her touch and not saying anything when she wanted only one of her extremely heightened sense to be addressed.

'You are a nymphomaniac, you know that, don't you?' He told her once, much later, much much later, when he had stopped saying things that she wanted to hear and started speaking out exactly what he really wanted to say. Things that *he* truly thought. By then she had begun to long for those days when he would say the right words even though he had not meant them. She did not want to hear the words that he really meant. The hurtful words. The sadistic words. The true words expressing how he truly felt. Truth, she thought, is an overrated, overhyped, and in the end, entirely expendable virtue. Or at least truth between people is useless. That is probably the reason why every human society has established rituals of politeness, of etiquette and of ways of living so that everybody can anticipate how everybody else is going act in a particular situation and everybody can go through the motions of interacting with each other, turning the wheels of human society, without putting too much effort, without saying

what they actually mean or behaving how they really want
to behave at that particular moment.

She realized *she* could not pinpoint the moment or
event or conversation when the descent in her relationship
with Deepak began. Or perhaps her relationship with
Deepak was always on a descending slope; only she had
been too self-involved, wallowing in her own loneliness
and betrayed by the needs of her treacherous body, to
have noticed it before. She began to notice it soon enough
though. In fact, not long after Deepak had moved in.
There was no mistaking it. Perhaps it began when Deepak
had rolled his eyes and stopped her in the middle of her
excitedly telling him about the sonnet by Petrarca she
had discovered that had been used almost word for word
by another poet two centuries later. A poet whose birth
centenary had recently been celebrated with much pomp
and whose brooding, bearded, bespectacled pictures had
adorned the cover of almost every magazine with any kind
of literary pretensions—'Do I have to keep hearing all this
still?' Deepak had said to her then, stopping her words
halfway between her throat and her lips, cauterizing her
enthusiasm instantly. 'Have I not heard enough? Don't you
understand that I am not interested in all this nonsense
about Petrarca that you harp about? I was not interested
in him before and I am not interested in him now. But
no, no. You don't have to stop. You go on ahead like you
always do and continue yakking away—yak yak yak yak—
while I can lie here pretending to listen to you like I have
always done. Only this time I *will* shut my eyes when I
go to sleep at your boring conversation skills unlike before

when I had to keep my eyes open although my mind had been fast asleep.'

Or had the descent started when Deepak had woken her up with a sharp kick on her ankle when she had slept on her notes at the table after working on them for almost the entire night? 'You are drooling all over. It is the most disgusting thing that I have ever seen,' he had said. Or when he said, 'You are so tiring that I think your father drove his car deliberately into a truck just to avoid seeing your stupid face again.'

Once she began to notice the slide, she could not confuse the interaction between them for anything else. She could not make any excuses. Not for him. Not for herself. She could not explain his words away as the occasional bad temper, or anger, or anything else but as a deep animosity he had towards her. But in all his time, despite all his words and his cruelty, he always stayed close to her and she felt the soft rise and fall of his chest when he was relaxed, the more agitated expulsion of his breath when he became irritated in the early days at someone else's inept driving or inefficient service, and later by almost anything in relation to her but she never saw him completely lose his temper. Not earlier, not later. When she remarked upon it, he said he did not believe in enslaving himself so deeply to his emotions that he lost control over his actions. It was then that he told her about how he had once, only once in his adult life lost his temper so completely that he had ended up having a physical fight with his opponent. He did not tell her the reasons of his brawl (although from what little he told her, she surmised that it had something to do with drugs, a habit that he seemed to have kicked since).

But he did tell her in great detail—almost punch for punch—about how he had won even in the fisticuffs until the bastard had pulled out a knife, which had tilted the balance in his opponent's favour and it had all ended with the other guy stabbing Deepak in his stomach multiple times and leaving him to bleed to his death on the road.

'Although obviously fortunately for me and unfortunately for you, my tall, uncoordinated darling,' he said, 'I did not die then but my stomach was so badly cut up that the tissues there still continue to be like little trellises barely able to protect and contain my insides, as my doctor who probably read a bit of T.S. Eliot in her free time told me rather poetically. Look here it is. The weakest part of my body. My Achilles heel. One hard kick there and I am gone. Out like a light.'

Although she did not completely believe his story, especially the part about him initially winning in the open-handed fight, she could not doubt the injury, the remnants of which he proudly showed to her as a largish patch on the right side of his stomach which looked like an intricately carved and painted ink blot with its uneven texture and its multiple hues ranging from deep red to deep purple to black and bits of yellow. She touched it with the tip of her fingers. His Achilles heel. That piece of embossed skin.

But Deepak's interactions with her were never tempestuous, at least not from his side. He was in complete control of his actions and words. Even when he was torturing her physically or mentally.

'Good women are not supposed to want sex,' Deepak told her once after particularly intense love-making as she lay flushed next to him. He was sliding a finger over the dark line running vertically down the middle of her torso. 'You are supposed to be submissive, granting the man his wishes because *his* body needs to have that avenue to vent *his* biological needs. It is *his* hormones that need satiating. A good woman's hormones, on the other hand, are subsumed under her maternal, her nurturing instincts. But you don't have any nurturing instincts, do you? You are a harlot, a nympho. A bad woman.' He had laughed at her discomfort then and had sucked on her navel hard. His laughter reaching his eyes making them shine with a kind of devilish glint that she had thought existed only in other people's imagination—in Poe's stories, in Mary Shelley's novels. But here he was, leaning over her, kissing her, the embodiment of every horror that she had flinched from as a child.

'Shameless. That is the word that will be hurtled at you. That is what you will be called.' He said. 'Shameless. A harlot, a nymphomaniac. A fallen woman. Do you think in our country where rape in a marriage is not even considered a possibility, let alone an offence, anybody will be at your side when you go out and shout out that I have abused you? Oh poor little me! Darling, what we have is very, very immoral but very, very consensual. You can't say otherwise. Who will believe a woman who has so willingly invited a strange man to live with her? Who do you think will come to your aid? Do you think Mr Deol who came so sanctimoniously to scold you for having a man in the house will believe you or help you or even listen to you? What did the notice say? Ah yes. "Rules for Safe and Virtuous Living in Bellevue Boulevard." Haha! He wants a note from you explaining your relationship with me. Actually, *I* will love to see that note. I will love to see what you will call me. The tormentor-in-chief? Or the lover-in-chief? The person who kills you with ecstasy or the person who murders you with misery.'

'You are stuck with me, my darling, as I am stuck with you. You have blunted my killer instinct. I have decided that I am too old to go looking for any other place to live in. I am very comfortable here. All these empty rooms suit me fine although living in this chaste middle class place does cramp my style a bit, it is a good, safe place to operate from. You have made me invest in keeping you. I am very comfortable here. I have begun strategizing. Something that I had promised myself I would never do because it takes too much of my time. But here darling, just to prove that I am serious. To make you give up on any ideas you may have about going to the police or the court or wherever else poor battered women go, let me show you these.'

'These' were printed pictures of her asleep and naked, with the bed covers twisted around her—looking like the shameless harlot he had called her.

'They are lovely pictures, are they not?' He said, running his finger along the outlines of her body, along her waist, along the insides of her thighs in the one photograph in which she slept with her legs splayed apart. 'I know this is the age of digital images and believe me I have these in digital form too—the better to spread it around the world with,' he had made the grandma wolf face. 'But there is something delicious about having physical prints. Like in old movies where the private eye hands over a large manila envelope to his client with pictures of his adulterating wife spilling out. I was almost tempted to print your pictures in black and white to make them even more in character but unfortunately that would make them less realistic, so I had to give up on that. See, I gave it all so much thought. I told you, you have made me invest in you. I took the trouble of actually going to a photo studio to get these printed. Don't worry I took care to go to one of the places that specializes in art photography. So they did not ask me any questions. I bet they have seen more bizarre stuff than these tame pictures. You know that I don't want to use these pictures, darling. Not unless you make me. You know I *will* use these pictures and tell so many little stories about your ways. I will tell you enticed me into your house. I will tell them you *begged* me and when that didn't work you forced me to have sex with you. They will understand how as a man it would be natural for me to succumb to your enticement. I will tell them that you use these pictures to meet other men too. I will tell them so many little little stories that you will be hounded right out of this stodgy little mausoleum of a house that you have made. Your Dad's shoes. Your Mom's saris. Your *little* Neel's Legos. Geez, I can't believe you've kept them all. Your darling Mr Deol will probably call a meeting of Bellevue Boulevard Resident Welfare Association to shame you like they do in Khaap panchyats before they throw you out.'

Shameless. Brazen. Wanton. According to Ruth Benedict, there are shame societies and guilt societies. Theirs was a shame society. But shame for whom? Not for the corrupt policeman next door always on a buying spree completely disproportionate to his meagre policeman's income; not for the politician going in and out of jail because of one scam or the other; not even for the property agent paying no taxes but changing the colour, make and model of his car every other month; not for the IAS officer who everybody knows takes vast amounts of money to put his signature on any approval and yet who is feted in society and has his own membership of the designated Officers' and Gymkhana clubs in the heart of Delhi's most expensive areas. Not for godmen nor for trustees of temples and mosques and churches who deal only in cash and jewellery and on whom the swirling accusations of defilement of women, of children, of the environment never really settle. No, not for any of them. Only for the women in all places and in all circumstances. Always the women who are placed in the social web of judgement and expectation with hierarchies of authority where they obviously are the lowest rung. All women, any women, in all circumstances. Tangled in the web of looks, clothes, hair, behaviour, morality, honour. And shame. Shame and shameless. Layla had remained focused on that all evening. There was nothing else to focus on, was there?

She was not sure what she said later that night in her ritualistic phone conversation with Tanya that made Tanya pack her bags and return. Or had she not said anything and it was the intensity of all those unsaid words that had flooded inside Tanya's head making her hurry across the 1340 km and 341 days that lay between them and arrive at her door step two days later, looking exactly like

Layla was feeling at the moment. How could literally two embodiments of shame exist at the same place at the same time? And yet there they were. Twin sisters with their faces distorted by similar smiles. Mirror images with the same mouth, same nose, same hair and same overlarge stricken eyes, full of fear.

28 October 2014

25

The World Tilts

'I think we have seen all we need to see in this room.'
ACP Satya says and ignoring the living room goes
straight towards one of the bedrooms. Raman too,
curbing his usual instinct to linger among books, looks
only for a moment at the large number of them still lying
scattered in the living room exactly where they had left
them yesterday, follows Satya before stopping short at
the threshold of the same and yet a completely different
world that the bedroom is. After the clutter and mayhem
of the living room, the orderliness of the bedroom is almost
sacrilegious. Everything in the bedroom too is covered in a
thick film of dust but that is where the similarity between
the outside and the inside of the bedroom ends. In the
bedroom everything is exactly where it is supposed to be.
There are no toppled chairs or scattered books or clothes or
papers. The bed occupying a large proportion of the room
is properly made and in place, the dresser has bottles that
are arranged almost too neatly in order of height and not,

as far as he can tell, for ease of use; the cupboard is shut
tight and there are even two pairs of slippers placed under
the bed for the occupants of the bed to swing their feet into
as soon as they wake up. The room looks as if it has been
hit by the neutron bomb of his childhood—a bomb that
was deemed to be capable of taking out every living thing
while leaving all non-living things, including the man-
made ones—buildings, roads, bridges, infrastructure—
intact to spare the occupying forces the inconvenience of
having to rebuild after the war. He has, of course, found
out since then that the truth about neutron bombs is less or
perhaps more macabre (depending on your viewpoint) than
what his childhood soldier-uniform-arms-and-armament-
loving friends had imagined it to be. But here it certainly
looked like one moment its inhabitants had been peacefully
asleep on their bed and the next moment they were gone—
whoooosh. And, come to think of it, although the process by
which they had disappeared may not have been as dramatic
as being vapourized by a neutron burst, the outcome, when
it came to Layla and Tanya's parents, was from what he
had read in the newspaper reports, almost the same—
one minute they were driving their all-dressed-up-gift-
carrying-selves in their little car to a birthday celebration
and the next minute they were gone from the face of the
earth, crushed under the wheels of a large lumbering truck.
There is a picture of the family on the wall of the bedroom
with a little boy in the centre, Layla and Tanya rorscharch-
like on side of him and the parents standing on the outside,
reminding Raman of the tightly entangled fingers that
Tanya had compared her family to. Raman stands at the

door, wary of entering the room that looks like it has not been touched for nearly two years since the time Tanya and Layla's parents died. Although the dust on the floor looks disturbed, which suggests that a few pairs of feet had stepped on that turf quite recently. Had somebody looked inside the cupboard too?

'We have checked that,' Satya catches him looking at the cupboard. 'It contains all of their parents' clothes and things; the sisters seemed to have got rid of nothing. Like I told you, it is like a shrine for their parents. We also found their bank papers inside. I am sure you already know that the sisters have money. There was enough coverage in the media about that. But come here, I want to show you this. This is what I was telling you about yesterday.' Satya, who has reached the door of the en-suite bathroom, is pointing towards something inside the bathroom.

Raman walks across the room to him and sees that the bathtub he is pointing towards, instead of being filled with water, is incongruously filled up to the brim with hardened cement. The rest of the bathroom too looks like a continuation of the madness of the living room, the immaculate arrangement of objects in the bedroom seeming like an aberration in the house where everything else is in a state of frenzied, pulverizing, almost reassuringly familiar disarray.

Raman steps closer to the bathtub. It is obvious that the concrete inside was not filled by a professional. By somebody who professionally handles cement. There are protruding gray blotches of dried cement on the floor of the bathroom because of clumsily dropped concrete mix, and the top of the bathtub too is uneven and bubbled like somebody had amateurishly mixed the cement before pouring in the concrete layer upon layer without bothering to level the layers. There are cracks in the cement too. Long lines that run horizontally and vertically across the length and the breadth of the bathtub top. Something deep inside one of the larger cracks close to where Raman stands looks different from the rest of the surface. It looks darker and strangely textured. Is the concrete still wet? How is that even possible? Perhaps it is just a trick of the low light. Raman sees that Satya is looking at the rest of the bathroom, flicking through the tumble of toiletries that lie inside and around the bathroom sink. There is a switchboard near Satya.

'Do these lights work?' Raman asks him.

'I suppose so,' Satya flicks the switches, bathing the bathroom in the bright white of two CFL light bulbs.

'What are you looking at?' He joins Raman near the bathtub and bends his head close to Raman's.

'I am not sure. Looks like something got stuck in the concrete down below. It looks like a parchment or a piece of cloth. But it is probably nothing. Just some badly mixed cement.'

'No.' Satya peers into another large crack in the cement further up the bathtub. 'I can see something here too.'

'Do you think we should try breaking the concrete?'

'Yes.' Satya sounds grim and distant. He has begun to look like the policeman that he is. 'Stay here if you want to but don't touch anything anymore. I will get some tools'.

Raman stays, staring at his reflection in the mirror. He can sense the shadows of the bedroom behind him, the shrine

that Tanya and Layla have made for their parents, according
to Satya. Perhaps this is another reason why he is attracted
to Tanya, despite the apparent chaos and dysfunction of her
life, there is an inner coherence to her that probably comes
from the rock solid family life that she had had before things
seemed to have gone so terribly wrong for her. In that, she
is the opposite of him. His restlessness despite his otherwise
structured life as a successful award-winning journalist
probably comes from the complete lack of emotional support
that he received from his parents throughout his life and
although it feels a little juvenile and unfair as a thirty-seven
year old man to still attribute his lack of emotional depth to
his parents, what is undeniable is that they could be from
another planet for how much he understood them or how
much they have ever understood him.

He looks away from the mirror towards the bathtub.
Everything has gone strangely quiet as if all of Krishna
Colony, like him, is holding its breath. He can almost hear
the sound of the incandescent CFL bulbs whirring away.
No. He suddenly feels breathless. He wants to go out and
say to Satya. 'Let it be. Let us get out of this place while we
still can.' Why does he want to say that? Why does he feel
that the world is going to take yet another turn?

But of course he does not say anything to Satya when
he returns with his turbaned constables. One of whom—
Surinder or Parminder—Raman remembers the two
names but he is not sure who was who, holds a large black
bag, which he zips open. Raman sees that apart from other
sharp tools which look like surreally hooked and distorted
versions of everyday tools that he is familiar with at least in

the passing, the bag also contains a tiny crowbar, a miniature axe and a small hammer. The two men immediately put on their cloth masks, sit on their knees and get down to their task. Working surprisingly gently with their large hands, they break the concrete little by little, one small chunk by one small chunk, as if digging for precious artefacts at a particularly fragile archaeological site. Satya stands above them looking intently at what they are doing and giving them an occasional instruction to dig this or break that. He has not even glanced once at Raman since he has returned.

The bathroom is becoming increasingly hot and claustrophobic because of the presence of four people in that small space and because powdered cement has begun to escape the confines of the concrete slab of the bathtub, the air inside too has become cloudy but the men are all so completely focused on the task that is being undertaken bit by bit that it does not occur to Raman or to anybody else for that matter—because nobody suggests it—that he can step outside to allow him and the people around him literally a little more breathing space. Soon there is sweat trickling down the men's foreheads and their khaki-coloured armpits have begun darkening with moisture but even after over nearly half an hour of careful digging, there is nothing to show; just more concrete inside concrete. And then suddenly without any kind of forewarning, the deluge of things begins.

The first to emerge is a little piece of what appears to be a part of a stiff cloth or hard paper. It is so deeply encrusted with cement that it is difficult to be sure. Satya asks Raman to help him spread a large plastic sheet on the floor on which the constable carefully places the piece with his gloved hand but despite the precaution, the piece disintegrates like soot as soon as it touches the plastic.

'The lime in the cement is pretty corrosive. It almost completely burns things through,' Satya says.

More and more pieces of disintegrating paper or cloth come out of the concrete. Then comes a set of buttons still attached to a small slice of what could have been a jacket. They are badly eroded but unmistakably expensive brass buttons.

'What is going on?' Raman whispers almost to himself. Nobody replies. A nearly intact electric shaver came out next, its plastic casing melted but its wire still solid. A little metal box comes out that Satya, who has by now sat down on the floor, cleans with a liquid from the bag. The box contains a completely intact USB flash drive.

'You have your laptop here, don't you? Can you see what is on it?'

Raman holds out his gloved hand to take the disk.

'Raman, not a word of anything you see here should get out.'

Raman nods and places his backpack, that he still had on his back, on the floor before fishing his laptop out, placing it on the slab next to the sink and fitting in the pen drive. Deepak Rajvanshi (F:) it reads. Raman clicks on 'Open folder to view files' but before he can look closely at what seems like a series of images that the drive contains, he hears one of the constables say, 'Sir.' And something in his voice, something in the way he says the words tells Raman that the tilting of the world that he had feared, the ominous portent of that which he had felt deep inside him, has happened. He looks up from his laptop where a slide show showing a series of pictures of semi-or unconsciousness Tanya or Layla or both in various states of complete nakedness has begun and he sees that the constable is holding what is unmistakably a finger that is attached to a hand that is still encased in cement.

26

The Killer and the Killed

'The prodigal sister returns!' Deepak said when I returned to the house after staying in Rampachodva for eleven months. 'Let me introduce myself! I am Deepak, your sister's boyfriend,' he said. Boyfriend. Layla's boyfriend. He did not look like he could ever have been a boy. If he ever had been an innocent boy of two (which of course, he would have been thirty or forty odd years ago), that time had long passed and somehow, somewhere along the way, he had warped, and hardened so much that he seemed to have been born the wily thirty-five or forty or forty-five year old that he now was. And Deepak did nothing to dispel my notion of him appearing on earth as a grown man. He never spoke about his parents, his siblings, his relatives or anybody apart from himself.

But that was not why I thought that he was not the kind of man that I had expected Layla to be attracted to. There were other reasons. For instance, I am sure he had never read a book in his life, not even the manuals on cars that he seemed to be fond of—cars, food and alcohol being the only things that seemed to interest him. Although only slightly, like a diversion; an indifferent hobby that did not merit too much knowledge and not even too much attention. Not enough for him to take his concentration off Layla whose every action, every emotion, each word seemed to rivet him, making him poke into and feed on her in a twisted horrible kind of way, as if pulling each strand of flesh off her bone little by little. Making sexual innuendos out of any arbitrary thing that she said—basin, carpet, wall, light—anything, at any odd time; commenting on everything that she did, sometimes derisively, sometimes lovingly, sometimes lecherously but always always unpredictably; keeping her off balance with his responses. Once he kissed her full on the lips in front of me after she remarked cleverly on something, I don't remember what now. 'That's my bright girl,' he had said then, kissing her slowly, hungrily as if his very life depended on the elixir that those lips exuded. But often he would walk up to her, put his face close to hers and cut her off mid-sentence saying something childishly cruel like 'your dumbness is making you stink so much that I will suffocate in its noxiousness if I stay near you any longer.'

There was no pattern to his behaviour that I could discern. If there was a grand design that he was working on or a goal that he was working towards, it remained shrouded in the web of heightened emotions and overreactions that he managed spawn with his unpredictability and his cruelty. He swung from one emotion to the next, from one mood to the next, gnawing and gnawing and gnawing away at Layla in a way that I had not thought was possible for one human being to want to affect or be affected by another. Had I not been so deeply entrenched in the situation, had I not been so affected by it myself, it would almost have been fascinating to see the watchful, predatory stillness that settled around Deepak whenever Layla came into the room, even when he did not look at her, even when he did not move a proverbial finger in her direction.

But for all Deepak's disinterest in books, especially Layla's books about which he spoke almost as caustically as he usually spoke of and to Layla and for all his disdain for the written word, he was not stupid. He had this unmistakable shrewdness that surrounded him like armour with no chinks, leaving no space for vulnerability and allowing people to see only what he wanted them to see. He was polished and suave and smooth when he wanted, adopting a warm Clooney-esque twinkle that for all its insincerity, still felt deeply flattering. He was probably like that with Layla in the beginning and he was with me too for a few days when I arrived—charming, polite and attentive and funny. 'Two of the same kind or like they put it in old-fashioned movies, two peas in a pod,' he had exclaimed to me. 'How wonderful is that? I have real difficulty in deciding who is more beautiful,' he had said, all the while looking at Layla and making me laugh in a way that I had not laughed before and never wanted to laugh again. As if I didn't know everything about Layla and him already. As if who was more beautiful mattered any more. Mirror, mirror in the house.

Deepak left me mostly alone after that. His charm, his volatility, and more importantly his aggression continued to be directed at Layla. His aggression was reflexive, almost unthinking (although on second thoughts, nothing that he did was probably unthinking)—like a natural, obtrusive, unashamed part of him that he was as unselfconscious about wielding as he was about using his hands to pick up a fruit or using his mouth to chew on the said fruit. And for all its nonchalance, his aggression was large and devastating—capable of flattening anything that came in its way. I would look at Layla and want to ask her (although I never did because didn't I know it already?): 'How had she, my intelligent, my sharp sister not noticed that Deepak was so wrong for her? How had she landed herself in this situation? I knew Layla too was aggressive but her aggression was small, quiet, introspective and well thought out. I don't think her aggression was ever instinctive or impulsive and although it had not been evident for a very long time, it had never been completely absent either. Not until now with Deepak.

With Deepak, Layla was different. She looked the same, she went through the same motions, she spoke the words, she smiled at me and hugged me when I came back from Rampachodva and she didn't ask me any questions; I guess by now, there was no need for explanations between us. She showed me to Little Neel's room because she shared the room that she and I had shared earlier with Deepak now. Mamma and Papa's largish 'master bedroom' was still a place of too much reverence for us to use casually as a place to sleep. She stood still, smiling as I arranged my belongings carefully between Little Neel's clothes and Pictionary and Scrabble and his Lego dinosaurs, trying, out of habit, to disturb as little of his things as possible. She smiled for Deepak too whenever she could find the space between his cruelty, his derision and his demands. And yet she was different. She took all of Deepak's barbs steadily, facing him with her back characteristically straight but she looked distracted, puzzled almost. Somnambulant. As if she could not quite hear or understand what he was saying or was not even sure if he were speaking to her. Like a part of her remained switched off. As if she was using herself sparingly.

Those days were strange. The house imbued the sweaty, still discomfort of that particularly torrid April and May when temperatures, according to shrill TV reporters, were touching record highs. Hottest it has been in fifty years, no, hundred, the TV anchors proclaimed, intent on outdoing each other with their theatrics, accompanying their stories with images of thirsty birds flying with their beaks open, or of little boys jumping into the man-made, unnamed water body near India Gate, or of the orange-red shimmering envelope of heat surrounding a blazingly hot sun, or (and this image was looped endlessly) of an ingenious woman frying eggs in the heat emanating from her bare terrace floor in Andhra Pradesh.

We received two reminder notices slid underneath and four knocks on our door telling us of our obligation to the RWA and to Bellevue Boulevard and to the society in general and we were given till the end of the month to comply with the nation's notion of morality, as one of the men who came to our door told us, using the kind of lexicon popularized by a strident TV anchor and that I had never imagined anybody using in real life except in sarcasm. But the man was earnest; obviously there was no possibility of mirth in the situation, according to him. It was that kind of mood and it was that kind of weather and it was those kind of days that were passing one day closer to the deadline set by the BBRWA that Layla and I spent on a tiptoe, trying to be as unobtrusive as possible, trying to touch as few things as possible in the house whose every room, even Mamma and Papa's bedroom, where Deepak had begun to leave his shoes and bits of crumpled, used tissue papers, had begun to bear the marks of Deepak's presence, like territorial markings left by a particularly aggressive predator; making every familiar object reek with unfamiliar smells. Something had to change and something did. But only for the worse.

We had just watched the re-run of *Shakespeare in Love* on TV and Deepak was in a jovial mood. He was hovering around Layla and he chanted.

'I am thee puck, O beautiful Lady, for you to hit in any direction you want. Blessed am I thee puck.'

I had learnt to keep my distance from Deepak when he was in a jovial mood. I had learnt to keep my distance from Deepak when he was in any kind of mood but I slipped that day. Without even looking up from my reading, I corrected him automatically. 'It should be thy puck and not thee puck.'

'But that is not how my name is pronounced m'lady! I am Dee-pak and I can be thee-puck too if you would so like, for you to hit in any direction you want. Or better still to take me inside you. Show me m'lady if identical

twins' pleasure zones are also identical and if they are both
identically shameless nymphomaniacs!'

I continued to sit on the table with my chin on my
palm and continued determinedly to look into my book but
I shook slightly, like I had just experienced a little shiver
of an earthquake that everybody living in Delhi is familiar
with. The little tremor, the leftover from the tremendous
movement of the earth's plate that occurs thousands of
kilometres away somewhere near Banda Aceh in Indonesia
or in the Hindukush mountains or like the soft ping of two
black holes meeting that is heard thousands of light years
later, after travelling through the kind of continuum of
space and time that defies the boundaries and parameters
and even the imaginations of most humans. We all know
that Delhi is not safe. It lies in seismic zone 4 so the Big
One, as they call it, can happen any time. But meanwhile
we sit and measure the 7.8 quake on the Richter scale in
Afghanistan as tiny few seconds of shaking of the ceiling
fan in our living room—our own individual little LIGOs—
and we make elaborate plans for living in a world that may
soon come literally crashing down all around us.

A line was crossed that day and the facade of order that
our house and our things and the painting on the wall had
stoically held began peeling off bit by bit, like skin peeling
off the face of a perfectly normal, perfectly beautiful
heroine of a horror movie, one strip at a time, revealing
worms and maggots that had long been eating away her
insides. Deepak began to include me in his taunts and his
innuendos, spreading his cruelty equally between Layla
and I; fusing us in the way we had been fused together

in Mamma's womb. Except then we had shared the elixir of life that had emanated out of Mamma's umbilical cord to sustain us and now we shared the noxious exudation that came out of Deepak's mouth that diminished us little by little, word by word, action by action. The days were beginning to get clotted like congealed blood and there was no way to separate the various strands that constituted it, no way to isolate red blood cells from the white ones and no way to get to the platelets. We shifted and fidgeted and scratched and scratched till we drew blood but we refused to look directly at our wounds or at Deepak or even at each other.

I wish I could say that the day it finally happened was different from all other days preceding it. It wasn't. It was another hot afternoon and I had sat primed to take on whatever came my way, with sweat meandering down my spine and my shoulders squared.

There had been another knock on our door and the door-knocker, another of the generic old men, who took the responsibility of ensuring that all young women remained within the boundaries prescribed by him and the likes of him, had delivered his message. 'Only ten days are remaining till the month's end,' he had said. 'We don't want to be strict with you, beta, but you know we cannot allow this kind of behaviour. Don't force us to do drastic things.'

I was already familiar with that combination of patriarchal condescension and mafioso threats that had emanated in various forms for a long time around us now so, in that way too, the day was not unusual. But Deepak had responded differently.

'Let me make an honest woman out of you.' Deepak said to Layla that day after the man with the stern message had left. 'You and I will get married. And Tanya can come as a bonus wife. We can all live together. I am sure everybody from Bellevue Boulevard RWA will be very happy with a married couple, even one with a spare wife.' Deepak looked smug and pleased with himself and he looked at Layla expectantly, ready to receive the praise that he was sure he was entitled to for coming up with such an ingenious solution. As smug as, I am sure, the men who pronounce that a rapist marry his victim to be absolved of his crime look. Men who believe marriages are only about getting the women who have fallen or who could fall off (which would include any woman, all women) the society's moral ladder, back into the task of producing sons for their clans. And why spare a thought for the woman—having to live each day, every day with the person who inhabits her worst nightmare; cooking his meals and producing his children and hearing his snores each night—when the interests of the society at large are being so fruitfully met?

'No,' Layla said. Sounding quiet but very much there. She looked neither somnambulant nor puzzled. I sat up although I continued to stare resolutely at my book. This was the Layla I recognized. I waited to see if Deepak recognized her too.

'No? Are you sure? No to the marriage or no to sharing Tanya.' He, obviously, had never met this Layla before.

'No to both.'

'You know, those naked pictures of you that I have, can be hers too.' Deepak said almost conversationally but for the first time since I had met him, I could see flaming anger in his eyes that he could not quite camouflage. 'I could use those pictures against either of you. This is amazing, two harlots for the price of one! Like a salacious pizza deal!'

'But, wait. Perhaps I should check and see whether under the same-size pizza with the same toppings, the crust is different. Does Tanya look like you under her clothes too or does she have an extra wart on her stomach or an ugly, hairy mole on her breast that will make my pictures a lie?'

The blazing heat in the room moved. Like blizzard turned on its head, it made everything, dripping with sweat, stagger backward—even the two sisters in the painting looked decrepit and wilted. I did not want to see what I was seeing. I did not want to hear what I was hearing. I did not want to be where I was. I stood up and went into the bathroom of Mamma and Papa's room. Somehow, that space seemed a little less infected by Deepak, despite the used crumpled tissues. But what I did not hear or see or sense was that Deepak had followed me. He pushed open the bathroom door before I could bolt it and catching hold of my T-shirt he ripped it hard off me. Everything began to slow down. I turned around as if in slow motion. I could see him towering behind me in the mirror as I stood looking at the woman who stood in her bra in the mirror looking at herself and there was a person behind her, beyond the man who was exactly like her too. Like in the bizarre arrangement when you place a mirror opposite a mirror to produce thousands of replicating images one after another, each getting smaller and smaller as the distance from the mirror increases—there were thousands of Layla-Tanya in the mirror—one inside the other inside the other. 'Look what you sisters have made me do,' Deepak was saying from somewhere far away. 'I hate to lose control like this but I hate it even more when Layla defies me. But you know, I am loving this,' he said and tugged my bra off my back.

'No.' Layla's voice was so soft that I almost did not hear it except on my inside. And I knew it then. Layla was going to kill him. She had long meant to kill him. I could see it in her stance. In the way she held herself, the way she looked at him and later at what remained of him. Hers was not an impulsive, anger-ridden, spur-of-the-moment act. It was methodical. A culmination of endless shaping and reshaping of scenarios that had gone on in her head, in her dreams. For the first time in my life I could see Layla's dreams. They were not disturbed, restless dreams. Her dreams were not monochromatic like mine usually were, with hints and shadows, implications and inferences. Hers were bold graphic and technicolour. So true to life that I could be watching events unfold like in an old-fashioned movie where everything was explained—every emotion, every motive, every act painstakingly sketched out. A privileged viewer who watched as the scenarios took shape somewhere between her cortex and her eyes where dreams are born and sorted. They were an extravaganza of splattered blood—her dreams. Of severed limbs, of bloated bodies. Correction: one bloated body. And they were detailed. Purposeful, scenario-building dreams. Like a management guru doing complete justice to the enormous consulting fee that she has charged, Layla had built her scenarios immaculately. They differed in their details, in their little frills and embellishments but they all ended with Deepak's death. Her dreams and her consciousness were contiguous. I was not sure where one ended and the other began. Was she dreaming that she was holding the knife or was she actually holding the knife dripping with blood? It was the Japanese Sekiryu Deba knife that Papa had bought when he had decided, much to our collective delight, to cook a whole leg of a goat. 'They will give you the mutton leg cleaned and cut so you don't really need that humungous beast of a knife,' Mamma had laughed at Papa. But Papa had looked so important and serious using that knife for the first and only time, to clean out the minuscule bits of black hair that that none of us, apart from him, could really see, that we had stood around him solemnly and watched him ritually marinate the leg of mutton as he followed the recipe to the last pinchful of saffron—before cooking it slowly over the earthen angithi that he had also bought especially for the roast leg of goat.

How can the scattered images, thoughts, actions, emotions be assimilated and assigned? How can I establish the chronological order of all that had happened? Why am I even attempting it? Have the words that can describe what I want to describe, to say what I want to say even been invented? I can say whatever I want but will those words ever be accurate? Layla had come up behind Deepak and I had seen Deepak cry out even before I had heard the sound of his cry. He had turned to face Layla but by then it was too late for him. Layla knew his vulnerable spot, his Achilles heel that he had so proudly boasted about.

The embossed wound on the right side of his stomach that proved to be a very flimsy protection for one of his kidneys and all of his precious liver. He had staggered back and Layla had lifted the meat knife and methodically hacked at his stomach, her left arm swinging to cut through the skin and the bones and the fat and whatever bits of flesh she could get at. 'Swing, swing, swing' I think Layla was singing. I think she was singing *Norwegian Wood*. Why was she singing *Norwegian Wood* but I joined her in the singing because really what else was there to do? Swing, sing, swing, sing.

Deepak fell into the bathtub or Layla pushed him in or I pushed him. It did not matter. He lay splayed with his arms and legs spread out far apart like a particularly corpulent old man luxuriating in the satisfying warmth of the bath. If only he had no clothes on and if only his expression better matched his posture, I thought, the image of luxuriating corpulence would have been complete. But even as it stood, the image was no less impressive. As if finely choreographed for maximum drama. Deepak was dressed in black. Black trousers and black T-shirt that was tattered on one side with bits and pieces of his insides spilling out and there was blood. A lot of blood pooling all around him. The rest of the pristine white bathtub was untouched and I stood for a long time, half-naked with my T-shirt and bra tethered to parts of me that I had no inkling of, admiring the image that looked straight out of a Tarsem-movie and singing, *I once had a girl or should I say, she once had me . . .*

After the violence and the intense frenetic pressure of the preceding month and days and minutes, I wanted to stand there forever and revel in that afternoon that was suddenly purged of Deepak because whatever else remained in the bathtub, it was certainly not the Deepak of our nightmares. There was work to do but neither Layla nor I wanted to break the incredibly relieved hush of the afternoon and we were still silent with no need to say anything when we moved from the bathroom and quietly, methodically went from one room to the other, removing all the things that belonged to Deepak and replacing every object that Deepak had displaced back to their original positions. I put Papa's slippers back under the bed. Layla put Mamma's perfumes back on the dresser. We picked up every object that belonged to Deepak—his clothes, his shaver, his creams, his jackets, his shirt, his shoes, his tissues, Layla's pictures that he had cleverly hidden all around the house that we found one after the other—and put it in the bathub.

I wish I could say that we felt remorse then or guilt. We didn't. It was a relief to walk around the house without the possibility of Deepak coming up behind us or in front of us and saying whatever came to his mind at that moment. It was a relief to not feel his presence in the house because it did seem like an extremely efficient pest controller, Layla had cleared the house of his presence with one swoop—or ten or twenty—of her knife. The house was immediately back to being ours—Papa, Mamma, Little Neel, Layla and mine. We kept doing what we were doing, single-mindedly putting all of Deepak's belongings into the bathtub. Soon Deepak's face was covered with his things as was most of his body and the bathtub was more than half full by the time everything of Deepak's went in. It was beginning to

get dark but we had one more thing to do. I am not sure
who said it and to whom or whether we said anything at
all, but I knew and Layla knew what we needed to do. We
pulled the portable steel ladder from under Mamma and
Papa's bed and placed it against the wall. Layla climbed
up the ladder to reach the loft where we knew the bags of
cement that Papa had bought eons ago before Little Neel
was born, to build a refuge for himself on the roof, was
kept. Layla climbed into the loft and slid the 20 kg bags of
Ambuja cement down to me one after the other. She was
saying something about 1 kg of cement being enough to
fill .017 cubic feet and since the bathtub would be about
8 cubic feet in volume, we would have needed more than
470 kg of cement that is more than twenty-three 20 kg
bags of cement but since a lot of the volume of the bathtub
was taken up by Deepak and his things, we would probably
need only about 15 bags which was exactly the number of
bags that the loft held.

I only half-listened to what anyway seemed like a
conversation that she was carrying with herself, as we lifted
each bag and took them across to the bathroom—one
after another after another. I remember thinking that the
20 kg of solidness made the bag feel like a rock. One after
another we carried the bags of cement to the bathroom,
one after another we mixed the concrete with water in the
large bucket with the wrong end of the bathroom swipe
and one bucket by one bucket we poured the concrete into
the bathtub, that half flowing, half shifting, half settling
between the spaces left between Deepak and his things,
little by little turned the entire technicolour ensemble gray

until there was no Deepak and no belongings of Deepak left
to see. And yes, as usual, Layla was right in her calculations.
At the end of the fifteen bags, the bathtub was a mass of
semi-solid gray concrete and all I could do was not draw
a large skull and crossbones on the concrete. It was late
night by the time we finished. It must have been hours of
bone-tiring work but I felt light and springy. I was ready
to do another few hours of mixing and pouring, mixing
and pouring. I was ready to put any number of Deepaks
into any number of bathtubs and fill each one of them with
concrete. I knew Layla felt exactly the same—my mirror
image with her large shiny eyes that were glittering like an
animal's in the darkness when we finally switched off the
light, shut the bathroom door, breathed in the exhilarating
absence of Deepak from our once again familiar house,
switched on the AC of our living room, sat under *The Two
Sisters* and never mentioned Deepak again.

We should have done this long back, was all that Layla
said that night. All other words, all other emotions came
later—the next morning when Layla inexplicably started
doing the web searches on food and guns and death and life
and the next when we decided on our food experiment, and
the next and the next.

28 October 2014

27

The Improbable Accomplice

The newly acquired Delhi Police mobile forensic lab with its team arrives soon enough (Satya had immediately summoned them upon discovering the body in order to ensure that no mistakes were made in the investigation this time). Khaki-attired men and women with masks and gloves and brushes and cameras and ticker tapes and a lexicon of macabre that they use with chilling off-handedness—shattered bones, scattered blood, perforated lungs, protruding intestine. Nobody pays any attention to Raman who shuts his laptop and watches as the comings and goings and the incessant digging and cleaning reveal a tallish man's body. Raman tries to focus his attention on the body, not the person; shutting all other voices and describing it in his head for himself, for his article, like the detached journalist he is supposed to be:

The body belongs to a man 5 feet 9 or 10 inches tall (or long now, he thinks ghoulishly) who according to the preliminary estimates of the forensic team here was between thirty-five to forty-five years of age when he died. The lack of microbes in the cement has ensured that the body has remained surprisingly intact although not completely so, because there would have been enough microbes *inside* the body to decompose parts of it. Some parts of the arms and legs and head (with a generous crop of hair) have skeletonized but large portions of the body has adipocere formation—adipo–fat, cere–wax—caused by the anaerobic bacterial hydrolysis of fat in tissues which has sealed those parts of the body in a kind of soapy-waxy coating that takes some time to form in anaerobic or airless environments, which means that the corpse is at least four or five months old, if not older. And that kind of macabre Madam Tussauds kind of coating has also managed to make the injuries, the most likely cause of death, visible as clear, prominent knife marks on the right side of the torso as if somebody has repeatedly hacked into that part of the body.

Why attack that part of the body? Why not the heart or the middle of the torso as would be expected where it would be more effective? But perhaps more importantly, *who* attacked that part of the body? Who had killed the man? Raman realizes his journalistic detachment is a sham, a flimsy protection against the onslaught of the grim facts and grimmer surmises being discussed in dispassionate tones by the masked team of forensic experts that has turned the affable gentle soft-eyed Satya into the sharply angled, hard-eyed, calculating, assessing ACP Satya whose capabilities Raman no longer has any doubts about and those grim facts and grimmer surmises have also begun to twist his stomach with the dark, bottomless fear of losing that which has become the most important thing to him in the world. They find another set of jacket buttons on which the embossed 'V' of Valentino is still intact. They find shoes. They find the sharp Japanese knife, which is most likely to be the murder weapon, inside the cement too. And he stands in the corner of the bedroom watching the body being wrapped to be carried to the lab. All other pieces of evidence are also being carefully collected and collated and labelled. Nobody remarks upon or even notices the disarray of the house because Tanya and Layla's home has stopped being a home that had been used for living, sleeping, eating and sheltering five tightly entangled and deeply loved people. It has, instead, become the crime scene that a large group of people are going over with a fine-tooth comb taking photos, making notes, marking, labelling, encircling as if every little piece of furniture or every little displacement of dust on the floor, every book and paper would help them string together the saga of culpability that the experts would then have no trouble noosing around the guilty person's neck. You did it because our painstakingly collected evidence says so. Now that the pattern is beginning to emerge, Raman wants to jumble it all up again, jump in and muddy the water, remove every shred of evidence that will incriminate . . .

'Did you have a chance to look at the USB stick?' Satya asks, coming towards him.

Raman nods.

'And?'

And nothing. Raman thinks sadistically. See it for yourself. Time you were subject to those images too. You deserve to be haunted by them as much as I do. You too have thrown your emotions up in the air hoping that it will coalesce and condense and come down as rain to bathe you with its tranquil, rejoicing coolness. But what if the rain that actually comes down is acidic? What if it is so corrosive that it reaches in and chars your heart?

He wordlessly crooks his right knee, places his foot against the wall and supporting his laptop on his thigh switches it on.

'Oh God!' He hears Satya breathe beside him. 'We don't know anything yet, do we?'

'No, except that the USB belonged to Deepak Rajvanshi,' Raman replies, putting the USB in Satya's gloved hand. He needs to get away. He needs to go to Tanya.

'I am going to the hospital,' he says, turning to go towards the door of Tanya's house.

'Wait,' Satya says. 'My work here is done. The forensic team will wrap up whatever else needs to be done. I will come to the hospital too.'

They come out of Tanya's house into the clamour of journalists and camera persons who have gathered in hordes once again as the news of a body being found in the house of the freaks of nature has spread. They are asking Satya questions: Is it true that they have found a man's body? Do you know who he is? Was he found in the bathtub? Who killed him? Were the sisters engaged in witchcraft like some reports are suggesting? The story has obviously become twisted and exciting once again—a sad story about two ugly sisters did not attract high TRPs and therefore did not matter. But a whodunit in an upscale neighbourhood is the stuff that long running, successful TV series are made of. Nothing is going to be allowed to remain private any more. Every display of emotion of any kind would become a part of reality TV melodrama. The neighbours are once again being rounded up for another set of sound bites. Anyone with any connection to the women is once again in demand for comments and analysis, as are psychologist, doctors, criminologists, social commentators, as channels scramble to lure the most eminent or the most camera-friendly or the most dramatic of persons to their studios for their prime-time panel discussions. Raman catches sight of Mr Deol, for once looking a little harried—a murder in Bellevue Boulevard is more than what he had wanted to handle—and as he leaves the gates of Krishna Colony, Raman also sees Hariram, the guard who looks up from his strenuous endeavours to properly classify any legitimate visitor and hold off any illegitimate ones, and gives Raman a look of such unmitigated anger that Raman almost tells Satya to stop the jeep, fully intending to find out the reason for the guard's anger before realizing that his anger is not directed at Raman in particular but at all the likes of him—the privileged, judging, sanctimonious group of people who are as much, if not more culpable than the person who actually lifted that large Japanese knife and hacked the life out of a man. The man, who in all probability was the aristocratic, car-loving Deepak Rajvanshi (F:) who had been fitted for a short while into his laptop.

When Raman reaches Tanya's hospital room, she is talking to Dr Anita. He stops short at the door. Tanya *talking* to Dr Anita. Why is she talking to Dr Anita? He had been so intent on meeting Tanya, he had so much to tell her and ask her and he had been so sure that she would be alone for him to begin speaking with her immediately that he had not even bothered to knock.

'Can we come in?' Satya, who was a few steps behind Raman, stops at the door too. 'Or is it a confidential doctor-patient conversation?'

'No.' It is Tanya who replies, her voice stronger than Raman has ever heard it. Her bed is propped up completely and she sits straight on her bed. Perhaps that accounts for her louder voice? 'I want you to hear this.'

'Yes,' Dr Anita says. 'You can come in. I came to talk to her when I heard about the body. She is telling me about it. So, it is as much your territory, ACP Satya, as mine.'

Dr Anita looks flushed. She has an air of self-importance around her as if she has just cracked a particularly difficult exam. She is probably very pleased that Tanya is speaking with her, Raman thinks, with a bout of crazy childish jealousy. Or perhaps with perfectly rational jealousy because he wants Tanya to speak only with him, tell him her confidences. Especially now. Only he can protect her because he so badly wants to protect her. Oh, who is he kidding? Raman slumps mentally. How can he protect her? He has been so afraid for her, so afraid of saying the wrong thing that he had not wanted Satya to come with him and on the way here he literally had not said a word to him. And does she even want his 'protection'—a big word for the flimsy shell of whatever it is that he may be able to offer? But he does not want to share Tanya with Satya or Dr Vaidya and definitely not with Dr Anita who holds a utilitarian brown notebook in her hand that she had been writing furiously in when they came. He has no doubt that she would have written down every word that Tanya said. She is the kind of person who would have taken down verbatim the lectures of her professors in her medical college. Thank God for that, the more rational part of Raman's brain tells him; this way he will not miss anything that Tanya spoke about. And yet . . .

He knows what he is doing. He is once again focusing on the trivial, on the unimportant to temper the huge pulverising intensity of his emotions at the sight of that prone woman who has not moved an inch from that bed since he first saw her and yet she has come with him to every place that he has been to since then, sometimes taking up so much space inside his head that he has had difficulty remembering where he was and who he was speaking to. He is beginning to realize now at the ripe old age of thirty-seven that perhaps it isn't emotional depth he lacks (how can he when he has begun to feel so strongly for a person—who has given no indication that she even remembers his name—that everything else has started to seem soft-focused, light-weight and ephemeral), it is the fear of his emotions being thwarted as it has been since he was a child that has kept him constantly staying away from any emotional entanglements. But now although he knows Tanya could be the one who had murdered the man, that she can be a murderess, that she can be taken away from him forever and that knowledge lays like a physical weight inside his heart, he is not afraid of his emotional entanglement with her. If giving in to his emotions leads to a lifelong of hurt, a lifetime of waiting, he is ready for that too; he thinks rather dramatically—a small, more rational part of his mind once again marvelling at his newfound capacity for grandstanding.

Tanya begins speaking and there is no space for anything but her words in that room where three people listen, oblivious to the noises of the world outside the room where, despite the scores of TV cameras waiting just at the door of the hospital, it is just another day and people are going about their tasks as if nothing cataclysmic is being revealed so close to them.

Not that Tanya speaks like they are cataclysmic events that she is describing. When she tells them about what had happened with her and Layla and Deepak, her voice is calm, everyday. Her words dispassionate as if what she is saying has no connection to what or who she is. And when Raman looks into her large eyes with its still porcelain white cornea, he can sense that she is cutting herself loose—floating above everything and increasing her distance from everybody. She does not look at anybody when she tells the chilling tale of Deepak. About how he blackmailed Layla with her nude pictures and how he almost raped Tanya and how Layla protected her by killing Deepak. And as Raman listens, he realizes that despite the gruesomeness of the incidents that she is describing, there should have been some respite for him, some relief in the knowledge that it is not Tanya who has murdered the man, it is her sister Layla and yet the way she is saying it—her words coming one after another after another in a strange monotone—is making him even more perturbed than he had been when he had been afraid that she had committed the crime and she was going to be arrested for it. Is she retreating into the depths of the place where she had resided during her months of starvation? Will she lose her mind to those awful dark forces before he has even begun to get to know her as the person she must have been before all this had happened and the person he is sure she still is, or is capable of being, despite the drastic change in her appearance?

He wants to stand up and shake her physically but Tanya has finished saying what she wanted to say. She shuts her eyes, turns her back towards them and becomes suddenly quiet. For a few seconds nobody moves, still held under the thrall of the images invoked by her words, wondering if there is more to come, wondering if there *could* be more to come, until Dr Anita who had been sniffling as she wrote her words although her pen did not slow down even when she pulled out a tissue with her left hand to dab her eyes a few times, rises to her feet to check on Tanya.

'She is asleep. She is not going to wake up for some time. She is so weak. She must be exhausted after this long talk.' She says, gently cranking the bed down to allow Tanya to sleep more comfortably.

'Oh my God!' She breathes out softly, turning towards Raman and Satya. 'Perhaps we should all go to my chamber.'

Raman wants to continue to stay on in the room, stay close to Tanya to make sure that she does not float away like a dream after he leaves, or when he wakes up. But what can he say to Dr Anita and to Satya? His action is bound to be misconstrued or perhaps too accurately construed. And in any case, he tells himself sternly, he will probably be able to help Tanya better if he is privy to as many conversations about the case as possible with the man charged with solving it. So he fitfully follows them out of the room after taking one last look at Tanya and her monitor that shows a still weak but steady and even heart rate of 40.

Satya's phone had been on silent in Tanya's room but when he takes it out in the corridor, Raman sees over his shoulder that Satya has forty-two missed calls. Satya immediately begins to make a call, moving a little away when he starts to speak with somebody. Raman too has missed calls. Not as many as forty-two but at fourteen, it is still a fairly large number by his standards. There are a couple of calls from unknown, symmetrical numbers that end with zeros which are probably from phone marketers, five calls from his mother and seven calls from his CEO's office (what was it about the number seven after which his CEO's office stops calling him?) but he wants to speak with nobody. There are a couple of messages for him from his CEO too. These he reads—

> *I don't know where you are but it is IMPERATIVE that you follow the Starving Sisters' story. Forget all your other commitments.*

It is followed by another message:

> *You were right. This is a bigger story!*

This message ends with three exclamation marks and two thumbs-up signs.

Dr Anita's chamber is sparer, better lit and less crowded than Dr Vaidya's and it smells faintly of food. And although as Raman had expected, it contains only large stacked up piles of files and very few books, contrary to his expectations, there are no cute pictures drawn by her children and no photographs of her family anywhere in the room. In fact, apart from a small pen-stand with her name Anita Aditya embossed on it, he can see no personal stuff in her room at all. Everything appears to be standard hospital issue. Perhaps she does spend her evenings in night clubs, after all.

There are a few moments of awkward silence between them. A few seconds during which they each do not know where to begin and what to say. They have been brought together because of circumstances, both their heads are filled with the things that they have just heard and under normal conditions that should have been enough. Enough for them to find something to talk about but somehow they don't know where to begin. They have no small talk between them and in any case, what they have just heard precludes the possibility of beginning to talk about the weather. Raman could ask her about the state of Tanya's mind but like some superstitious idiot, he hesitates. What if his mentioning severe mental illness would cause Tanya to actually have it? And where can he begin? Which strand should he pick up first?

'Would you like to read my notes on the parts you missed?' It is Dr Anita who finds the first words.

'Yes,' Raman takes her notes. Her handwriting is small and neat. She would have been the teacher's pet in school, obeying all instructions without ever applying her mind, he thinks uncharitably before he begins reading and another

part of Tanya's world opens up to him. There are parts about
her and Layla and about Layla's first meeting with Deepak
and about their gradual but almost inevitable coming together.
The descriptions are broken up and patchy but Raman is sure
it is not because of any limitations in Dr Anita's note-taking
but because that is how Tanya must have spoken. That is
how she had spoken to them too. In that birdlike voice of
hers with bits of sentences and bits of descriptions and bits of
conversations that had painted a picture of the horrors that
she and Layla had to bear, the entire, horrendous magnitude,
the entire unfairness of which suddenly strikes him now with
its full intensity. Raman stands up abruptly making Dr Anita,
who had been doing something on her computer while he
read, look up at him enquiringly.

'I should go out,' Raman says.

'But isn't ACP Satya about to join us here?'

'I should go to Tanya's room.'

'She will not have woken up yet.'

'I want to take a look.'

Dr Anita looks at him steadily but if he is making his
attachment to Tanya apparent, if he is making a complete
fool of himself, he is beyond caring.

'No, no. Why do you want to do that?' She shakes
her head. He can see the censure in her eyes but boy is
he way beyond caring about that. There is a rush in his
head, threatening to macerate every rational thought in
its wake.

'Please sit down,' Dr Anita says.

'Why? What will I achieve by sitting down and letting
them continue doing what they have been doing as if those

are the rules set in stone that everybody has to abide by. Who will be punished for the murder? Layla? And guess who will go scot-free? The sanctimonious Mr Deol and his equally smug merry RWA men.'

There is a knock at the door and Satya enters.

'Are you okay?' he asks Raman distractedly without curiosity and without waiting for him to answer, sits on the chair that Raman has just vacated, with an exhausted, resigned thud.

'Everything that Tanya has said seems to check out. We had already established from the University Arts Library that a number of people had seen a man pick Layla up in his car quite often and from their description it is more than likely that the man was Deepak.'

'Do we know anything about him?' Dr Anita asks.

'Well, Deepak Rajvanshi belonged to the family of the Maharaja of some small erstwhile principality in Madhya Pradesh. Their family story is the usual one of all the wealth being squandered. As far as we have been able to find out he has no close living relatives. The few distant relatives that he has don't have any love for him. So, he was not really missed. Looks like there is a crumbling haveli somewhere near Chhindwara and he had lived a life of utter decrepitude. There are some drug related offences registered against his name although he was never convicted for anything, at least not here in Delhi. We are not sure which other states, apart from Madhya Pradesh I guess, he lived in but we are trying to gather that information.' He pauses.

'Yes, there is also a record of his being involved in a major fight about three years ago when he almost died.

So that part about Layla targeting the right side of his stomach where he had a previous injury also checks out. And then there are the photographs.'

'So now you have everything. What next?' Raman asks him.

'I don't know. I can't arrest Layla in the ICU, can I?'

'What about arresting Deol and all those resident welfare people, who pushed them into a corner, who threatened them that they could lose the one thing that was most important to them? The house where they had lived with their parents.'

'Do you want me to arrest everybody? All of them? On what charges? Abetting murder? And say if I am mad enough to do that, do you think the charges will not be thrown out in the first court of law if not by my superiors way before that? Grow up, man. Your outrage will not change the way law functions.'

'What will, then? Your complacency?' Raman almost shouts. He is standing over Satya looking down at him with intense anger.

'I am not complacent but I can't work outside the law, can I? Can I?' Satya too stands up, staring back at Raman.

'What are you two doing?' Dr Anita says. 'Baith jaiye. Please sit down. Both of you need to calm down.'

'If Layla was being blackmailed, there is a just cause, isn't there? Self-defence or defence of one's honour under Sections 96 and 97 or 100 and 103 of the Indian Penal Code? Aren't these mitigating circumstances that will allow her a lighter or even a suspended sentence?' she asks.

Satya turns away from Raman with a sigh.

'That will depend upon how well the lawyers present the case. I don't think you have seen the stories that are being circulated in the media at the moment: "the monster sisters who had no qualms about murdering a man and burying him in the very house where they lived." The sisters are probably being convicted by the media even as we speak. In any event, it will be a state vs. Layla Sharma case and as a government employee, my job will be to work with the prosecution.'

'How can you say that? How can you even allow such things to be said? Can't you bloody see the injustice of it all?'

'Yes I can, Raman. But I have to abide by the law whether or not I agree with everything that it stands for. I am not a private citizen although private citizens also cannot ignore the law.' The fight has gone out of Satya. There are criss-cross lines on his face that had not been apparent before. But he is wearing his policeman's mask now. He does not look angry, or agitated or even emotional.

There is another knock at the door and another man stands in a police uniform. He looks younger to Satya but more hardened and buffed up in an artificial, steroidal, cinematic kind of way.

'This is Inspector Sunil Bhalla. We are now doing a murder enquiry so he is here from the station to assist me.'

An alarm begins to buzz in Dr Anita's room, startling everybody.

'It is code blue,' she says. 'Probably coming from the ICU which means some patient needs critical attention. Our alarm system is very new. It has not been refined enough to buzz only in those rooms where the critical care doctors and nurses are.'

'Sir, the preliminary forensic report has come.' Inspector Bhalla says. 'It seems that the knife injury *was* the cause of death. It perforated the kidney and the liver and caused excessive bleeding. The injuries match the knife we found. The handle of the knife is quite corroded so we have not been able to lift any fingerprints from it but from the way the knife was used, we know that some left-handed person did it. We have found out from her professor that Layla is left handed.'

The world stills and quietens around Raman. The ACP, the Inspector, the doctor, the room fade. All he can see, all he can hear, is the image of Tanya drawing Phenylethylamine with her left hand on that piece of paper that he still carries with him like a talisman and he hears Tanya's voice telling him that she and Layla are mirrored twins. I am left- handed she had said, and Layla is right-handed. It is a left-handed person who killed Deepak. So did Tanya kill Deepak? And then it strikes him. Could Tanya be in the ICU and Layla in room 107? Has he been talking to Layla all these days while Tanya lies unconscious in the ICU?

'But,' he hears Dr Anita say. She is flicking through her notes and Raman remembers that he has seen mirrored twins written somewhere in her neat, small handwriting in the notebook that she had handed to him.

Stop. Raman wants to jump and tear out the notebook from her hands. Stop it. Don't read it. Don't say it . . .

Dr Anita looks up at him. Has he said those words aloud?

'You were saying something doctor?' Satya asks.

'Yes,' she says. 'The description checks out. It is exactly what my notes say.' She looks steadily at Raman as she says this and Raman looks away from her.

'Sir, should I go to Ms Tanya Sharma's room to take her formal statement?'

'No,' Satya says. 'Not yet.'

'Absolutely not,' Dr Anita says. 'Tanya is too psychologically weak and physically exhausted to make any statements now.'

The cadence of Dr Anita's stilted, formal, almost clichéd words sound like music to Raman's ears.

'Shall I go back to the police station then?'

'Yes, Bhalla, do that and let me know if any new reports come in.'

Dr Vaidya walks into the room just as Bhalla leaves.

'Layla is dead,' she says without a preamble. Shutting the door carefully behind her and leaning against it. 'She died of cardiac arrest. There was multi-organ failure due to malnutrition. There was too much stress on her heart.' she is continuing to speak.

Satya's policeman mask has dropped. His anguish is naked, unapologetic, tearful. He knows nothing about Satya's family, Raman realizes. Does he even have one? This time Raman does not look away from Satya's open display of emotion. This time he puts his hand on Satya's shoulder, who holds it for only for the briefest of moments before letting go and moving away.

'Well, nobody can prosecute Layla now,' he says. 'There will not be any case.'

This time it is Raman who stares straight at Dr Anita and this time, it is she who looks away. Why had she not told ACP Satya that it is Layla in Room 107 and it is she who has committed the murder? Dr Anita turns towards Raman again and he sees deep sympathy in her eyes. She knows. She knows his task—loving a woman who is a killer—is not going to be easy. There is a lot he will need to talk about with Dr Anita, Raman thinks. A lot of things on which they will have to work together to save the woman lying in room 107 who is still asleep.

Raman's phone that he had left on Dr Anita's table, when he had leapt up wanting to go to Tanya's room, rings and he sees it is his CEO once again. He picks up the phone and turns it off. He knows he is never going to write the Starving Sisters' story.

28 October 2014

Denouement in Delhi

I know she is dead. My head is quiet now. Not filled with the incessant chatter that has filled my insides literally since even before I was born. I can feel a part of me become still. Wrapped up, mummified. There is no more living up to. No more looking down upon. No more second-guessing. No more first-guessing. No explanations to give. No promises to keep. Nobody to take care of. There are no whispers coming from inside my head. No screams either. No more patting my back. No more same-DNA different-fingerprints. No more carbon copy of me. No more less shiny, shinier, more beautiful, less beautiful doppelgangers. No more, 'Gosh, how alike you are!' Although nobody has said this since we came to the hospital. Perhaps we did not look so similar anymore. Or maybe because we had been separated from each other physically. Or perhaps there was so much to exclaim about, so much to stare at that our identical twinship had become secondary, insignificant. The LIP of us. The Least Interesting Part of us. Like a stubbed toe in a major accident, or a fallen signal in front of a train wreck. So noticeable when the trains are trying to run smoothly by following the signal's dictates and so insignificant in front of messily cast about parts of the people and the train after a train crash.

Time has become sliced with pieces of it falling haphazardly all over. There were people in my room when I told my story. There was Raman and the policeman and Dr Anita who was writing furiously. I had begun to tell it to Dr Anita because I knew she would write it down. It was essential that she write everything down. All the truths and all the lies. When you have to tell a lie, when there is no other way, keep it as close to the truth as possible—this was another ILL—another Invaluable Layla Lesson. Keep everything around the story absolutely, meticulously accurate, change only that crucial bit that really matters—that little lie will survive within the safety net of all the truthful details. They were piecing together my words, my sentences and my story while the solid rock on which I had lived my life—competing against, drawing strength from, being envious of, sharing secrets with—the rock that had held *me* together all my life was crumbling slowly into sand. Sculptures in smoke, drawn meticulously but ephemerally. She was dying and I knew she was holding back till I had completed my story—the kernel of lie inside the epidermis of truth.

But was it really a lie? 'Layla', I had called out to her, trying out the sound of my name on my lips, rolling it inside my mouth. Layla, I liked the aftertaste of it. 'Tanya', she had replied, knowing instantly. Looking exactly like me. Perhaps Pollux-like, one half of the Greek twins—one of us should have given up a part our immortality or more accurately, a part of our morality for the other. Spend half our lives in Hades and half in Olympus. But we were not quite allowed that bargain, were we? For us, it had to be all or none. No half-ways for us. Complete morality or utter depravity. Whole life in Hades or forever in Olympus. Because we had killed a man. We had put a knife through him and buried him in cement. But who had killed and who had not? Which one of us was moral and who was immoral? Did I kill Deepak or did she? Was I kissed in that sucking out life kind of way or was she? Did my clitoris tremble against Deepak's hardness or did hers? Did I face Deepak's cruel eyes and words or did she? Did I feel the softness of Deepak's flaccid dead flesh so different from his live taut, strung-out masculinity or did she? A man was dead and someone had to pay. Whatever the provocation, whatever the justification, despite there being nearly seven billion of us on earth—each life matters. It is for each individual that hospitals are built, each person that doctors save, each individual that lawyers fight for, each individual—each convicted criminal—whose death sentence is sought to be commuted. Even a collective comprises individuals. Many, many, many each individual. Who were we to remove one individual from the network of lives, species, organisms that makes up the earth and our tenuous ecosystem? Nobody has that right. Someone had to pay for it and someone paid. But who? Who paid? Who is who? Who is alive and who is dead? Is Layla dead and Tanya alive or is Tanya dead and Layla alive? Or is one simply a continuation of the other separated after birth and yet having shared the same amniotic fluid, the same moments of panic, the same

pangs of hunger and fulfilment, the same shades of light
and darkness, the same exquisite taste of the dark chocolate
milk that Mamma had at night, the same soft lullaby that
she sang, the stories that Papa read, the occasional holding
of each others' hands, the spooning together despite all the
efforts to turn the back against the other, during that most
important time when they were being assembled one cell
by one cell, can never really split away from the other?

There are more comings and goings in the room. I can
feel them. I can hear them. I can see them. Dr Vaidya comes
in and the policeman and Dr Anita comes in too. 'She has
very high fever,' I hear Dr Vaidya say. And I see Raman who
stands alone looking at me for a very long time. He starts to
say something and stops. Layla, he says and stops again. He
realizes that I know Layla is dead, like I know when I look
at him that he knows about Layla and me. He knows things
that no other human being apart from Layla and I know. Or
does he? I had called her Layla one day, I wanted to tell him.
Or had she called me Layla? I had said I was tired of being
the older sister. The first-born. The decider of decisions.
The maker of mistakes. The committer of crimes. I did not
want to be that person. I wanted to be the other person.
The one who does not make the decisions, the one who
splays out her fingers on the grass and sits dreamily for hours
watching little ants walk up and down the unexpected crests
and troughs, the hillocks and valleys made by her fingers.
Or had she said that she was not going to be the decider
of decisions? And had I called her Tanya and said that she
does not need to be the first L of ILLs, the formulator of
important lessons? It had been very difficult but somehow

also very easy. We became zygotic twins in the truest sense of the words—as entwined inside as we were outside. That is what I would like to believe but we had not quite succeeded even in that, had we? She was gone. She was no longer available to make the decisions or to make up stories. And I had to say that she had murdered Deepak whether or not she had because I knew she was dead. Even before her heart stopped, even before she breathed her last. She told me. She told me to tell the story the way it needed to be told. One of us needed to survive.

One critic, Louis Peisse, had written about *The Two Sisters*. I remember almost every word, 'M. Chassériau wanted, perhaps unnecessarily, to undertake a difficult thing, to do a painting with two figures of women, both full length, of the same height, both in dresses of the same colour and the same fabric, with the same shawl, posed in the same manner, and to sustain that gamble of sorts without using any artifice of light or effect, solely through the authority of style, form, and character. Did he succeed adequately? I do not think so. Nevertheless, he executed that tour de force with a resolution and skill that deserved to prevail.'

Is that how Layla and I were? A particularly ambitious but not entirely successful project of nature—same face, same body, same hair, same walk, same talk, almost the same DNA. And yet we were the gamble that could not quite be sustained—not with our different minds and our different destinies.

According to the legend, the twins Castor and Pollux became part of the stellar constellation Gemini. They are the two brightest stars in the group. Castor became Alpha Geminorum and Pollux Beta Geminorum and sailors believe that they appear as St Elmo's fire—as the bright glow on their masts during stormy weather at sea to protect them.

They are leaving my room. Dr Anita and Dr Vaidya. And Raman.

'Don't go,' I say to Raman. 'Don't go yet.'

Isn't the story about St Elmo's fire beautiful? I want to ask Raman. That's Tanya. She was always beautiful, always a better person, always by my side to make me stronger I want to tell him. I want to tell him about *The Two Sisters* and about Petrarca and Rampachodva. But when I begin speaking again, the words stumble and lose direction and fall out as droplets of water. Ok. Perhaps I am not ready to speak yet. In time, but not quite just yet. Or perhaps never. I am so tired. I shut my eyes and I feel Raman put his hand on my forehead. His hand is cool and light and for the moment that is enough.

Acknowledgements

Where is a novel born? Where does a novel rest? *So All Is Peace* came from the people I met, the stories I heard, the incidents I read about, the emotions I encountered, the feelings they evoked. But it would not have happened without the support of family and friends who encouraged me, read my drafts, gave me refuge, provided me coffee, allowed and understood (somewhat!) my moods, forgave my absences, accepted my silences and were there for me when I needed them, in just the way I needed them.

Kamal Thakur, my charismatic Class 8 English teacher in Sacred Heart School, Ranchi. For being the first to tell me that my rambling, unconventional essays made *perfect* sense.

Rekha Gupta Menon, for being my first friend, my lifelong friend. For reading my earliest Enid-Blyton-style letters and my first draft and attempting to figure out who is who!

Swati Rai, for the gentleness and for being the friend who matters.

Aoife Smith, for weaving a web of intricate Irish tales. For trying to make me pronounce Irish names. For taking me out for hot chocolate and marshmallows on biting-cold Oxford mornings!

Marcel Robischon, Giovanni Cordoba, David Jensen. For friendships that last through distance and time.

Deepa and Nevin Wilson. For the love and warmth, and the home and hearth.

Amita Baviskar, for reading the initial draft. For the incisive, intelligent comments.

Anthony Horowitz, for understanding my excitement. For making me believe.

Geraldine McDonald. For reading my writings. For teaching me how to live. I will miss showing you the finished book, but I know you will always be with us.

Caroline McDonald, Michael Swain and Simon Mark, for setting the bar of workplace fulfillment so high that nothing has ever matched it. For reading my first, tenuous draft. But mostly, for being my friends.

Pradip Krishen, for making me think. For making me laugh. For inviting me into the beautiful world of soils, trees, plants, fantastic music and funny, moving, wonderful words. And for dal-e-Bari Aam!

Bharat Dube, for reading my draft and telling me, 'not a word needs to be changed!' Words that meant more than I can ever express. And Siddharth Dube. For believing.

Shreyasi and Jatin Singh, for giving me a little corner to hide and write at Skymet. And for the friendship.

Apurva Narain, for reading the very first draft and telling me, with some surprise: you are a writer! For inveigling a little space for me to write at the IHC.

The gang. Golak, Ruchi and Vijay, Jashodhara and Abhijit. For the sheer joie de vivre!

Ma, Papa and everyone else in the Lal, Nigam and Singh family. For being the people I can count on blindly. Unthinkingly. And especially Shaily Didi and Chetan Saheb for providing me refuge to write whenever I needed it; Subhodh Mama, Ashok Mama and Kumkum Mami for reading the initial, tentative draft. And Kabeer for the photographs.

Jessica Woollard, my wonderful agent. For having faith and for the conversation that began at Pali Bhavan and has continued unabated since.

My fabulous publisher, Penguin Random House. Meru Gokhale, Ranjana Sengupta, Manasi Subramaniam, Shantanu Ray Chaudhuri, Hina Khajuria, Niti Kumar, Shruti Katoch. For explaining, for polishing, for believing. Ahlawat Gunjan, designer par excellence, for literally giving shape and colour to the mood of the book. And of course, Anushree Kaushal—my super editor. For flooring me with her enthusiasm and her determination. For being patient with my moods, for honing and sharpening and making the book what it is today.

My family. My bedrock. My sentinels. Mummy–Daddy: Ibha and Ramashray Singh, Didi–Jijaji: Anjana and Ajit Prasad, Sis-in-Law and Bro: Meeta and Kumar Saurabh; and my adorable little car-loving nephew, Aryav. I love you.

My love. My life. Pranay—for widening my horizons, for making me see the connections, for bringing the beauty of science into my life. For being there always. For being mine. Aria—for being the daughter that dreams are made of, for sharing the chocolate cakes and the confidences, for polishing my aesthetics, for initiating me into the latest music, for solving all my tech problems! Avie—my Mogu pillow, my source of all scientific information. For making me love every creature in the world, for never allowing me to get bored or feel lonely. For the hugs. For being my son.

And finally, my readers. For choosing to read this book. Thank you.